Uncorrected ARC
B.O.H. Exclusive
Limited to 310 Copies

B.O.H. Uncorrected ARC

ISBN: 978-1-940250-60-1

Interior Layout by Lori Michelle
www.TheAuthorsAlley.com

Printed in the United States of America

Visit us on the web at:
www.bloodboundbooks.net
https://www.bloodgutsandstory.com/

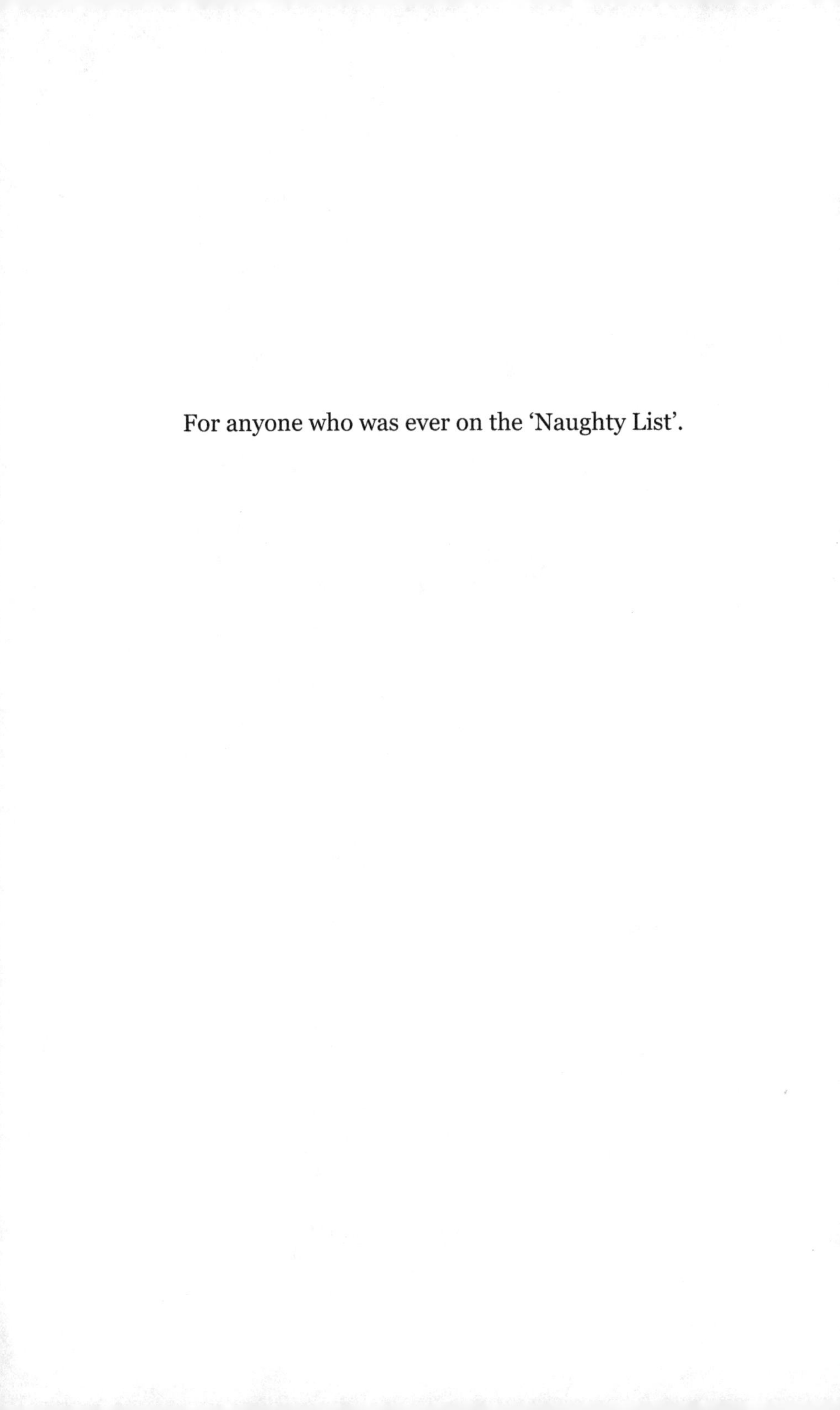

For anyone who was ever on the ‘Naughty List’.

A NOTE ON TERMINOLOGY

St. Nicholas—a small town in northern Canada

Saint Nicholas—something else

I.

ON THE MORNING of the 23rd, knowing he was expected at the elementary school at noon, Father McHattie limited himself to only two beers with breakfast. On an average weekday it was hard to find an excuse not to throw back a shot or two of hard liquor by mid-morning. Around the festive season it became something more like a necessity. A regular medicinal measure of Crown Royal was required at the start of the day and every hour hence to make it through the cavalcade of speeches, ceremonies, functions and frivolities foisted on him by the town. He was careful with it, prescribing himself just enough to lift his mood and numb the agony of existence without turning him into a belligerent, stumbling, vomiting inebriate. He always stayed on the right side of the line. With the children, however, he felt it important to maintain a certain edge. A brighter sparkle in his eye. A shinier sharpness to his diction. He owed them that much. After all, he had quite a story to tell and they, unlike the few poor wretches who still attended his sermons, could actually be expected to listen. So he drank a beer while waiting for the coffee to percolate, then ate some toast and a couple of stale doughnuts left over from a meeting with the new town refurbishment committee, followed by one more beer and that was all. And he found he didn't even miss the liquor until he was walking across town, navigating fresh snow piled high as his waist in places where it hadn't been cleared. He missed the whiskey's warmth then. But it was only a short walk to the school.

The teacher who greeted him in the foyer was new. A pretty young thing she was, like all the recent newcomers. The priest suspected this was down to the Bingzhen corporation's hiring policies—in culture if not explicitly stated in its contracts—and he wondered how many of the other townsfolk had noticed. With the arrival of each new employee, their community grew a little more attractive. And anyone old, fat, or downright ugly could, at a glance, reliably be judged to have been a resident since before the town fell into the hands of private enterprise.

This interloper had red hair, long legs, and a charming accent the Reverend made no effort to place. She spoke quickly, telling him how delighted she was to meet him and how excited the children were about his visit—both statements he doubted in the extreme. Leading him to the classroom, she asked if it would be all right if she ducked out for ten minutes to prepare lunches for the children and he said certainly it would, explaining he had taught Sunday school lessons for over thirty years and anyway, there wasn't a child in her class he hadn't known all their lives.

They were a ragtag bunch, the pupils of St. Nicholas Elementary. There were fewer than twenty of them; the youngest seven years old and the eldest just turned twelve. Anyone younger was typically schooled at home, while anyone older attended secondary school at MacArthur Point, some 400 miles east, typically through a mix of boarding and online learning. Despite his assurances to their teacher, McHattie knew only a few of the children by sight—and fewer still from his Sunday school classes—but he bid them hello as though they were all old friends and they echoed the greeting with a similar level of warmth.

Taking a seat on a red plastic chair beside her desk, Father McHattie showed the teacher a wide smile full of yellow teeth and told her, "I think we're going to be just fine, dear."

She nodded, a nervous scratch of her arm betraying her slight hesitance, then stepped out, shutting the door behind her and disappearing down the hall toward the canteen.

Sucking air in through his nostrils and puffing up his chest the way he would at the pulpit, the Reverend surveyed his audience, their cherubic faces blank, their bright eyes fixed in anticipation. "Well now, children. I think you all know me."

"You spoke to us last year," said one of the boys.

"That's right, I did. And the year before that and the year before that, going all the way back to when I came to this town as an interim priest, filling in for the late Father McCarthy. I thought I would be here a few months, a year at most. But for nearly four decades now, I've been coming here on the last day of school before Christmas to tell a story. Usually, I'll tell the story of the Nativity or I'll tell the story of Saint Nicholas of Myra, the original Santa Claus."

At mention of this name, a few heads perked up, as the priest had expected them to.

"But today . . . " He licked his dry lips. "Today I think I'd like to tell you a different story. A story that's not often told aloud, but passed down through families from one generation to the next. I don't suppose, with the way things are going, there are too many people left around these parts who know it—or, soon enough, anyone who'll care. But that's why it's important for me to tell it to you, so it will at least be known by the last children of St. Nicholas. It's the story of how this town got its name and it focuses on the town founder, a man by the name of Boyd McCulloch. Are there any McCullochs present?"

One of the youngsters raised his hand—the same boy who'd spoken before. He might have been the eldest in the class—lanky and heavily freckled—but his bowl-shaped haircut and primary-colored clothing, decorated with cartoon characters, made him appear juvenile.

"What's your name, son?" the priest asked.

"Devon," he answered.

"Well Devon, your ancestor Boyd McCulloch was a homesteader, lay preacher, and prospector who, more than a hundred years ago, bought a parcel of land stretching from the foothills of Mount Coldwell all the way down to the Carrick River, hoping it might yield a fortune of a kind he couldn't guess. In the meantime, he settled here with his wife and six children and raised hogs and planted an orchard. And he called the land Applecross. And come Christmas time, he would travel out across the hills to visit farms and towns in the valleys beyond to spread good cheer and tell stories of the festive season, much as I'm doing today. And he took with him baubles and trinkets and toys he had fashioned, which he would share among the children, along with cups of cider and strips of smoked pork. And in his breast pocket he carried a handwritten copy of the popular poem 'A Visit from St. Nicholas', better known to you, probably, as 'The Night Before Christmas', and a cartoon etching of Santa Claus which he would have the children pass among themselves while he read aloud the verse.

"And it so happened that in the Year of our Lord 1877 he ventured out to make just such a trip, hoping to spread some

Christian cheer when, crossing the hills, he was caught in a blizzard as sudden and terrible as the one that struck here last night. It was a maelstrom so fierce that it drove the huskies to panic, and in the confusion, McCulloch was thrown from his sled. He walked blindly, helplessly, through a wall of white until, apparently by the grace of God, he staggered into the shelter of the woodlands on the southern slope of Mount Coldwell. Now, you kids may be young, but I'm sure your parents and teachers have taught you well enough to know that if you find yourself lost and alone in the bitter cold, the very last thing you ought do is fall asleep. But poor Boyd McCulloch, after hours of stumbling through the trees in search of some sanctuary, succumbed to exhaustion and collapsed on the ground, falling immediately into unconsciousness.

"Yet when he awoke, he found himself in a soft padded cot in a warm candlelit room, being tended to by a large, shadowy figure. Bleary-eyed, McCulloch blinked up at the shape before him, but no matter how he strained, the image would not resolve itself into a form and countenance of which he could make sense. Yet seeing that his girth nearly filled the room and he was dressed all in fur, from his head to his foot, McCulloch, still brain-sick from his ordeal in the snow, said to the man—if man he was—he said, 'Can you be Saint Nicholas?' And his savior replied, in a soft, deep voice, 'That is my name, if you say it is so.' McCulloch blinked again, straining once more to see through the low light, and through steaming tears of debilitation and disorientation, he saw, taking shape before him, the visage of a rosy-cheeked old man with a bushy white beard, a pipe 'twixt his teeth, and bells on his collar. And McCulloch proclaimed, 'It is you! You are he! You are Saint Nicholas!' To which the fat fellow gave a wink of his twinkling eye and replied, 'Yes indeed, good sir. As you say.'"

McHattie paused now, casting an eye around the room to check all were still listening. It was easy to lose youngsters these days in the telling of a tale. They had no attention span for it, too easily distracted by whatever fantastical thoughts lit up their heads. Yet all before him now appeared focused and attentive, urging in their own quiet way—with twitching brows and nibbled lips—for him to continue.

"So for two nights Boyd McCulloch was nursed by his savior, fed broth and mulled wine and soothed with Yuletide hymns till the storm passed and he regained the strength to move on. He asked his savior how he would find the way home and the man assured him, 'Follow your feet and you'll get there, with good fortune hurrying on your heels'. He asked what he could do to repay the man for saving his life and was told, 'Rename your land in my honor so that when I am weak and starving I may claim whatever grows upon it as my own, share in your bounty, and be fortified'. Of course McCulloch agreed and, when he arrived back at his farm, was as good as his word, renaming the land 'St. Nicholas'.

"Over the following months, he made many trips back up the mountain, searching for his savior's cabin to bring him gifts of food and drink. But he could never find it, and the friends and family with whom he shared his remarkable story reasoned it must have been a dream or guardian angel, for no man could make a life up on that unforgiving rock.

"The next summer, McCulloch's land yielded gold and in a few months, he had a working mine and a whole town to support it. The town of St. Nicholas, named in recognition of the man or saint or angel who made it possible. But it wasn't until three years later, on Christmas Eve, that McCulloch finally saw his savior again. With another blizzard buffeting the town, he answered a knock at the door and found the same grand figure standing there in his garments of red and white, laughing behind his snowy beard, bells in his furs jingling with the motion of his big, round belly, and a burlap sack in his hand. He told McCulloch of how hungry he was and reminded him of the deal they'd struck, that for as long as the land bore his name he could claim all that grew there as his own. And McCulloch—in no need of being reminded for he had not forgotten—welcomed the man into his home, introduced him to his family and led him on a tour of his expansive pantry, bidding him take his pick from its rich bounty. And such a bounty it was, children, for McCulloch's winter larder, primed for the Christmas feast, was stuffed from floor to ceiling with such nourishing delicacies derived of fruit, grain, bird and beast, and all grown on the land which bore the name St. Nicholas. And he told the man, 'Take your pick.'

"And so doing, the man snatched up McCulloch's two youngest, plumpest children and bundled them into his sack. Then he threw them over his shoulder, stalked off into the snow, and carried them up the mountain, never to be seen again by living eyes.

"And poor McCulloch, though he loved his babies well, there was nothing he could do but stand and watch. For as I'm sure you all know, from all the tales you've been told, whether it's fairies, trolls, spirits, serpents, genies, goblins, Santa Claus, or the devil himself . . . a deal is a deal."

A stunned silence filled the room and the priest drank it in, his eye roving across the faces of the children before him, each one twisted in horror. Internally, he reveled in their shock and discomfort. As a younger man, relying on the Good Book, his oration had saved and inspired, infuriated and repelled. With a well-told tale, he could nudge a man toward charity or degeneracy. These days, his only hope of seeing any reaction at all to his words was when scaring schoolchildren. And he lapped it up without shame.

"Well?" He grinned, his gaze coming to rest on the face of Devon McCulloch. "That there is a true story. What did you all think?"

For a brief, all-too-wonderful moment, he thought the boy might cry. His shoulders heaved with panicked breaths. His wide, black eyes watered. His gaping mouth quivered, his entire face on the verge of erupting into a hot, red wail of a terror tantrum.

But then the kid cut the act. His face relaxed. The gasps ceased. He leaned back in his chair, eyes narrowing beneath a brow creased in contempt as, sneering, he said, "We've heard it already."

Father McHattie's ear twitched at the sound of a click from behind him. He turned in his chair to find one of the children had somehow snuck past him during the story, gone to the door and locked it. He turned back to see all the rest rising from their chairs, stepping to the sides of their desks, their expressions hard and mean, all eyes on him.

Unable to comprehend what was happening—beyond some dim recognition of a coordinated effort against him—he wondered, briefly, if he too should stand up.

But then they rushed him. And he saw it was already too late.

2.

CURTIS WAS IN the basement. Curtis had been in the basement for two weeks, practically from the moment he'd arrived in St. Nicholas to begin his exciting new career as a school custodian. The previous custodian, Mr. Elliott, had been, so Curtis was told, "something of a pack rat". These were the words the school's acting principal, Miss Gulliver, had used in alluding to the first task he was to be set—clearing out all that had been left behind by his predecessor. On venturing into the old building's subterranean depths, Curtis had quickly concluded 'pack rat' to be too gentle a term. Mr. Elliott had been a hoarder—and a dangerous one at that.

The basement's walls were lined with shelves, every one groaning under the weight of the rusting tins and strongboxes piled upon them. In front of the shelves were shoulder-high bins, filing cabinets and metal drums, each overflowing with a perplexing profusion of uncategorized odds and ends which the old man had somehow judged worthy of preservation. Though there existed a clear—albeit narrow—path from the basement steps to the furnace, every inch of the stone floor around it was occupied with a crate, a can, a pallet, or a cage, none of them empty and many piled up in crooked towers, giving the room the feel of a dense jungle thicket fashioned from sheet metal, hardwood, and cardboard.

And that was only the furnace room. Curtis had been raking through the junk for more than a week before he'd cleared away enough to reveal the opening in the brick wall leading into a second chamber twice the size of the first, stretching out beneath the gymnasium. Here, Mr. Elliott had concealed the star treasures of his collection. These included three complete home backup generators, five portable generators, and enough spare parts to build a half dozen more from scratch. All models were several decades old, bordering on vintage, but they appeared to be functional. It seemed that during his time in St. Nicholas, Mr. Elliott had lived in perpetual fear of the power going out during a snowstorm—not only at the school but at his own home and the homes of his friends and loved ones. He had eased his mind by keeping a constant eye on the local second-hand equipment market, snapping up all reasonably priced generators in good condition he could find, along with a plethora of consumables to suit. And he'd amassed a stockpile of fuel to feed every machine—natural gas, propane, gasoline and associated oils—storing them down here, alongside the school janitorial department's forgotten supplies of cleaning solutions, flammable solvents and combustible chemical compounds.

When Mr. Elliott got started down this road, Curtis had to imagine it had all been well organized and safely stored, a place for everything and everything in its place. But as his obsessions had driven him to accumulate more and more and more, everything had spread into everything else, piling one item atop another without rhyme or reason until it all became one sordid jumble that, with a stray spark in the wrong place, stood a good chance of erupting into an inferno to rival the worst firestorms in Canadian history. All this he had achieved while failing miserably in his custodial duties, allowing the school building to fall to rack and ruin. None of the radiators on the upper floors worked. The roof had turned into a colander. Water ingress had warped the gymnasium floor so badly that staff and students alike had been banned from entering lest it crumble and collapse completely, dropping them into the dungeon-like vaults beneath.

Mr. Elliott (now happily retired to the shores of scenic White Rock, British Columbia, so it was said wasn't solely to blame for the building's deterioration. The school board, PTA and town council each deserved their portion. But it seemed there had been a general acceptance across St. Nicholas—until its recent reversal in fortune—that its population and properties were in steep decline and would remain so until the fast-approaching day when the whole shebang was finally, mercifully, wound up.

That had all changed now. With the Bingzhen corporation signing the checks, much of the town's buildings, primarily in residential areas, would soon be demolished. However, the most historic and aesthetically pleasing—among them the school, church, town hall and police station, each one, unusually for the region, constructed from stone rather than timber—were to be refurbished to an exacting standard.

As custodian, Curtis was relieved he would be playing no part in the repair of the building's plumbing, wiring, roof, or the gymnasium floor. So far, all he had been asked to do by way of contribution to the project was empty the basement of all Mr. Elliott's abandoned chattels in time for the student body's return from winter break. It hadn't sounded like much of a challenge the way Miss Gulliver had described it. Yet after two weeks of toil and barely a dent made, Curtis was struggling to see any likelihood of completing the task before next year's Christmas.

Still he pressed on, and was carrying a crate of jam jars and broken flashlights up to the first floor when he noticed the new schoolteacher quietly weeping on a bench down the hall. He'd seen her once or twice before through her classroom window or as she was dashing out to her car, but they hadn't met. Miss Gulliver, the only other staff member currently working in the school, had apparently seen no reason to introduce them, which he'd taken as a bad sign, indicative of a workplace culture which saw him, a mere custodian, as being unworthy of an introduction. It was doubly frustrating as she was the only person he'd seen since arriving in town who looked worth being introduced to. She had long red hair and fair skin, wore tight blue jeans and knee-length leather boots and was a far cry from any kind of teacher Curtis had known when he was growing up back in Mobile. Now she sat, bent forward with her head in her hands and shoulders shaking. Alone, upset and vulnerable.

It wasn't how he would have liked to make her acquaintance, least of all while dressed in his dirty overalls and work boots, cobwebs in his hair and his skin shiny with sweat and grime. He considered walking away before she noticed him or even dashing to the nearest faucet and dousing his whole head beneath it before dashing back. But then he heard her whimper echoing along the cavernous hallway and his gentler nature overtook him.

"Hey." He approached slowly but noisily, trying to make her aware of his presence before he spoke. It was impossible to guess how some white people would react to being surprised by a 6.5-foot Black man who looked like he'd crawled up from a tomb. "You all right?"

She lifted her head, sniffing loudly and blinking up at him through her tears. "Who are you?" She asked it without intonation, hardly sounding like a question at all.

"I'm Curtis, the custodian." He indicated his overalls, relieved not to have frightened her. "Are you okay? You need help?"

She shook her head, face creasing as she fought back a sob. "It's not me. It's . . . Father McHattie's dead."

"Oh." He didn't know who Father McHattie was. Likely some dear family friend back in her hometown who she'd left behind to start her new life in St. Nicholas, but he tried to sound sympathetic. "I'm sorry to hear that."

"It's my fault. I shouldn't have left him."

"Hey, don't say that. Don't blame yourself. How did he die?"

She shrugged. "Heart attack, I think. I only left him for a little while to help Beatrice with the lunches. But when I got back all the children were crying and he . . . he was lying dead on the floor."

"Wait." Curtis was confused. "When did this happen?"

She sniffed and shrugged again. "I don't know. Maybe . . . twenty minutes ago?"

"Shit." He moved away from her, stepping over to the double doors leading to the main entrance and pushing one open. "Oh shit."

The foyer was littered with distraught children being inadequately comforted by whichever parents had been able to drop whatever they had been doing and rush across town when Miss Gulliver called. Miss Gulliver herself was trying to fend off the barbs of a woman who appeared to hold the school somehow responsible for what had happened, while simultaneously dealing with a middle-aged man Curtis figured for the town sheriff. Though he had no badge or gun, he wore an air of authority and an outfit—from his polished black boots to his khaki shirt and clip-on tie to his green bomber jacket and tan Mountie hat—with the look of a police uniform. A second, younger, heavier man, identically dressed minus the hat, stood in the doorway to the children's classroom, his eyes pointed at the floor, his face screwed up in contemplation.

While Curtis was staring at him and before he could get away, the younger man turned about, locked eyes on him, thrust a black-gloved finger in his direction and called, "Hey you! You the janitor?"

Curtis swallowed a sigh. "Custodian."

Without acknowledging the correction, the man snapped his fingers and waved him over. "C'mere."

Curtis cast an eye toward the red-headed schoolteacher—who had already returned to her sobbing—then stepped reluctantly through the door. He followed the man into the classroom and around the desk to where Father McHattie's body lay. Not having known the man in life, Curtis could only guess at how much better he might have looked when his heart was beating, but it sure seemed like he had suffered an ugly death. His face was wrenched in pain, bloodshot eyes bulging and tongue hanging out of his mouth. His hands were set like claws on the ends of arms that, like his legs, stretched out from his bent body like they'd been flailing in every direction. He couldn't keep himself from imagining the old man writhing on the floor, kicking and howling, froth spraying from his mouth and the children screaming, helpless and afraid. All while Curtis had been downstairs, sorting through boxes of superglue and thumb tacks.

"You got anything we could put him in?" the young cop asked.

"What?"

"We've got the van out front, but we need something to carry him out in. We can't just haul him out like this, in front of the kids and everybody. A body bag would be good, but we don't have any."

Curtis looked at the cop, then at the body, then back to the cop. "You mean like a tarp?"

"A tarp would be great. You got one?"

"I think I could find one, sure."

"You're a real lifesaver." The cop glanced briefly at the body at his feet, appearing to realize the stupidity of what he'd just said, before shrugging it off. "What's your name?"

"Curtis."

"Pleased to meet you, Curtis. I'm Dan. Hey Owen!"

Answering the cry, the man in the hat strolled into the room. "What is it?"

Dan pointed to Curtis. "Owen, this is Curtis, the new school janitor."

"Custodian," Curtis said, shaking the man's hand when he thrust it toward him.

"Good to meet you, Curtis. Owen Dupont. Where you from?"

"Mobile, Alabama."

"No kidding! You've come a long way. You know, for years people around here acted like I was something real exotic and I only came from Thunder Bay. Changed days, I guess."

"You're an outsider too?"

"Yeah, you could say that. Transferred here as a young recruit in hopes of career advancement. Didn't quite work out that way, but I can't complain."

"Sorry, I don't understand. Ain't you the sheriff?"

The man bristled uncomfortably. "Technically, chief of security. I was senior officer with the RCMP detachment stationed here up until . . . Y'know. Things change. It's pretty much the same role as a sheriff, but chief of security is what they're choosing to call it for now. But it's fine, y'know . . . Can't fight progress." He sighed, and in the awkward silence that followed, Curtis had time to wonder at the psychological wound he'd just poked.

Then Dan said, "Curtis here's going to grab us a tarp then the two of us are going to load the Reverend into the van."

"We are?" Curtis heard himself say it, but no-one else seemed to.

"That's great," said Owen. "I'll see if I can clear these kids out and give Gertrude another call. See where she is."

Owen left the room and, a moment later, resigned to carrying out the instructions so carelessly dropped upon him, so did Curtis. He returned to the basement and grabbed a piece of tarp from atop a pile of them and brought it back upstairs along with a piece of thin rope. Then, with only a little help from Dan, he spread it out on the floor and lifted the priest's body onto it. They settled on folding the material over him rather than rolling him up in it, using the rope to secure the parcel tight. Then Dan grabbed him by the shoulders and Curtis picked up his feet and together they took him out through the main entrance, across the schoolyard and into the street, where a beige utility van was parked. Curious passers-by, aggrieved parents and even some of the children still lingering by the entrance, watching intently as they carried the body out. After another halfhearted attempt to disperse the onlookers, Owen jogged over just as the priest was being placed inside.

"You need the tarp back?" asked Dan from inside the van, where he was hunched over the body.

"That's okay; you can keep it," Curtis told him.

"Gertrude's on her way," said Owen. "Her truck got snowed in, so Morgan's giving her a lift." He'd no sooner said this than a black SUV rolled around the corner toward them. The driver honked the horn and Owen waved. "This'll be them!"

First to jump out was a short, boxy, middle-aged woman in a puffy coat and knitted pink hat. She carried a traditional leather doctor's bag, not that it was likely to do the priest much good.

"Well it's about time," Owen said.

"You know damn well I can't be in two places at once," she answered. "Where's the patient?"

"Inside." Dan climbed down from the van so she could take his place.

Following along behind Gertrude was a stocky, balding blond man of around the same age, wearing a fluorescent blue ski jacket over a shirt and tie, with a briefcase slung over his shoulder and a clipboard in his hand. He was grinning as he stepped out of his car, grinning on the walk over, and grinning as he put his hand out toward Curtis. It seemed very much like the grin was a permanent fixture on his face. "Morgan MacLean, pleased to meet you."

"Curtis Tate."

The grin got wider. "Of course! Curtis Tate from Arkansas!"

"Alabama."

"That's it! You're the school's new . . . "

"Custodian."

"Right. We spoke on the phone at least once. I'm COO of Coldwell Slopes. When did you get into town?"

"About two weeks ago."

"Really, that long? Sorry I've not been out to meet you, but it's just been one thing after another lately. Speaking of which . . . " He stepped over to the back of the van. "What's the verdict, Gertie?"

The doctor had unwrapped the tarp to examine the priest's body and was now staring down at his face, lips pursed in contemplation. "You said he had a heart attack?"

"That's what we heard," Owen answered. "Is it not?"

"Could be," she said. "Looks more like he choked on something. Eyes are all bloodshot."

"McHattie was a drunk," said Morgan. "His eyes were always bloodshot. And I don't need a cause of death right now."

"Then what do you need?"

"Well . . . is he dead?"

Gertrude made a face like it was the dumbest question she'd

ever heard. Then, speaking slowly and clearly, she answered, "Yes, Morgan. He is dead."

"Thank you." Morgan scribbled a note and checked a couple of boxes on his clipboard then handed it to her. "Your signature here, please."

Sighing, she signed her name. "A proper examination would tell the tale. Such as would usually be customary in a case of sudden death."

"There'll be time enough for that," said Morgan. "If the church allows it."

"Where do you want him?" asked Dan.

"The clinic," said Gertrude, climbing down from the van.

He winced at the suggestion. "Funeral home's closer."

"Funeral home's closed." She eyed Curtis and, seemingly for his benefit, explained. "They shut up shop due to lack of business. More fool them." She patted Dan on the arm. "Come on. Take us up to the clinic and you can help dig my truck out the snow."

Dan groaned. "That's what I was afraid of." He closed the van's rear doors, nodded his thanks to Curtis, then went around to the front.

Curtis was backing away when Morgan sidled up to him again, the same grin resolute on his round face. "Don't get the wrong idea about our little town. I doubt the past couple weeks or today have given you the greatest impression, but it's important to remember we're in a transitional period at the moment. Things are a little chaotic, to say the least. Locals are running short of patience while newcomers are trying to find their feet and nobody's quite sure what's happening from one minute to the next, but it's all temporary. This time next year, you won't recognize the place. It's going to be incredible. Believe me."

"I don't doubt it."

Morgan chuckled. "You know about Wintertainment?"

"Uh . . . "

"It's not much. Just a little Christmas party we're throwing in the town square tonight. Starts at 7pm. Very informal. Free food, music, a few drinks—a chance for people to feel like a community. Plus, I hear Santa Claus himself will be swinging by to hand out a few presents. Now tell me I'll see you there."

"You might."

"I'd better!" Morgan was moving back toward his SUV now

but stabbed a finger in Curtis's direction. "Curtis the custodian," he exclaimed, his grin fixed and phony as a game show host's. "I like it!"

Curtis felt dazed as he walked back to the school and went inside, unable to process the whirlwind of experiences in which he'd briefly been caught up. Crossing the now empty foyer and going through the double doors on his way back to the basement, he was surprised to find the sobbing schoolteacher exactly where he'd left her. She'd stopped crying now but sat staring at the wall, her expression blank, her mind lost in the kind of thoughts Curtis couldn't hope to guess at, except they were probably dark.

He watched her a moment or more, then said, "Hey."

She flinched at the sound of his voice, apparently unaware of his presence, then turned to face him. "Yeah?"

"What's your name?"

She blinked and frowned, like it was taking her a moment to remember. "Um . . . Shona."

He nodded. "There's some kind of party happening in the town square at seven. Want to go?"

She stared at him for what felt like a long time, her expression blank, her big, brown eyes betraying no feelings whatsoever. Then she shrugged and said, "Sure."

3.

ST. NICHOLAS TOWN HALL was designed, built, and paid for by the McCulloch Mining Company early in the second decade of the 20th century. Generally regarded as the finest building ever to grace the town, its red brick and marble edifice contained a grand hall in which the townsfolk could enjoy entertainments like plays, concerts and social gatherings, while also serving as a place to hold elections and ceremonies and provide emergency relief. The floors above housed the company's administrative offices until the late 1970s, when the mine was purchased by a conglomerate operating out of Toronto. Since then, until very recently, they had been utilized by the mayor's office, town council representatives and their staff. Effective, volunteer civil servants receiving token salaries for taking on parcels of tedious bureaucratic responsibilities in addition to their day jobs, these men and women joked often about the mocking grandeur of their surroundings which seemed excessive even during the town population's peak around seven thousand. As that number fell sharply in the years following the mine's closure, the situation had seemed more absurd still. The various mayors and councilors who occupied the offices spent most of their time on a desperate, feverish quest to attract some kind of industry to their dying town, all the while being taunted by their mahogany desks, crystal chandeliers, and oil paintings of town elders and long-dead mining company executives in ornate gilded frames.

It was through an improbable collision of hard work, persistence, opportunism, and luck that the Bingzhen Group had entered the fray and emerged as the town's potential savior. The Chinese financial firm was aggressively pursuing the ambition of becoming the world's leading luxury hotelier and had set its sights on securing a ski resort somewhere in North America to add to its growing portfolio. By chance, someone in the company's New York office learned of St. Nicholas and its desperate fight to avoid becoming a 21st century ghost town. And by good fortune, this individual had imagination enough to see the potential. Rather than buy an existing resort and refurbish it for an upmarket clientele, they could buy the entire township of St. Nicholas and associated lands, carve their own piste into the side of Mount Coldwell, and transform this isolated Canadian community into the world's must-visit winter holiday destination.

That enterprising individual was Ling Wong, the Bingzhen Group's head of business development for North America, newly minted CEO of Coldwell Slopes and, currently, the town hall's sole occupant. On arrival, she had claimed the former mayor's office as her own, making no changes save for swapping out his computer for hers and having the huge painting on the wall—depicting scores of men proudly marching into the McCulloch gold mine circa 1919—replaced with an artist's rendition of Coldwell Slopes, illustrating—with colorful cartoon styling—the first-class, world-beating ski resort St. Nicholas was set to become. In the top right corner, watching over the town with a warm, fatherly smile, was its new mascot, Coldwell the Singing Snowman. The same face adorned thousands of dollars' worth of caps, T-shirts and assorted merchandise securely stored in empty buildings throughout the town.

Ling had visited St. Nicholas frequently over the last 18 months as plans for its future took shape shape. The first trip had been purely speculative, touring the area's charming properties and meeting with community leaders. Later, she had returned with a survey team to explore the mountain's ski slope potential. She had been present on the day Bingzhen made its offer and when the town's property owners voted by majority to accept. At the end of November, she had bid a fond farewell to her New York apartment and relocated her life to St. Nicholas, where she would be living for at least the next five years. She moved into one of the finest homes on leafy McCulloch Lane, recently vacated by one of the wealthier residents—now even wealthier—and on the morning of December 1st marked the town becoming the official property of the Bingzhen Group with a breakfast of poached eggs and champagne. She regurgitated it all a short time later when the stress and anxiety of her situation overwhelmed her, but in the moment it had been glorious.

Every hour of every day since had presented a fresh angle on the scale of the challenge before her. While her superiors pushed for the resort's opening day to be brought forward, she saw little hope of the transformation project being completed without spiraling far beyond budget and falling way behind schedule. Central to the problem was a lack of people. The population of St. Nicholas had fallen to fewer than one thousand by the time Bingzhen made its offer. Coldwell Slopes would still require cooks, cleaners and retail workers, schoolteachers, lawyers, utility workers, dentists, and doctors, just like any other mountain town, and it was hoped many of its residents would choose to remain and become a part of their community's wonderful regeneration, albeit now living in properties rented from the Bingzhen Group. Instead, many deposited the checks offered for their homes and fled, leaving a glut of vacancies to be filled. Efforts to recruit for these roles were ongoing, but presently the town itself was desperately short-staffed.

Then there were the local infrastructure problems, of which there were many—the result of decades of underinvestment. Ling had engaged dozens of contractors to carry out a comprehensive suite of improvement works—from roads to the power network to phones, internet, water, sewage, building integrity, and amenities—but the majority of technicians and their project managers would not be arriving until the new year. The few already in town were belligerent, unhappy about missing Christmas with their families and delivering work which, though the tasks set them were relatively minor, was far below the quality expected by Bingzhen.

Compounding Ling's stress was the fact she felt woefully unsupported. It was, she thought, quite a bold thing to uproot oneself at fifty-two years of age, leave behind the greatest city in the world and move to a small, broken town in the mountains of northern Canada, committing yourself to remaining there for the next five years. She had come alone and no-one had offered to come with. True, there were platitudes from her superiors and colleagues, assuring her they would help however they could with whatever she asked. But there was a clear expectation that she would not ask. Coldwell Slopes was her idea. Her mission. It would succeed or fail by her hand.

She had hoped it would be different. She still hoped things would improve come the new year, but her first few weeks as CEO had been challenging in the extreme. There had been an informal agreement with the mayor and the town council—such as it was—that they would remain in St. Nicholas for the first few months of the handover to ensure things went smoothly. In the end, they'd all taken the money and run, with the mayor leading the exodus. The only former councilman to stay behind was the one who applied for and secured the position of chief operating officer in the Coldwell Slopes regime: Morgan MacLean. At least Ling could count on him for an ally, though as of yet, his worth was difficult to gauge.

On the afternoon of the 23rd, Morgan entered Ling's office a few minutes after 1pm. She heard him before she saw him.

"Ling Wong merrily on high; in Heaven the bells are ringing," he sang, bouncing through the door with coffees and bags of food. "Ling Wong verily the sky is riven with angels singing!"

"You're feeling brave," she told him, not a trace of warmth in her voice or a smile on her lips.

"I'm flush with the spirit of the season!" He laughed, setting his provisions down on the desk. "And I bring tidings of . . . Well, not great joy. But I bring news."

While he dragged a chair over from the corner, she said, "Please tell me it's about the roads." The roads out of St. Nicholas were currently closed, the result of the blizzard that had struck the previous day, the heavy snowfall rendering them impassable. Such blizzards and resultant road closures were not unusual in the town, but for the roads to still be closed twelve hours after the blizzard had ended was.

Morgan's semi-permanent grin morphed into a grimace. "Oh, about that. Yeah, those roads aren't getting plowed any time soon."

"What?"

"I had to go through Lortie's old emails to find out." Lortie being the name of the former mayor, now retired to romantic Kingston, Ontario. "Seems when you bought the township of St. Nicholas and the surrounding lands, you bought a good few miles of the roads out of town into the bargain."

"What?" Ling said again.

"They're now private roads. Not the responsibility of the province."

"So nobody's coming to clear them?"

"They are not."

"How are we just learning this now?"

Morgan shrugged as he picked up one of the coffee cups and passed it to Ling. "We haven't had decent snow in a month, nothing that would ordinarily trouble the maintenance crews. Lortie knew about it and should have made arrangements, found a private contractor to take over the responsibility. But . . . I guess it slipped his mind."

"Meaning he didn't give a shit. He could at least have warned us before fleeing town. It's negligence bordering on criminal." She took a sip of coffee and winced. "That's awful."

"It's an easy enough fix. I can make some calls, find a couple crews who'll be only too glad of the work. Only it won't happen for a couple of days, what with Christmas and all."

"There's no-one in town can do it?"

Morgan shook his head. "Clearing roads in St. Nicholas is a one-man operation. His name's Izaak Strauss and he doesn't have the kind of equipment to tackle a highway job."

"So we're stuck here; is that what you're saying? No way out?"

"For anyone who doesn't have a sled, a snowmobile or a helicopter, yes, that's pretty much how it is."

"Well that's unacceptable."

Morgan chuckled. "It's not as big a deal as you think it is. People here are used to getting snowed in once in a while. Hell, some of them live for it. And there's no better time it could happen, believe me. Everybody's got a full pantry and nobody's going anywhere." He opened up one of the food bags and held it out to her. "You can afford to relax a little."

She peered into the bag, not masking her suspicion. "What is it?"

"Bannock. Fresh made. Still warm."

"I don't think so."

"It's just fry bread." He jostled the bag under her nose. "Come on, it's not going to kill you."

Reluctantly, Ling plucked out one of the rounds of fried dough and bit into it, washing it down with another mouthful of coffee somehow even worse than the first. "I want the roads open on the twenty-sixth."

"No, I doubt anyone will agree to come out on Boxing Day."

She frowned. "What's Boxing Day?"

He frowned back. "The twenty-sixth."

Deciding to let it go, she took another bite of bannock. “The twenty-seventh, then.” She chewed. “Are there raisins in this?”

“There are.”

“Not my favorite.”

He held out the second bag. “Have a doughnut.”

She rolled her eyes and swallowed. “Carbs on carbs? This is what you bring me?”

He shrugged apologetically. “Lunch options were limited.”

Despite her complaints, she reached into the bag and retrieved an old-fashioned. “But this wasn’t the news you were going to tell me?”

“Oh yeah, that.” Morgan spoke with his mouth full. “Father McHattie’s dead.”

“The priest?”

“Yep.”

“He’s dead?”

“Yep.”

“What the hell happened?”

“Heart attack while telling a story to the schoolchildren.” He slapped his palm on her desk. “Dropped dead right there in the classroom.”

“Oh, for Christ’s sake, Morgan!”

“It’s nothing worth getting upset about. Yes, the children were somewhat traumatized and yes, the timing could have been better. But he was an old man in poor health and a drunk into the bargain. These things happen.”

“Bingzhen won’t see it that way. They’ll view it as an omen.”

“Bingzhen aren’t here. And they’re not likely to come here any time soon. They’ve effectively got you doing two jobs—CEO and town mayor—that involve a tremendous amount of unknowns and variables. It’s inevitable that a lot of things are going to happen outside of your control. What matters is not that you allowed them to happen, but how you respond to them.”

“You’re a sage.” She said it in a heavily sarcastic tone, though, in truth, she appreciated the pep talk. “How do you propose I respond to the death of the town’s priest two days before Christmas?”

“Since you ask, I do have a suggestion.”

“Go on.”

“You know McHattie was due to speak tonight at

Wintertainment? His death leaves a rather significant hole in the program."

Ling cringed. "Oh, Morgan, no. I don't think I'm ready for that. I don't . . . I don't even know these people."

"This is your chance to get to know them. All of them! McHattie's speech would have been his usual sanctimonious guilt trip about how everyone's forgotten the true meaning of Christmas and how the church shouldn't be ignored eleven months out of the year—though, of course, he's much missed and his memory will be treasured in all our hearts. But you could say something that actually brings people together and gives them hope for the future. They need that now. And people will want to hear what you have to say."

Ling sighed and leaned back in her chair. "You're probably right." She ran her fingers over her brow, trying to massage away the worry lines. "I hate public speaking."

"It'll be a breeze. I could throw a little speech together if you want. Something simple."

"Yeah, you do that. And give me another doughnut."

4.

IN THE GRAND HALL below Ling's office, as darkness fell, children gathered, unseen by adult eyes. They came from all corners of the town, those same youngsters who had been in the room when the priest died. They scurried in through the doors like rats in bobble hats and clustered in the corner by the stage, communicating in high-pitched, over-excited whispers.

"Do you know what time he gets here?"

"Is he coming on a sleigh?"

"Will we meet his reindeer?"

"I know their names. I know all their names!"

"I hope he brings presents."

"He said he would. He said he'd bring toys."

"And chocolate."

"And surprises. Lots and lots of surprises!"

The children of St. Nicholas Elementary had all gone home shortly after the events of that morning. Gone to the safety of their living rooms and dens, to be served crackers and cocoa and be comforted in the arms of their loving parents. They had all appeared mightily distressed in the aftermath—as one would expect—and so their mothers and fathers fussed over them, worrying that they had been forever changed by the kind of trauma that scars in deep and unknown ways. Some of them held the school itself responsible, promising Miss Gulliver there would be hell to pay for what she had allowed to happen under her roof. And of course they worried their darling progeny's Christmas had been ruined—for that much, if nothing else, seemed certain.

Yet how their little angels had rallied. In little more than an hour, their tears had all dried, the rosy glow had returned to their chubby cheeks and their eyes once again sparkled with all the excitement of the festive season. And not a one would be dissuaded from performing that evening.

In years gone by, St. Nicholas Elementary had boasted a fine choir—the kind of choir that was proudly dispatched to other towns and cities to compete in competitions and perhaps even return with a prize. Presided over by the endlessly patient and enthusiastic Ms. Beaverbrook, the choir had disintegrated with the town's decline and the draining away of its young families heading off in search of fresh opportunities. But as the Bingzhen deal became a reality and Christmas approached, Ms. Beaverbrook—now retired and half deaf but still living in St. Nicholas—was persuaded to take the school's remaining students into her hands and, from their raw, minimal talent, craft a choir that could at least take the stage in the square and lift a few hearts at Wintertainment.

Most of their parents fully expected the performance to be canceled under the circumstances, the children much too traumatized to sing. But the youngsters would not hear of it. They insisted the show would go on and they would attend the final rehearsal in the town hall. Their mothers and fathers could only gaze in misty-eyed astonishment at their heirs, so impressed with their strength and fortitude for ones so young, as they bundled them up in coats and scarves and waved them out the door.

Now they jostled each other in their little crowd, whispering of rumor and expectation and all they had planned for the coming days. Only one stood apart—an eleven-year-old by the name of Lucas Grenier. While the rest chatted and squealed, he shuffled his feet with his hands in his pockets, staring at the floor. He looked up when Cindee Joyce—a girl two years younger than him with curly brown hair and a glittery purple coat—approached and asked, "You okay?"

"I don't know," he admitted, his voice small and faltering. "I can't stop thinking about what we did. His face . . . "

"What did you do?" The question came not from the girl, but from Devon McCulloch. He spoke from the center of the huddle, hidden from view by a couple of the girls, who were taller than him. They stepped aside as he moved forward, slipping off the star-patterned mittens on his hands and letting them hang from the string through his sleeves as he locked his black eyes on Lucas. "Well?"

Lucas swallowed. "We . . . "

"Not we," said Devon. "You. What did you do?"

"I . . . "

"You did nothing. Melody locked the door." He pointed behind him to a skinny girl in pig-tails. "The others jumped on him and held him down, while I pulled a plastic bag over his head and held it tight as he fought and kicked and his eyes bulged and he gasped for breath and tried to beg for his life and prayed to Jesus to save him and then, finally, died. But you didn't do anything. You just stood there."

"Feels wrong," said Lucas.

As soon as he said it, a sound went up from the cluster. A communal intake of breath, not quite a gasp and not quite a moan. More like the filling of the lungs a band of soldiers or sports team would make in the second before entering the fray.

Devon's reaction wasn't as aggressive. He smiled. "It feels wrong because you didn't do anything. You knew what you were supposed to do, but you chickened out. And now you feel guilty and confused." He turned to the others. "Anyone else feel what we did today was wrong?" Answered by silence, he turned back to Lucas. "You see? When you have a purpose and you're given something to do, and you actually do it, it doesn't feel wrong. It feels right."

Lucas scanned the faces of the kids standing behind Devon, then looked to Cindee, then at the floor. He shrugged. "I guess so."

"You guess so." Devon spoke through a sneer. "You believe in God, Lucas?"

Lucas flinched at the question, his face creasing in confusion. "What? I don't know."

"I don't know either," said Devon. "Father McHattie, he believed in God. And if he's right, all I did today was send him to Heaven to spend eternity with his creator, who he loved more than anything on Earth. And if that's true, good for him. Because I don't know if God is real. But do you know who is real?"

A few seconds passed in silence before Lucas realized an answer was expected. "Santa Claus?"

A sigh of awe rose from the cluster at mention of the name. Devon grinned. "That's right. Santa Claus. All our lives and all around the world, people say that God is real, but nobody knows. Santa, though . . . The world tells us he's just a story, made up to fool little kids. There are no churches to Santa. There are no priests praising Santa. They want us to think he doesn't exist, but he *does* exist. We all know it. We've all seen it. He's real, but the world would rather pretend he's not. How crazy is that?"

"It's . . . pretty crazy, I guess." Lucas nodded along.

"Right?" Devon stepped closer. "You can't allow yourself to be fooled by the world grown-ups have created. That's how people end up believing that God is real and Santa Claus isn't. It's up to us to hold on to what we've seen and what we know and put our trust in the only higher power who's proven he's there for us. That's why I say: I reject God and I worship Santa Claus. Say it."

Lucas cleared his throat. "I, uh . . . I reject God and I worship Santa Claus."

Devon turned to his meager congregation. "Say it with me. I reject God and I worship Santa Claus!"

The children chanted in unison, "I reject God and I worship Santa Claus."

Devon's face flushed with joy. "Amen."

The arrival of Ms. Beaverbrook put an end to the sermon. "Oh goodness, you're all here," she said, coming through the doors and unwinding the scarf from around her neck. "Good, good, good. We haven't very much time, so we'd best get started. Everyone get into positions."

The children did as instructed, forming up into their practiced rows at the foot of the stage.

"Well now." Ms. Beaverbrook's thick glasses were fogged. Taking them off to clean them, she said, "Let's take it from the top, shall we? Santa Claus is Coming to Town!"

Up to the north-east corner of St. Nicholas, on the outskirts of town, where snow was piled high between abandoned homes and on roads where nobody drove anymore and where starlight shone on a scene of cold, lifeless tranquility, something moved.

It emerged, twisting and shivering, from the snow itself, punching an opening from deep in the drift and lurching awkwardly forward before disappearing back beneath the white. It moved on, proceeding uncertainly, turning this way and that through car lots that had stood empty for years and behind properties in which every door and window was boarded, revealing itself infrequently by sending up puffs of powder where it briefly broke the surface.

At last it arrived at a part of the neighborhood where bulbs still shone in the streetlamps and the road's plowed and salted asphalt gleamed black beneath their glare. Here, the moving thing emerged once more, bursting from the neat wall of plowed snow at the roadside and immediately collapsing. It lay flat and ugly as roadkill for a minute or more, then reared up, seeming to discover legs beneath its ragged frame. It stood only briefly, however, before falling again and moving forward on its belly.

It half slithered and half scuttled, propelling itself on with deranged corkscrew motions as it navigated a route through suburbia, clinging where it could to the deep shadows cast by homes, trees, and hedgerows. It was passing another house, nearing the edge of the next street, when a truck swung into the road, the beam of its lights swooping across the front yard. The moving thing threw itself against the nearest fence and lay there in a crumpled heap, looking to anyone who might chance to see it like nothing more interesting than a discarded bag of trash.

When the truck was gone, the thing resumed its expedition, finding legs once more and using them to limp over the road and through the facing lot to reach the house on the next corner over—the one with the glowing reindeer on the roof and the twinkling snowmen on the lawn.

The thing paused for a moment to watch the snowmen, who waved with clockwork movements, their translucent plastic bodies turning green, then orange, then blue in the glow of the ever-changing lights strung up across the house. The thing surveyed the scene, nodding and clicking with something that might have been a tongue, as though seeking to share an opinion with itself. And the snowmen, though their necks were not animatronic, slowly turned their heads in its direction and regarded it with their cold, black, lifeless eyes.

Then it lumbered on, around the side of the house and into the garden, to hide among the evergreen bushes. Wherever its feet touched the snow, they left putrid stains of red and black. And when the thing gave a shiver and sought to settle itself among the shrubs, the rusted bells on its cuffs and collar made a dull, despondent jingling sound.

5.

CURTIS AND SHONA had agreed to meet in front of the church. It had been Curtis who suggested it, purely because it was the most obvious of the town's landmarks—beyond the school—they were both likely to know. He only realized his error when he was standing before it, staring at the spiked iron railings running across its stone facade. Word of the priest's sudden passing had clearly spread throughout the afternoon, as anyone would expect it to. The community's more sensitive souls had reacted quickly, tying flowers and ribbons to the spikes and building a small tribute from candles and cards on the church steps.

Curtis felt a stab of self-loathing when he saw it, asking himself: *How can you be such an idiot?* In the moment—and for the rest of the afternoon into the early evening—all he'd been thinking about was meeting her. The death of Father McHattie had already been forgotten. This, he knew, was exactly how he'd ended up in this crazy town with his ludicrous job. His selfishness. His single-mindedness. His analytical and emotional shortsightedness had cost him every serious relationship he had and left him alone and all the way out here.

But there was still time to salvage this, he thought. If he managed to guess in which direction Shona would be coming from, he could intercept her and they could walk to the square together without her ever reaching the church. This desperate plan was in his mind as he turned, ready to run back the way he'd come, and found her standing behind him.

She was swaddled in layers of winter clothing much like he was, but her face was uncovered, her eyes bright and aimed up, over his head at the church steeple. "It's missing a cross."

He turned around and tried to see where she was looking. "What is?"

"The spire. There should be a gold cross at the top."

"Maybe it got blown down?"

"Maybe." At the suggestion, her gaze immediately lowered and she saw the makeshift shrine to Father McHattie. She stared silently for a few moments, during which Curtis tried and failed to think of some comment to make. Then she said, "We should go."

They started along the street in the direction of the square, with Shona leading the way. Though it was the center of town, it was a place Curtis was yet to visit. The days following his arrival had been spent going back and forth between the school, his apartment and the dismal supermarket down the street. He wasn't curious enough to go exploring in the biting cold on foot and he didn't feel comfortable taking the truck he'd been gifted for drives on the snow. Thus the charms of the town square and its many historical features had remained unknown to him until tonight.

"I'm okay," Shona said, when they'd gone a few steps in silence. "Really, I'm fine now. I was upset earlier. Obviously, you saw what I was like, but that's not like me. I don't cry ever, for any reason, normally."

"I get it."

"Yeah, it was . . . rough. But I calmed down, had a good chat with Beatrice . . . "

"Who's Beatrice?" He recalled her mentioning the name during their first conversation.

She gave him a look of mild confusion. "Beatrice Gulliver?"

"Miss Gulliver? The principal?"

"You call her Miss Gulliver?"

"She introduced herself as Miss Gulliver. Never told me her first name."

"Oh." Shona appeared to give an uneasy shrug, though it was difficult to be sure with all the layers she wore. "Well . . . "

"It's fine." He smiled thinly. "I don't need to dig too deep into that one."

They continued in silence for a few more steps before she said, "The children call me Miss Fleming. You might want to remember that, in case you ever find any graffiti about me . . . "

"Leave it up?"

"Only if it's really filthy. I have a reputation to maintain."

He smiled and repeated the name, so as to remember it. "Miss Fleming. You've worked in other schools?"

"A few brief stints."

"And did you ever do any socializing with any of the custodians there?"

"As a matter of fact, I did not. No, the teaching staff tended to do their drinking separate from other departments. And there were a lot of cliques. Worse than the kids. That's not to say I wouldn't have gone should a member of the custodial team have invited me somewhere. But they never did."

"Well I'm pleased you came tonight."

"Ah, it's nothing." She gave him a playful nudge with her elbow. "You looked like you were in need of someone to take you out on the town and show you a good time."

Now he laughed and nodded. "That I am. That I am."

Curtis hadn't expected much from the town square. It was true that once you got past the sprawl of gray and wilting properties littering its outskirts and approached the center, St. Nicholas had some beautiful buildings to behold—or at least buildings that must have been beautiful in their prime. The school, certainly, was one, and the church, with its proud sandstone spire and elaborate stained glass windows, was another. But impressive as they appeared from the outside, they were both impractical, uneconomical and well on their way to ruin. The refurbishment and improvement work required to make them fit for the current century—and the machinations of the Bingzhen Group—were staggering. So Curtis had prepared himself to be met by a similar level of dilapidation in the square. The reality, then, was a pleasant surprise.

Like something from an old Technicolor movie, the square was flanked on two sides by rows of quaint buildings of various sizes and styles, including the bank, police station, stores—most of them boarded up—and diner on the corner, the sidewalks lined with small trees and cast iron lamp posts. The square had a bandstand in the center and a twenty-foot Christmas tree at the top, facing onto the town hall. Fairy lights had been strung from every available branch and eave, glittering in various color combinations. Beneath their glow, crowds milled between hot food and drink stands, their hands clutching cups of coffee, cocoa, mulled wine, doughnuts or bannock or bowls of poutine as, up on the bandstand, the children's choir of St. Nicholas kept spirits high with a selection of festive favorites. Overhead, the night sky was clear and full of stars, while the crisp air carried the soothing scents of cinnamon, hot chocolate and fried dough.

Curtis doubted the town's entire population had come out for the event, but it felt close to it. A few hundred people were clustered in groups, talking, laughing and getting caught up on the latest gossip—in which he was certain both he and Shona featured.

"Ever get the feeling you're being watched?" she asked, doing her best not to return the gaze of any of the heads turning her way.

"No, I'm not that vain," he joked.

They grabbed a cup of mulled wine and a doughnut each and wandered over to one of the fire pits that had been set up near the center. The men gathered around it wore hats and scarves branded with the Bingzhen Group logo and Curtis guessed they were from the group of contractors hired to improve local infrastructure, currently lodging at the old hotel on Samuel Street. Better to stand with them, he reasoned, than anyone else. They could all be outsiders together.

They didn't speak much while the kids were singing, instead choosing to respectfully observe the performance. Curtis was sure that if one of the kids looked out and saw Shona in the crowd, they wouldn't want to see her talking or laughing. They'd want their teacher to be paying attention—something she clearly understood, as her eyes didn't waver from the bandstand.

Watching alongside her, he couldn't help but be impressed by the choir. They weren't all great singers—not at all—but they remembered all the words, singing loudly and clearly and with obvious enthusiasm. When they sang 'We Wish You a Merry Christmas' it felt like they really meant it. He couldn't help but be reminded of school recitals he'd attended at which his own children had performed, how much they hated it—as most of their classmates had—and how obvious their disdain and embarrassment had been from out in the audience. St. Nicholas truly was a long way from Alabama.

The townsfolk must have known 'We Wish You a Merry Christmas' was the final song, since they erupted into applause as soon as it was over. Curtis held Shona's cup so she could join in. The contractors, their backs to the stage, didn't bother.

As the youngsters were ushered off, Morgan MacLean bounded up, clapping as enthusiastically as anyone in the crowd, then produced a microphone on a stand. "How about that?" His voice resounded from speakers positioned at all four corners of the square. “The St. Nicholas Elementary School choir. Soon to be the Coldwell Slopes Elementary School Choir.”

The applause reduced dramatically at the mention of Coldwell Slopes, community members obviously uneasy at the thought of their town’s corporate re-brand.

Morgan’s grin didn’t falter. “We’re having such fun tonight. Isn’t everybody having a great time?” He didn’t leave much of a pause for the smattering of halfhearted cheers that answered his question before continuing. “Now I want everybody to please make sure to get yourself a cup of cider, a cup of mulled wine or coffee or cocoa. Get yourselves a waffle, a hot dog, whatever you want. Go right ahead. It’s all free, courtesy of the Bingzhen Group, so go crazy. It’s Christmas, after all.” He looked over to his left and nodded to someone standing near the bandstand. “Now, we’ve got a lot more fun and fellowship planned for this evening. I know we’re expecting a visit from one important celebrity in particular, so you’re going to want to stick around for that.” At this, parents made theatrical noises of excitement for the benefit of their children, encouraging them to guess who the ‘celebrity’ might be. “But first, I want you to please welcome the person who made tonight possible. The same person who brought us a new vision for this town, this community, and who is here now to ensure, over the coming months, that vision becomes a reality. Please join me in giving a warm welcome to the CEO of Coldwell Slopes, Miss Ling Wong!”

Now the applause—whether sincere or not—was thunderous. People knew better than to openly show any kind of scorn toward their new Chinese-American overlord. For Curtis, this was his first chance to see the woman whose name had been signed on his contract of employment, and he was surprised to see she was almost exactly as he imagined. A slim, attractive Asian woman of indeterminate age with high cheekbones and jet-black, shoulder-length hair, elegantly dressed in black high-heel boots, black winter coat, black gloves and black ushanka-hat. She was the physical embodiment of a cold, calculating corporate envoy.

When she spoke, it was with a flawless mid-western American accent, in a voice softer and more hesitant than her audience might have expected. “Thank you.” She cleared her throat and consulted a sheet of paper on which her speech was typed. “I feel tremendously honored to be speaking here tonight.”

"Ha!" The exclamation came from somewhere in the crowd and it wasn't immediately apparent if it was intended as a rebuke to Ling's statement or unconnected.

It was clear she heard it, but she kept her eyes on the words on the page. "This event is not only a celebration of Christmas. It marks the conclusion of a long chapter in this town's history and the beginning of a brave new one."

"Hogwash!" It was the same man who yelled, making his disdain quite evident now. He stood on the other side of the crowd from Curtis and Shona, who craned their necks to get a look, but could only see the top of his near-bald head. A few others turned in his direction, muttering for him to be quiet.

Ling cleared her throat again, obviously perturbed, before resuming her speech. "As excited as I am about the future, I know there are many of you who have mixed feelings."

"You're damn right!" There was fury to the heckler's voice. He raised his fist and shook it over his head, ignoring the many people who aggressively shushed him.

Ling's hands and voice were shaking, but she pressed on, refusing to acknowledge the man's outburst. "And I know it feels strange to be celebrating on the day we so suddenly lost this town's long-serving and much-admired priest, Father McHattie."

At mention of the name, a few hats were removed and heads were bowed, in a show of respect. Even the heckler stayed silent. However, Curtis's eye was drawn to a group of teenagers, one of whom let out a scornful laugh at the phrase 'much-admired', crossing his eyes and raising his hand to his mouth to imitate a drunkard taking a swig from a bottle. The brunette beside him—a girl in a silver snowsuit and matching earmuffs—immediately slapped the hand away from his face and hissed at him to shut up.

Ling licked her lips and continued, "Indeed, I know if not for today's tragic events, it would be Father McHattie addressing you now, instead of me. But it's at times like these we need the comfort, strength, and support of community to see us through." She looked out over the crowd in its many huddled packs and put on the best approximation of a smile she could muster. "This is an odd sort of community. Looking around I can see people born and raised in St. Nicholas, others who came from outside but chose to settle and make their life here. I see contract engineers and technicians who may only be in town a few weeks or months but are nonetheless celebrating Christmas with us, away from friends and family. I see the first influx of Coldwell Slopes employees—the new residents destined to shape this town and secure its future for generations to come. I'm sure some of you must constantly be asking yourselves if you made the right choice. The same way everyone who was born, grew up or chose to make their life in St. Nicholas is now wondering if this is still your home. Your town isn't just changing its name. It's changing its whole identity. That makes this a strange and scary time. But it is also a time for hope and excitement. I'm excited."

"Ah, bull-pucky!" It was the same man from before. The folk around him didn't even bother telling him to shut up, deciding it was a lost cause.

Ling kept going, determined to get to the end. "I'm excited for the journey ahead and all the challenges and opportunities it presents. Tonight, we begin that journey. Here and now, we begin forging the bonds of friendship that will foster a new community and build the foundations of a bright and prosperous future. And I promise you this—it's a future that's going to be worth sticking around for. So trust that it comes from the bottom of my heart when I say to you all: have a very merry Christmas and a happy new year."

There followed a round of polite applause as Ling stepped away from the mic, then rushed back up to it. "Oh, and I promise we're going to have those roads cleared on Tuesday." Now the applause strengthened, garnished with a few more whoops and cheers as generic old-time Christmas music faded in through the speakers.

"Inspired yet?" Curtis asked.

"Too sober for that," Shona knocked back the last of her wine and motioned to his cup. "Another?"

"Thanks."

"I'll see if they can put some alcohol in this time." She took his cup and turned around, almost immediately colliding with a young girl. "Oh, sorry!" The child was standing in her shadow—had perhaps been there for some time. When Shona stepped aside, the light from the fire pit revealed her face. "It's Cindee, isn't it?"

The girl stared at her, standing her ground. Her expression was blank, but her eyes held an intense seriousness. They almost looked scared. "Miss Fleming?"

Shona frowned, suddenly a little concerned. "Cindee, are you all right?"

The girl took a few short breaths but didn't look away. "I'm sorry about Father McHattie."

"Oh, sweetie, I know just how you feel. But it's not your fault. It's not anyone's fault. It's just . . . one of those things."

Cindee pursed her lips and continued to stare at Shona for a long moment, eyes unblinking, appearing to consider her next words very carefully. When she spoke, it was at half her previous volume. "Miss Fleming, can I ask you a question?"

"Of course." Shona bent down to hear better.

Now the girl's eyes flicked left and right to make sure no-one else was listening. "Is he real?"

"Is who real?"

Again the girl hesitated, before spitting it out. "Santa Claus."

In defiance of her worst impulses, Shona did not laugh. She knew how serious the subject could be for a child of Cindee's age. "What do you think?"

"I don't know."

"What do your parents say?"

"They say he's real."

"Then he's probably real, don't you think?"

Now the girl sniffed, her eyes watering, and Shona thought she might cry.

She reached out to her. "Hey, Cindee . . . "

And there was a sound like cannon fire—a cacophonous fury that flooded the air and shook the ground beneath their feet, causing all gathered to cry out in shock and throw their hands over their ears. Someone standing at the controls to the sound system turned a knob and the ear-shredding wail resolved into the sound of jingle bells.

"Girls and boys, do you hear what I hear?" Morgan's voice sounded over the speakers, still slightly distorted. "Can it be? I think it is . . . Yes! He's here! The one! The only! Santa Claus!"

At the mention of his name, a spotlight—positioned on the roof of the building opposite the police station—flashed into life, throwing a beam of white to the other side of the square, onto the stoop of what had once been a bargain clothing outlet but was currently being retrofitted to become the first Christmas store in Coldwell Slopes. Captured in the circle of white, like a convict caught trying to scale the prison walls, was a portly man in a Santa Claus outfit, a huge, obviously fake silver beard hiding his face and a bulging sack slung over his shoulder. As 'Santa Baby' blasted from the sound system, he waved to the cheering crowd, jumped into a waiting ATV and began making his way toward them.

Shona couldn't help but laugh at the spectacle, the grandiose silliness of it all. At the same time, it was nice to see an effort being made. But when she looked to Cindee, the girl was neither laughing nor smiling. Her face had hardened into a mask of pale terror—lips tight, eyes wide and nostrils flared as they fought to suck air into her lungs.

"Hey," Shona said, reaching out to her. "Hey, it's okay. It's not the real deal. It's only someone dressing up for fun. Okay?"

The girl shook, shoulders jerking with panicky breaths, but she blinked, swallowed, and appeared to understand, her relief apparent.

"Everything's okay, sweetie, honestly," Shona told her. "There's no reason to be afraid of Santa Claus."

Now Cindee let out a long sigh, expelling the last of her momentary panic and fixing her teacher with a strange look somewhere between disgust and pity. "You're wrong. You're so wrong." Then her head snapped to the right, like a wild animal reacting to the approach of a predator.

Shona followed her stare and saw one of the boys from her class, Devon McCulloch, standing with his mother a few yards away. His eyes serious and trained on Cindee. His blank expression lasted but a moment, then his gaze shifted to Shona and his face flushed with warmth, his mouth opening into a big smile as he raised his arm and waved. Shona waved back and, when she turned away from him, Cindee was gone.

Curtis put a hand on her elbow. "You want to go get a real drink?"

"You have a place in mind?" She opted not make any acknowledgment of the strange encounter, though her eyes continued to search the crowd for Cindee.

"There's a bar nearby." He decided against mentioning it was also on the way to his place. "I've seen it, but not had the courage to go in by myself."

"Aw, that's so cute. And also quite pathetic."

"Thanks. You want to go?"

"Lead the way," she said, casting an eye toward the bandstand. The man in his mall Santa costume had climbed off the ATV, ascended the stage and was now seated on a wide chair, handing out presents to each of the children as they approached him. It didn't look to her like there was anything frightening about it. Or maybe she just wasn't looking closely enough.

6.

LING STOOD OFF to one side of the bandstand, in an area the spotlights didn't reach, grateful for the comforting blanket of shadow. She watched Morgan, doling out presents to the children, wondering how she could have been so stupid as to let him talk her into making such a fool of herself. Her stomach roiled and hands shook from a feeling so intense she couldn't tell if it was anger, embarrassment, or both.

"That was some speech." The man stood only a few feet away from her, sharing the same shadow. His silhouette was back-lit in the glow from the Christmas tree, revealing a tall, thin, crooked frame, one fist clutching the handle of a walking stick. Wisps of hair, silver in the light, clung to a bald pate as pale and cracked as the moon. The reflection of a far-off flame caught the gleam in his dark, unblinking eyes, their fury trained on Ling. If she didn't know any better, she might have taken him for the specter of death. But she knew better.

"It's Mr. Hodgkiss, isn't it? I don't think we've had the pleasure."

"So you do know my name." He growled in the same harsh tone as when he'd interrupted her speech. "You must have received my letters then. How curious that you wouldn't respond to any of them."

"I know you by reputation. I know you're highly regarded."

"Oh hogwash!" He sneered. "You've been ignoring me and I know why. Hoping I'd go away or die of old age. Knowing that if I was given the proper forum, I'd have made damn sure nobody signed away this town's future."

"I haven't been hiding away, Mr. Hodgkiss. There have been several public meetings at which you would have had ample opportunity to . . . "

"Public meetings your lickspittle worked like the devil to make sure I never knew anything about." He wagged a bony finger at Morgan on the bandstand. "I'd watch him, if I were you. I've known Morgan MacLean since he was six weeks old, and a more ambitious, deceptive, greedy, self-aggrandizing, two-faced, power-hungry, backstabbing son of a bilge rat I have never had the misfortune to meet. And you, big city, high-flying corporate hotshot, who damn sure ought to know better . . . *you* give the weasel a job! I mean . . . " He let out a bitter chuckle. "It defies all reason."

"Mr. Hodgkiss." Ling clenched her fists, battling to maintain a calm, measured tone. "Whatever your opinion of me or Morgan or Coldwell Slopes, the deal is done. It is happening. I would suggest you try to adopt a more positive outlook as that's the only way—"

"Miss Wong." He took a step toward her. "They say the Chinese respect their elders, is that right?"

She frowned, uncomfortable with the direction he was steering their conversation. "Certainly."

"Well I'm ninety-one years old. I am the eldest of all the elders in this town and I've lived here all my life. So while you may not have any respect for the opinions of humble country bumpkins, perhaps, on this one occasion, you might listen to what I have to tell you."

Ling glanced around hoping she could catch someone's eye but discovered, remarkably, no-one was paying them any attention. All the others in the square were too involved in their own conversations or watching Morgan's theatrics to notice her or the old man who had her trapped. "Of course."

He stabbed the end of his cane into the snow and leaned over it. "You will fail. This whole ski resort fantasy of yours was doomed from the start and you're going to find out, sooner than you think. You're going to crash and burn and the great tragedy is you're going to take a lot of people here down with you. People who are too soft and naive to know an idiot's enterprise when they see one. And after you return to New York City, defeated and humiliated, you may well be able to pick yourself up and start again somewhere else. But the people of St. Nicholas, this once great community, they will be utterly, irrevocably destroyed. And it'll be on your head. Be in no doubt about that."

With every word spoken, Ling felt the cold permeate a little deeper into her flesh, as if his speech was stripping away her clothing, leaving her exposed to the biting elements. When he finished, she opened her mouth to respond, but her own faculties for argument had deserted her. "Well . . . " She coughed, swallowed. "Obviously, you're entitled to—"

"Have a good evening, Miss Wong." Hodgkiss turned about and shuffled away, passing the steps to the stage at the same moment Morgan was descending.

"Why it's Jake Hodgkiss," he exclaimed in his best, booming voice. "I'm quite sure you've been a good boy. Whatever would you like for Christmas?"

The old man sucked at his teeth, his dark eyes flicking to Ling, then back to Morgan, looking him up and down, taking in the full scope of his ridiculousness. "Unbelievable," he muttered, then continued on his way.

Morgan gave out a half-hearted little "ho-ho-ho", then went over to Ling. "Somebody's full of the joys of the season."

She was shaking with impotent rage. "How dare you."

He frowned. "What's that now?"

"I have been roundly humiliated tonight. And for what? You sent me up there as your warm-up act!"

"Hey, Ling, come on. It went great. Don't listen to what Ol' Man Hodgkiss said."

"For you! It went well for you! Meanwhile I look like a fool. And that's probably just how you planned it!"

"Ling, no." He held out his hands, gesturing for her to keep her voice down. "You're way, way off. I'm on your side."

"Nobody's on my side," she hissed, on the verge of tears. "No-one. I am utterly alone."

"Miss Wong?" She spun around to find they had been joined by two young women. A blonde in a gold snowsuit and a brunette in a silver one. Both aggressively pretty and heavily made up. It was the blonde who spoke. "We wanted to say we liked your speech."

"Thank you, girls," said Morgan, turning to Ling. "There now. Don't you think that's a lovely thing for them to say?"

"Yes." Ling sniffed, quickly regaining her composure. "Thank you very much."

"We thought it was cool," said the brunette. "All the stuff about the future. About helping to shape Coldwell Slopes and make it a success."

"And we were like . . . we definitely want to be a part of that," said the blonde.

"Do you really?" Ling nodded. "What are your names?"

"I'm Bailey," the blonde answered. "This is Kendra."

"We were thinking about what a new holiday destination needs to be successful in the modern world," said Kendra. "And then we realized—it's obvious!"

"It is?" said Ling.

"Influencers," said Bailey. "You need young, hot people on social media telling everyone how awesome the resort's going to be."

"And working with brands to promote the bars and restaurants and all the high-end products that will be available in the stores," said Kendra.

"Sportswear and equipment . . . "

"Food and drink . . . "

"Cosmetics, hair products . . . "

"Shoes, jewelry,"

"Swimwear, lingerie . . . " Bailey glanced Morgan's way at mention of these last suggestions.

"We can do that."

"We can do *all* of that."

Morgan turned to Ling, a lascivious grin behind his synthetic beard. "Well I'm sold."

Her own face betrayed nothing. "I see. How old are you girls?"

"Eighteen," Bailey answered, without hesitation.

"Six- . . . eighteen," said Kendra.

"Okay," said Ling, ready to bring the conversation to a close. "Thanks for your suggestion. I'll think it over."

"We could start right now, y'know, building the hype and stuff," said Kendra.

"Yeah, we've loads of ideas for content," said Bailey. "Instagram, TikTok. We've already got tons of followers." Her friend elbowed her in the ribs and she backtracked. "I mean . . . we would have, if the internet worked."

"Ah, the internet, yes," said Ling. "I can only apologize for that. We did think it would be operational again by now. Morgan—perhaps you'd like to go find out what the latest is with that?"

Morgan was slow to respond; his attention trained on the teenagers, both of whom were casually pulling poses like models at the end of a catwalk. "Oh yeah, sure. I'll . . . I'll check it out."

“We can talk later,” she said, waving him on his way as he stalked off toward the nearest group of contractors.

“So you’ll think about it?” Bailey asked her.

“Oh certainly,” Ling said. “It’s good to know we have such enthusiastic, enterprising young people in the community.”

“We’re serious when we say we can start any time,” said Kendra. “Like . . . if you were planning to throw a party over Christmas or New Year, like . . . at your mansion? We could come along, post about it, make it look really, seriously cool.”

“I will . . . certainly keep it in mind.”

That seemed to satisfy them. The girls went off, arm in arm, giggling and whispering excitedly about the bright new career they’d conjured up for themselves in Coldwell Slopes. Ling remained behind, in the shadow of the bandstand, too numb from the cold now to feel the nausea in her gut.

A party. What a ridiculous notion. Morgan was the partying kind, certain to have some big celebrations planned he wouldn’t bother mentioning to her, not wanting to trouble her with irrelevant little details—as usual. She was no leader of the community and when she tried to play at it, it just felt hollow. There would be no parties at her home this year. Christmas for her would be quiet and lonely and fraught with anxiety.

For a few minutes more, she watched the crowd from the shadows, the families, the old friends and the new, the easy way people had with each other. Then, when she was quite sure no-one was looking, she moved off to the edge of the square, crossed the street and went home.

7.

THE MALAMUTE WAS a wooden hut on stilts that had been grafted onto the side of a truck repair shop, currently unoccupied. The steep staircase leading to the door looked treacherous as hell and had surely seen some painful drunken falls in its time, but at least its heightened position meant there was little chance of the bar being snowed in. The red and blue neon sign in its only window advertising Molson Canadian was visible from the far end of the street, shining like a beacon through the dark of night. Curtis and Shona stepped into its pulsating glow and ascended, laughing to themselves over thoughts of the absurdities potentially awaiting them at the summit.

On the inside, however, the Malamute looked just like a million other cheap watering holes scattered across North America. Three booths near the door. A few more running along the left wall. Opposite them stood the bar, a few wooden stools in front of it and a tiny galley kitchen behind. At the far end of the hut were the restrooms, one for men and one for women, though, looking around the place, Curtis doubted the one for women saw much use. The man behind the bar was heavy-set with a red face, gold-gray beard and ponytail. Were it not for the gray knitted sweater and leather apron he wore, he'd have looked more like Santa Claus than the one in the square.

Seated in a booth with one full beer and four empties was a young man wearing a green army jacket and a sour face. Giving off the perfect impression of a loner, he did not look up when Curtis and Shona entered. The two men seated at the bar did look round, if only briefly. They wore heavy work-wear and were both too tanned to be locals, marking them out as more contractors. The one furthest from the door chuckled once at sight of the newcomers standing hesitantly in the doorway and softly whistled the opening strains of 'Dueling Banjos'. The reference was not lost on Curtis.

Everything in the place was made of metal, cracked leather, or wood painted black to hide the stains; the lights kept low for the same reason. There was no TV, no jukebox, no radio, no music, and no atmosphere. Immediately regretting his decision to invite her, Curtis turned to Shona and was about to ask if she wanted to leave, when he saw she'd already slipped off her hat, scarf and gloves—tossing them into the nearest booth—and was now working on the buttons of her coat. When she looked up and saw his eyes on her, she said, "I'll have a gin and lemonade, thanks."

"Sure thing." He crossed to the bar, ordered her drink and a whiskey and soda for himself. The barman nodded cheerfully and went to prepare them as one of the contractors shifted around on his stool.

"New in town?" the man asked. Only three words, but from the way he slurred them and the way his eyelids drooped when he spoke, it was clear he and his friend had been enjoying themselves for several hours.

"Yeah, I just took a job at the school."

The other man leaned over, waggling his finger in Shona's direction. Having unleashed her hair from the confines of the bobble hat, she was working at it with her hands, trying to get it into shape, studying the reflection in her pocket mirror. "You, uh . . . together?"

"Colleagues," said Curtis, wishing the bartender could be quicker with their drinks. "We only met today."

The man sighed wistfully, eyes still on Shona. "And already making friends. Some guys have all the luck."

Changing the subject, Curtis asked, "You guys with the team staying at the old hotel? On Samuel Street?"

"We are indeed," the man answered, raising his whiskey glass. "I'm Richie. This is Sergio."

"Curtis."

"What do you make of the town, Curtis?"

"It's got a lot of potential."

Sergio laughed. "Potential? It's a fucking ruin! I said to my boy Richie, earlier, I said: when I read the job listing it was for a telecommunications engineer, not an archaeologist! Somebody fucked up, huh?" He laughed again, then made a show for the bartender approaching, coughing to conceal the laugh, though the bartender hadn't been more than two feet away and had heard every word of their conversation. "I don't mean this place, Einar. You understand? This place is . . . It's great."

The barman snorted as he set down Curtis's drinks. "Don't get used to it. Pretty soon this place will be bulldozed, and I'll be managing a ski lodge up on the mountain. Oh yes, Bingzhen has big plans for Einar." He spoke with a heavy Nordic accent and, whether he was joking or not, Curtis could certainly imagine him welcoming guests fresh from the slopes with brandy and hot chocolate. "I apologize for the lack of music," he said, speaking to Curtis. "It's an internet jukebox, but the internet went down about an hour ago."

"Not my team," Sergio stated to the room, like he'd already been hearing complaints.

"A few guys are still out there," Richie explained to Curtis. "They've had teams working round the clock to upgrade cable routes while the snow's off. Periods of outage are to be expected."

"I'd put the radio on," said Einar. "But we're not picking up any stations."

"Not my team," Sergio repeated.

"Probably the local tower was damaged in the blizzard," said Richie. "That'll be an easy fix once we can get somebody out to it."

"Maybe you're right," said Einar. "I could phone someone to find out, but my cellphone has no bars."

"Not my . . . " Sergio began, then hesitated. "Wait . . . *Is* that my team?"

Richie shrugged. "Look . . . it's tough out there, okay? We've got a hell of a lot to get through. You guys have no idea." He looked to Einar. "You still have a two-way, right?"

"Sure, for emergencies."

"So what are you complaining about? Enjoy the peace and quiet. Who needs emails and phone calls at Christmas. This!" He tapped his glass. "This is all you need."

"About that," Curtis said, "What do I owe you?"

Einar held up a hand and smiled, his cheeks reddening as he did so. "Those two are on the house. Welcome to St. Nicholas."

"Coldwell Slopes," Sergio corrected him.

"Oh já! Coldwell Slopes!" Einar laughed. "I can never remember that name."

Curtis took the drinks back to the booth. As he approached, he saw Shona clutching something—a document or photograph, staring at it intently. Before he could get close enough for a decent look, she folded it up and slipped it into her pocket.

"Friendly sort of joint," she said, deflecting any questions before he could ask them.

"Better than what I'm used to." He sat down.

"You mean back home in . . . the United States?" She said it like she was solving some big mystery. "The American South?"

"Mobile, Alabama, to be specific. And you are from . . . " Ireland. It was definitely Ireland. Every electrical impulse in his brain screamed Ireland. "Scotland?"

She gasped through a grin. "Right first time. Well done. Most people guess Irish."

"That's crazy. You don't sound even a little Irish. Where in Scotland are you from?"

"Inverness. In the Highlands. You know it?"

"I know it's a hell of a long way from here."

She nodded, staring into her drink. "Some six thousand-odd miles, as the crow flies."

"How did you find your way to Canada?"

"Oh, that was my fiance's idea."

Curtis felt a sharp stab of disappointment in his gut. This wasn't a date. He'd never said anything to suggest it was a date, nor had he truly considered it to be one. He'd hardly given any thought to whether Shona might be the kind of person he would be interested in dating. Still, the immediate sorrow he felt on hearing the word 'fiance' was acute—and told him something. His eyes darted—discreetly, he hoped—to her hands, looking for a wedding ring, but there was none. "You're married?"

"I almost was. To a forestry contractor. He drove one of those big beasts that haul timber out of the woods. A specialist in that field can work just about anywhere he wants—if it has trees—and he wanted to come to Canada. He thought there were huge opportunities for us out here. So we came and did our best to make a go of it. And within a year he wanted to go home. Not that the opportunities weren't there. He just got homesick, I think. And I did not want to go back. So we split. I've been working temporary teaching posts, nothing permanent on the horizon. I couldn't afford to keep living where I was without him, so I started looking for any job I could apply for that was long-term and would allow me to stay in the country. And I read about this place, which couldn't have been more perfect."

"Why didn't you want to go home?"

"Because it's not my home. It's hard to explain, but . . . just because you're born somewhere, doesn't mean you belong. At least, that's the way I feel and what I believe. It's just where you start. And all my life I never bothered to look beyond it. I just accepted what was offered, whatever was easiest and within reach. I allowed myself to assume the shape of a life dictated by a home I didn't choose, a family I didn't choose, friends I didn't choose, even a fiancé I didn't choose. Not really. He chose me. And it was his idea to leave, not mine, but once I did, I knew I couldn't go back. I didn't begin to breathe until I left. I think you have to cut all ties to where you came from before you can understand yourself, who you really are and what you want. And only once you know yourself can you figure out where you belong."

"You think you belong here?"

She shrugged. "Maybe. It's too soon to say." She turned her head to look out the window, past the neon sign to the icy gray desolation of the town beyond. "I get the impression there weren't very many applications for my position. People read up on this place and to them it sounds like a nightmare. The cold, the dark, the isolation. The fractured community full of lost people in search of a future. Everything changing. Nothing certain. If there's one thing people fear, it's uncertainty. But to me? Certainty's what I'm trying to break away from. So this sounded like exactly where I needed to be." She sipped her drink. "Time will tell, I suppose. What about you? I know it's not Scotland, but Alabama's still more than a bus ride away."

"I needed work."

"That's not the whole tale."

"No, it's not. But I don't know that we want to get into all that."

"Oh come on! I've just given you my whole tragic origin story. The least you could do is share yours."

He shifted a little uncomfortably. "It's more the kind of story you tell after three drinks."

She snorted at his discomfort and shrugged. "Okay, fine. Then I guess we're not going anywhere."

There followed a brief silence as Curtis struggled to think of something to say, broken by the rapping of knuckles on the bar top as Richie, doing his best Bing Crosby imitation, burst into song. "It's beginning to look a lot like Christmas," he crooned. "Everywhere you go . . . " He appeared to forget the lyrics after that but continued the melody with some "ba-bum-ba-ba-bum-ba-bums", accompanied by Sergio a half-beat behind.

The kid in the army jacket turned slowly to face them, not a trace of amusement in his expression. "Hey," he barked and the singing ceased. "Cut it out."

The duo shrugged apologetically and went back to their drinks.

"I guess somebody doesn't like Christmas," said Curtis.

"I love Christmas." Shona made the statement in a sad, quiet tone. She appeared not to have taken any notice of the singing and was staring out the window again. "Are you religious, Curtis?"

It was a surprising question to ask without preamble, but he supposed her mind was on Father McHattie again. "I was raised Baptist, but . . . I'm not a believer, no. You?"

She shook her head. "I don't agree with organized religion in general. Those who make people believe absurdities can make people commit atrocities, as Voltaire would say."

"Voltaire, right," he murmured encouragingly.

"I absolutely fucking love Christmas though."

She was silent a while, just staring out the window, and Curtis watched her, studying her profile. Anyone who knew him would not have considered her to be his type. She was a little taller than average and much skinnier than the more voluptuous ladies of his romantic past. He typically preferred striking facial features to prettiness. Mean-looking women were a sure-fire turn-on. Shona didn't look the least bit mean and was undeniably pretty, but in a tired, somber way that appealed to him. He found world-weariness a beguiling quality, more so now than in his youth. Perhaps because it relaxed him to see his own traits written on the faces of others. As he looked on, a tear collected at the corner of her eye and rolled down her cheek. She blinked, sniffed, and wiped it away.

"Shit," she groaned through a halting sigh. "I'm sorry."

"It's okay."

"I don't cry. I never cry." She snatched up a cocktail napkin and dabbed at her eyes, both of which were suddenly streaming. "What you saw this morning would have given you a completely inaccurate impression of the kind of person I am, because I don't cry."

"Exceptional circumstances."

She sniffed again, taking a deep breath and blowing it out through her mouth before taking a long drink of gin. The combination worked. The tears stopped. "There is currently no cafeteria staff employed at the school. You might have noticed that?"

"I think I did."

"It's fine. The kids all bring packed lunches anyway. But today? Today was special. The last day before Christmas. The last day for St. Nicholas Elementary before becoming the Coldwell Slopes Academy for Gifted Little Angels, or whatever they want to call it. So Beatrice decided they should have a lunch to remember, with roast turkey and mashed potatoes and Yule log and Christmas crackers and something absolutely horrific for the vegan kid—we still have one, bless her. Cruel thing to inflict on a child." She sighed. "It's a lot of work for one woman, to do all that. And Father McHattie? He seemed like the kind of person who could handle a roomful of perfectly polite children for fifteen minutes. So I went to give her a hand. And by the time I got back . . . " She didn't need to complete the sentence.

"There was nothing you could have done."

"Well see, that's the thing." She took another sip of her drink. There wasn't more than a half inch left in the glass now. "As well as a teacher, I am a trained nurse."

"Seriously?"

"Nearly fully trained. Almost qualified. See, in my family, tradition dictates that if a woman can't figure out what to do with her life, she goes into nursing or teaching. And that means every last woman in my family is a nurse or a teacher, because not a one has ever been able to figure out what do with herself. And me, being even more unable to figure out what to do with myself than most, I did both. Nursing first. I dropped out in my third year and switched to teaching, but I learned a lot before I did. It never bothered me before. A good teacher must possess a wealth of useless information. Or useful only insofar as it can be passed on to others. But maybe, if I'd only stayed in that room, I could have helped him. I could have fucking saved him."

"You don't know that."

"No. And that's the—"

"Sandwich?" The interruption came from Einar, appearing at

the end of their table with a platter of thin unimpressive sandwiches, cut into neat triangles. He leaned in so the light from the lamp above them caught his face, illuminating his over-eager grin. "They're free."

"Oh, um . . . thank you," Shona said, the distraction doing a sterling job of completely shattering her train of thought. She eyed the platter suspiciously. "What's . . . what's in them?"

Einar's smile wilted. "Caviar and smoked salmon. It's a free sandwich."

"No, I appreciate that. I'm not trying to be ungrateful. It's just . . . there's no mayonnaise, is there? Because I can't have mayonnaise."

"You're allergic?" Curtis asked.

"No, it's just disgusting."

"Turkey and cheese," said Einar, his patience wearing thin. "The ones on the left have butter. The ones on the right, no butter. And no mayonnaise at all."

"In that case, thank you very much," Shona said, gathering up enough to make a decent stack, while Curtis politely declined.

"You're very welcome," Einar sighed, struggling and failing to plaster the smile back across his face. "I hope it compensates for the lack of atmosphere."

From over at the bar, Sergio called, "Hey Einar! If it's atmosphere you want, we can provide!"

He nudged Richie, who lifted his head and, without any further prompting, began to croon, "He's the little boy that Santa Claus forgot . . . And goodness knows, he didn't want a lot . . . "

Once again, the kid sitting in the booth turned his angry face their way and yelled, "Hey, shut up!"

But Richie continued. "He wrote a note to Santa for some soldiers and a drum . . . It broke his little heart when he found Santa hadn't come . . . "

Now the kid bolted up from his seat, grabbing the neck of one of his empty bottles, raising it like he was about to smash on the table. "I said shut the fuck up, God damn it!"

"Hey, hey," Einar interjected, holding out one arm in a calming signal while balancing his sandwich platter on the other. "That's enough. Take it easy." He turned to the men at the bar. "No more Christmas songs, okay?"

Richie and Sergio nodded, their eyes on the kid. "Whatever you say, Einar," said Sergio.

Einar nodded to the kid who, though he still looked angry, sank back down into his seat, apparently mollified. Einar turned back to Curtis and Shona, and in a lowered voice explained, "Will doesn't care for Christmas because he lost his mother at Christmas."

"Oh, that's so sad," Shona said.

"I didn't lose her," the kid called from across the room. "She was murdered." His gaze passed from Shona to Einar, then to the men at the bar, before finally coming to rest on the table in front of him. "By Santa Claus."

Richie and Sergio's faces immediately crumpled into laughter, though they did their best to conceal it, clamping their fists against their mouths, shoulders heaving and kicking their feet as they slowly doubled over.

Einar sighed deeply and said to Shona, "This time of year is a hardness for some people. The cold, the dark. The loneliness. We get a lot of blizzards here, like the one last night. Sometimes things get so bad in a person's head, all cooped up inside, all alone, they decide they'd rather take their chances with the blizzard and are never seen again. Happens more than you might think."

"It wasn't the blizzard," Will yelled. "And she wasn't alone. She had me." The room was silent, everyone's attention on the kid, waiting for him to tell the tale. After taking a moment to compose himself, he did. "I wasn't born in this town. My mom could see there was no future here, so she worked like hell to get herself an education and get out. Went to college in Vancouver, where she met my dad and where I was born. But when he left us, she didn't have any option but to come back to this shit-hole. And I wish every day she hadn't." He snatched up the only bottle with a little beer left in it and drained it, gasping when he lowered it from his mouth. "I was eleven years old the night he came for her. She let him right in and gave herself up to him. She couldn't see him for what he was, but I could. I saw." He stood and waved a finger around the room. "See, the people born in this town, they're under a spell. They can't see what's happening right in front of them, right before their eyes. Only outsiders. Outsiders like me . . . and you. When he reveals himself, if you're still here, you'll see him for what he is. But it won't help you. And it won't save you. Cos if you see him at all, it's already too late." He rose slowly from the booth, unsteady on his feet, and staggered across the floor, heading for the restrooms.

As he passed, Sergio held out a hand to stop him. "Hey, man. If all that's true and your mom was killed all those years ago, what are you still doing here? Why not leave?"

Will squinted at him, struggling to focus with all the alcohol in his system. "I have to be here. This is where I have to be. So when he comes back—and he *is* coming back—I can kill him."

His piece spoken, the kid continued on his way. In the moments that followed, the only sound in the bar was the shuffling of his feet across the floorboards, till he finally reached the door to the men's room and disappeared inside.

Then Einar turned back to Shona and Curtis, nodded to their glasses and asked, "Another round?"

8.

DEVON MCCULLOCH WALKED all the way home from Wintertainment hand-in-hand with his mother, only letting her go when they entered the porch and had to take off their boots.

"You know, you could have stayed if you'd wanted to," she said. "None of your little friends seemed in a hurry to leave." Indeed, all the other schoolchildren had remained in town, splitting into groups and chasing each other through the streets, obviously making mischief. "Or you could have lent a hand on the cider stand. I'm sure your dad would have appreciated the help."

Devon winced. He hated it whenever anyone referred to Ryan Wray, hot-shot real estate lawyer and his mother's husband of the last year and half, as his dad. "I know, but I'm tired."

"Aw, honey. It's been a tough day, I know." She ruffled his hair and led him inside, to the warmth of the hallway. "How would you like a cup of cocoa before bed?"

"Yes please." He shrugged off his coat, wandered through to the living room, and turned on the TV. The cable was out—as he knew it would be—so he scrolled through the DVR and picked one of the dozens of Christmas movies he'd saved. It didn't matter to him which one it was. As long as there was snow and Christmas songs and actors dressed as Santa Claus. He didn't need more than that. He couldn't pay attention to the plot anyway. His mind was elsewhere, howling at the agony of time's lethargic crawl, the way he was forced to wait. The seconds always ticked by more slowly the closer it came to Christmas. He was well used to that. Used to the pain of waiting. But this year was so much worse, because the thing he awaited was so much grander and more wonderful than anything he'd looked forward to in his life.

The doorbell rang.

Devon felt his stomach tighten and his skin prickle with goose-flesh as he turned around.

"Expecting someone?" Leaving the cocoa on the stove, his mother came down the hallway. He watched her quickly check her hair in the mirror by the stairs, then go to the door and open it. "Oh my. It's you!"

"Season's greeting's, Mrs. Wray. Mind if I come in?" From where Devon stood, he could only hear the man, not see him. But his voice—deep, rich and buttery—flowed through the room, warming the air.

"Of course." Devon's mother, eyes wide and mouth agape, stumbled back without looking away from their visitor. She kept one shoulder against the wall, relying on it to keep her aloft, her legs quivering and threatening at any second to buckle. She knocked a couple of framed family photos from their hooks as she brushed past, but made no effort to pick them up.

The man now crossing the threshold and closing the door behind him, either not seeing the photos or not caring, stepped forward and crushed them beneath his shiny black boots.

Devon trembled with the thunder of his own heartbeat, the panting of his breath. For a moment, he thought he would never be able to get enough air into his lungs to speak, but then he said it. "Santa?"

A head of luminous white curls beneath a jaunty red hat turned his way and eyes twinkling with all the magic and music of the stars found his. "Hello Devon."

He was everything the movies, songs and stories had made him out to be, and so much more. Tall in height and wide in girth, yet with a build that looked strong, like a champion power-lifter. Not fat at all. He was old enough to have white hair, yet his gentle, handsome face was flushed with the wonders of youth. His suit of scarlet velvet and white fur trim was finer than any worn by multitudes of impostors on the street, stage, and screen. And when he moved, the bells sewn into the fabric jingled with a sound like an ode to charity and fellowship.

"You really came," said Devon.

Santa chuckled. "Of course! I come every year." He leaned toward Devon's mother. "I hope you don't mind I'm a night early on this occasion."

"Not . . . not at all." She appeared to swoon under his gaze, wilting against the stairs and grasping the banister for support.

"I did everything you told me to, Santa," Devon said, stepping closer. "We're going to have everything set up, just the way you want it."

The big man grinned—and when he grinned, it sent a ripple of wonder through the atmosphere, changing the nature of the light in the room so that every edge and every surface gleamed as if it had been cleaned and polished that afternoon.

"That's just grand, Devon," he said, and when he spoke, the Christmas cookies on the kitchen counter spun and the ornaments on the tree did a dance of delight. "And you may call me Santa if you wish, but seeing as we're such close friends, how about you call me by my true name?"

Devon hesitated, unsure for a moment what he meant, then understood. "Okay, then I will . . . Saint Nicholas."

The man's grin widened and the fire in the hearth—where there had been no fire only moments ago—burned brighter than it ever had before. "Good lad. You and I have got a long night ahead of us. There is much to be done! But first . . . " His glittering eyes settled on Mrs. Wray once again. "Your mother and I need to go upstairs for a little while."

"Oh," Devon's mother said, breathing heavily and blinking like she couldn't quite comprehend where she was. "Yes. Yes, of course."

Saint Nicholas took her hand into his. "Lead the way, my dear."

She moved unsteadily, like the floor was tilting beneath her feet, and began climbing the stairs, Santa Claus at her back. Devon made to follow them, but the big man turned to address him.

"Don't let the cocoa burn, boy."

Devon looked into the kitchen, saw the pot boiling over on the stove and ran to save it. He turned the heat down, grabbed a spoon and began to stir, while over his shoulder the radio—though it wasn't switched on—began blaring carols, the volume growing louder and louder. Almost loud enough to obscure the sounds of struggle from upstairs.

He was still stirring the cocoa some time later, when he heard the front door slam. He looked and saw his stepfather crouching to collect the broken photos from the floor. For him to be home meant Wintertainment was over, which meant at least an hour had passed since Devon and his mother got back. Could he really have been at the stove stirring cocoa for an hour? It had only felt like moments.

"Hi, Devon." Mr. Wray entered the kitchen holding up the photos in their shattered frames. "What happened here?"

"An accident."

His stepfather nodded and set them down on the counter. "Where's your mom?"

Before Devon could think up a reply, there came a scrape and thud from over their heads, as of a heavy piece of furniture being shoved against a wall.

Devon was sure his face would betray his panic, but Mr. Wray, tired from a full day at the office and an evening spent manning the cider stand—a way of subtly promoting his legal services to the townsfolk—gave no indication of concern. He only stifled a yawn and turned away, moving toward the stairs and the source of the sound.

It took Devon longer than he could reasonably explain to peel his hand away from the wooden spoon. He knew he should chase his stepfather, get his attention somehow. Stall him. Get him out of the house, if possible. Yet his grip remained tight on the spoon, continuing to stir the cocoa, now too thick and dark to be drinkable after all its time simmering over the heat.

He heard footsteps going up the stairs.

"Erin?" His stepfather's voice.

It took an unlikely amount of concentration, but at last his hand sprang open, the spoon dropping into the pot. He took a step back from the stove in the same moment Mr. Wray opened the door to the master bedroom.

Devon only heard what happened next. There was a sound like the screeching of a pack of wild animals, followed by a furious pounding as of a stampede of hoofed beasts from one corner of the room to the other. Barely audible through the chaos was the startled, perplexed cry of Mr. Wray, immediately silenced as the stampede reached him and became a fury of howls and thunder that rattled the walls of their home.

Devon ran for the stairs, halting once he was on the bottom step and could see what lay at the top. His stepfather's body was sprawled across the landing, his feet twitching in the open bedroom doorway. His decapitated head rested against the wall, face frozen in terror, while the ravaged remains of his neck gushed blood in a river cascading down the carpeted steps.

Devon felt a rush of panic through his body, his breath

immediately faltering, chest seizing like it was being clenched in a demon's fist. He didn't know if he would scream, faint, or puke.

But then he blinked. And realized his mistake.

Mr. Wray wasn't dead. He was asleep, dozing comfortably with his hands clasped over his stomach, rising and falling with his calm, contented breaths. Far from being separated from his body, his head, still entirely attached, was merely propped against the wall, his gently smiling lips fluttering as soft snores passed between them. It was surely a pleasant dream he was enjoying, for his feet twitched the way a dog's would when submerged in fantasies of parks and rabbits.

Devon was briefly baffled, wondering how he could have misinterpreted the scene so badly, but then relief overwhelmed him, carrying with it an irresistible sense of calm, and he let his concerns evaporate, the horrific vision immediately forgotten.

He climbed to the top of the stairs—ignoring the strange sensation of warm liquid gushing over his stockinged feet—and peered into the bedroom.

His mother and Santa Claus lay together on the bed. She sprawled seductively beneath him, sweater pulled up and pants pulled down to reveal lacy underwear and the sheen of lustful sweat on her taut torso. Her eyes were closed and lips pouting in anticipation of his kiss. Santa loomed over her, his red hat casually tossed away, the belt to his tunic unbuckled, his body heaving with visible pants of passion. Before proceeding, he turned his head in Devon's direction.

"You should go," he said, not unkindly. "Call the others. There's work to be done."

Devon knew enough to know this was a private moment between adults and not the sort of thing to which he should bear witness.

"Okay." He nodded, reached for the door and began to pull it shut. As he did, he was briefly assaulted by another hallucination. It was fleeting, only the flash of an image, lasting no more than a fraction of a second. But in that instant he saw his mother lying dead, split up the middle from her crotch to her neck and splayed open, organs spilling from the gaping cavity, the bed and walls hosed in her blood. Her glassy eyes bulging into oblivion, mouth wrenched open in a scream drowned by a torrent of her own frothing fluids. And, perched above her, something monstrous.

Something inhuman. Something huge and ugly and covered in jagged edges only half-hidden by molting red rags. Something that had more in common with a lizard or an insect than any kind of man. Something that rasped and chattered as it drove its mouth and upper limbs into the red mess of her corpse, plunging through the gore with ravenous fury.

A vision there and gone.

Devon descended the stairs, shaking his head in bafflement at the wild, insistent fancies his imagination presented. By the time he'd reached the last step, he'd forgotten all about it.

He found his schoolbag in the living room and dug out his two-way radio—a brightly colored red and green model, adorned with stickers of snowmen and candy canes. "This is North Star calling Joseph. North Star calling Joseph. Come in Joseph."

After a moment, he heard the voice of his classmate, Sam Ellison. "This is Joseph. Go ahead North Star."

"The plan is a go. Send the word. All return to Bethlehem. I say again. All return to . . . "

He silenced himself at the sound of a key being turned in the front door. He heard voices as it swung open—soft, low, conspiratorial. The last thing he expected. The *very* last thing he wanted.

His bitch of a sister was home.

9.

"UH OH." Shona grinned, staring out the window. "Here comes trouble."

"What is it?" Curtis leaned forward, but from where he was sitting couldn't see anything.

He heard before he saw. The door slammed open and a man cried, "Ho ho ho! Merry Christmas!" Curtis turned to see the Santa from Wintertainment strolling into the room, his arms held out in theatrical greeting.

A cheer went up from the men at the bar. "Now it's a party," called Sergio.

"Usual is it, Morgan?" asked Einar.

"Morgan?" the Santa said, attempting to deepen his voice. "You must have me confused, sir. I am Santa Claus! I don't know any Morgan. But he sounds like a fine, handsome fellow and a generous tipper."

Einar gave a sarcastic laugh and reached for the bourbon.

Morgan turned, surveying the room, and saw Shona and Curtis in their booth. "And what have we here?" Hitching up his belt, he stomped his way over to them, eyes sparkling mischievously behind his ridiculous silver beard. "Fellowship? Camaraderie? Bacchanalia? 'Tis the season!"

Shona grinned. "You were at the Wintertainment celebration."

"I was. You were there? Both of you?"

They nodded.

"Fantastic." Morgan pulled down his beard to show his face. "That's just fantastic. That's exactly what we need." He aimed a finger at Shona. "Shona Fleming from Scotland."

"Correct," she said.

"And Curtis Tate from Arizona."

"Alabama," said Curtis.

"That's it. Well . . . " Morgan waved his hands toward the pair of them. "This is exactly what I love to see. You've both come so far, you don't know anyone, you don't know what to make of the place. But here you are. You've had . . . quite the rough morning, I know. And you could have stayed home. But you've come out, joined in the celebrations, come for a drink at the local bar . . . You're connecting, meeting people . . . This is how a community rebuilds. This is exactly it. Right here."

"We're happy to do our part," said Shona.

"I'm serious. I want you to know we couldn't be happier to have both of you here. It takes a lot of guts to do what you've done. And right now, you're probably both wondering if it was the right call. But don't judge the place on what you've seen so far. A year from now, you won't recognize it. We're building something amazing and I just know you're going to love it."

"You sure sell it well," said Curtis.

The grin semi-permanently plastered to Morgan's face suddenly vanished, replaced with an expression of deadly seriousness. "Because I believe in it, Mr. Tate. Because I believe in it." He patted his belly. "You might think this is just a costume, but not me. When I put this on, I swore an oath to live up to the highest ideals of Santa Claus. I intend to make sure this Christmas every man, woman and child in St. Nicholas gets exactly what they want."

"That's a lofty ambition," said Shona.

"Try me. What do you want for Christmas?"

"I honestly haven't given it much thought."

"Well give it some thought. And tell me later. Now . . . " He tugged the beard over his mouth. "How about the rest of you?" He strolled over to the bar. "What are your demands?"

"A vacation would be nice," said Einar. "I'd like to get away from St. Nicholas for a while."

"Let me make a note of that." Morgan produced a notepad and pen. "And yourself, sir?"

Richie smirked. "Since you ask, I notice you don't have a masseuse in town."

Sergio laughed. "And I bet I know just the kind you'd like. Swedish, blonde, naked . . . "

"God damn it, no," Richie yelled over his friend's laughter. "I'm serious. My back's a wreck. And the cold doesn't help."

"A back massage." Morgan made a note. "I'll see what I can do. Sergio?"

The contractor raised his glass. "Another drink would satisfy me."

"That I can do right now," Morgan said, slapping the counter. "Barkeep! Another drink for my friend here. In fact . . . " He glanced around the room. "A round of drinks for everyone in the place!"

"Thank you, Santa," Shona called and took a long sip from her glass. She stared at Curtis. "Coming up on three drinks. You know what that means. Soon be time for you to spill your guts."

He showed her something between a smile and a wince. "Don't set your expectations too high. It'll bore you to tears."

"Oh no. No more tears from me this year. Today was plenty."

There was a howl of laughter from the bar and Morgan stepped back. "Wait, wait, I've got a better one. Hey!" He waved to Shona and Curtis. "You listening? This morning, as I was preparing to leave the North Pole, Mrs. Claus told me to remember my umbrella. When I asked why, she said, 'Because it looks like rain, dear.' Get it?"

Shona raised her glass and, over the cackling from the contractors, called out, "We get it!"

"Don't worry if you don't like it," said Morgan. "I've got a ton more!"

"That's okay."

"Seriously. I went online and wrote a whole bunch down. Give me a second, though. I've got to pay a visit to the little elf's room." He threw back his drink and told the two contractors, "When I return, you can tell me all about how you're going to repay me by getting our internet back up and running. Tonight."

"Knew there was a catch," Sergio muttered as Morgan wheeled away from the bar, heading for the restrooms.

"Wow." Shona looked at Curtis as she reached for her stack of turkey sandwiches. "Dinner *and* a show. You really know how to treat a girl."

There was a sound of commotion from the far end of the bar. Curtis and Shona both looked to see Morgan and Will in a tussle, grunting and struggling. Everyone turned to watch the pair wrestling their way across the room, before Morgan cried out and fell backward, hitting the floor. His face twisted in rage, Will jumped on top of him, pinned him in place and screamed, "This is what you get, you fuck!" Then he slammed his fist into his body.

"No," Morgan yelled, his arms flailing defensively. "Help! Help me!"

Will raised his fist and brought it back down a second time. Then a third, punctuating each blow with a screamed word. "Merry! Fucking! Christmas!" Only on the fourth time he raised it did Shona see his hand was wrapped around a knife. The blade was coated in blood, casting an arc of crimson splashes as he swung it upward.

She launched herself from her seat and across the room, delivering a swift kick to Will's wrist. He cried out as the blade flew from his hand. "Bitch!" He shoved her away, then put his hands back on Morgan, clamping them around his throat.

Shona fell back against the bar, looked to Curtis and was shocked to see him still sitting in the booth. "Curtis!"

His eyes flashed with a kind of nervous, embarrassed panic and he stood up. "Right. Sorry." He rushed over to the kid and tried to pull him off Morgan. When Will wriggled out of his grasp, still strangling the other man, Curtis drew his fist back then drove it hard into his nose. It connected with a crack louder than Morgan's screams and sent Will tumbling backward. He snorted blood as he scrambled up, back onto his feet and spotted the knife over against the wall. He lunged for it at the same moment someone racked a pump-action shotgun and yelled, "Freeze!" He turned his head to find the barrel of Einar's sawn-off 12-gauge aimed at his eye.

"Don't move," the barman told him.

"Kill him," Will replied, drunkenly slurring the words through the blood pouring from his nostrils. "We've got to kill him! It's our only chance!"

Morgan was writhing on the floor, kicking his legs and whimpering. Shona knelt down at his side and put a reassuring hand on him. "Calm down. Don't move."

"Stabbed me," he spat, patting weakly at the wounds in his torso. "The little shit stabbed me!"

"You're going to be okay," Shona said. "Just lie still. We're going to get you help." She looked at Curtis, narrowing her eyes. "What the fuck was that?"

He wasn't sure if she was referring to the kid's explosion of violence or him freezing up in the booth, so didn't answer. He stepped around Will and picked up the knife from where it had landed. It was a narrow flick knife with a blade around four inches long, still stained with blood. He closed it and put it in his pocket, then looked to Einar. "You got a first-aid kit?"

Einar nodded to his left, without taking his eyes or the gun off Will. "Under the register."

Curtis went behind the bar, found the kit and tossed it to Shona, who opened it, found a pair of disposable gloves and slipped them on. "It's all going to be okay," she told Morgan, now shivering and whimpering. "You've got nothing to worry about."

Up at the bar, Sergio sipped his drink and sighed. "Well that's a hell of a way to ruin a perfectly pleasant evening." He turned to Will. "Hey kid! What'd you have to go and do a stupid thing like that for?"

His face turning paler and eyes growing wider by the second, Will appeared to be quickly sobering up, the drunken mania that had overwhelmed him now evaporating from his system. "I . . . I thought . . . " He licked his lips, tasting his own blood. "I thought it was Santa Claus."

"Jesus," Richie groaned. "That's a dumb fucking thing to think."

Curtis kept looking behind the bar until he found the CB radio. "This work?" he asked Einar.

"Better pray it does," the man replied.

Curtis gave it a go, switching it on and putting the microphone to his mouth. "Mayday, mayday!"

"Mayday?" Richie repeated. "Is the plane going down?"

"Anybody come in," Curtis continued. "This is . . . " He turned to Einar. "Where is this?"

"The Malamute!"

"This is the Malamute. Someone's been stabbed. We need urgent medical assistance. Can anyone hear this? Respond please, over."

They waited and were silent, all except for Morgan, who continued to moan as Shona lifted up his Santa coat and peeled back the blood-drenched padding to reveal his wounds.

Then the radio crackled. "Malamute, this is Gertrude. Read you loud and clear and I'm on my way. ETA fifteen minutes. Over."

She made the journey in ten, blasting the horn as her truck pulled up outside, but it took her another three minutes to climb the stairs. Curtis could do nothing but watch from the doorway and call for her to hurry, though he was tempted to race down, lift her over his shoulder and haul her up.

"I'm coming, I'm coming," she snapped back, one hand on the railing and both eyes on her feet as she carefully navigated each step. "Whole place is a god-damned death trap."

At last, she made it into the bar and went over to where Morgan lay, still being tended to by Shona. A few feet away, in the corner, Will sat with his head in his hands, while Einar kept a watchful eye on him. Sergio and Richie had not moved from their stools.

"What's the damage?" Gertrude crouched down, setting her medical bag on the floor.

"Three knife wounds," Shona answered. Her blood-smeared hands were clamped on Morgan's stomach, applying pressure to the deepest cut. "I think the bleeding's under control. There was some hemostatic gauze in the first-aid kit, so I used that."

"Well, well." Gertrude looked in Einar's direction. "I'm impressed."

The barman shrugged. "I try to prepare for all eventualities."

He didn't take his eyes from Will, who muttered, "I . . . I thought it was Santa Claus."

Gertrude squinted at him, perplexed, then refocused her attention on Morgan and his blood-soaked costume. "Easy mistake to make, I suppose. And how's the patient?"

"I'm fine," Morgan answered in a weak voice, his lips trembling. Shona had rolled her coat up and slipped it under his head to make him more comfortable. "Except for the stabbing . . . That I could have lived without."

"He's been telling me Christmas jokes," said Shona.

"Is that so?" Gertrude took a closer look at his wounds and the efforts Shona had made to patch them up. She touched his skin, finding it cold and clammy. "Got one for me, Morgan?"

He thought for a moment, then answered, "You know what the technical term is for Santa's little helpers?"

"What's that?"

"Subordinate Clauses."

Gertrude cringed. "Jesus Christ, Morgan. You write that yourself?" She looked at Shona. "You've done a good job here."

"Thanks." Shona smiled. "I trained as a nurse."

"That's lucky. Could you come with us?"

"To the hospital?"

Gertrude shook her head. "He's not making it to a hospital tonight. We can go up to the clinic, but I'm the whole staff. I'd appreciate the extra pair of hands."

"Sure."

Morgan cleared his throat and wheezed, "Remind me to recruit more medics."

"That's a good idea, Morgan," Gertrude told him. "Now . . . do you think you can walk?"

"Walk?" he said.

"Is that wise?" asked Shona.

"I've got a stretcher in the truck," said Gertrude. "But with those stairs, it could take thirty minutes to get him down. If he can walk, we can get up to the clinic a whole lot faster. And faster, I think, would be better."

Steeling himself for the ordeal, Morgan nodded. "I can walk." Gertrude got Curtis, Sergio, and Richie to pitch in, helping him up onto his feet and then half-carrying him out the door and down the steps. When they got to the truck he was nearly moving entirely under his own steam, but they eased him in back onto the stretcher. Shona was climbing in when another vehicle pulled up behind them. Curtis recognized it as the brown utility van he'd helped load Father McHattie's body into that morning.

The engine cut out and Owen and Dan emerged, followed by Ling Wong. She ran past them to reach Gertrude's truck. "Morgan? Morgan, my God!"

"Hi, Ling." He waved weakly from the stretcher, poking his hand out the side of the blanket Shona had thrown over him, voice muffled by an oxygen mask. "How are you?"

Gertrude slammed the back door before she could answer and moved around to get in the front. "We don't have time to talk," she said. "We're going to the clinic. Anyone who wants to can follow us."

"Wait," Ling called. "What happened?"

"They'll tell you." Gertrude pointed at Curtis, Sergio, and Richie, standing sheepishly together on the sidewalk, then jumped in the truck, started it up and sped away.

"All right then." Owen adjusted his Mountie hat as he turned to survey the trio. He puffed up his cheeks and blew a thick white cloud into the air, shaking his head. "I honestly . . . I can't believe I actually have to ask this, but . . . who stabbed Santa Claus?"

Across the street, hidden in the shadows beneath a half-collapsed fence, two children observed the unfolding drama with interest. Bringing a radio up to his face, one whispered, "Balthasar calling Gaspar. We're outside the Malamute. There's something happening here."

10.

KENDRA WRAY'S HOLIDAY was not off to the greatest of starts—but she was set on changing that. For weeks she had been looking forward to celebrating the season with her school friends at MacArthur Point, but the blizzard and road closures had screwed with her plans. She was reduced to attempting to make the best of the depressingly dull Wintertainment party with other St. Nicholas teens like Bailey McLuhan, Noah Fessenden, and Marshall Boyd. While she didn't hate their company, none could be described as especially smart, funny or cool. Bailey's dream of becoming an online influencer and brand ambassador for Coldwell Slopes was cute, but delusional. Kendra went along with it for fun, but in her head, she still saw Bailey and the guys the same way the more fashionably elite of MacArthur Point High did, dubbing them 'the St. Nick Nobodies'.

Kendra was *not* a nobody. She was a temporarily dispossessed somebody—a product of the big city, which was where she belonged. Her involuntary relocation to the back end of nowhere only happened because of her father's unlikely romance with and eventual marriage to former civil servant and property developer Erin McCulloch. Kendra could see no reason why the new family unit couldn't be based in MacArthur Point, but her father insisted on moving the two of them in with Erin and her son Devon, much preferring the thought of his 'impressionable' teen daughter living a quiet, boring, uneventful life in St. Nicholas.

With a population of just over twenty-five thousand, MacArthur Point was no great metropolis. But it had a cinema and a mall and bars and nightclubs and strip clubs and violent crime and prostitution and drug dealers and above-average rates of teen pregnancy for the territory. While Kendra complained loudly and often about the boredom and indignity she was forced to endure as a resident of St. Nicholas, her father was comforted by the thought that he didn't need to worry about his darling princess falling under the sway of bad influences. In this town, she *was* the bad influence.

Tonight, she aimed to prove as much. She had played the part of an innocent and wholesome young woman at Wintertainment, engaging with the locals, keeping Noah's loud mockery in check, making a polite introduction to Ling Wong, even helping her dad on the cider stall toward the end. She'd asked him then if she could stay out a little later and he'd agreed, unaware her friends had used the distraction of the event to source a heated basement in an abandoned property where they could party the night away, engaging in whatever illicit and immoral activities their young hearts dared. The cellphone service blackout (far from the town's first) meant no-one could hound her to come home and, in the morning, she could offer up any excuse she cared to invent. However, while her friends had succeeded in securing a venue, they proved woefully inept at sourcing either drugs or alcohol. And regardless of how enthusiastically Noah or Marshall might proclaim its virtues, she would not be reduced to huffing paint.

So Kendra had returned home on a mission. Bailey had followed along behind her, loudly whispering as they crept through the front door. "Why are the lights on? I thought you said they'd all be asleep."

"They will be," Kendra assured her, silently slipping off her chunky winter boots. "Dad and Erin are always dead by ten. Probably left the lights on for me."

"How sweet. My mom locked me out of the house for a whole weekend once while she was at a Rush concert. I was ten."

"Shit."

"She still says it was my fault. Says said she'd arranged for me to stay a couple nights with Miss Gulliver and I must have forgot or not been listening to her in the first place, 'cos I'm stupid like that. Funny thing though, 'cos Miss Gulliver didn't know shit about it either." Bailey peered into the living room as Kendra advanced toward the kitchen. "I like your tree."

"Thanks. Now shut the fuck up." She moved down the hall like a ninja, prancing on the balls of her bare feet.

"How do you make it move like that?"

Kendra didn't know what she meant or why her voice had

suddenly taken on such a hazy, spaced-out quality, but didn't want to encourage her to talk more by asking, so she kept her own mouth shut. She moved into the kitchen, pausing briefly at the stove to ponder the pot of burnt, black gunk atop it, then went to the corner closet. Erin and her dad were only moderate drinkers, so stealing alcohol from them was an impossible task for most of the year. However, around Christmas, thanks to their work they were inundated with bottles from clients—so many that the bottom shelf of the corner closet had been designated for overflow. As Ryan refused to drink clear liquor and Erin disliked dark, there was a fair amount of trading, with a good number of bottles eventually re-gifted. Nobody kept track of every last one. Searching through the assortment now, Kendra found a bottle of spiced rum she felt sure would not be missed. She slid it down the front of her silver snowsuit, where it nestled insecurely and uncomfortably between her breasts, then zipped up and stood.

"Hey Kendra," Bailey called, making no effort to keep her voice at a discreet volume.

"Shut up," Kendra hissed, hurriedly doubling back across the kitchen floor. She wondered if her friend had already taken something but hadn't told her.

"Y'know, your bro—" Bailey's voice was suddenly drowned out by the kitchen radio, blaring into life as Kendra came past.

Jooooy tooo the world, a choir exulted at maximum amplification. *The Lord has come!*

The shock caused Kendra to jump like she'd been stabbed with a cattle prod. She snatched the radio up and turned down the volume, but it made no difference to the sound roaring from the speakers. She turned the tuning dial, but it had no effect. She slapped at the on/off switch, but it was futile. Only when she grabbed for the power cable and yanked the plug from the outlet was the choir finally silenced.

She cringed, cursing under her breath and listening for the inevitable sound of her father's footsteps on the stairs.

But the only sound she heard came from the living room. A slow, insistent, repeated *thunk*.

"Bailey?" Kendra whispered. She placed the radio back on the counter and moved into the hall, tip-toeing her way to the living room, the thunks growing louder and wetter as she approached. *Thunk, thunk, thunk*. Stepping into the doorway, she met a scene that took her more than a couple of seconds to comprehend.

Bailey laid face down on the rug with Devon on her back. His hands gripped her head, pulling it up and slamming it into the hard edge of the fireplace. Her skull had split open along her forehead, spraying blood across the marble. High above her head, over the mantel, Christmas cards fluttered like flirtatious butterflies. The lights on the tree changed color in time with each violent crunch of bone and brain. And the porcelain figures crowding Kendra's stepmother's ornamental nativity scene jumped and cheered.

"What the fuck?" Kendra said, unable to make sense of any part of the images dancing before her.

Devon spun around to face her, his hands still clutching Bailey's blonde hair, now streaked with red. The specks of blood on his cheeks were difficult to distinguish from the freckles. "I tried to hide." His voice sounded even more childish than normal, almost infantile. "But she found me."

"Dad!" Kendra turned and ran to the stairs.

"Don't," Devon called after her, rising as he let Bailey's head fall, her face landing in a frothing pool of her own blood and brain matter. "Don't do it!"

"Dad?" She ran up the stairs, but stumbled when she saw the sticky, mangled mess waiting at the top. She gasped, squeezing her eyes shut against the sight, slipped and lurched backward. She half fell, half staggered the rest of the way down, not opening her eyes again till she was back in the hallway. When she did, she was met by Devon, but all she saw was the image of the mutilated body on the landing, its twisted limbs and plucked, wretched head. Though it had the look of her father about it, she knew it couldn't be him. It couldn't be.

Devon regarded her with an expression approaching embarrassment. Sheepishly, he aimed a bloody thumb over his shoulder, back at Bailey's lifeless body, still leaking fluids onto the hearth rug. "Sorry. I guess I didn't have to do that. But I panicked."

Kendra gave him a shove that knocked him straight on his ass and bolted for the front door. She'd only made it three steps when a stabbing pain shot up through her foot. She cried out, hopped, pivoted and fell against the wall. Sliding down to the floor, she grabbed at her foot and found a narrow sliver of glass jutting from the sole—a fragment from one of the broken family pictures. Adrenaline pumping, she snatched the jagged shard between thumb and forefinger and yanked it from her flesh, ignoring the searing shriek of pain and the hot jet of blood that spurted from the wound.

"Kendra." Devon was suddenly at her side, reaching out to her, his face racked with concern. "Let me hel—"

"No!" She slapped him away, kicking at him with her good foot.

He fought his way through her flailing limbs and delivered a punch to her jaw. She fell sideways from the blow, shocked by its power, and grasped at the zip of her snowsuit.

"Don't fight me." Devon's voice was a snarl. "I don't want to hurt you."

Her hand closed around the neck of the rum bottle. She pulled it out from under her suit and swung it hard at his head. It connected with a harrowing crack and sent him staggering, striking the back of his skull against the banister. He slumped to the floor, eyes rolling back in his head, and didn't move.

In the moment, Kendra didn't care if he was alive or dead. She dropped the bottle, dragged herself up to her feet and started hobbling for the door. Putting any kind of pressure on her pierced foot caused pain to radiate all the way up to her hips and made stars dance before her eyes. She felt dizzy and nauseous and wasn't sure if she might faint, but she kept moving, hopping her way to the door, throwing it open and launching herself onto the porch.

Six of Devon's classmates were waiting for her.

They pounced as one, throwing their full weight into her, knocking her back into the house and sending her sprawling onto the floor. Then, with howls of insane rage, they rained blows upon her, pummeling at her head and body with tiny, balled fists of fury.

She stayed conscious just long enough to ponder the novelty of being murdered by a pack of feral schoolchildren. But then it all got very dark indeed.

11.

"THAT'S A LOT of blood, for damn sure." Standing in the middle of the floor in the Malamute, Owen kept the beam of his flashlight trained on the puddle of red at his feet a second longer, then swung it toward Will. "You got something you want to tell me?"

The teen's wet, pale, blood-caked face was ghostly in the flashlight's glare. "I . . . I thought . . . "

"You thought he was Santa Claus?"

Will nodded despondently, then let his head fall forward, staring at the floor.

"What does that mean?" Ling stood at the bar next to Sergio and Richie, who had returned to their stools and their drinks.

"Young William here has a problem telling fantasy from reality where Santa Claus is concerned," Owen explained. "It's well documented."

"You mean this has happened before?"

"Nothing this bad. Not for a long time." Owen crouched down to the boy's level, still aiming the flashlight at his face. "Been taking your meds, Will?"

Without lifting his head, the kid replied, "They don't do anything."

Owen nodded sympathetically and looked to Ling. "We did have a shrink in town who'd been taking care of him. She moved out about a month ago, after her contract was terminated. I don't know what stage things are at with getting a replacement. You'd need to ask Morgan about that." He glanced again at the pool of blood. "If he lives."

"Christ," Ling groaned. "What do I do?"

Sergio pointed at the rack of bottles behind the bar. "Have a brandy. Best thing in a crisis."

"Feel free to help yourself, Miss Wong." Einar still had his shotgun trained on Will. "I'm a little occupied here."

"I think we can put the gun away now, Einar." Owen edged closer to Will, his voice brimming with sympathy. "Nobody else is going to get hurt, are they Will?"

Now the kid lifted his head, tears streaming from his eyes. "You don't understand. He's here. He's close. I can feel him."

"Who's that?" asked Sergio. "Sandy Claus?"

Richie chuckled and, keeping his voice low, started to sing. "You better watch out, better not cry . . . "

Will ignored him, focusing his attention on Owen. "I'm serious. You've got to listen to me. It's not like the other times. Not a dream. He's here. He's coming for you. He's coming for all of us."

"Better not pout, I'm telling you why . . . "

Ling slammed her fist on the bar, making Richie jump. "Shut up," she told him, then looked to Owen. "I can't deal with this right now. I should be with Morgan. Can you give me a ride?"

Owen shook his head, his eyes still locked on Will's. "No, I think our top priority is for Dan and me to get young William here into a nice safe and secure cell, where he can't do anybody any more harm."

Will let out a sob, his head falling forward once again. "You don't believe me," he moaned. "Nobody believes me. You're all going to die."

Coughing to conceal a belch, Sergio raised his whiskey glass to Ling. "We'd help you if we could, boss," he said, indicating Richie. "But in all honesty, I don't think we're in any condition to drive."

She eyed the two men with obvious disdain. "I appreciate the sentiment."

Curtis stepped forward. "I can take you." Until now he'd been standing by the door, observing the others, saying nothing. "My truck's parked at the end of the street."

Ling gave him the kind of look that suggested she hadn't known he'd been standing there and didn't know who the hell he was. Then, after a moment of awkward silence, she said, "Well you'd better go get it."

She didn't speak another word to him until nearly twenty minutes later, as they climbed the steep road to the clinic.

"This truck's a piece of shit," she said.

"It was provided courtesy of Coldwell Slopes," he answered, fighting with the stick shift.

She let out a dry laugh and put a hand to her brow. “That figures. Christ my head hurts.”

“We’re nearly there. I think, anyway.”

“It’s Curtis, isn’t it? The school janitor?”

“That’s right.” He didn’t bother to correct her about his job title.

“Bet you’re wondering what kind of shit-show you’ve landed yourself in by coming here.”

“It has been a . . . challenging day. But not all bad. It’s actually been kind of exciting, if you want to know the truth.”

“Doesn’t make you homesick?”

“Not as such.”

“And where is home?”

“Mobile, Alabama.”

“I’ve never been. How does it compare?”

“It’s warmer.”

“You miss the heat?”

“I do miss the heat.” He stole a glance out the driver’s side window, at the dark, foreboding wilderness along the roadside. “As for the rest, I don’t know yet. It’s some kind of country. Feels like a different world.”

“They say God was tired when he made it.” Ling smiled to herself. “It won’t always be like this. It’ll get better. That’s what Morgan would say. A year from now you won’t recognize the place.”

Curtis nodded. Morgan had told him exactly that less than an hour ago.

“I tried telling it to myself,” Ling continued, staring out her own window now, watching the snow falling through the night. “But somehow I can’t make it sound quite so convincing. The truth is, more and more I wonder if all I’ve done here is saddle myself with a clusterfuck of such epic proportions they’ll write books about it. I mean . . . who builds a multi-million-dollar ski resort during a climate crisis? Who does that? The wholesome little community I thought I was buying has all but fled. I’ve inherited a few crumbling buildings and mendacious employees and a plan for development that suddenly looks like such . . . absurd fantasy. I’m afraid all I’ve managed to build is a method of destroying my career and reputation in the most elaborately humiliating way possible. And every move I make to try to save myself seems only to make it that much more certain this place will fucking kill me.”

In the seconds following her confession, Curtis offered no reaction, doing everything he could to mask his discomfort. Eventually, he managed to mutter, "Yeah, well, it's . . . Y'know . . . Everybody has . . . thoughts. About . . . stuff."

"I'm not an idiot," she said. "I did my due diligence. I always knew the risks of this project. But when I came here before there was a magic to the place. The potential was more than obvious. It was crystal clear. It was tangible. I could see it. I could reach out and touch it. Now it's like I'm caught in a blizzard and drifted so far off course I can't even imagine how my destination might look. When I try to picture it, all I can see are a thousand different forms of failure, each one more catastrophic than the last. And I was supposed to have a team! I was supposed to have support! Who did I have? Morgan MacLean, the Master Manipulator! And if I don't even have him, well . . . " She put her hands over her face, her rant degrading into a series of theatrical moans Curtis assumed were part of some stress management breathing exercise.

"Morgan will be okay," he said, his hands tightening on the wheel. "You'll see. Everything's going to be okay."

She didn't respond. A little later, they arrived at the clinic, pulling into the parking lot alongside Gertrude's truck.

Curtis killed the engine, then looked to Ling, who stared out the window, her expression unreadable. "Shall, uh . . . Shall we go in?"

She took a slow, deep breath, then turned and showed him a smile that didn't reach her eyes. "You repeat a single word of what I just told you, to anyone, and it's your ass. Understood?"

He nodded. "Yes ma'am."

12.

KENDRA AWOKE TO a stabbing pain in her foot and a sound like a milkshake's dregs being slurped through a straw. She opened her eyes—the left opening no more than halfway—and tried to kick at the blurry figure kneeling before her. But her foot didn't move. He gripped it in both hands.

"Relax," Devon told her. "Struggle and you'll just wind up hurting yourself."

Trying to move her arms and legs, she found they were bound in tape and her body strapped to the living room couch. At least her mouth wasn't taped shut—a relief, since both her nostrils were plugged with dried blood. "What are you doing?"

"Tending to your injuries." His hands moved, gradually coming into focus as her vision cleared, and she saw he was winding a bandage around her foot. He rubbed a finger playfully against her big toe. "I never realized how small your feet are."

"What?" She squirmed but could barely move beneath the restraints. The fog of unconsciousness was receding, but it didn't leave her feeling any less confused or scared. Her head and torso ached where they'd been pummeled by tiny fists and boots. She remembered what had happened before she blacked out, but still couldn't make any sense of it.

"My feet are bigger than yours," Devon said. "From the moment we met you've only ever treated me like a stupid little kid, but the truth is: while I may be younger, I'm bigger and stronger and smarter than you are."

"The fuck is this?" She hated how her voice sounded—weak and afraid—but it was a fair representation of how she felt inside.

"There's that potty mouth. So immature." He let her foot drop and climbed up onto the couch, positioning himself on top of her. His fingers toyed with the slider on the zipper of her snowsuit, open to the navel. "You're lucky you didn't knock me out with that bottle. The others would happily have beaten you to death, but I stopped them. You know why?"

"Cut me loose." She seethed, straining at her bonds. "Let me go."

His eyes roved up and down her body. She could see his hands twitching, eager to do the same, but he didn't touch her. "Y'know, a lot of kids made fun of me when you moved in. They said I was so lucky to have such a hot piece of ass for a step-sister. And you know what? I agreed with them." He lowered his face toward hers, getting so close she could smell the hot chocolate and marshmallows on his breath. "I always thought you were so pretty, Kendra. Prettiest girl I'd ever seen. But you had to act like such a total bitch. It's kind of a turn-off."

She winced, trying to pull her head away from his, but there was nowhere to go. "Get. The fuck. Off me."

His lips curled into a mean smile. "See, what I'm hoping for is that once we understand each other better, we might find a way to improve that attitude of yours. But this isn't a great start."

"I want my dad." She could feel tears forming. "Where's my dad?"

For a brief moment, Devon looked utterly baffled, like he'd forgotten she even had a father. "Oh, him. Don't worry about him. He's fine."

"That's a lie. You hurt him, didn't you?"

"I haven't done anything to him. He's upstairs, chilling. Same as . . . " He trailed off, appearing to struggle to remember the name of the person he was referring to, before it came to him. "Same as Mom."

"You're lying. You're a liar and a psycho and a fucked-up little perv."

He rolled his eyes. "And you're a big drama queen. Is this all because of what happened with Bailey? She's going to be fine, silly. Don't worry. She's in good hands. He's going to fix her right up."

She studied his face, unable to tell if Devon was teasing her or if his own tether to reality had snapped. "Who is?"

He grinned and looked past her, over at the tree. "Who do you think?"

There was that slurping sound again.

Kendra tried to turn her head and look at the source of the

sound, but the armrest blocked her view. She had to move her whole body, twisting like a worm in her restraints, shifting a fraction of an inch at a time.

"I wrote to him," Devon said, while she squirmed. "I told him what they were planning to do to his town, what they were going to make it into, and he was horrified. Of course he was. It's *his* name on all the signs. His home from home. But it's all going to be okay. He can put things right. You know he can. All we need to do is help him with a few problems, get rid of a few people, and then he can turn this town into a paradise. Christmas every day, forever and ever. You can be a part of it, if you want. I can introduce you. But you have to promise to be nice."

At last, straining all her muscles to push her way up, she got her head above the crest of the armrest to see exactly what Devon had been staring at. It took more than a moment for her eyes to make sense of the scene.

The children were gathered together on the floor, sitting or kneeling around an armchair and gazing beatifically up at the thing which perched atop it. A thing of spines and scales and glistening black edges, its body wrapped in filthy rags of red and white that did little to hide the leathery amber sacs pulsing along its undercarriage. Bailey's corpse was cradled in its multitude of gnarled limbs, her clothes torn away and belly split open. The gaping crater revealed a torso robbed of all organs, leaving only bone and blood, which poured out slow and thick with every quiver of her cold, dead flesh. The creature clutching her pressed its head against hers, something that might have been a mouth closing over the crack in her skull. With a furious hunger, it sucked her brains out through the wound, shivering with delight as her meat flooded its throat. And its eyes, like every one of the lights on the Christmas tree, burned blood red.

"A word of advice," Devon whispered in Kendra's ear. "You'll want to call him Santa Claus. But he prefers Saint Nicholas."

If he said anything else she couldn't hear it over the sound of her own screams.

13.

"HE'S GOING TO be okay. I think." Gertrude met them in reception wearing a surgical smock over her clothes.

"You think?" said Ling.

Gertrude made a face like she'd stepped on a nail. "I never give guarantees. Not in this game. But I'd say I'm ninety percent sure he'll live. The wounds were not deep and he was fortunate to have some, uh . . . natural padding to protect him, if you know what I mean. The bleeding was not severe. His blood pressure is stable. The only issue that gives me concern . . . "

"Yes?"

"I think he might have experienced a cardiac event."

Ling gasped. "A heart attack?"

"He's showing all indications. And not surprising, in the circumstances. It's hard for me to make a conclusive assessment with the facilities we have here, but I would say it's at the lower end of serious."

"Oh God." Ling put a hand to her mouth, swaying unsteadily on her feet, and for a horrible moment, Curtis feared he might be required to catch her.

"It's okay," Gertrude said, fighting to make herself heard over the rising hum of Ling's hysteria. "We patched him up, he's resting, his vitals are holding steady. Obviously, it's important we monitor him for at least the next forty-eight hours and, at the first available opportunity have him fully checked out by a cardiologist, but I think for tonight we're in the clear."

"Right." Ling was breathing rhythmically, trying to maintain her composure. "Right. Okay. Obviously, not that I don't trust you, but I'd prefer he was being looked after in a proper hospital."

Gertrude smiled. "I completely agree with you, in an ideal

world, yes. However, the nearest facility is in MacArthur Point and all the roads there are currently closed."

"Then request a helicopter. I'm serious. I want him properly treated."

The smile grew a little more strained. "Well, now . . . Yes, MacArthur Point does have a chopper, but we are right at the very limit of their range up here. In any case, I tried to reach them on the radio a little earlier, just to make them aware we had an emergency case, and I couldn't get through. I'm guessing the weather's to blame. Phone lines and internet are down too, which, to be fair, is not unusual."

"Shit. Shit! The satellite phone!" Ling spun toward Curtis, grabbing his shoulder. "I have a satellite phone back at the town hall. We need to get it."

"Well, sure." Gertrude held out her hands like she was placating a startled animal. "I'll bet a satellite phone will work like gangbusters, but if the storm's bad enough to screw with the radios, they're not going to send their chopper out in it, certainly not if there's a danger their tank might run dry before they get here. So there's no rush, is there? Honestly, right now, this is the best place for him. And the best place for you to be, if you're so concerned, is right here at his side."

"Okay." Ling nodded, letting go of Curtis's jacket, settling down. "Okay."

He was checking his sleeve for puncture marks when he saw Shona walk out of one of the rooms down the hall. She wore green medical scrubs and her hair tied in a pony-tail and looked like she'd been on shift for ten hours. "He's asking for you," she told Ling, who nodded and followed her back into the room.

"It's, uh . . . some place you've got here," Curtis told Gertrude, to break the silence that descended when they became the only two left in the corridor.

The clinic was bigger than he'd expected, comprising a network of interconnected buildings, including separate wards, operating theaters and offices, most of which were unmanned and in darkness. Power had been restricted to the reception area and a few consulting rooms.

"In its heyday it was a top-of-the-line private facility," Gertrude explained. "Built by the mining company, serving miners and their families, which, at the time, was pretty much everyone in town.

Offered a full range of services—oncology, gynecology, psychiatry, the works. Fully equipped emergency room for dealing with mining-related incidents. That's why we're so far out of town. After the mine closed, the clinic was sold to Medicare, which is how I got posted out here. We had other staff . . . for a while. Now? Only what you see."

"Well it's a good thing you stayed. Going to stick around?"

"Why? You having second thoughts?"

He shrugged. "Not yet, but . . . "

"I hear you," she said, nodding sagely. She sank into one of the uncomfortable-looking chairs scattered along the hallway and gestured toward the room where Morgan was being treated. "Those two make all kinds of promises. Him especially. A sparkling new medical center in the heart of town, all modern conveniences, nothing but the best, blah, blah, blah. Sounds nice, but if it means more days like today, I just don't know. I prefer the quiet life."

"So . . . you *are* a doctor then?"

She raised an eyebrow. "You doubt it?"

"No. No, it's just . . . I noticed nobody calls you 'Doctor'."

She snorted. "Doc. That's what they called me when I arrived. But I soon put a stop to that. You come to a place like this, ass-end of nowhere, stranger in a strange town, surrounded by strange people, the least people can do for you is call you by your name. If they don't, you might just forget who the hell you are."

"I hear you."

She nodded, giving him a look like she could see straight into his soul and everything it did or did not contain. "I bet you do."

Morgan lay on his back in a narrow bed, still wearing his Santa suit, the fabric dark where his blood had soaked through. The tunic was open to reveal his broad chest, strapped up with bandages and dotted with electrodes attached to a heart monitor. His skin looked gray and greasy beneath the fluorescent lights. His watery eyes focused on Ling as she entered and he groaned. "Ling. I'm dying."

She looked at Shona, who shook her head. "He's not dying. He's doped up. You'll be lucky to get any sense out of him."

Ling turned back to Morgan and put her hand on his arm. "You're not dying, Morgan."

"I am. But it's okay, really. I'm not in any pain. And I have no regrets. None at all. Except . . . " His gaze drifted away from her, aiming off into space, as if he were watching a playback of all his memories, all his hopes and dreams. "Except . . . I suppose I just wish my life could have been . . . just . . . *completely* different."

"You're going to be fine."

His eyes narrowed, getting mean. "And I wish I'd done something about that punk Will Douglas. A long time ago. Someone needs to put that kid down. He's a menace."

"Morgan . . . "

"Here I thought he would leave town if his shrink left. What else did he have to stick around for? Stupid. If I only had the chance now and a blade in my fist, I'd gut him like a . . . "

"Morgan!"

He blinked and gave her a startled look, like he'd forgotten she was at his side. "Oh, Ling. Ling, I'm so sorry. I'm so sorry for you . . . "

She smiled, stroking his arm in an attempt to deliver some comfort. "There's no need to feel sorry for me, Morgan."

With a show of great effort, he swallowed and woozily shook his head. "No, no, there is. There is. Because . . . when I'm dead, you will be . . . fucked. You're going to be so fucked, Ling."

Though she tried, she couldn't quite maintain the smile. The stroking of his arm ceased. "Thanks Morgan."

"Listen to me now, I'm serious. You're fucked, Ling. You're so fucked. Even if I'd been around, you'd probably have been fucked. But now? You're super-fucked. There's so much I've kept hidden from you. So much you should have known, but it's too late for you to learn. I was only looking out for myself, you understand. You've got to be careful with information if you want to get ahead. You want to be the king, you've got to play the game, only . . . I didn't mean you any harm. I really, never meant you any harm. But now . . . Now, you're so fucking fucked!"

Wishing she'd done so a few seconds earlier, Shona cleared her throat. "So, um . . . I'm going to go."

"That's fine." Ling didn't turn to face her. "Thanks for everything." Once the schoolteacher had slipped awkwardly from the room, Ling dragged a chair over to the bed and sat down. "You were saying?"

His eyes fixed on the ceiling, Morgan took a long, dramatic breath. "I'm dying."

"Morgan, listen to me." Now she pinched his arm, and he winced and turned to gaze stupidly in her vague direction. "This is your terrifying corporate she-devil of a boss speaking to you now. You are not going to die."

"I'm not?"

"No. Because that would disappoint me greatly. And you know what happens to people who disappoint me?"

He shook his head.

"Neither do I. Because no-one has ever been stupid enough to dare to find out. Do we understand each other?"

He grinned, his head sinking back into the pillow and he began to sing. "Ling Wong merrily on high, in heaven the bells are ringing . . . "

She groaned, bowing her head. "Ah, Jesus."

"Bing bong berrily ba-daaa . . . Wing-wong, ling-bing . . . " In the midst of massacring her name to music, his eyelids fluttered shut and he drifted off to sleep.

It was a little after 2am before Curtis and Shona got back into town, the truck gliding through dark and empty streets, brightened intermittently by homes and businesses festooned with fairy lights. Ling had elected to stay at the hospital, maintaining a vigil at Morgan's bedside. Gertrude, who apparently spent most nights at the clinic, said she would be glad of the company, though Curtis wasn't entirely convinced.

Shona was curled up against the door, head turned toward the window, and Curtis was certain she was sleeping until she suddenly said, "I could really do with a drink right now."

Hoping she didn't notice his jump of surprise, he replied, "Yeah, no kidding. Been a hell of a night."

"Hell of a day."

"Even if the Malamute was still open, I wouldn't argue for going back."

"No, it might be tempting fate. And I'd rather not have to deal with any more stabbings." She sighed, letting her head roll back against the seat. "There's no way I'm going to sleep though. Not now. I wish I had some wine at my house. I should have stocked up."

Curtis nodded and made a sympathetic sound while biting his tongue and keeping his mouth shut. A voice in his head told him: *Don't say it. Don't say it.*

And a moment later: *But why not say it?*

And then: *You may as well say it. What's the worst that can happen?*

And finally: *Oh just say it already!*

"There's a bottle of bourbon back at my place."

He kept his eyes on the road, refusing to allow himself so much as a glance in her direction during the interminable wait for her reply, which, to him, seemed to last a silent eon, but was probably no longer than five seconds.

At the end of which, with staggering ease, she said, "Aye, that'll do."

14.

"GATHER ROUND, CHILDREN. Don't be shy." His round belly jiggled with mirth as Saint Nicholas reached deep into his velvet sack and produced a tall, golden flask.

"What is it?" asked Lucas Grenier, his voice nervous, bordering on cynical.

Saint Nicholas unscrewed the cap and snatched up a mug. "Eggnog. My own special recipe. I want you all to have a cup." As he poured, the air filled with the sweet aroma of vanilla and nutmeg.

The boy wrinkled his nose. "I don't like eggnog."

Saint Nicholas grinned, his rosy cheeks growing rosier. "Oh, you'll like this one, my boy. The secret ingredient is magic. All my elves drink it, and it fills them with strength and vitality and cleverness. It'll give you superpowers. Wouldn't you like to have superpowers, young man?"

He held forth the brimming mug and the boy peered into the liquid's thick, glossy surface. Feeling the apprehensive eyes of the other children on him, he tilted his head forward and drank.

"There now," Saint Nicholas cooed. "How does that taste?"

Stepping away, Lucas licked his lips and nodded. "Good. It tastes good."

"Didn't I tell you?" Saint Nicholas cast an eye over the children seated on the floor, all gazing up with the same looks of starstruck awe they'd worn from the moment they'd first laid eyes on him. "Now line up. There's plenty for everyone."

They did as asked, politely taking their turns, making small murmurs of delight as the thick, warming liquid touched their lips, coated their tongues, and oozed down their throats.

On the other side of the room, still strapped to the couch, Kendra made an agonized howl just loud enough to be heard through her gag. If any of the kids gathered around Saint Nicholas heard her, they didn't show it. The only one to pay her any attention at all was little Cindee Joyce, who'd been ordered to stand guard over her while Devon was out of the room.

It proved to be an easy assignment. Cindee found herself transfixed by Devon's step-sister, whose whole body quivered frantically, her every muscle tensed with a kind of wild panic. She had screamed from the moment she had seen Saint Nicholas. Nothing Devon or anyone else had said could calm her down and so finally she had been gagged with her own Christmas stocking. But though the sounds of her hysteria had been muffled, it remained bright and apparent in her face—the skin drained of color and shiny with sweat, her eyes bulging in depthless horror as she watched the parade of youngsters receiving their dose of medicine from jolly old Saint Nick.

"Young Cindee," he called, holding the mug aloft like a sacrificial chalice. "You too. There's an awful lot of work to be done and I need all my little helpers to be strong and powerful if they're to see it through."

"No thank you," she said.

"Oh come now. You don't like eggnog either? Lucas here will tell you how delicious it is."

His own protestations completely forgotten, Lucas eyed the mug hungrily. "It's delicious."

Saint Nicholas beamed. "See?"

"I can't have eggs," Cindee said. "I'm vegan."

Saint Nicholas didn't show any obvious reaction, but behind him the decorations on the tree flapped indignantly. Slowly, his grin widened—wider than seemed natural. "Don't be difficult, Cindee. Difficult is only a hair away from naughty. And we know what happens to naughty little girls, don't we?" His gaze shifted to Kendra, who shrieked through her gag when his eyes met hers. "Come drink your eggnog."

Cindee looked to Kendra, who made a garbled attempt at communication that sounded vaguely like, "Don't! Don't do it!"

Not that it mattered. It was plain for all to see Cindee didn't have any choice.

But then Devon appeared in the doorway and said, "Saint Nicholas? Can I talk to you please? It's important."

Saint Nick's eyes lingered on Cindee as he set the mug down, then put the lid back on the flask. "Certainly." Taking the flask with him, he stepped over Bailey, curled up like a cat while she dozed in front of the fire, and followed Devon out of the room.

Cindee stared uncertainly at the mug, knowing what she was expected to do, understanding this was a test and afraid to imagine what might become of her if she failed.

She felt a gasp of relief escape her lips as, before she could make up her mind over what to do, Lucas greedily picked the eggnog up and drank it down.

Devon led Saint Nicholas to his stepfather's study at the rear of the house. For most of his life it had been his playroom, but Mr. Wray had needed a place to get work done in the evenings and anyway, his mother had said, Devon didn't need all those toys or space to play with them anymore. He was growing up now and far more interested in video games. Though he hadn't said anything at the time, Devon had found her contention both hurtful and inaccurate.

He'd rarely stepped foot in the room since and doing so now caused a spasm of revulsion in his gut. The brightly-colored walls he'd once known, decorated with crudely rendered jungle animals, had been unceremoniously muted with coats of magnolia paint. The toy chests, beanbags and play-sets he'd loved had been replaced with filing cabinets, plastic crates full of files, and heavy furniture the color of tobacco. Pinned to the wall above the desk was a map of the town, highlighting Mr. Wray's existing clients and ones he still hoped to secure. Sitting on the leather couch against the opposite wall was an eight-year-old by the name of Blair Brodie, aka Balthasar. He stood up when the other two came in.

"Hello Blair," said Saint Nicholas.

The boy attempted to formulate a reply, but his mouth betrayed him. He was too stunned to be in the presence of Santa Claus to do anything but make a few meaningless sounds.

"Get a grip," Devon told him, then turned to Saint Nicholas. "Something has happened. Morgan MacLean, one of our key targets, has been taken to the clinic outside of town. Ling Wong has gone with him."

"Is that a problem?" Saint Nicholas asked.

"Our plan was to deal with them first. They're very dangerous to us, especially the woman. She's pretty much the boss of the town and she's an outsider. But the clinic is too far away for any of us to reach on foot." He pointed to the clinic's location in the top right corner of the map over the desk. "Anyone we sent would probably freeze to death before they got halfway there."

"I see." Saint Nicholas smiled. "Well, that shouldn't be of any hindrance to us. Blair, would you be a gent and fetch us a couple of glasses from the kitchen?"

Like a soldier rushing to carry out the orders of his general, the boy leaped from the couch and ran from the room.

Saint Nicholas immediately lowered himself into the vacant seat. "Tell me about this Morgan character. Do you know what's happened to him?"

Devon nodded. "Will Douglas stabbed him for wearing a Santa suit."

Saint Nicholas chuckled. "Oh, dear me. This Will Douglas . . . he doesn't care for Santa Claus?"

"No."

"Well, we'll have to do something about that." Saint Nicholas ran a hand contemplatively through his feathery-soft beard. "This . . . Morgan. He's a big man?"

"I guess."

"That's something that could be turned to our advantage."

"What do you mean?"

Blair returned with the glasses.

"I'll tell you." Saint Nicholas unscrewed the lid on his flask. "But first, I want you both to have a drink of this and tell me it's not the most delicious thing you've ever tasted."

15.

"WHO THE FUCK did you piss off?" Shona asked. She stood at Curtis's living room window, staring out at the street below, which sloped down at a ludicrously steep angle.

"I haven't had time to piss anyone off," he replied as he went around the room, lighting lamps. "I don't think."

"You're at the very top of Nugget Hill, Curtis. The top!"

"I don't know what that is."

"It's the steepest hill in town. Most of the buildings up here are from prospector days. Heritage pieces. Nobody lives in them. You know why? Because in winter, nobody can make it up the fucking hill!" She laughed. Their own circuitous route from his truck to the building had been a ridiculous one, taken to avoid having to climb up the steepest part—and still they'd both slipped and nearly fallen on their asses more than once.

"It was Miss Gulliver who found me the place," he said, shrugging off his coat. "Same as with the truck and . . . ah, hell!"

"What is it?"

His hand had slipped into the pocket of his coat as he was taking it off. Now he took it out, holding up Will's flick knife. "I forgot all about it."

Shona gasped. "The murder weapon!"

"He's not dead."

"Even so."

"I'll give it to Owen tomorrow." He put it back in the pocket of his coat and hung it up, then went into the kitchen to grab his bottle of bourbon and two glasses. He returned to find Shona had unzipped her own coat and taken something from the inside pocket—the same folded piece of card she'd been studying ever-so-briefly in the bar. "What's that?"

She smiled without looking up. A sentimental kind of expression. “The children made me a Christmas card. Presented it to me on my first day.” She tilted it toward him. “See?”

He saw an abundance of glued-on stars and the words ‘Merry Christmas Miss Fleming’ above a crowd of crudely drawn characters, each one scrawled by a different hand, arrows leading back to their names.

“They all drew themselves,” she said. “I’m supposed to carry it around with me, so I can teach myself who they all are, what they look like.”

“Does it help?”

“Not at all.” She sighed, studying the card again. “But it’s a nice gesture. Apparently their idea. They worried about me coming to a new town, not knowing anyone. Didn’t like the idea of me being lonely at Christmas. Not when it means so much to them.”

“I think it means a lot to most kids.”

She shook her head. “No, not in the same way. St. Nicholas . . . it’s a town that’s been on the verge of death for years. Businesses failing, friends and family leaving, those who are left behind fighting and scrapping among themselves to try and salvage something from the wreckage. The people in this community have been under a lot of stress, for a long time. Children pick up on all that. They soak up all the anger and resentment like a sponge. Christmas is the one time of year they’re guaranteed relief from it all. When everyone makes the effort to treat each other with kindness and decency and seems . . . happy. That’s why they all cherish Christmas so dearly. And this year they don’t even have that.”

“Wait till they hear about poor Santa Claus, getting stabbed by a drunk in a dive bar.” He cringed inwardly as soon as he said it, sure it would cause offense.

But she didn’t seem to mind. Gently, sadly, she set the card down on the windowsill. “Poor Morgan. I liked him.”

“He’s not dead.”

“No, I know. Even so. It’s a terrible shame.” She took off the rest of her winter layers and hung them up while Curtis found a seat on the couch.

“It is, yeah,” he said, without emotion.

She frowned. “You don’t like him?”

He began pouring the drinks. “I didn’t say that.”

"But . . . ?"

"I think he gave me diabetes."

She grinned. "How?"

"Everything he says is a sales pitch on the future. Everything's going to be great; we're all going to do such amazing things; we're going to create the most incredible place and have the most wonderful time. And all said with a sugary sweet smile. It makes me . . . " He faltered over his next words, trying not to be overly unkind about a man currently in a hospital bed—even if he had heard Ling call him a 'master manipulator'. "Let's just say a little goes a long way."

"I get that. Constant positivity can be sickly. But perpetual cynicism isn't much better."

"I prefer realism. Seeing things the way they are and saying it how it is. No bullshit."

"You think the way you see reality is exactly how it is?"

He nodded, holding out a glass of whiskey. "I think I've got a pretty good handle on it, yeah."

Shona smirked and took it. "Then congratulations. You might be the only one. And what does your keen perception of the world tell you about Morgan?"

He thought it over. "Just that . . . he is not exactly what he presents himself to be."

"And who among us is? You?"

"I try to be that much, if nothing else." He sat back, regarding her intently and openly. "You too, maybe."

"Me too, what? What am I?"

"Honest about who you are."

She blushed, bowing her head to her drink. "Aye, that'll be fucking right."

He gave a sigh that sounded like a laugh. "You sure do swear a lot."

She raised an eyebrow. "For a woman?"

"For a schoolteacher."

Now it was her turn to laugh. "Oh no. Not nearly enough for a schoolteacher. You must be new to custodying. Does it bother you?"

He smiled. "No, it doesn't bother me."

"Good. Because I wouldn't give two fucks if it did." She reached out with her glass to clink his and said, "*Slainte.*"

"That's what you say?"

She nodded, taking a sip. "What would you say?"

He tried to recall. "I honestly don't think I've ever said anything."

"How sad." She took another sip as she toured his living room—effectively a circuit of the coffee table—inspecting his sparse furnishings. "Would you describe yourself as . . . utilitarian?"

"I don't think so."

"Minimalist?"

"No."

"How would you describe yourself?"

"I don't think I would, if I can help it."

She smiled. "Fair. Trying to define yourself is like trying to bite your own teeth. So said Alan Watts."

"Right," he nodded, like he knew who she was talking about.

"But you get my point?" She waved a hand around, indicating his bare gray walls, the empty bookcase, the TV balanced on a stool opposite the beige two-seater sofa.

"This is all stuff left behind by the previous tenant. And I've only been here a few weeks."

"So if we were to see it a year from now, how would it look?"

He considered the question. "Probably the same."

"That's what I thought. Someone who really cared about their home comforts would have spruced things up in here by now. I've only been here a few weeks, but you should see my place."

He thought of a reply to that, but decided to keep it to himself. He drank his whiskey, watching as she took another lap around the room.

"No tree," she said. "No lights, no tinsel, not even a dancing Santa Claus."

"No mistletoe either, but I wasn't anticipating company."

"Clearly." She joined him on the couch. "You don't like Christmas, do you?"

He winced. "It just seemed like a lot of work to decorate the place for myself."

"And you don't like Christmas."

"And I don't really care for Christmas," he admitted. "But I know you do."

"Love it." She grinned. "The lights, the songs, the terrible movies, and the ugly jumpers. I love everything about it. It makes me feel cozy."

"You've never worked retail."

"Ah, you've got me there. You have?"

"I have."

She narrowed her eyes, studying him intently. "But that's not really why you hate Christmas, is it?"

Curtis, though he considered himself a fairly open book, was beginning to feel slightly uncomfortable with the interest she was taking in him. A certain kind of interest wouldn't be so bad, but this bordered on a psychological evaluation. "I guess . . . " He rolled the whiskey glass between the palms of his hands. "I don't like that it comes with all these expectations."

"From whom?"

He shrugged. "You know."

"Family? Friends? Lovers? Wives?" She raised her glass and lowered her voice. "I don't know if you noticed, pal, but we're three drinks in."

"You're right. I'm impressed you could keep track in all the excitement."

A sparkle of pride shone in her tired eyes. "Time to get real, don't you think?"

He took a deep breath, leaning forward to set his own glass on the table then clasping his hands between his knees. Staring at the wall, he said, "Yes, I had a wife."

"I knew it."

"And kids."

"The plot thickens. How many?"

"Two. Boy and a girl."

"How old?"

"Nine and seven, now."

"What happened?"

"I'm . . . not sure I can answer that."

"You left?"

"I was told to leave."

"Why? What did you do?"

"Nothing. I didn't do anything."

"That sounds . . . unlikely."

"No, that's just it. I didn't do anything." He spoke slowly, struggling to find the words to explain. "I didn't take the job seriously. I didn't make any effort to include them in my life or make myself a part of theirs. I worked, I paid for things, but I wasn't . . . I wasn't *there*."

"You think you took them for granted?"

He nodded. "It's not like I didn't know what it took to be a good husband and father. But I didn't do it. Not that I didn't care. But I couldn't bring myself to make the effort. Too scared or too selfish, I don't know. Maybe both. Finally they all had enough."

Shona made a skeptical sound. "Okay. Sounds a little extreme. You didn't . . . Not to be crass, but you weren't cheating on her or anything?"

"No," he answered, without showing any sign of offense. "She cheated. But I get why."

"Oh." Shona's eyebrows jumped. "Okay . . . So . . . she started hooking up with someone else, told you it was all your fault and ordered you to leave?"

"It's not as simple as that."

"Obviously, but . . . still. When did all this happen?"

"We divorced a couple years ago."

"And ever since then you've been carrying this around with you? Beating yourself up? Convincing yourself it was all your fault and you're a terrible person?"

"A man ought to own his mistakes."

"A man can be a little too keen. Fuck sake, Curtis, leave some blame for the rest of the world. So where are they now? Back in Alabama?"

"Her new husband, he . . . moved them to Toronto."

"Oh shit."

"I couldn't stop it. But I wanted to do my best to try and stay in their lives. So I started looking for work that would keep me close to them. Only that turned out to be a lot tougher than I thought. Canada tends to like its immigrants to have college degrees and money in the bank. This place was the one exception I could find. At least we're in the same country."

"Barely."

"It's a start."

"No, I get it. It's admirable. And pretty far removed, I would say, from the actions of a selfish man."

Curtis was silent for a long moment, a catalog of responses cycling through his head—dismissive, sarcastic, irate, abstract. In the end, he opted for a simple, "Thanks." He surprised himself with the sincerity of it.

"Shit, though." She chuckled, stifling a yawn. "No wonder you don't like Christmas."

He showed a hint of a smile and, seeing both their glasses were empty, reached for the bottle. "Honestly? I've had a lot worse."

16.

IN HIS DREAMS, Morgan danced with people he recognized but had never met, in places he knew well, but had never been. He bucked and swayed in a swirling ocean of vague impressions and half-finished thoughts, warmed by the soothing waves of his own subconscious, their currents rippling up and over and through him, but only gently. No rushing. No jostling. He was in a state of painless bliss in which he would be content to float forever more.

Until something that felt very much like a claw closed around his neck and he was unceremoniously ripped from the comforting flow of meaningless sounds and images and catapulted up into a cold, black sky.

And suddenly he was plunging through roiling clouds to emerge halfway down the slope of Mount Coldwell, swooping and soaring over the tips of the snow-dusted trees and high over the town of St. Nicholas. The community was fast asleep, their homes all in darkness. Yet in the streets and alleyways he could see movement. Figures darted across the snow—small and dark and purposeful. It was difficult to tell what they were up to, but he spotted a few gathered at the entrance to the Samuel Street Hotel. And another scaling the fence to reach the yard in which Izaak Strauss kept his snowplow. Morgan thought he saw some tinkering with generators, trucks, and snowmobiles, but all he caught was a glimpse before he began his rapid descent into the town square and was then pitched, head-first, like a missile, straight through the roof of the bandstand.

He closed his eyes a moment before the crash—and felt nothing. He opened them again to silence and darkness.

"What's happening," he heard himself say. He sat in a chair, facing a wall of black. "What's . . . going on?"

A booming voice answered, coming from somewhere out

beyond the darkness. "Ladies and gentlemen, boys and girls, residents of Coldwell Slopes," it proclaimed. "Presenting the new CEO of the number-one ski resort and Christmas holiday destination in the world, the man who makes dreams a reality, the one, the only . . . Morgan MacLean!"

A black curtain fell and white light flooded in, burning his eyes. He squeezed them shut, his shocked, pained cry obscured by the ecstatic roar of the crowd.

"Mor-gan! Mor-gan! Mor-gan!"

He eased his eyes open, jaw dropping as the brightly colored blur before him came into focus, revealing a sea of cheering faces. Young, attractive, flawless faces. It was no kind of crowd he'd ever seen outside of a movie, the people too unbearably beautiful to gather in such numbers. Yet here they were, filling the town square, yelling and clapping for him.

He was back on the bandstand. He could recall being there only a few hours ago, dressed as Santa Claus, handing out presents to the local children. Glancing down, he saw he was dressed as Santa Claus once more, but the suit was cleaner, fancier, better quality in truth than anything in his wardrobe. The chair in which he sat was an ornate, gilded throne. And he wasn't alone on the stage. For the first time in living memory, St. Nicholas's bandstand had a band.

He jumped as the trumpets and trombones blasted a fanfare, announcing the presence of the swing band to his left, before segueing into a softer, slower, jazzier melody he knew. He'd played it himself, earlier in the evening, when he'd made his grand entrance on the ATV. When the vocals kicked in, he expected to hear Eartha Kitt. But it was someone else.

"Santa baby, slip a Sable under the tree, for me . . . "

She stepped out from behind the band, redheaded firecracker in a little red dress. And little meaning *little*. Not much more than twice the width of the black belt cinched tight around her waist. Strips of silver fur along the bust and hemline covered most of her modesty, but a lot was still on display. The red stockings she wore drew his eyes down to her milky white thighs, watching their approach as she seductively danced her way toward him.

"Been an awful good girl, Santa baby . . . " He didn't look at her face till she leaned forward, dropping her cleavage into his eye-line, playfully pouting her lips over the mic. "So hurry down the chimney tonight!" It was the new schoolteacher, Shona Fleming. From the first moment he'd seen her, he'd suspected she had hidden talents, but this was something else.

"Hiya," he said.

She leaned closer, brushing her soft cheek against his, purring into his ear, her breath warm and moist on his skin. "Time for presents, Santa?"

He swallowed. "I . . . I don't think I have any . . . "

"Oh sure you do!" It wasn't Shona who answered, but young Bailey McLuhan in her golden snowsuit, its fabric thinner and more form-fitting than he remembered. She was arm-in-arm with silver-suited Kendra Wray, the pair of them marching onto the stage.

"I've got a gift for you, Santa," the second girl said as she reached his throne. She grabbed his hand, unzipped the front of her suit and slid it inside, pressing it to her breast. "Right there!"

Aiming to go one better, Bailey grabbed his other hand. "It's not about what you can give . . . " She put it between her legs, clamping her thighs around his fingers. "It's about what you can take!"

"Oh, he can give plenty," Kendra moaned, eyes closed, whipping her long hair against his face as she pulsed and writhed theatrically beneath his touch.

Morgan let a few puffs of air out through his lips, attempting to speak, but failing for the first few times to form any words. "G-g-girls," he managed, eventually. "Please!"

Shona laughed and tapped a fingernail against his nose. "All the girls love Santa Claus." She spun away from him, striding up to the edge of the stage, addressing the crowd. "Isn't that right, ladies?"

Every last woman in the audience—every one of them young, pretty and willing—let out a sound somewhere between a cheer and an erotically charged shriek. The girls grinding against his hands echoed the noise with ecstatic sounds of their own, their movements growing more intense, their bodies on fire.

Breathless, sweating, his heart pounding, Morgan felt on the verge of something himself, but couldn't be sure if it was an orgasm or a heart attack. He glanced around, trying to make sense of the extraordinary scene. "What . . . what is this?"

Shona turned to face him, showing him a smile as beautiful as it was mean. "This? This is everything you could have had."

He blinked and they were gone. Day was night. He stood in the snow, in the middle of the square, all alone. He shuddered, though it wasn't cold. He glanced at his hands, still outstretched, then turned around, looking frantically in every direction, searching for the girls who only a second ago had been so aggressively determined to seduce him. "Hello?" He was surprised by the sound of his voice. Though he shouted the word across the open square, it sounded as though it was being muttered in a cramped room. "Hello? Hello!"

"Hello Morgan."

The response came from the bandstand. Someone else sat there now in his gilded throne. A man who looked very much like himself, dressed in the same clothes, a warm and welcoming smile on his bearded face.

"Who are you?"

"Don't you know?"

"Santa Claus?" It felt ridiculous to say it. "You don't exist."

The man's smile widened. "Neither do you, Morgan. Not anymore."

"What?" Morgan felt a chill go through his bones that had nothing to do with the weather. In fact, though he was standing in snow on a night when the temperature was well below zero, he didn't feel cold at all. "Where did everyone go? The . . . the girls . . . "

"They were never here, Morgan. Just a dream. Just your brain treating you to a delightful little vision of your fantasies realized, the future you could have had as it fires its last few synapses, winding its way down to a state of inanimation."

"What does that mean? What's happening to me?"

Somewhere, far off in the night, somebody screamed. Santa let the smile fall from his face as he stood up. "I think you know. And it's time you admitted it to yourself."

"No." Morgan glanced around, searching for help, for a way out of the conversation, but his feet were rooted to the spot. "Don't say it."

"I don't have to say it." Santa strolled down the steps from the bandstand, moving toward him. "You already know it's true."

"I . . . " Morgan's voice cracked. "I'm dead?"

"For what it's worth, I am sorry."

"No. Oh no." He tried to turn, to run away, but his legs gave out beneath him. He collapsed onto his hands and knees. "No, it's not fair. It's not fair!"

"It very rarely is."

Through the shimmer of tears in his eyes, he saw the black boots of Santa Claus crunching across the snow. He squeezed his eyes shut. "You don't understand. I was so close. I was going to transform the town. I was going to be rich. I was going to be loved. It was all . . . It was all going to be so different. It was going to be good. At last, it was going to be good."

"Yes. It would have been. But that's all over now. And all because of . . . "

"Will Douglas." Morgan spoke the name through gritted teeth, his hands balling into fists.

"Yes, Will Douglas. A pity you never did anything about him while you had the chance. But now he gets to go on living in your perfect little town . . . and you're dead."

Morgan let out a sob, his body shaking. He opened his eyes, blinking away the tears. Something scurried across the street, at the edge of the square—a small shape, with a blade that shone bright as its yellow eyes. There and gone, off to make mischief. But Morgan wasn't watching it. His focus was on Santa Claus. "Is . . . Is there an afterlife?"

"Not for you, I'm afraid. For you there is only a brief window in which to understand and reflect before your consciousness disintegrates and melts away to nothing, like a snowflake on a fingertip. In this way, your death mirrors your life. Heaven, as you mortals like to call it, is reserved strictly for those who amounted to something on Earth."

"But I would have. You would have seen. I was so close. If I only had more time . . . "

"You squandered all the time you had, Morgan. No sense crying about it now."

"I was building something."

"Building? You destroyed your community. You sent its meek and docile citizens scattering and gave their jobs and homes to hardhearted outsiders. You tricked those that remained into signing their lives and property over to a heartless monopoly and exploited the generosity of its envoy to try and ensure that when she failed—as you aimed to make sure she would—you would be in prime position to take her place. In doing so, consumed by avarice, ambition and yes, even your own shameful lust, you condemned yourself to oblivion."

Morgan dug his fingers into the snow, wishing he could dig down far enough to reach the earth. If he could get his hands around it, he'd never let go. Death would not claim him. "I didn't know I was doing anything wrong."

"Wrong? You betrayed the children of St. Nicholas, Morgan. What could be more wrong than that?"

"No," he exclaimed, clambering back onto his feet. "It's not fair, god damn it! It's not fair! Can't you let me go back? Give me just a little more time! Please!"

Santa chuckled—an oddly humorless sound. "Oh come now, Morgan. What makes you think I can do that?"

"You're Santa Claus. You can do anything!"

Now the big man's face lit up. "Are you trying to tell me you believe in Santa Claus?"

"I do. I believe!"

"Oh come now. You're a rational man. You must assume I'm a figment of your imagination, another random firework display by a brain in its last death throes . . . "

"No! It's not true! You're real! I believe in Santa Claus! I believe in Santa Claus!" Morgan reached out and snatched at the man's tunic, frantically rubbing its velvet between his fingers, slapping at his broad chest, proving to himself the man was real. "I do believe! I do! I believe! I believe, I believe, I believe!"

Santa tore his hands away. "All right, all right. You say you believe. But what use is that if you won't do the things I tell you?"

"I will! I'll do anything!"

"You'll serve me?"

"Command me! Command me and I'll do it!"

"Worship me?"

Morgan dropped to his knees, bowed his head, and knitted his hands together in prayer. "Hail Santa! Hail Santa!"

The laughter of Saint Nicholas echoed across the square and through the town. "Oh, very good. Yes, very good indeed." He sighed, regarding the pathetic specimen huddled at his feet. "Even so, it would be highly irregular."

"But you can do it!" Morgan spoke without lifting his head, his voice half muffled by the snow. "I know you can. You can do anything. Please. Please! Let me go back. I'll make it right. I'll make everything right. I'll do everything you tell me to do and I'll fix it. Please. Please, please, please. Let me show you the man I can be."

It was darker now than when their conversation had begun. If Morgan had bothered to lift his head, he might have noticed the town around him changing, the scenery growing less defined as the shadows crowded in. He might have caught the distant sounds of violence, of whimpering men and giggling children. Or been confused by the sight of the buildings bordering the square and how closely they appeared to resemble the walls of a hospital room. He might have wondered if he was making a mistake. But all he was interested in and all he cared to hear were the next words out of Saint Nicholas's mouth.

"Very well, Morgan. I can allow you one more chance."

"Oh thank you!" He sprawled forward, into the snow, grabbing at the big man's boots and kissing them. "Thank you! Thank you! Thank you!"

"But it's conditional. You must rid the town of outsiders."

"I will!"

"You must deal with Will Douglas."

"I shall!"

"You must aid the children of St. Nicholas."

"Of course. Yes. I'll do it. I'll do anything you ask. Thank you. Oh thank you. Thank you!"

Saint Nicholas crouched down and took Morgan's head in his hands, turning it toward him, getting a good look at his puffy, tear-stained face. "Maybe we'll make something of you yet."

"Please."

Saint Nicholas cocked his head to one side, his smile like a lizard's. "You wanted to make a name for yourself, but the name you have is worthless. You need one with some value behind it. So I'll tell you what I'll do. I'll let you share mine."

Morgan's eyes widened at the thought. "You will?"

"I will. Now one thing more. I'm going to send you back now, to your bed in the clinic. In a few moments, your heart will begin to beat once more and your eyelids will flutter open. And when you look to your right, you will see a cup . . . "

17.

SOMETHING EXTRAORDINARY WAS happening to Devon. In the study, he'd said the clinic was too far away for any of the children to reach on foot. He said it because he believed it, certain any who attempted the journey would lose their way in the dark and freeze in the biting cold.

Then Saint Nicholas had offered him a cup of eggnog. The drink had looked like liquid gold and Devon had sucked it down, relishing the sensation as it poured into his stomach and seemed to burst, coursing through his body, flooding his veins with a curious energy.

Something changed in him then. What moments before had seemed impossible now felt entirely within his grasp. He could run to the clinic himself. Of course he could. It would hardly take him any time at all.

And that's just what he did, jumping into his boots, slinging his backpack over his shoulder and tearing from the house, off into the night. He traversed the snow with a kind of light-footed grace he'd never known and a speed he'd not thought possible. Reaching the woods on the outskirts of town, he found the flashlight he'd packed completely redundant. Though it was pitch black, he could see his way through the trees as clearly as on the brightest summer day. At no point did he stop to rest. He did not tire. The cold did not trouble him. He raced up the hill and arrived at the clinic with a feeling like he could keep on running and running and running until he had circled the globe and arrived back in the same spot. He imagined it would hardly take him a day.

This was how Saint Nicholas did it. This was the power that allowed him to visit the homes of all the Earth's children in one night. A power he'd shared with Devon and the others, infusing its magic in an ambrosia fit for angels. Thinking for half a second of how lucky he was made him want to cry. But he didn't have time for that. There was work to be done.

He sneaked into the clinic through the main entrance. The overhead fluorescents had been turned off, but amber mood-light strips lined the walls, diffusing everything with a soft, warming glow, so he stayed low and moved slow, clinging to the shadows to avoid being seen.

He needn't have bothered. The Bingzhen woman—Wong—was in the reception area, curled up on three chairs pushed together, fast asleep. He watched her from the corner, briefly transfixed by how innocent she appeared. She'd made a pillow of her ushanka-hat and a blanket of her overcoat. At rest, her face was as soft and serene as a child's and, were it not for the soft snore she emitted, she might have passed convincingly for an ivory doll.

It would be easy to kill her now, Devon thought. Easier than killing Bailey—though, of course, she had recovered in Santa's care. Easier even than killing Father McHattie, who had crumpled like a paper bag beneath the children's onslaught. He wondered if he should.

Though he despised the woman for what she was and the effort she'd made to rip the heart out of his town—the town his own ancestor had founded—he knew she had unwittingly played a part in bringing Saint Nicholas into his life. For that, he should thank her. Then again, she was dangerous.

He decided he would compromise by thanking her before he killed her. Or perhaps during, if she woke up. But he had a mission to complete first.

He crept along the hall until he found the room in which Morgan had been tucked away. The fat man was still asleep and reeked of blood, sweat, and antiseptic. His fingers twitched and eyes shifted under the lids, and Devon wondered if, in his dreams, he was speaking to Saint Nicholas right at this moment. He wished he could remember their first conversation, the first time Saint Nicholas had paid him a visit in his sleep, but it was lost to him now. He had been able to remember the whole thing when he'd woken that morning but had dismissed it as a pantomime thrown together by his subconscious. It had taken weeks of visitations before he allowed himself to admit the truth —Santa Claus really was talking to him in his dreams and desperately needed his help.

Once convinced of the reality of the situation, he had

committed himself wholeheartedly to the cause. How could he not? How could anyone not, who truly honored Christmas in their heart?

The latest task he'd been set was a relatively simple one, compared to those early days of recruitment, reconnaissance, and weapons gathering. He took the Rudolph thermos from his backpack, unscrewed the cap and poured the contents into a plastic cup, filling it all the way to the brim. It had the gloss and consistency of melted white chocolate and its aroma quickly overpowered the room's sweaty stench of fear and panic, turning the air sweet. He set the cup on Morgan's bedside table and backed away, his job done.

Before leaving the room, he looked into the flask and saw the half-inch of eggnog swirling around the bottom.

"It's a concentrated mixture," Saint Nicholas had told him. "Very powerful. You must ensure Morgan gets a full cup. That means no stealing any for yourself."

Naturally, he'd agreed, but Morgan had a full cup and there was still a little left. Only a mouthful, in fact. Certain Saint Nicholas wouldn't want it to go to waste, Devon tipped the flask back and drained it.

Immediately re-energized, he left the room and started walking back to reception, eager to put an end to Ling Wong while he had the opportunity. From his backpack he drew a knife—a cruel-looking blade his stepfather had said he kept for hunting, though Devon had never seen him hunt. Even in the hazy glow of the lamps its silver surface sparkled.

He was turning the corner into reception, close enough already to hear her snores, ready and willing to strike, when something overcame him. An exhaustion like he'd never known washed through him like a wave, soaking into his limbs. He fell against the wall, his legs buckling and arms going limp as gravity pulled him toward the floor. He fought to stay upright, using the wall to prop himself up as he dragged his failing body back the way he'd come, into the first room he could find. He staggered through the door—knife clattering to the floor, backpack sliding from his shoulder—and slumped to his knees. All the energy he'd felt rushing through his veins had evaporated, replaced by an unbearable heaviness—the kind of sensation he couldn't resist for long.

He was in a break room of some kind, with some dilapidated vending machines and two sets of tables and chairs. It didn't look like it was in much use. There was a chance he could hide here. With what little strength he had left, he shoved the door closed and crawled under one of the tables. His whole body shook as all its processes suddenly, violently, shut down. He had time enough to pray this was only sleep and not death coming to claim him. And then he was gone.

18.

SHONA WOKE WITH the taste of whiskey on her tongue. She opened her eyes and saw her glass on the coffee table, still with half a measure left. She lay on the couch, fully clothed, beneath a knitted blanket, and the sunlight was in her eyes. It hovered just above the sill of the living room window, magnesium white in a silver sky, and Shona didn't know if it was rising or setting.

Throwing off the blanket, she sat up and searched the room until she found her phone. It told her the time was 11:20 a.m., which in St. Nicholas, in December, meant dawn had just broken. The day could be expected to last around five hours. That was all the information she could gather from her phone as reception and wi-fi were still down. There was a time when being cut off like this would have caused her serious anxiety, but she was starting to get used to it. Still, she knew there would be hell to pay if her mother didn't hear from her on Christmas Day, so she hoped it would be repaired soon—not that meeting Sergio and Richie in the Malamute had filled her with much confidence in Bingzhen's team of expert contractors.

She rose groggily and went in search of the bathroom, finding it at the end of the hall. She passed Curtis's bedroom on the way. His door was ajar, just an inch or two, and, though morally dubious, she couldn't resist a peek inside. He was still asleep, lying face-down on the bed, dressed in long underwear and sleep socks. Not the most ruggedly sexy of images, perhaps, but she had to admit he looked comfortable. The only decoration in the room was a framed photograph on the nightstand of two children with big, open-mouthed smiles, in matching sweaters, staring off-camera. It occurred to her she hadn't asked their names the previous evening and she made a mental note to do so at the first opportunity.

In the bathroom mirror she locked eyes with a woman who appeared to be on the verge of collapse, suffering from nervous exhaustion and a likely Vitamin D deficiency, not to mention the early signs of halitosis. On a shelf by the shower was a basket of toiletries—a welcoming gift from the Bingzhen corporation, similar to one she had received—and she was relieved to find it contained an unused toothbrush.

After freshening up, she went into the kitchen, hunted around to see what food was available, found nothing but protein shakes and supplements, made a pot of coffee, poured a cup, and returned to the living room. Roused by the coffee's aroma, Curtis appeared a few minutes later. "What are you doing?" he asked.

She sat with her feet up on the table, blanket around her shoulders, cup in hand and watching his TV, which was on, displaying a screen of solid blue. "I'm watching my favorite show."

"Cable still out?"

"Everything is still out." She raised her cup. "But there's coffee."

"Thanks." He left, went to the kitchen, poured himself a cup and returned, joining her on the couch. "So tell me about this show."

"Well, there's not a lot of plot. It's more of a vibe. I guess you might call it a 'hang-out' show. Very easy to jump in at any point. You don't need to know any of the backstory or characters, so that's a big plus. It's mostly blue."

"Mostly? Does it change color?"

"It hasn't yet. But who knows? Maybe it could. That's the hook that keeps you watching." She sipped her coffee. "You know there's no food in your kitchen."

"There's mayonnaise."

She shuddered. "Yes, I saw. You can't eat mayonnaise for breakfast."

"I don't eat breakfast."

"You don't? That's mad. Where do you find the energy for all your . . . custodying?"

"I get by."

"Madness." She pointed to the window and the sun, now cowering behind gathering clouds. "The good news is it's nearly lunchtime. Don't tell me you don't eat lunch."

"I'm sure we'll be able to find a place." He spoke with a

confident smile that almost immediately collapsed. "I hope. Actually . . . I don't know."

"I don't think you can afford not to have food in your house in a town like this. It's not like there's a Taco Bell on the corner."

"That's a fair point."

"We should go back to the clinic. Raid the vending machines."

He laughed. "Yeah, we can do that."

"And check in on Morgan and Gertrude, of course. I'm not totally heartless."

"Sounds like a plan to me."

She set her coffee cup down on the table and turned her whole body around to face him. "Don't you find this aggravating?"

"What specifically?"

"This!" She waved a hand at the TV. "Being isolated from the world. Completely cut off from all forms of media, news, friends, and family. Doesn't it drive you insane?"

"It's an adjustment, sure. But I wouldn't say it's all bad. Has its pros and cons."

She nodded, and for a few moments more than was socially acceptable, nobody spoke. They sat together, sharing the passing of the seconds in absolute silence. Shona was the one who finally broke it; her speech slow and considered. "Isn't it mad to think that for most of human history, this is what it was like? No internet, no TV, no radio, no phones. This was entirely normal for most people who ever lived."

"I guess that's true."

"Makes you wonder what they did all day . . . to fill the time."

On this occasion, he left no room for awkward silence. He leaned over and kissed her. A kiss that was soft and polite and might have been brief and tentative, if it wasn't so warmly received. She leaned into it, hungrily pressing her lips to his, both of them tasting of coffee and toothpaste. She put her hand on the back of his neck and pulled him close, letting out an involuntary moan of excitement. His fingers disappeared into her hair, fulfilling a need to caress it he'd felt from the first moment he saw her but hadn't wanted to admit, even to himself. Moment by moment they drew closer, touching more confidently, encompassing each other more completely.

Somewhere in the midst of it all, his forehead nuzzled against hers, he managed to mutter, "So this is happening?"

She smiled and said, “It’s happening.”

A minute later she was straddling him on the couch, their lips locked, tongues entwined, her hair cascading over his face and hands down the front of his shirt, stroking his chest, hips grinding against his erection, which strained potently against the fabric of his thermal underwear. One of his own hands had slipped shamelessly down the back of her jeans and beneath her underwear to clutch her ass, while the other more demurely pawed at her left breast over her clothing.

She broke the kiss suddenly, her face flushed, to suck in a breath and ask, “Bedroom?”

He nodded—too lost in arousal to formulate words—and she jumped to her feet, grabbed him by the wrist and very nearly dragged him from the room.

19.

ALL WAS QUIET in the McCulloch house.

Kendra didn't know what time it was. She hadn't slept, but she had spaced out for a few hours. Somewhere in the midst of the grotesque horror show she'd been forced to endure, her gaze had focused on a single bulb on the Christmas tree and remained there while her brain, overloaded with too many sounds and images it could not make sense of, simply switched off. It was like she'd hypnotized herself into escaping reality and it made for a blissful period of non-thought, but it couldn't last. Slowly, she returned to a state of comprehension, fully aware of her surroundings—the sights, the smells, the silence.

The room was dark except for the twinkling bulbs on the tree and hazy gray daylight around the edges of the drawn curtains. The floor was littered with formless shapes that could have been furnishings, presents, people, or monsters. Her eyes searched the shadows for signs of the thing Devon had called 'Saint Nicholas', but she couldn't see it. The very thought of it caused an involuntary whimper, stifled by the stocking in her mouth. Instinctively, she tried to lift her hand and take it out, forgetting about the tape and ropes tying her to the couch. Amazingly, her hand came up and removed the gag. She tried lifting her other limbs and found all the ropes loose, the knots untied, the tape slashed. Someone had set her free.

For several minutes, she was too afraid to move. It felt too easy, too much like a trap. She feared the instant she climbed off the couch, the lights would come on and Devon and all the others would be there, laughing at her. One final, cruel, childish prank before Saint Nicholas pounced from his hiding spot and turned her inside out.

But she had to try. Her head throbbed and her bruised and

battered muscles ached from the beating she'd received, but she stiffly raised herself into a sitting position and swung her legs over the side of the couch. Standing up was a delicate affair. Pain lanced through her pierced foot when she put weight on it. Her legs trembled and she felt dizzy, but moving slowly and keeping one hand on the armrest, she managed to rise to her full height.

Several obstacles lay on her path to the hallway door. It took some time, staring down at it through the gloom, before she worked out what the first one was. Bailey's eviscerated corpse had been arranged on the rug in what appeared to be a perverse imitation of a sleeping pet. Kendra had to step over the emptied-out husk of what had once been her friend to make her escape. Two steps on was another body—and a third beyond that. Only these two, both friends of Devon, were actually sleeping. It looked like exhaustion had overwhelmed them in the same instant and they had fallen where they stood.

Kendra silently limped her way around the dozing children and into the hall. A few steps to her left was the front door and freedom, but she didn't dare risk it. Suppose Devon had posted guards on the porch? She'd soon be back on the couch, gagged and waiting to be fed to Saint Nicholas.

So she headed for the back door. She fought the instinct to look up when she passed the stairs, to the mess at the top she strongly suspected was her father, but as she neared the door to her bedroom, she paused. It was, so she'd been told, the house's master bedroom, yet Erin and her father had gifted it to her. It had a lock on the door and an en-suite shower room and, being on the first floor, offered a little more privacy than the others—all things that were important to a girl of her age. For a long time, it had been her sanctuary. Now, a sound came from within. The slow, regulated breathing of a slumbering beast. Its snoring made ripples in the air around the door and caused vibrations in the floor under her feet. She knew what it was.

She limped on into the kitchen, going straight to the knife block, but finding it empty. She searched a couple of drawers and scanned the counters, but it looked like anything with an edge or point sharp enough to be used as a weapon had been removed.

Briefly, she wondered whether if she had been able to find something, she might have doubled back, sneaked into her room and gutted the thing as it slumbered in her cotton sheets. But it was only a fleeting fantasy. She hobbled over to the back door and peered out through the window, checking for sentries. In the noonday light, the snow-covered yard appeared serene as a Christmas card. Mouthing a silent prayer, she zipped up her snowsuit, eased the door open, and stepped outside.

20.

LING FOUND GERTRUDE in the clinic's radio room, seated at a terminal that looked more than fifty years old. She reclined, almost horizontal, in a tarnished leather desk chair, eyes closed and hands clasped across her stomach, either asleep or dead.

Ling cleared her throat. "Gertrude?" Her voice was rough from a night spent sleeping in reception, far from the comforts to which she was accustomed.

"I'm just resting my eyes," the doctor replied, without opening them.

"Any luck with the radio?"

"Nothing from MacArthur Point. Could be the storm did some damage on their end."

"And Morgan?"

Now Gertrude did open her eyes, looking reluctantly at her watch. "I guess I could go check on him."

"If you wouldn't mind." Ling tried to make it sound polite, but couldn't keep an edge of irritation out of her voice. If Gertrude were an employee, she would feel a lot more confident in making demands. And perhaps she *was* an employee, but Ling couldn't be certain. The takeover had created so many gray areas where such roles were concerned. She decided it would be one of the first things she asked Morgan when they next spoke.

Groaning from fatigue, Gertrude eased herself out of the chair and led the way to Morgan's room. As they approached, she pointed ahead to a closed door at the end of the corridor. "There's a kitchen in there. You'll find a coffee pot on the counter and everything else you need in the cupboard above."

"You want me to make coffee?"

Gertrude showed her a gently mocking smile. "If you wouldn't mind."

Ling didn't argue, walking on as the doctor disappeared into Morgan's room and arriving at the door to the kitchen. Pushing it open, she was surprised to see a knife and a backpack on the floor. She crouched down and picked up the blade, clearly out of place in a culinary setting. She turned it in her hand, studying its design and the way the light glinted along its sharpened edge. It wasn't any kind of bread knife or chopping knife, but more like something a soldier would carry. By contrast, the brightly-colored backpack, adorned with cartoon characters and stickers, looked like it belonged to a child. She reached for it when an alarm sounded.

She jumped back and wheeled around, unsure at first where the noise was coming from or what it meant. Back in the corridor, she saw a blue light flashing over the door to Morgan's room and her heart sank. She ran toward it, telling herself there was no need to panic. It could be a mistake, an accident, Gertrude hitting the wrong button or pulling on the wrong wire. Morgan would be all right. She'd already said so.

A few steps from his room she heard a crash so loud and violent it sounded like a piece of equipment had been hurled against the wall. She froze, suddenly afraid to enter, though she knew it couldn't be as bad as she imagined. Perhaps something had been tipped onto its side, knocked onto the floor. It surely sounded worse than it was. Then came another crash and this time the door shook in its frame. Ling felt its vibration and instinctively stepped back. The light above the door kept flashing, but the sirens cut out.

In the silence that followed, Ling could hear a voice, strained and pleading. "Help . . . Please help." It was so low and muffled, she couldn't be sure whose voice it was.

"Gertrude?" She pushed open the door to illuminate a scene of chaos, Morgan's bed upended and smashed to pieces, its broken parts piled in the middle of the floor. Monitors and other machines had been torn open and their insides scattered across the room, like a violent tornado had manifested itself within its confines and dissipated a few seconds later. This much was visible in the rectangle of light cast through the door from the corridor. The rest of the room was hidden by shadow. "Morgan?"

On the other side of the broken bed, something moved. One of the bed-sheets, torn and dangling from a broken railing, fluttered as something behind it took a deep, rasping breath. "Ling . . . "

It was too dark on that side of the room for her to tell what she was looking at. She put a hand to the wall on her right, reaching for the light switch—and something grabbed it.

"Run!" Gertrude sprang toward her, into the light, hand clamped around her wrist, her eyes crazed and face smeared with blood. "Get away!"

Ling jerked her hand free in the same moment something behind Gertrude moved. From the darkness behind the bed it reared up and struck out, thrusting a spear of darkness across the room. Gertrude cried out as it struck, her whole body seizing as something pierced her back and burst from her stomach, spraying the air between them with a thin mist of red.

Ling stepped back, gaze darting between Gertrude's agonized face and the darkening stain on the front of her sweater, from which four long, thin rods now appeared, their tips dripping blood. They emerged slowly from the wound in her belly, like the stems of newly-planted flowers in search of the sun, then appeared to wilt, folding in on themselves to dig back into her flesh. Only when Gertrude's torso was pierced for a second time and four more stalks sprouted beneath the first set did Ling realize what they were—fingers.

Two hands were deep in Gertrude's body. She quivered helplessly as they shifted in her guts, one on top of the other, holding her upright as she bucked and blood frothed through her gritted teeth. They ground one against the next, working at the wound, pushing to pry flesh from fresh, till both hands clamped down, fingers finding purchase in muscle and, like unlocking jaws, they split her open. The sound of splashing blood echoed down the hall as, with terrifying strength, Gertrude's upper half wrenched away from her pelvis.

Savagely separated from the rest of her body, her legs and hips dropped wetly to the floor, trailing a short length of vertebrae from her shattered spine, while her torso—head and arms already hanging limp—pitched toward the ceiling, loops of her entrails unraveling from the ragged cavity beneath her rib cage. Ling's focus was locked on Gertrude's face, watching as she was lifted high and unceremoniously dropped like a sack of rotten meat, hoping against all sense for a sign she might somehow survive. But her features had frozen at the peak of her torment and her bloodshot eyes were dead.

The hands that had torn her apart lingered in the doorway, like a magician's awaiting applause in the wake of performing some elaborate trick. Coated in blood, strands of muscle and viscera dangling from their nails, they more closely resembled claws—the fingers unnaturally long and double-jointed, the bones narrow and crooked beneath skin that was loose yet paper-thin. They were attached to arms that stretched all the way back to the other side of the room and behind the broken bed, to the shapeless lump that crouched there, half-hidden by shadow. "Ling . . . " It spoke with a voice she knew. "Please . . . help me."

"Morgan?" She heard herself speak his name, but didn't feel her lips move, couldn't feel anything; her whole body turned numb from shock.

The hands, swaying on the ends of his comically elongated limbs, gestured to her in a kind of invitation. "Praise me." He beckoned her with blood-slick fingers. "Help me *live*."

He made a grab for her, lurching forward with his grasping claws. Ling brought her own hands up to defend herself—forgetting one of them clutched the hunting knife she'd found in the kitchen—and slashed his palm open.

Morgan cried out and retreated, the wound in his skin gushing blood that was thick, viscous, and yellow. It pattered on the floor, fizzing as it mingled with the red puddle of Gertrude's emptied fluids. Attempting to flee, Ling slid in the blood and nearly went down, but managed to stay on her feet, running down the hall while looking back over her shoulder, watching for Morgan, in whatever form he'd now assumed, to emerge from the room.

She was still looking behind her when she collided with another body. She quickly jerked back, swinging the knife up to defend herself, but another hand clamped around her wrist before it could do any damage.

"What the hell?" Curtis searched her face for a sign of recognition, the beginning of an explanation, but all he saw in her eyes was madness.

"Gertrude?" Shona stepped past him, hands over her mouth, eyes fixed on the mutilated corpse spattered across the entrance to Morgan's room. "Oh my god."

"Run! Get away!" Ling unknowingly parroted Gertrude's final words, the only ones she was able to choke out through her near-paralyzing fear. Her hand was locked tight around the handle of the knife and Curtis had to fight to get her to lower it.

"What's going on?" he cried, attention switching back and forth between the crazed woman in his arms and the one walking slowly ahead of them, nearing the open door.

"Run," Ling repeated, shaking free of his grasp. "Run!"

Before he or Shona could ask why, Morgan answered the question for them. The sound he made was like the trumpeting of an enraged elephant as he came barreling from the room, swinging his bloodied fists like anvils and gouging holes in the walls and ceiling.

Briefly obscured in a cloud of debris, he heaved his enormous bulk around and took one faltering step forward. Curtis and Shona stared at the beast emerging from the plume of plaster dust, both struggling to comprehend what they were seeing, neither of them guessing it was Morgan. Though he still wore the soiled and ragged Santa suit, his transformation had left him unrecognizable as human. The skin over his entire body appeared to have separated from the muscle and bone beneath, so his skeleton now shifted independently of the tissue in which it was encased. He turned his head and his limp, lifeless face sloughed across his skull. His belly was like a deflated air balloon, dangling awkwardly between his malformed legs, its contents gone elsewhere to serve other parts of his anatomy in its ongoing reinvention. Each step and swing of his arms was punctuated by the sound of bones snapping and resetting, finding their place in the new order. If the process caused him pain, Morgan could not show it. His screams were muffled by a mask of his own migrating flesh.

"Run," Ling repeated, and this time they listened to her, turning around and racing back the way they'd come, down the corridor, through reception, out of the main entrance and across the parking lot to reach Curtis's truck.

"God damn," he said as he jumped behind the wheel. "God damn, God damn!"

"Go," Ling ordered from the seat behind him, covering her face with her hands, too scared to look back. "Go, just go!"

Curtis started the engine and slammed his foot on the accelerator. The truck's wheels spun uselessly for a few seconds, then found purchase. It lurched across the lot then swung back around, plowing through a snow drift in his haste to reach the road. Only once did he steal a glance back at the entrance, expecting to see the beast smashing through metal and glass in its pursuit of them. But all he saw—or *thought* he saw—was a child stepping through the door. It was barely half a glimpse, snatched while the truck was hurtling across the ice, just before it reached the road, and he knew he had to be mistaken. Whatever he'd seen, it hadn't been that.

"Ling." Shona was in the passenger seat, too confused by what she'd just witnessed to be terrified. She reached back and put a hand on the other woman's shoulder. "Ling, what was that?"

Ling was leaning forward, head between her knees, doing her best to ignore the existence of the world around her.

"Ling!" Shona gave her a push, tried to shake her into making some kind of response, but it had no effect. Giving up, she turned her attention to Curtis. "What the fuck was that?"

"You think I know?" His heart raced and beads of flop sweat dripped down his face, pouring into his eyes. The truck bounced and skidded along the road and he had to fight to keep it from veering into the trees. He knew they were going too fast, but he was afraid to slow down.

"Oh Christ," Shona groaned. "You don't think . . . It couldn't have been . . . " She let the sentence trail off as something dashed out of the woods ahead of them. "Look out!"

Curtis saw it a split second after she did and slammed on the brakes. The truck slid and swerved for nearly a hundred yards, coming to a reluctant stop just a few feet from the figure now standing directly ahead of them in the middle of the road.

Shona leaned forward, staring through the windshield, her mouth falling open in disbelief. "Is that . . . Devon McCulloch?" Nobody answered, but they didn't have to.

"Where did he come from?" asked Curtis.

"From the woods." Shona grabbed his arm. "Curtis, we have to help him."

"Don't," said Ling, her tone flat. "Don't you dare."

Shona turned to face her, but Ling wouldn't meet her gaze. Her eyes were locked on the McCulloch boy, regarding him the way an animal would a hunter. If her mind had snapped from what she'd witnessed at the clinic, Shona couldn't really blame her. "He's just a wee kid."

"Want to bet?" Ling gave Curtis a nudge. "Drive."

Curtis didn't hit the gas, but nor did he open his door. He sat with his hands clamped on the wheel, momentarily paralyzed by fear and confusion.

"He's just a wee kid," Shona repeated, staring at Curtis, willing him to move. When he didn't, she let out a growl of frustration, turned, and reached for her door handle.

"Wait," Curtis told her. "Don't. I'll go."

"I wouldn't," Ling warned and held out the knife. "But if you're going you should take this."

Shona shot her an irritated look, but didn't argue. She couldn't deny something strange and dangerous was happening here. At the same time, she couldn't bear the thought of leaving a child in the woods to freeze.

Curtis eyed the knife a moment, clearly tempted, but brushed it away. "I'll be fine. You two stay here." He didn't like the way the words sounded coming from his mouth. They had an air of finality about them. With one last, encouraging nod from Shona, he opened the door and stepped out, into the road.

Devon hadn't moved in the time they'd been talking. He stood perfectly still, watching the truck. As he moved closer, his boots crunching through the fresh snow, Curtis was able to get a better look at him. He was tall for an elementary school kid and extraordinarily pale, even by the standards of St. Nicholas, with skin so bleached it had a sickly translucence to it, like lemon sherbet. The jacket and pants he wore looked two sizes too small, his scrawny limbs stretching far beyond the fabric, exposed to the elements. As for his face . . .

Curtis didn't pay much attention to the students coming and going from the school. He spent most of his days in the basement, of course, but even when topside he wasn't interested in learning who the kids were and being able to tell them apart. Even so, if he'd seen this particular child in the halls, he was certain he would have remembered him.

The kid's head was shaped like a white turnip—bulbous at the top, tapering to a sharp point at the bottom—with features that seemed too small and tightly grouped for his face. His mouth, nose, and mean little eyes were all tiny, yet his ears were big and pointed. It took more than a moment before Curtis realized what he reminded him of, but then it came to him.

An elf, he thought. *Kid looks like a damn Christmas elf.*

"Hey," he called, while still a few steps away. "You okay?"

Devon didn't look at him. His gaze remained fixed on the truck. Curtis took a look and figured out exactly what his attention was focused on. Ling Wong was directly in his sights, and she was staring straight back.

"Listen," Curtis said, his own eyes still on the truck. "I don't know what's going on here, but . . . "

Devon struck while his head was turned. Curtis's first clue he was in trouble was Shona jolting up in her seat and flapping her arms in panic. He turned too late to keep the kid from leaping up onto his back, clamping his legs around his waist and wrapping his arms around his shoulders.

"Hey! Get . . . " Curtis stumbled, grabbing at the kid, but afraid to do him any real damage. He managed to get a hold of his sleeve and pulled his arm away from his chest. Devon's hand, tensed like a claw, passed briefly in front of his face and he watched, horrified, as the fingertips exploded, spears of sharpened bone sprouting through the flesh. In the next instant, the sleeve slipped from his grip and the bones plunged into his chest, digging through several layers of clothing, skin, and muscle in an attempt to gouge through his breastplate and tear out his heart.

Curtis cried out from the shock and pain and could hear Shona, slightly muffled from within the truck, echoing him with a scream of her own. He could feel the kid's hooks in his flesh, forcing their way deeper. He spun around, slapping and pulling at the kid's arms, trying to rip him free, but it made no difference. Falling back against the truck and pinning Devon there, he turned his head to see the kid's tiny black mouth opening wider and wider and wider, two rows of jagged fangs ready to bite down on his neck and sever his head from his body.

He didn't even think of Will's knife. It was like his hand remembered all on its own, snatching it from his pocket, flicking it open, and planting the blade in the kid's forearm, all the way to the hilt. In the moment, it felt like the most satisfying action he'd taken in his entire life.

Devon's eager mouth warped to form a howl, his hot breath forming a white cloud of agony in the icy air. He immediately peeled away, his claw sucking free of Curtis's chest and legs uncoupling from his back. He scuttled backward across the hood of the truck, clutching his wounded arm, his howls turning to childlike whimpers, and dove into the snow.

Curtis, hand pressed to his own wound, blood oozing through the holes in his jacket, clambered back into the truck and started it. Pushing through the pain rippling across his chest and ignoring the perplexed and terrified sounds of the woman in the seat beside him, he got them moving again, hurtling their way back down the hill toward St. Nicholas.

They'd almost reached town before anyone said anything. Ling was the one who spoke.

"Told you so."

21.

THE ST. NICHOLAS POLICE STATION—recently re-branded the Coldwell Slopes Security Department—was a four-story brick building in the middle of the row flanking the west side of the town square. Having undergone only superficial refurbishment throughout more than a century of operation, it retained many historic features, including its two iron-barred jail cells, adjoining the main office, which looked like they were straight out of a western.

Will Douglas had spent the night in one, grimly shaking his head and muttering to himself about Santa Claus. Owen Dupont had taken the other, managing to get a few hours' sleep in the cot, for which he was grateful, before the start of the morning shift. His own bed was only a few streets away, but he knew he couldn't go home. Not with the town's communications down and Morgan MacLean out of commission. He'd known, once she eventually returned from the clinic, Ling Wong would come marching through the front door, barking orders—and that's exactly what she did. What he hadn't expected was for her to be brandishing a hunting knife and to be accompanied by the school janitor pouring blood from a hole in his chest. He had his arm around the new schoolteacher, Miss Fleming, who half carried him into the room and put him in a chair before yelling to the small contingent of security officers, "I need a first-aid kit!"

"Again?" Stepping out of his cell, Owen cast an eye toward Will. "At least I can't blame you this time."

The young man only shrugged, indifferent to the unfolding drama.

Dan Hoxton and Terry Cabot, the only other full-time members of the Coldwell Slopes security team, had been at their desks when the trio entered. Now Dan stood and fetched the first-aid kit for Shona while Terry simply looked on in bafflement.

"What's going on?" Owen walked between the desks, approaching Ling. "What's with the knife?"

Her face was screwed up in thought, like she was battling to figure out a way to tell him something. "Mr. Dupont, do your men have any guns?"

"Guns? We . . . we don't keep any guns here. It's not that kind of operation anymore. But we can get some. Why . . . why would we need guns?"

"There's something up at the clinic. Something . . . Some kind of . . . It attacked us."

"Some kind of what? An animal?"

"Animal?" Ling looked to Shona who, in the midst of tearing open a pack of gauze, could only give a helpless, wide-eyed stare back. Both knew she couldn't tell them what they'd really seen. There was no way they'd believe it. "Yes, I think so. An animal of a kind."

"So . . . a bear? A wolf?"

"More like a bear than a wolf."

Terry Cabot, who still hadn't moved from his desk chair, let out a skeptical snort. "A bear attack in the middle of winter? It's unheard of."

"Whatever it was," Ling snapped. "It was big and it attacked us. Look!" She pointed to Curtis, now shirtless, pressing a wad of bandages to his mutilated chest. "Plus . . . " She winced, struggling over how to tell the next part, before blurting it out. "It killed Gertrude."

The gently bemused smile on Owen's face suddenly melted away. "Gertie?"

She nodded.

"Gertie's dead?"

Again, she nodded.

Owen, Dan, and Terry exchanged looks, all of them sharing the same expression of mingled grief and shock. Dropping into the nearest chair, Owen asked, "What about Morgan?"

Ling hesitated a moment before answering. "Yes, it . . . Him too, I think. Yeah, he's . . . Morgan's gone."

"Shit." Owen shook his head in disbelief. "Shit." He reached for the desk phone and put the receiver to his ear. "Shit!" He slammed it back down. "Still out. Come on, we'll try the two-way." He took Ling over to the corner of the room where the radio terminal sat.

At the same time, Shona began the process of cleaning and disinfecting Curtis's wounds.

He smiled as she leaned in to tend to him, her face a mask of concentration, serious as a pallbearer. "I suppose if we hadn't already had sex," he said, keeping his voice low. "This could have been one of those heavily charged erotic moments you get in films, the heroine tending to the battle scars of the handsome hero."

"Sad to say, I don't find the sight of blood a turn-on."

"That's a pity." He shrugged, then winced.

"Don't shrug," she snapped, her brow furrowing in anger as she mopped up a fresh spurt of blood. "Fuck sake, what did he use to do this?"

"Your star pupil? He used his hand. That's all."

"That's impossible."

"I saw it. His fingers grew claws and he used them to try to tear my heart out. How is it?"

"Not as bad as it looks. In the movies they'd call it a flesh wound. Still . . . you're lucky you're in good hands."

"I hear that." He let his head fall back, exhaling a long breath, then whispered, "What the hell is going on, Shona?"

"I don't know," she said, the question obviously frightening her. "Not a clue. I do not have one fucking clue."

"You want to know what's happening?" Will yelled the question from behind the bars of his cell at the back of the room. Curtis and Shona had both been whispering, so there was no way he could have heard them, but he must have guessed what they were talking about. "I can tell you."

"Keep it to yourself, Will," Terry told him. "No-one wants to hear it."

Will laughed the statement off. Even from a distance he could see how scared Curtis and Shona were, their worried eyes trained on him, afraid that this time, when he spoke, he might say something they believed. "This is only the start. You'll see. You can't hide. You can't get away. He's coming for all of us. And it's too late now to do anything to stop it. Way too late. All we can do is wait."

His piece spoken, something approaching a sadistic smile on his lips, he let go of the bars, strolled over to his cot in the corner, lay down and turned to face the wall.

In the time it took Shona to get Curtis provisionally patched up, Owen managed to reach a couple former volunteer constables by radio who were only too happy to escape the boredom at home by grabbing a hunting rifle and coming to the station.

"What do you intend to do?" Ling asked him as he put on his coat and grabbed his hat.

"While there's still some daylight left, I want to drive up to the clinic and see what we can find."

She shook her head. "No. The priority should be reestablishing lines of communication. We need to get the phones working again and the roads cleared. Then we can get some real help down here."

"That'll take hours. If there's a killer *bear* on the loose . . . " He spoke the word with an obvious tinge of skepticism. "It could already be on its way to town. With no quick way to warn people we're putting them at serious risk. We need to find it fast and deal with it."

Ling tried to imagine Owen going up against the thing Morgan had become. The way the scene played out in her head wasn't pretty. "I don't want anyone going up there. And you work for me, Mr. Dupont. Don't forget that."

He bristled at the statement, but it was true. He wasn't chief of police. Not even a constable. He was a paid employee of the Bingzhen Group and, as such, was in no position to call the shots. "What would you have me do?"

"There's a satellite phone in the town hall. We can use it to contact MacArthur Point. I intend to go get it. I require an escort."

"An escort?" He couldn't hide how ridiculous he found the idea. The town hall was only a two-minute walk across the square.

"Preferably armed." Ling was careful with her tone, ensuring there was no way anyone could doubt she was serious. "From there we'll go to Samuel Street and talk to those contractors, find out what the hell they've been doing for the last two days. Maybe we can persuade them to do their jobs and fix the phone service."

"Fine." Owen sat on the edge of the desk and folded his arms. "Lonnie Price and Hank Steins are bringing some firepower over. We'll just have to sit a while and wait for them to get here, but once they do, I'll be only too happy to escort you myself."

"Good." She turned from him, ignoring his frustrated head shake, and walked over to Shona and Curtis, who'd put his bloodied shirt back on over his bandaged torso. "As for you two, you should go home. Stay safe. Lock your doors."

They both nodded, quite happy to step aside and let others deal with whatever crisis was unfolding. Leaning forward, careful to ensure she couldn't be heard by Owen or his men, Shona asked, "Ling, do you have any idea what's happening?"

"I don't know," she said, and they could both see she was telling the truth. "But what I do know is, if it wasn't for the two of you, I'd almost certainly be dead right now. So thank you."

"You're welcome," said Curtis. He tried to make it sound sincere, but there was a flatness to the words. An emptiness that resonated through all three of them, recognizing there was little worth in giving or receiving thanks at this time. Yes, they were all still breathing, but how long that could be expected to last felt deeply uncertain. What they all understood, on a palpable, instinctual level, was that whatever nightmare they'd stumbled into was far from over.

22.

DEVON STAGGERED THROUGH the open door of his home to find the other children and his stepsister gone. Cradling his wounded arm, he entered the living room to meet with the sight of Saint Nicholas occupying the couch to which Kendra had been tied. Devon wasn't sure, at first, if the old man was still alive. His eyes were closed and his skin gray, with a sheen across it that might have been cold sweat or rot. He sat very still, and his round belly did not jiggle with mirth or even breath.

"Santa?" Devon didn't recognize the sound of his own voice, so much higher in pitch and raspier than normal. "Santa Claus?"

A sigh. "How many times must I ask you not to call me that?"

Devon winced. "I'm sorry. Saint Nicholas. Where is everyone? Where's Kendra?"

Saint Nicholas did not open his eyes, but sighed again, his head slowly falling forward. He appeared to be dozing, the conversation requiring more energy than he could muster. "The girl escaped."

"That's impossible. When?"

"While we slept. It couldn't be helped."

"The others should have been watching her."

"They were asleep." Saint Nicholas sucked in a slow, deep breath. "Sleep is important. So important. Rest fortifies the mind. It is when the body is repaired, strengthened, *developed* . . . We all need sleep. And now, when I rest, so must you. This is the bond we've made. Don't blame the others. It couldn't be helped."

"Where are they now?"

"Some went to recapture the girl. Others in search of more . . . entertainment. Everything in hand. Nothing to worry about." Now one of his eyes eased open, the pupil rolling lazily around to find Devon. "And you?"

Devon swallowed. It was a question he wasn't sure he could

answer. He felt disconnected from the world around him and from himself. The superior senses he'd known the previous evening had dimmed, leaving him unsure of his surroundings and his own abilities. His head pounded and he felt like he was seeing Saint Nicholas through the wrong end of a telescope, the rest of the room in darkness. His lip trembling, he said, "I don't know. I . . . I went to the clinic. I tried to eliminate the woman, Wong. But there were others. They hurt me. They got away. I failed."

"You delivered the eggnog to Morgan? He drank it?"

"Yes."

A smile. "That's all I asked you to do. The rest matters not."

"But they got away."

"We'll get them. We'll get them soon enough. When we're ready." Saint Nicholas opened both eyes and studied the boy, looking him up and down. "You drank some of it too, didn't you?"

He didn't try to deny it. "I know I shouldn't have. I . . . I feel strange."

"It's quite all right. Means you'll develop a little faster than the others, that's all. But you shouldn't be afraid. You'll feel much better soon."

"What do we do now?"

"Where's Morgan? Still at the clinic?"

Devon nodded.

"Then we must bring him here. But first, I must feed. Food is as important as rest."

Devon turned toward the kitchen. "I can make some sandwiches . . . "

Saint Nicholas put a hand on his arm, fingers digging into the tender flesh around his knife wound. "No, child, no . . . " His deep chuckle only halfway hid his impatience. "This has all been good fun, but try your best to understand me now. I need . . . to *feed.* Real food. Where do you think we might find such a thing?"

Devon stared at him for several seconds, telling himself he didn't know what the man's words meant or what he wanted. Then, under his idol's penetrating gaze, quite without preamble of explanation, as though he'd known all along and had simply been denying its existence, the answer presented itself.

"The Boyles are home," he said. "They live not far from here."

"The Boyles." Saint Nicholas teased out the name, his mouth opening into a grin as he did so. "Who are the Boyles?"

"Mechanics. Mom, dad, son. It's a family business. Mostly truck maintenance and repair, but they can fix anything. They're . . . on our list."

Saint Nick's grin widened a little more. "Locals?"

Devon nodded. "St. Nicholas born and raised."

With a show of tremendous exertion, the old man lifted himself from the couch. "Then I say we absolutely must pay them a visit."

23.

"YOU SHOULD SEE my place," Shona had said, the previous night, when they were drinking whiskey in his living room. She'd made the comment in reference to Christmas decorations, but even from the outside, the difference between her home and his was stark.

She lived in suburbia, a mile from the center of town, in a detached three-bedroom house with an expansive yard and garage. In winter, half-buried in snow, a little of its elegance was lost, but come summer Curtis could easily imagine Shona out on the veranda, sipping from a tall glass of gin and lemonade. Meanwhile, he'd be sweating in his walk-up one-bed apartment with no air conditioning and windows that didn't open all the way. *You should see my place,* indeed.

Beatrice had found it for her, she explained. In fact, Beatrice—Miss Gulliver to him—was her neighbor, living only two doors down the street. She explained how she understood how hard it was, being the new teacher in a strange town. She'd been in exactly the same position herself, thirty years earlier, and so knew exactly how unappealing St. Nicholas could be for new arrivals. It helped to have a neighbor nearby, someone you could rely on. And the house, now the property of the Bingzhen Group and in terrific condition, would only be sitting empty otherwise. Better to have someone living there, even if she was only by herself, to ensure it was heated and the roof didn't spring a leak and none of the pipes froze.

Curtis understood all this. But it didn't explain why Beatrice, who also found him his accommodation, chose to put him where she had. He had many demonstrable skills that could be put to use on the upkeep and renovation of a historic townhouse or sprawling mansion. Instead, Beatrice—Miss Gulliver to him—had chosen to deposit him in a one-bed walk-up over an abandoned barbershop at the top of the steepest hill in town. You'd have to be a fool not to take it personally. Despite knowing next to nothing about Curtis, she clearly took a dim view of him. Whether that was because of his ethnicity, his job, or simply the fact he was a man, he didn't know. And he wasn't particularly interested in finding out. But it riled him, nonetheless.

It dominated his thoughts as he parked the truck at the end of the drive, navigated the icy route to the front door and took off his boots to cross the wide hardwood floor of the living room to take a seat in the plush leather couch to which Shona had directed him. Then, in the midst of his internal fury, he wondered if he was only letting it preoccupy him so because he didn't want to think about anything else. Especially not the boy with the razor fangs and heart-gouging claws or the monstrous thing they'd briefly caught sight of at the hospital. It was a welcome distraction to have anything else to focus his attention on.

"Take off your shirt." Shona called to him as she was running up the stairs.

He obliged, wincing as he tugged the ruined garment over his head before shouting back, "I don't know what you've got planned, but I bet I don't have the energy for it!"

He was alone for a minute—just long enough to survey the room and its disconcerting abundance of Christmas decorations. Ornaments, cards, and candles on every surface. Garlands and poinsettias adorning every wooden frame and mantel. Snowflake decals crowded the window panes while string lights threaded the curtains. Her tree—real and surely too large to have been carried into the house by human hands—stood in the corner, groaning under the weight of its innumerable baubles. On a table beside the TV a gingerbread house had been constructed, through the windows of which he could see a gingerbread family, staring back at him. Though their eyes were mere beads of frosting, he sensed something strangely judgmental in them.

Then she returned and tossed him a t-shirt. "Here."

"I doubt I'm your size."

"It belonged to my ex."

"You want me to put on your former fiancé's shirt?"

She gave him a mockingly seductive look. "I used to sleep in it on nights he was working away from home. And send him pictures. Sexy ones."

"Don't tell me any more." He studied the lettering. "What's a Caledonian Thistle?"

"A football team."

"A good one?"

She nodded. "The best."

He shrugged as he pulled it on. "That's all right then."

She started moving again, heading to the kitchen this time. "Can I get you something to eat?"

"Not for me."

She doubled back immediately, head poking incredulously through the doorway. "What's the matter with you? You never eat."

"I eat."

"I've never seen you eat."

He grinned, instantly reminded of conversations with his mother. "I eat, okay? I'll get something later on."

"It's not healthy."

He sighed. "Well, I don't know what to tell you, Shona. I guess I'm not really in the mood right now."

She came and sat down beside him, her expression turned serious, body language serious, ready for a serious conversation. "What's going on, Curtis?"

He shook his head. "I don't know."

"I can't be sure what we saw this morning, but I don't think it was human. And the way Devon was acting, the way he looked, what he did to you . . . "

"It's okay." He could see she was getting upset. "Whatever it was, it's over now."

"It's not. The phones are still down, the roads are still out. And Devon . . . Fuck, Curtis, he has a family."

"Hey." He pulled her close and—with no small amount of pain—put his arm around her. "Take it easy. Don't think about that."

"They could be looking for him now. His poor parents . . . "

"It's nothing to do with us. And there's nothing we can do about it. We've just got to let Ling and the cops . . . the *non*-cops . . . do their thing."

She nodded in forlorn agreement and rested her head on his chest. He didn't complain, though it hurt a little. They stayed that way for a minute or two, feeling like their Christmas might yet turn out not to be so bad, as long as they could hold each other close on the couch. Then Shona asked, "Should I put the fairy lights on?"

Curtis didn't get to answer. The frantic pounding of a fist at the front door put an end to the tranquility. They both sat up, but neither stood, both too afraid of what might be awaiting them if they went to answer. Then, from outside, they heard a woman cry, "Shona! Shona, please! It's an emergency!

Shona let out a sigh that wasn't entirely one of relief. "It's Beatrice! What could she want?"

Curtis watched her as she stood and went to the door, wishing she wouldn't. Sensing instinctively it would be better if they both stayed where they were. "Doesn't sound good."

The hammering of fists on wood continued right up to the moment Shona opened the door and Miss Beatrice Gulliver rushed inside. A scrawny, fastidious woman in her mid-fifties, who Curtis had never seen without a cashmere cardigan buttoned to the neck, a razor-sharp crease in the legs of her pants or with a jet-black hair out of place. But she looked a disheveled mess now, her tousled hair half-hidden by an awkwardly angled beanie hat, glasses askew and padded cream Parka hanging off her shoulders. And she wasn't alone.

She hurried Kendra inside and slammed the door behind them. The girl limped in boots that were too big for her, arms folded across her bruised ribs, swollen face concealed by curtains of long hair wet from sweat, blood, tears and snow.

"Thank God you came home," Beatrice said, gasping to catch her breath. "My truck wouldn't start and there's no-one else on this street who . . . " She paused in the middle of her sentence when she noticed Curtis, still sitting on the couch in his Caledonian Thistle shirt. "Curtis?"

He nodded his head in greeting. "Miss Gulliver."

"Beatrice, what on earth's going on?" Shona asked, reaching for the girl, eager to see if she was injured, but Kendra only twisted away from her, hiding her face as though ashamed.

Beatrice, forcefully swallowing her obvious distaste at finding young Miss Fleming and the school's new custodian together, took her by the arm and led her a few steps forward, nowhere near far enough away to be out of Kendra's earshot, but enough to make it look like they ought to be. "She just showed up at my door." She spoke the words in a stage whisper. "Banging, screaming, crying for help. I don't know what happened to her. She babbled nonsense for five minutes then collapsed. Hasn't said a word since. I don't know what she's gotten into, if she's been beaten, raped or what." She waved a hand in the traumatized girl's direction. "I mean I assume drugs of some kind were involved, but I don't know what. I expect this is the comedown now."

"Who is she?" Shona did her best to keep her own whispered words between the two of them, feeling awkward to be talking about the girl in the abstract while they were standing in the same room with her.

"Kendra Wray." The name meant nothing to Shona, but Beatrice was good enough to explain without her asking. "Not a local girl. Comes from MacArthur Point. Who knows what kinds of debauchery she could have got mixed up in there. Moved to McGee Street after her father got involved with Erin McCulloch."

Now that was a name she knew. "McCulloch? Devon McCulloch's mother?"

Beatrice nodded excitedly, happy to be gossiping. "One and the same."

That changed things. Before knowing who she was, Shona had been prepared to welcome the girl in, give her a place to rest, any first aid required, let her gather her thoughts while they waited for the phones to be fixed. Once they were, she'd give Owen Dupont a call to come collect her. But the stepsister of Devon McCulloch? That was someone who had to be dealt with immediately. "Curtis?"

He was already getting up, wincing at the pain it caused him. "Yeah, I know."

"You'll give her a ride?" Beatrice asked. "The clinic would be my first stop. I had to lend her my old boots, you know. She turned up at my door in bare feet. Who knows how long she was out in the snow—no hat, no gloves, no boots. Can you imagine? You'd have to be high."

"We'll get her some help." Shona handed Curtis a football scarf to match his shirt and his blood-stained jacket, while pulling her own on. "Don't worry."

"Good. Just don't take her to McGee Street. That was my first instinct, but then I thought . . . well, what if whatever it was that happened to her happened there? What if it's not over? And with the phones down . . . I mean, I could take a walk over there now and find out. Let them know she's okay . . . "

"I wouldn't." Shona opened the door and ushered Beatrice and the girl outside. "I'd suggest going home and locking your door.

When we get back, if the phones still aren't working, I'll come see you."

Curtis turned to look back into the room before following them out, then paused. Frowned. It was a strange feeling that came over him, but for a moment he was quite certain that in the few seconds between him leaving the couch and putting his coat on, every single Christmas ornament, light and decoration in the room had ever-so-slightly changed position. Almost as though they'd begun creeping toward him while his back was turned.

"Curtis!" Shona's voice broke the spell. He followed them out, closing the door behind him.

They walked in a group to the truck, Kendra at the center, passively going wherever she was led, like a heavily drugged mental patient. Shona guided her into the back seat before getting in beside Curtis in the front. Nobody noticed the trail of fresh, child-sized footprints through the snow up to the fender.

"Heck of a start to the holidays, huh?" Beatrice poked her head in through Curtis's open door.

"You're not wrong," Shona replied, while thinking: *You don't know the half of it.* She suspected, however, that Beatrice was glad of the excitement. All she'd been anticipating was another Christmas alone in her big empty house.

"You'll come see me later? Bring me an update?"

"We will," Shona assured her.

"Okay then." She nodded, stepping back from the truck. "Okay. Thank you, Shona. Thank you, Curtis."

The personal thanks caught him by surprise, but he tried not to let it show. "Any time." He closed the door and put his key in the ignition.

Beatrice was walking away now, waving to them. Shona waved back, muttering, "What the fuck is going on?"

Curtis turned the key. Nothing happened.

"No," said Kendra.

He tried again. And a third time. Nothing happened.

"What's wrong?" Shona asked.

"I don't know," he answered honestly.

"No, no, no," said Kendra, her voice getting louder all the time.

"Hey, it's okay, we . . . " Shona turned to face her and saw it wasn't the truck's uncooperative engine that had her so concerned.

She had her face up against the window, hands on the glass, staring out at Beatrice. "No, no, no, no, no!"

Shona leaned forward to look through Curtis's window, spotting the school's principal a few yards away, standing in the middle of the road. It looked like she'd been walking back to her house and had stopped to talk to someone Shona couldn't see. Only when she pushed herself up in her seat and craned her neck did four small children come into her line of sight. Kids from her class, of course. Not that she could tell which ones from this distance. They gathered around Beatrice, assembling first at the front. Then, as she spoke to them, they gradually moved to encircle her, drawing in close.

She was too far away for anyone to hear what she said, but it was clear she was confused by their behavior, if not yet afraid. In spite of Kendra's increasingly frantic cries and all they'd seen that morning, Shona wasn't afraid either. She'd spent more than a decade teaching children. She knew every one standing around Beatrice now. To fear them felt like an impossibility.

Right up until the moment they drew their knives.

24.

LING SLAMMED ANOTHER drawer shut. "It's not here either." It was the fourth desk she'd tried. She'd begun at her own, certain the satellite phone had been safely tucked away at the bottom, but after five minutes of rifling couldn't find it. She'd then gone through Morgan's, then—acting out of pure panic—searched two more that weren't assigned to anyone.

Owen had stood watching her throughout, rifle slung over his shoulder, wishing he'd brought someone else along on their mission to the town hall so he would have someone to exchange weary looks with. "And you're quite sure you left it here? You didn't stash it somewhere else? Take it home with you maybe?"

"No, God damn it!" Her tone was sharp, making clear she found the question patronizing.

"Okay . . . " He rolled his eyes. "What about Morgan? Could he have grabbed it last night, before everything that happened? Maybe there was someone he wanted to get in touch with?"

"I don't know." She didn't find the scenario plausible, but couldn't argue against it. She pressed a hand to her head, gloved fingers drumming nervously against her temple. "I don't know, I don't know."

"All right, so maybe we try his place next?" His calm, logical thinking was infuriating given the circumstances, but she had no idea how to explain to him what they were.

Ignoring his suggestion for the moment, she wandered the room, weaving between disused desks before returning to her office, eyes roving hopelessly over every surface in case she saw something that might save them. Eventually, her gaze drifted up to the painting on the wall—the artist's rendition of Coldwell Slopes as it would look when her project was complete. Even now, the vision was tantalizing; a dream of joy, community and prosperity she yearned to achieve. And she could sense, at a primal level beyond human understanding, as though peering through a veil in reality to see the secret workings of a world beneath the world, that someone was trying to take it away from her. The depiction of the resort's mascot, Coldwell the Singing Snowman, stared at her from the corner of the painting. For the first time she interpreted something cruel and mocking in his huge grin.

She didn't know who or why, but she understood—with a certainty that permeated her bones—that she and everything she'd worked for were under attack. It was a concerted, coordinated effort and she would be a fool to let herself imagine for even a second that it was not.

Knowing that rendered any further search for the satellite phone pointless. She already knew where it was. In the hands of the enemy.

"Where you going?" Owen asked as she walked briskly past him and out the door.

"To talk to the contractors. Hurry up. We don't have much time."

The Samuel Street Hotel was in the south-west corner of St. Nicholas, overlooking the Carrick River. A traditional bunkhouse with popular restaurant, it had for many decades offered clean, comfortable, and unpretentious accommodation to travelers on a budget. Now all thirty rooms across its three floors were occupied by members of the first team of contractors to have arrived in town. It had been chosen so the new arrivals would be within walking distance of all local amenities, but still at a safe remove from the heart of the community, in case their off-duty drinking and carousing became too abrasive.

It was around fifteen minutes from the town hall on foot and Owen would have preferred they double back to the security station and take the truck, but Ling was in no mood for doubling back. She marched across the square and down Fifth Avenue, her boots thudding heavily on the wooden boardwalk lining the storefronts. It was the only sound to be heard in the streets, which were even quieter than normal.

Sound traveled far in St. Nicholas and it wasn't unusual, while walking down Fifth Avenue in daylight hours, to be able to hear vans, trucks or Izaak Strauss's snowplow all the way over on Eighth. Today, however, the silence was eerie.

"How ya doin', Owen?" He jumped, fumbling for his rifle, before realizing the question had come from the other side of the street. Jake Hodgkiss stood there, arm in arm with his wife Hilary, each one supporting the other. They had been married over seven decades and claimed the secret to a long life, loving relationship and surviving the harsh Canadian winters was to keep moving. As a result, they could be found most days making a patrol of the streets around their home, stopping to talk to whomever they happened to encounter. Hilary was deaf as a post, so Jake was the one who did most of the talking.

"Good morning," Owen called back, waving.

"Lookin' forward to Christmas?"

"Sure am!" He smiled, but kept walking.

"Swing by and say hello if you get the chance!"

"Will do, Jake!"

"Who's that with you?" Hodgkiss asked, squinting to get a look at Ling. "Is that . . . ? Oh." The smile slid from his face when he recognized her, but he forced himself to be polite. "Merry Christmas, Miss Wong!"

Ling didn't respond. She didn't even look in his direction. She had halted at the edge of the boardwalk and was staring across the street, to the parking lot of the Samuel Street Hotel. Owen was briefly outraged, taking offense on the old man's behalf. It was one thing for her to be rude and dismissive to her employees, but to so rudely ignore the town's best-loved elders was another matter entirely. He felt like telling her exactly that, regardless of the dressing down she might give him in return. But then he caught up with her and understood why she hadn't said anything.

A body lay in the entrance to the hotel parking lot. A man's body, dressed in the Bingzhen-branded workwear of a contractor, the fabric crusted with frost. He lay face down, the snow around him stained red with blood.

Owen cocked the rifle, looking up and down Samuel Street in search of . . . what? A bear? He didn't know. Either way, there was nothing to see. "Miss Wong?"

Without responding, she stepped off the boardwalk, striding

across the road to reach the body, staring down at it with cool detachment, the way a botanist might inspect unusual flora or fauna. Owen chased after her, swinging the rifle around in an arc to guard against any assassins springing from the snow. He tried to get a look at the dead man but couldn't see his face. Instead, his eyes lingered on the myriad wounds gouged into his back.

"Miss Wong . . . What's happening here?"

She shook her head, like the question had no answer, then turned toward the hotel. Blood dappled the snow in a trail leading from the body to the restaurant. She looked at Owen. "If I tell you to use that gun, you'll use it, right?"

Only after he nodded did he think to ask, "On what?" But she was already moving away, marching toward the restaurant. Owen snatched the radio from his belt and put it to his mouth. "Dan, this is Owen. Come in."

A moment passed in which he heard nothing but static, then Dan's voice. "Go ahead, Owen."

"Get your ass to the Samuel Street Hotel. We've got a real situation. Bring Terry with you. Bring the truck. And don't forget your rifles."

Posters in the window still advertised the restaurant's Thanksgiving menu, offered throughout October, despite the proprietors having long-since sold up and left. The people who cooked, cleaned and managed the hotel now were all residents on temporary contracts, like soldiers maintaining their own barracks. Ling understood the meals they provided were several grades above Army fare, if not quite up to the standard of the rotisserie turkey feast with free salad bar and pumpkin pie advertised on the poster. It was the first thing she noticed as she approached the entrance, followed by the red streaks on the glass.

Christmas music greeted her as she pulled open the door. *Jingle Bell Rock* by Bobby Helms. A CD player was hidden somewhere in the restaurant, an album of classics playing on repeat. Moving through the foyer, Ling could see the room had been prepared for a festive celebration. Lit fairy lights were strung around the booths and glittering cardboard stars, angels and reindeer had been pinned to the walls. The number of open liquor bottles and dirty glasses scattered across the tables led her to suspect this was where many of the men had come after Wintertainment, continuing to drink through the night and into the early hours of the morning. Somewhere, at the back of her mind, she tried to imagine the scene of merriment and conviviality that might have existed here, only a few hours ago, back when they were all still alive.

It wasn't so easy an image to conjure up now. Not with three men sprawled dead on the floor, a fourth sitting in a booth with his throat slashed and a fifth carved open on the counter. Ling suspected the man in the booth had been the first to die. He still gripped the handle of the half-full stein in front of him. He'd felt no panic when strange hands had grabbed him and pulled his head back. Perhaps he'd thought it some prank, not realizing the truth till after a blade plunged deep into the side of his neck and was then wrenched forward, slicing through his esophagus, windpipe and carotid artery, unleashing a torrent of gore across the booth. Some of his companions had tried to escape then, scrambling out of their seats and into the clutches of other killers—for there had to have been others, there must have been a whole gang. They must have sprung from their hiding places in the shadows and under tables, striking first at thighs, knees, and ankles, doing precise and merciless damage to bring their enemies down. Once the men were on the floor, the fight was as good as over, their attackers driving weapons into their chests, necks, and faces with such speed and ferocity that defense was impossible. The only course of action affording a chance of survival would have been escape. One of them had tried, managing to stay on his feet even as strips were torn from his legs. Charging out the door, he'd made it as far as the end of the parking lot before his pursuers caught up with him and brought him down.

Other attackers must have remained behind—there must have been at least five of them, probably more—to set upon the last man. Perhaps he was frozen in shock, too scared to move. How else to explain why he remained at his stool by the counter, watching as they encircled and closed in on him? Had he tried to reason with them? Whatever he might have said, it didn't work. They hauled him up onto the countertop, pinned him down, ripped his shirt open and eviscerated him. It was clear they'd taken their time, enjoying themselves. His organs had been ripped out and dumped on the floor. Knives and forks had been forced into his eyes and mouth, the silverware visibly bulging in his throat. Arterial blood had spurted high and thick, drenching the ceiling fan which, in turn, had cast drops in a playful spiral pattern around the room.

Whoever or whatever they were, Ling could see they must have been strong to do all this. Fast and vicious and evil, but above all, strong. And yet the footprints in the blood looked so small. Like children's.

"Oh my God." Owen was behind her, his voice dry and hollow. "Oh my. Oh my, oh my . . . " He reached up and removed his hat, suddenly finding it too tight for his head. "Ling, what is this?"

She didn't answer, but stepped to the side to let him get a better view of the carnage.

"Ling . . . " His voice cracked and he coughed, trying to get some moisture into his mouth. "This . . . No bear did this."

She tried to think of a reply that wouldn't sound sarcastic, but the best she could come up with was, "You know what? I think you might be right." She went behind the lunch counter and found the CD player tucked away on a shelf. Still playing *Jingle Bell Rock*. She'd never known it was such a long song.

"What . . . what could do something like this?" Owen's voice echoed in the sudden silence.

Ling was asking herself the same thing. Though it was savagely violent, the massacre didn't marry up with what she'd seen from Morgan. Even if the boy who attacked Curtis had been helping him, they couldn't have killed everyone. Someone would have got away. And, while she was no police detective, Ling had enough clues to be able to deduce the killings had taken place hours ago, likely in the middle of the night, perhaps while she had been asleep in the clinic. They'd picked their moment, stolen the satellite phone and killed the people responsible for restoring communications. A plan was being carried out. She didn't know by whom or what its ultimate goal was, but it seemed plausible—even likely—her death was part of it.

"We need to check the rooms," she said. "In case anyone survived."

Owen nodded dumbly, too dazed by the butchery around him to offer any suggestions of his own. She led the way, into the corridor connecting the restaurant to the hotel building. It brought them into a rec room with pool and ping-pong tables, from which they could access sleeping quarters.

It was a similar scene to the one they'd found in the restaurant. They went room by room, finding one man after another dead in his bed, their faces, necks and chests hacked open, white sheets stained brown by dried blood. They gave up the search before reaching the third floor. Owen, his face sickly gray and hair matted with sweat, began to sway in the stairwell, reaching for the wall to prop himself up.

"You need to sit down?" Ling asked.

"I'm okay." His breaths were heavy. He squeezed his eyes shut and tried to think of pleasant, calming images.

"Need to puke?"

"I'm fine."

"We should get out of here."

He nodded enthusiastically and grabbed at his radio. "Dan? Dan, where the hell are you?"

There was an uncomfortable silence while they waited for a response, before Dan's crackling voice finally answered. "There's, uh . . . Sorry, Owen, we're still at the station. There's some kind of problem with the truck."

"What? What problem?"

"Not sure exactly. Give us a minute, Owen. We're working on it."

"No! Dan, damn it, fu-fuck!" Owen spat, fear and confusion making him stutter. "Fuck the truck. Grab your guns and get your—"

He was interrupted by a sound echoing up from the floor below. A child's voice. "Hello?"

Ling and Owen briefly shared a look of panic, before his practical nature, police training and natural decency took over. If she could do it telepathically, she would have told him to keep his mouth shut and follow her silently into the hallway, away from whoever had called out. But then he leaned over the railing and it was already too late. "Who's there?" he called. "This is Owen Dupont. I'm a police officer. I'm here to help."

Somewhere in the back of Ling's managerial mind flared a desire to once again remind him he was not, in fact, a police officer, but a security operative in the employ of a private company, but she ignored it. Her overriding impulse was to run. "Owen . . . "

"Hello?" The voice came again, louder this time, stretching out the sound of the 'o' with a kind of vibrato that shivered up the stairwell and chilled Ling's skin. It sounded like a little girl.

Owen began moving, taking the stairs down. "Are you injured? Do you require assistance?"

"Owen!" Ling tried to shout his name, but it came out more like a choked whisper.

"Scared," the girl said.

Owen paused on the stairs, again peering over the railing, eyes searching the darkness below for a frightened child. "You don't have to be scared," he said. "I'm here to help."

"No," the girl replied, and there was something in the way she said it, something about the tone of it, that convinced Ling they were both about to die. "I mean *you* sound scared." Then she laughed. "And you should be."

She moved like lightning, tearing up the stairs from the shadows below, the sound of her rapid steps echoing like machine-gun fire. Owen had time enough to see her coming and turn to look at Ling, his expression making clear he knew he'd fucked up. There was time enough to raise his rifle, aim at the girl and fire, but he made no effort to do so. The very idea of pointing a gun at a child was abhorrent to him. That left him effectively defenseless as she pounced, her whole body colliding with his and throwing him back against the wall. She was less than a third of his size, a girl of around six or eight, with braided blonde pigtails and turquoise boots with pink unicorns. But she was strong and vicious as a wolf, opening her mouth wide and sinking her teeth into Owen's jugular. He screamed and fell back, sinking to the floor as she whipped her head away, a good chunk of his neck in her mouth. Ling made a sound of horror and the girl turned to face her, scraps of Owen's bloodied flesh hanging from her lips, still connected to the wound in his neck by strings of red tissue. Her yellow eyes blazing with excitement, she sucked the meat into the back of her mouth, then bit through the connective cartilage, chewed and swallowed. She grinned in triumph, displaying a mouth crowded with crooked crimson teeth.

Ling didn't wait for the girl to come after her. She turned and ran, dashing back into the hotel's second-floor hallway, racing past open doors to rooms in which men lay murdered and mutilated in their beds. The girl's laughter pursued her, echoing down the passageway, growing more discordant and maniacal the further it traveled. It was a sound Ling knew she would remember for the rest of her life—however short that turned out to be. The worst sound she'd ever heard. But then a second laugh joined it. A boy, lurking somewhere in the hotel, answered the girl's hysterical noise with a crazed, sadistic giggle of his own. Seconds after he started, a third voice chimed in.

Turning into the stairwell at the opposite end of the building and sprinting down it into the lobby, Ling couldn't tell where all the laughter was coming from. But she was certain they all knew exactly where she was and would be coming after her, just as soon as their hilarity subsided.

She burst through the main doors and ran into the parking lot. She charged across the snow, blinking away tears of terror to search the streets beyond for signs of life, but seeing no-one. It would be a great moment for Dan to appear, flanked by Owen's volunteer deputies, each one of them armed to the teeth, but it didn't look like anyone would be showing up.

"Help me," she yelled, hoping someone somewhere might hear it, then tripped and fell face-first into the snow.

From behind her came the sound of the hotel's doors being kicked open, followed by peals of childish laughter resounding across the lot. Ling rolled over, shaking snow from her face and hair, to find it was the Bingzhen contractor's frozen body that had tripped her up. Beyond him, at the entrance to the hotel, the pig-tailed girl crouched, eyes on Ling, her smile sparkling silver in the light of the setting sun.

Ling kicked at the body, using it for purchase as she scrambled back to her feet, turned and ran. The girl gave chase, closing the distance between them in seconds. Ling was nearly out of the lot when she looked back to see the girl only a few steps behind, the width of a parked SUV all that separated them, her grinning mouth already open wide, ready to clamp down on whichever body part she could grab first. Ling was as good as dead.

A gunshot roared and the SUV's rear windshield exploded, showering the snow with broken glass. Ling and the girl both halted in their pursuit, spinning back around to see Owen in the window of one of the second-floor bedrooms. His face white and half-painted in his own blood. His clothes were similarly stained, his neck gushing from where the girl had wounded him. Yet he'd found the strength to stumble into one of the rooms and over to the window before lining up a shot with the rifle.

He worked the slide to eject the spent casing and load another round, then took aim again, calm as his sights found the girl. She stood still, not smiling any more, but not scared. She looked annoyed to be inconvenienced, forced to pause her attack while waiting for Owen to bleed out or be tackled by her male allies, both of whom could be seen crawling down the side of the hotel toward his window, their clawed fingers digging into the wood as effectively as climbing spikes.

Poor Owen. Ling would have kissed him if she could. At the very least, it would have been nice to thank him, but there was no time. In a few seconds he would be dead and if she didn't take her chance, she would soon join him.

She turned and ran, fleeing the hotel and racing back up Fifth Avenue in the direction of the town square and the comparative safety of the police station. She passed Jake and Hilary Hodgkiss on the way, now nearly back home following their afternoon stroll around the block. Jake waved to her, his wizened face bright red from the cold, and called, "Merry Christmas Miss Wong!"

She didn't answer this time either. And when she heard the crack of Owen's rifle, she didn't look back.

She knew what it meant.

25.

THE FIRST KID to stab Beatrice did so from behind, sticking his knife into the soft flesh of her thigh. It wasn't a large blade and didn't go deep, but there was no question she felt it. She let loose a shriek—more of shock and confusion than of pain—and lurched forward, but the children in front drove her back, thrusting their own knives into her flailing arms and stomach. It was unclear to the observers in the car if they managed to penetrate the thick fabric of her winter coat and pierce the skin, but she screamed just as loudly as if they did.

"Oh Christ," Shona groaned, horrified by what she was witnessing. "Curtis!"

He turned the key in the ignition for the fifth or sixth time, without the hint of an effect on the engine. "It's not working."

She grabbed his arm, her eyes still locked on the unfolding horror outside. "Curtis!"

"It won't start." He didn't look at her, focusing all his attention on the key, while a voice in his head reminded him they'd been here already, only a few hours ago, her urging him to do something, get out the truck and do something. He'd barely scraped through that encounter with his life, yet here they were again. Not that he resented her for it. Not that he wouldn't act, if he had to. Not like he was afraid or anything. He just really, really wanted the engine to start.

"Curtis!" She slammed her fists against his arm, incensed by his inaction as, through the window behind him, she saw Beatrice whirling through a barrage of bladed attacks. There was blood on her coat now—in the front, back and sleeves, little stains growing bigger. She screamed for help. "Fuck!" Shona couldn't bear to sit helpless in the truck a second longer. She opened her door and turned to jump out.

"Wait," said Curtis.

She was going to tell him to fuck off, but before she could, something jumped out from under the truck. A creature of frightening speed and dazzling colors, it let loose a maniacal cackle like something between a wildcat and a jackal. Its face twisting in fury and claws already swinging in attack, it was almost on top of Shona before she realized it was another child.

The retina-scarring overcoat he wore belonged to Theo Deuling, a sickly seven-year-old whose mother dressed him in fluorescent colors for fear of him being lost in the snow. He was short for his age and on the thin and frail side, which caused his family no end of worry. They would have been shocked to see him now, with limbs so long and muscles so swollen they'd burst the stitching on his coat to expose the white padding beneath. His face was red and angry as a hemorrhoid and his left hand clutched the truck's ignition coil, while his right held a knife. And not a stubby paring knife like the kitchen utensils his friends had scavenged, but a twelve-inch machete, its edge sharpened to perfection. Dried blood was gathered at its base. Shona had just enough time to see and comprehend all this as the blade swung into her leg, slicing through her shin and glancing off bone.

The pain was instant and excruciating, sending an eruption of agony through her body. Riding its coattails was an overwhelming wave of adrenaline that caused her to yank both her legs back into the truck and pull the door shut—hard. It slammed into the side of the kid's head, crunching it between the door and the chassis. As red and bloated as it was, his head did not pop. He made a dreadful choking sound, spittle flying from his lips as his jaws cracked together.

"Sorry!" Shona cried, watching as his yellow eyes glazed and he fell backward. She hadn't meant to do it and was immediately horrified by her actions, but as he slumped woozily to the ground, his skull slipping clear of the door, she pulled the handle again, slammed and locked it.

"Shit, Shona!" Curtis's voice.

She turned to face him, panting from shock. "Yeah?"

He tried to speak, but could only stammer, directing a finger to the gash in her shin, leaking a torrent of blood, already forming a small pool in the footwell.

"Oh for fuck sake," she moaned, tearing the scarf from around her neck and quickly fashioning it into a tourniquet.

The truck rocked as Kendra shifted suddenly from one side to the other, putting her back up against the passenger-side window, staring stricken out the driver's side and crying, "No, no, no, no!"

Curtis looked and saw Beatrice hobbling toward them, her coat now soaked in blood, scarlet spatter on her knitted hat and face. Tears of terror made streaks through the red. "Help." She made the word long, dragging it out with a voice turned low and weak from pain. "Help me . . . "

She limped toward the car, trailing blood and the children. They marched in single file, a few steps behind her, jumping and kicking their legs and waving their hands and their bloody knives, like they were part of a holiday parade. And they were singing. The closer they came, the louder they got, soon drowning out Beatrice's mournful whimpers with an off-key helium-happy rendition of 'Jingle Bells'.

Curtis watched her come closer, shaking his head, pleading with his eyes for her to stop, to turn back, to take the danger away from him, as far away as she could get before bleeding to death. Then he felt something tighten in his chest and a voice in his head said: *This is pathetic. You are pathetic. She needs help. You're a grown man. They're children. Help her, you fucking coward. Help her.*

Beatrice reached a hand toward his window, blood pouring from her glove.

He gripped the door handle.

Theo Deuling jumped between them. Having quickly recovered from his brain-crushing experience in Shona's door, he'd rolled from one side of the truck to the other and sprang from under the rocker panel, swinging his machete upward in a display of kinetic fury and striking Beatrice. She spun completely around, revealing, as she whirled back into Curtis's line of sight, that her face had been split by the blade. A narrow cut ran from her chin to the brim of her knitted hat. Narrow, but deep. The machete had cleaved through her jaws and between her front teeth, bisecting her tongue and carving her nose open right up the middle. Her brain surely could not have evaded the blade's path. Curtis thought he could see pink matter throbbing through the wound in her forehead. It ought to have been enough to kill her, but she was still screaming, spraying blood from her ruined mouth in a hot jet that painted Curtis's window, obscuring the rest of her torture behind a cascade of red.

Kendra didn't announce the fact she was leaving. She simply got out the truck and ran, heading away from the house and toward the center of town.

"Shit!" Shona had only just managed to stem the bleeding from her shin and knew she had no hope of running as fast as Kendra. But there was no question the kid had the right idea. Giving herself no time for second thoughts, she threw herself out of the truck, started running and managed three steps before the agony drove her onto her knees. Sucking icy air through her teeth as she fought to keep from screaming, she looked back to the truck and was surprised to see Curtis in his seat, still transfixed by the slow and brutal murder of Beatrice. She had assumed he would follow after her. "Curtis!"

She had to call his name twice more before he turned his head, blinked and realized he was the only one still in the truck. Shona waved him over, the grimace on her face equal parts fear for their lives and burning rage. He shuffled into her seat and out the door, pausing only briefly when the truck was rocked by a thud against the driver's side. Beatrice had fallen against his door, her bifurcated face pressed against his window, her screams reduced to a wheeze of red foam. She slid from view as the children lunged for her, ready now to deliver the killing blow.

Curtis didn't run to Shona. He moved in a crouch, staying low to the ground and keeping one eye on the truck, waiting for the kids to come leaping over it at any second. But they didn't come. Their song had ceased, but they were laughing now. Laughing as they slashed and stabbed at Beatrice's wilting body, making a pincushion of what remained of her mutilated form. Curtis was glad he couldn't see what they were doing to her, but it sounded, from their cackling chorus of glee, like they were having the most fun of their young lives.

Without saying a word to her, he grabbed Shona under her arms and lifted her up, slinging her over his shoulder—the one Devon hadn't torn any flesh from—then started walking, briskly now, following Kendra's footprints through the snow.

It was nearly dark by the time they caught up to her, shivering at the corner of Lennox and Fourth Avenue, unsure of which way to go.

"Hey," said Curtis.

The moment he spoke, a neon decoration over their heads blinked into life. Hung on wires strung from one side of the street to the other, it was part of St. Nicholas's Wintertainment festival decorations and depicted Santa in his sleigh being pulled by three prancing reindeer. The sight of it made him oddly queasy.

"Hey what?" Shona asked, speaking from over his shoulder.

"It's the girl." He directed the comment to her ass, then gently set her down so she could see for herself.

She painfully limped her way over and put a hand on Kendra's shoulder, opting for the same greeting Curtis had tried. "Hey."

The girl turned to face her, revealing a mask of hopeless panic, fresh tears running down her bruised cheeks and her split lip trembling. "Where is everyone?" Her voice was a whisper. "No cars. No people. What the fuck? Are they dead? Are they all . . . Are they all fucking dead?"

"They're not dead," Shona told her, hoping she was right. It was true that in the few weeks she'd been in St. Nicholas, she'd never seen its streets so empty, not during the day. It never got busy, but there was always *someone* around. Right now it was twilight on Christmas Eve and in their flight from Curtis's truck they'd seen nobody. Even if there was nobody in sight, they should have at least heard the echoing rumble of diesel engines, of music and laughter. But there were no signs of life at all. She turned to Curtis, looking over his shoulder to check none of the children had followed them, and saw no-one. They'd been too preoccupied with the murder of Beatrice to notice their escape. "We need to get off the street. Don't you think?"

He nodded and pointed north-east. "Police station's that way."

This time his words were punctuated by the sound of a gunshot. A crack of rifle fire sounded, too far away to make any of them dive for cover, but close enough that they all flinched.

"What was that?" said Shona, though she knew what it was.

Curtis looked down Fourth Avenue, toward Samuel Street. "I think . . . I think it came from . . . "

A second shot, its sound like distant thunder as it echoed through the deserted streets. And there was another noise, fading in as the rifle's report dissipated. A sound of boots drumming on a boardwalk, getting louder and louder as they came closer and closer.

All heads turned at the same time to look across the street, into the alley linking Fourth to Fifth and seeing Ling Wong's silhouette leap across the far end—there and gone in a flash. The kind of sprint a person only does when they're running *away* from something. They didn't have to guess at what might be pursuing her. They heard that, too. A shrill scream as loud and piercing as the gunshot that mutated into frantic laughter. And it was getting louder.

Kendra was first to move, bolting across the street and up the alley, chasing after Ling.

"Ke—" Shona tried to give chase, but managed only two steps before the pain forced her to halt. She didn't fall this time, but looked helplessly toward Curtis, throwing up her hands in a signal of defeat.

He understood, snatching her up and cradling her in his arms the way a comic book superhero would a stricken child. Then he ran. It was fewer than five hundred yards, darting down the alley and up the Fifth Avenue boardwalk to reach the square, but he ran all the way, suddenly unspeakably thankful of Shona's waif-like proportions. She wrapped her arms around his neck, offering no audible complaints about the obvious pain she was in, but digging her fingers into the fabric of his jacket, clinging on for dear life and peering over his shoulder at the strange forms racing up the street to catch them.

They had the shape of children. Children she knew. Children she had taught and cared for. And yet . . . they could not possibly be children. Could not be human. Not the way they moved. The noises they made. Coming closer and closer and closer . . .

26.

"CLOSE!" LING CHARGED through the entrance of the security station, waving a hand behind her. She had wanted to yell 'close the doors' but had only been able to get enough breath into her lungs for one word. She collapsed, hitting the tiled floor with a slap, and lay there panting, shivering and afraid.

Dan, Terry Cabot, and the two volunteers—Lonnie Price and Hank Steins—stared at her with bemusement. "Everything all right, Miss Wong?" Dan asked.

She would have yelled something fiercely derogatory at him, but she couldn't spare the breath. Sucking another lungful down her throat, she pointed again and yelled, "Close the doors!"

"Yes ma'am." He was holding a mug of fresh-brewed coffee and he sipped from it as he casually strolled across the floor and around Ling to reach the entrance, unlatching the hooks that held the reinforced iron doors—historic features, much like the building's jail cells—in place. "Where's Owen?"

He was pulling the first door shut when Kendra rushed in, just managed to avoid plowing into him, then tripped over Ling and went sprawling on the floor.

"Ouch." Dan winced and went to help her up, but Ling got between them, fixing him with a glare that could have killed.

"Close the fucking doors!"

He backed off, holding up his hand in a placating gesture. "Okay, okay. Jeez . . . " He returned to the doors, bolting the first shut then reaching for the second. Curtis and Shona made it just in time, knocking Dan's arm out the way and spilling his coffee. Curtis carried her in like a new husband ushering his bride across the threshold. Shaking coffee drips from his hands, Dan muttered, "Congratulations to the happy couple," then slammed and locked the second door.

Curtis managed to stagger to a chair and lower Shona onto it before his legs gave way beneath him and he collapsed, joining Ling and Kendra in a breathless pile on the floor.

Terry Cabot cast an eye over the ragtag bunch, noting the lower half of Shona's left pants leg was soaked with blood. "First-aid kit?"

She nodded. "Please."

He went to go fetch it. "Hope there's something left."

Lonnie and Hank had been sitting in desk chairs eating gingerbread cookies when Ling had burst in. Despite all the drama, neither man had risen from his seat. The owner of the local sporting goods store, Lonnie had come dressed for a bear hunt, but didn't look the least bit concerned by the group of obviously distressed and injured people now spread out before him. "You folks having a good Christmas?"

Ling glared at him, coughed and spat. "That supposed to be a joke?"

He chuckled and told Hank, "Guess not."

Dan set his coffee down, then went to Ling and helped her up. "Owen didn't come back with you?"

"Owen's dead."

The news elicited some reaction from Curtis and Shona, but Dan only gave a gentle smile and said, "Sure. So . . . does he still want us at Samuel Street, or . . . ?"

"He's dead! Aren't you listening? He's fucking dead!"

"Oh, okay. Okay." Dan nodded like he understood, but the look on his face told another story. "So, uh . . . Hmmm. Okay."

"Owen's dead?" said Lonnie.

Ling aimed a look of fury his way. "Yes."

"Owen Dupont?"

"Yes! Yes!"

"Huh." Lonnie reached for another cookie. "How'd he die?"

Curtis was the one who answered. "Children." He said it while dragging himself up, onto his feet, and looked at Ling. "That's right, isn't it?"

She nodded. "They came after you, too?"

"They killed Beatrice," said Shona. "It was . . . " She swallowed, trying to maintain her composure. "I don't know what's happened to them, but they're not children anymore."

"Beatrice Gulliver?" said Dan.

"They chased us here." Ling walked to the window. "They'd

have killed us too if they'd caught us." She pointed through the iron bars on the other side of the glass. "They're outside! Look!"

Dan strolled over to her, picking up his coffee mug on the way back, and peered outside. Three children stood close together at the edge of the square, facing the building.

"What do you see, Dan?" Lonnie asked, through a mouthful of cookie.

Dan sipped his coffee as he nodded. "Sure enough. A few kids outside. Looks like they're . . . I dunno. Just standing there." He turned to Ling. "Want me to go talk to them?"

She gave him a look like he was nuts. "Didn't you hear what I just told you?"

Terry returned with the first-aid kit. "What are we looking at?"

"Some kids outside, causing mayhem," said Lonnie.

"They're just standing there," said Dan.

"They're killing people," said Shona, her voice ragged from pain and fear. She grabbed the kit from Terry's hands and aimed a bloody finger at him. "Don't go out there."

He showed her a patronizing smile, like he'd decided this was all part of an elaborate practical joke and he might as well play along. "Okey-dokey." He called over to Dan. "What's Owen's opinion on all this?"

Dan shrugged. "That's what we're trying to find out."

Ling stamped her foot and screamed in frustration. "He's dead! He's fucking dead! Why won't you assholes listen to what I'm telling you?"

"Okay, okay," Dan said, in his most soothing voice, while eyeing another cookie. "Don't worry, we'll get to the bottom of it."

"Get to the bottom of what? He's fucking dead!" Ling looked at each of the men in turn, their blank, passive faces and sagging bodies, eager to find a recliner to sink into. Then she addressed Curtis and Shona. "What the fuck is the matter with them?"

Will Douglas called to her from across the room. "You wanna know?" He leaned up against the bars of his cell, a mean smirk on his youthful face. "They're stoned. Anyone who was born here gets the same way whenever Santa's in town. Like a contact high. They get sleepy, unfocused, high on all the fuzzy feelings of Christmas. Can't hold a piece of information in their heads for longer than two minutes. And the closer he is, the worse it gets."

"You're not helping," Ling told him, in no mood to entertain such nonsense.

He let out a humorless snort. “Lady, even if I wanted to, there is not a damn thing I can do to help you. You’ve pissed him off big time and he wants your head. And that’s all there is to it.”

“Did he say we’re stoned?” Dan narrowed his eyes in confusion, struggling to follow what was being said. “Miss Wong, I can assure you I am not stoned. Owen himself will tell you how seriously we—”

“Owen’s dead,” she said.

His look of confusion intensified. “Oh . . . Uh . . . How do you mean?”

And Will laughed, if it could be called that. A kind of sick, wheezing, joyless sound veering between a madman’s cackle and sobs of despair. For a few seconds its sound filled the room, everyone else too scared, traumatized or bewildered to speak. “It was the same with my Mom,” he said. “No-one would listen to me. Or if they did listen, they couldn’t remember. It was days before anyone would accept she was really gone and nobody would so much as consider the idea she’d been murdered. It’s like he’s got everybody in this town hypnotized so they can only see what he wants them to see. He can even fool outsiders most of the time. But when you get scared . . . that’s when you see how things really are. And you’re all feeling pretty scared right now, huh?”

“I’m not.” Hank Steins shoved his chair back and stood up. A military veteran who’d come to the territory with dreams of living a survivalist lifestyle, he owned a log cabin several miles up the river, though typically spent most of winter in an apartment in town, making himself available to the security department for patrols of abandoned properties and other light duties. St. Nicholas had more than a few men of his type, who hated being told what to do but would gladly accept any position of authority if it gave them an excuse to harass vagrants and teenagers. “But if you’re saying Owen’s dead, I’m going to need a little more evidence than your word. So where is he?”

“The hotel,” said Ling. “But you don’t want to go there. Trust me.”

Hank had a long fur coat and a fur hat that made him look like a 19th-century trapper. He pulled them on and nodded at Dan. “Someone’s got to go take a look.”

“It’s not just Owen,” said Ling. “They killed everyone who was staying at the hotel. All the contractors.”

“And Miss Gulliver,” said Curtis.

"And Miss Gulliver," she repeated. "Who knows who else? Half the fucking town could be dead by now!"

"At the hands of a bunch of schoolchildren?" Hank was a big man. Naturally tall and broad-shouldered, with the muscle mass of a practicing power-lifter. It was hard to imagine what kind of opponent might intimidate him, but the kids of St. Nicholas Elementary were unlikely to qualify. He turned to shout across the room at Will. "Now I wasn't born in this town, so I know I'm not Christmas drunk or whatever the hell you want to call it. But that?" He waved a finger at Ling. "That just sounds like a whole heap of bullshit to me."

"Why don't you open your eyes, man?" Curtis, still on the floor where he'd dropped, yelled at him, gesturing at himself, Kendra, and Shona, still tending to her wounds. "Look at us! You think we did all this to ourselves?"

"See?" Will yelled. "This guy believes me! And he punched me in the face last night, so . . . y'know, it's not like we're friends or anything."

Hooking a thumb at Will, Hank said to Curtis, "So you're buying all this?"

Curtis hesitated. While he'd seen a lot of crazy stuff in the last few hours, blaming it all on Santa Claus was still a stretch. "I . . . No, that's . . . That's not what I'm saying."

"You should," said Kendra. While everyone else had been talking, she'd crawled across the room and found a place for herself on a bench by the wall. Sitting there, hugging her legs to her chest, head resting against the wall and eyes closed, she looked like she could be sleeping, but she was wide awake. "It's all true."

"What's true?" said Hank. "You saw Mommy kissing Santa Claus?"

"Saint Nicholas," said Kendra. "They call him Saint Nicholas."

"You saw him?" said Will.

Kendra shook her head, squeezing her eyes more tightly shut, like she was replaying the scenes of the past twenty-four hours behind her eyelids. "Not *him*. I saw *it*. To those kids it looks and sounds like Santa Claus, but it's not. It's big and ugly and evil. It tore my Dad's head off. It sucked my friend's brains out of her skull. And they all tied me to a couch and made me watch as, one by one, they went up and sucked poison out of its tits!"

"Good lord," Lonnie exclaimed, with some distaste.

"It changed them," Kendra continued, her voice quivering with emotion. "Whatever it fed them fucked them up worse than before. I think it's turning them into . . . more of itself. They're not even human now."

Hank walked over to the girl. All trace of scorn and skepticism had been scrubbed from his face. "What do you mean . . . not human?"

She opened her tired, haunted eyes and turned them on him. "Monsters."

He leaned in and lowered his voice. "You mean like . . . aliens?"

She stared blankly at him a moment, then said, "Sure, I guess."

He studied her a few seconds, nodding to himself in a considered sort of way, then straightened up and, with grim seriousness, told the room, "Well that changes things."

Ling let out a stunned laugh. "Oh, so glad to finally have you on board! Whatever convinced you?"

He said, "Look, school kids and Santa Claus sounds like a lot of bunk, but extra-dimensional entities? That's a whole different kettle of fish. I don't want to get into it, but when I was in the service I had some experiences, that, uh . . . Well, anyway . . . this stuff is no joke."

"Okay." Ling looked to Dan, Terry, and Lonnie, all of whom appeared to have lost interest in the discussion and were now adrift in their own thoughts. Whether she liked it or not, Hank Steins was now the closest thing to a sheriff the town had. "So what do you suggest we do?"

"Can't go off half-cocked," he said, stroking his beard in a contemplative way. "Not against these sons of bitches. There's three ways out of here—the front, the back, and the roof. We need to make sure they're all secure and make an inventory of weapons and supplies so we can hunker down in here till we figure out what's going on. We need to put a call out to everyone with a radio, see if we can get any kind of support at all. And while somebody's doing that, you, you, you and you . . . " He pointed to Kendra, Ling, Curtis, and Shona. "Are going to talk us all through exactly what it is you saw."

Curtis nodded. "That . . . actually sounds like a plan."

"Sound good to you, Dan?" Hank asked.

The deputy blinked, as though woken from a daydream, and said, "What? Yeah. Oh yeah, sure. Sure, but uh . . . Don't you think we ought to wait for Owen to get back first?"

"That's right," said Terry, popping the last piece of the last Christmas cookie in his mouth. "Owen always knows what to do."

Hank sighed. "How about you just make us a fresh pot of coffee, huh Dan?"

Dan winked and nodded. "You got it." He began striding across the office, blissfully happy to have been assigned a task he could handle.

Shona grabbed his sleeve as he came past. "Hey Dan. Any more cookies?"

"Sorry, no. That was the last of 'em."

"Well would you happen to have any other snacks or sweets or . . . anything? I haven't eaten all day and I've lost a fair bit of blood." She directed his attention to her slashed shin.

"I doubt it. I'll see what's in back, but it's not a restaurant."

He pulled his sleeve away from her and she let him go, muttering, "I'm going to starve to death."

Will was the next one to make a grab for Dan as he came past, reaching through the bars of his cell to snap his fingers. "Hey Dan! Seeing as how the situation's changed and we all need to pull together and everything, how about letting me out of here?"

"Oh, right." Dan scratched his head. "Yeah, I don't know about that, Will. After all, you still stabbed Morgan . . . "

"Honest mistake. Honest mistake. Hand on heart, it won't happen again. But if shit goes down, I could be a real asset to you."

Dan thought it over. "Well, sure, I guess so. It's just . . . " He winced. "You know what? Owen's got the keys."

Will's face fell. "Owen?"

"Yeah." Dan nodded, resuming his march to the break room. "But I wouldn't worry about that. He ought to be back any minute now."

As Hank began ordering Terry and Lonnie about—keeping his sentences short and his instructions simple, so as not to confuse them too much—Ling returned to the window, anxiously appraising the scene outside.

"They still there?" Curtis asked her.

She nodded. "Yep. Just standing there, same as before. Only there's five of them now."

27.

DEVON SAT AT the table in Izaak Strauss's kitchen, staring at his hands. Not long ago they had been plump, pink things with stubby little digits that frustrated him whenever he had attempted to learn a musical instrument. Now they were big and ugly, with pale skin as tough as aged leather and fingers as long and thin as knitting needles. Sharpened bone still protruded from his fingertips, but his frayed flesh had curled itself around it, fusing to and strengthening the base. The bones themselves had developed curves like fish hooks—or candy canes—and when he dragged them down the table they gouged furrows in the surface of the wood. *Hardly hands at all now*, he thought. *More like claws. Santa Claws*. And then he giggled to himself.

Christmas Eve was not going quite as he had imagined it. After all his careful preparations of the last few weeks, his intelligence gathering and marshaling of the other children, he'd expected a blitzkrieg with Saint Nicholas leading the charge. A single night should have been enough to rid the town of anyone who might have stood in their way. By now he thought they'd be celebrating their victory and welcoming those they had chosen to save to the New North Pole and its promise of eternal happiness.

Instead, his troops were scattered, pursuing whimsical skirmishes while he and Saint Nicholas slunk from house to house for reasons that remained opaque. They began with the Boyles. The family had welcomed him in just as Devon's mother had, before all sat down in the living room. Saint Nicholas went to the master bedroom and, one by one, each member of the family was called in to see him. Only Saint Nicholas emerged.

From there they went to the home of Ethel and Myra Greenwood, sisters-in-law and widows both. This time Devon had remained in the hall while Saint Nicholas escorted the ladies down to the basement. He did not see them again before leaving.

Now it was Mr. Strauss's turn for a private audience with Santa Claus. They arrived to find him tinkering with the engine of a snowcat the children had sabotaged during the night—one of several crippled vehicles littering his yard. Given his age and interests, Devon hadn't expected the man to give a hoot about Christmas. But as with so many others, when his eyes fell on Saint Nicholas his whole face lit up with child-like glee. And so he had led the way inside his house and down the hall to the bedroom at the back, Saint Nicholas following and closing the door behind them, while Devon took a seat at the kitchen table and studied his hands.

It wasn't only his body that was changing. His mind was developing in ways that excited and unsettled in equal measure. His preoccupations in advance of his hero's arrival—with toys, games, candy and other trivialities—had melted away, their space in his thoughts now taken up by interests darker and more perverse. He was developing new and strange appetites. And there was a new clarity to his thinking. It ebbed and flowed in unpredictable waves, but it felt like the more time he spent in the company of Saint Nicholas, the clearer his thoughts became, the fog rolling back to let him see the world the way it really was. The colors of the decorations no longer shone quite as bright. The air had lost its warming sweetness. He couldn't hear Christmas carols any more. They had played in his kitchen while Saint Nicholas had been upstairs with his mother. He'd heard them again, waiting in the homes of the Boyles and the Greenwood widows. Now all he heard was Terry Cabot's voice crackling over Mr. Strauss's radio.

"Izaak? Hello? Come in if you're there, Izaak. We need your help. Something of an emergency. Got some injured folk here and some . . . strange goings-on. Hate to put you out like this, but we're going to need you to take a run out to MacArthur Point, if you're able. If you're there. Like I say, it's . . . kind of an emergency. Give me a holler if you—"

With a click the voice was silenced. Devon turned around to see Saint Nicholas with his finger on the mute switch. In contrast to the weak, sickly figure languishing on the couch that morning, he appeared to be in rude health. Whatever conference he'd enjoyed with a succession of Devon's neighbors looked to have left him physically and spiritually restored. The rosy hue had returned to his cheeks and his eyes sparkled with renewed vigor. Yet there was obvious concern there, too. Approaching the table—and taking note of the fresh grooves in its surface—he said, "Everything all right, my boy?"

Devon stared at his savior a moment, waiting for the comforting clouds of confusion to return. But they never did. The sensation was not unlike waking from a dream. When he spoke, his voice sounded cold and quite different to the one he'd known all his life. "Mr. Strauss is dead, isn't he?"

Saint Nicholas hesitated a moment, then put a hand on the boy's arm, sinking into the chair beside him. "Yes, I'm sorry to say he is."

"And the Boyles and the Greenwoods. They're dead."

Saint Nicholas nodded.

"And my Mom."

A long and deep sigh. "Yes, Devon, I'm afraid she is."

"You lied to me."

"About certain things, yes. Not everything."

"You lied about my parents. You killed them and you ate them."

"I did, yes. But not because I wanted to hurt you. I did it because I had to. It's where my power comes from. It's what allows me to do the things I do. It makes it possible for me to show people the world I want them to see. The world *they* want to see. That same power now flows through you." He squeezed Devon's forearm, a touch that sent a shiver of electricity through the boy's flesh. "You can feel it, can't you? That's real magic coursing through your veins. You're special in ways beyond description. You don't need silly things like parents anymore. You're already far beyond all that. Trust in good old Santa Claus."

Devon pulled his arm away. "There's no such thing as Santa Claus."

Saint Nicholas showed him a sympathetic smile, its synthetic sweetness still powerful enough to spread a wave of warmth through the room. "Perhaps not. But I am the closest thing this world will ever know. And I can deliver everything I promised you. Everything you ever wished for. Boundless entertainments. Eternal happiness. Strength. Charisma. Kendra."

At mention of her name, Devon's elf-like ears perked up.

"Oh yes," Saint Nicholas purred. "I know what you want. You want her warm, young body pressed against yours. You want to taste her plump, pink lips and feel the softness of her ripe flesh. You want her heart. And you shall have it. You can have her. Her and so many more besides, should you wish. You deserve it for being such a good boy."

"How?"

Saint Nicholas leaned back in his chair, spreading out his big, thick arms. "My power is a part of you now. Give me time and I'll teach you how to use it to get anything and everything you want. All you have to do, for now, is keep the faith." He leaned in close. "You still believe, don't you, Devon? Tell me you believe."

"I believe."

"There's a good lad." Saint Nicholas rose from his seat, then cringed, putting a hand to his stomach. There was a sound of something bubbling within. He belched. "Oh dear."

"Are you okay?"

"I need to rest," he said. "One more time, before the feast. I'll need my strength for that."

"Rest? That means I'll go to sleep too? And the others?"

"Not for so long this time. Just long enough for the completion of certain . . . digestive processes. Then we can celebrate the season in earnest."

Devon stood. "Not yet. The Bingzhen woman is still alive. She's trapped with the others in the police station."

Saint Nicholas gave a dismissive chuckle, the bells on his suit tinkling with his movements. "They can't get in our way now."

"They can. They're trying to send for help. I heard them on the radio. We have to deal with them."

Saint Nicholas yawned, appearing bored with the conversation. Keen to rest. "Then go, if you think it's so important. Kill them all. You're more than capable."

"You're not coming?"

He grinned, showing teeth as white and bright as cake frosting. "I can support you better at a distance. But don't you worry. You'll have allies."

28.

WHEN ALL THE exits had been checked and all the guns counted and Terry had been assigned a list of townsfolk to try to reach by radio, Hank went around the room getting everyone to tell their stories, trying to build a picture of the threat they were facing. He started with Kendra, and it was Kendra he came back to after all the others had spoken, asking her to describe the creature she had seen in more detail.

"You said it had . . . tits?" he asked.

"I don't know what else to call them," she groaned. "It had these bulging sacs under its arms, with spouts on them so the kids could suck out whatever was inside. Kinda like a cow's udders, I guess."

"And how many arms you say it had?"

"I don't know. Four? Six? More than two. And more than two eyes in its head. With these big, moving things above them like antennae."

Hank nodded, sagely. "Insectoid."

"You know what this thing is?" Ling doubted it, but after all she'd seen in the last day she wasn't about to dismiss him out of hand.

"Just an inkling," he answered. "See there's several different alleged alien species. You've got the big ones everybody knows about, your standard humanoid, your grays, your little green men, the Venusians, and the Reptilians. But then there's the more obscure like the Insectoids, where there's not as much evidence, but what there is is some of the most compelling of all."

"Insectoids?" Though still trying to keep an open mind, Ling hated how ridiculous the word sounded coming out of her mouth.

"They've been here for thousands of years. The Hopi Indians called them 'Ant People'. An advanced race of beings who lived underground, sustained on vast food reserves, but who had their origins either in the skies or the far future. And there were stories told in Sumeria of Anunnaki, the astronaut gods who looked like ants and were thought to have genetically modified humanity to advance the species. Ancient Egypt too had tales of insect deities ruling over kingdoms of men, commanding their respect through wisdom and benevolence."

Kendra scoffed. "This one is very un-fucking-benevolent."

"Yeah." Hank sucked air in through his teeth. "But we're a long way from the deserts of Arizona or Egypt or Mesopotamia. Could be he's been hiding out here for centuries, all alone, struggling to survive without being discovered by humans." He turned to Ling. "And then he finds out you're planning to build a ski resort on top of his home. Could be he's not too pleased about that."

"Fuck him," Ling said, sternly rejecting the idea she bore any responsibility for their situation. "Do any of these myths and legends of yours tell you how to kill one?"

He clucked his tongue. "I'm no expert on Insectoids. Just read a few things here and there. But I've got to imagine you could kill one same as killing an ant. Take his head off or crush him. Hell, maybe if you shot him enough times that'd do the trick. Bullet in the brain kills most things."

"You'll never get close enough," said Will. "He won't let you. One of his elves will kill you before you ever get a look at him."

Ignoring his comment, Ling asked, "Why would an ancient alien be masquerading as Santa Claus?"

Hank smiled. "Now that's an interesting question. I've got a couple theories . . . "

Curtis, who up until this point had been politely paying attention, now stepped away from the conversation, ambling over to Shona, who sat on the floor with her back to the wall. "How are you feeling?"

She gave him a miserable look. "Have you ever had to sew stitches in your own leg?"

"No."

"It doesn't put you in the best of moods. Nor does being desperately hungry. Do you think we can get the fuck out of here?"

"And go where?"

"Back to my place?"

"Surely we're safer here. We've got guns, a radio, other people . . . "

"But my place has cheese, peanut butter, frozen pizza. I have an entire cooked lasagna in the fridge. Have you ever had a lasagna sandwich?"

"What's that?"

"It's a big piece of lasagna between two slices of buttered white bread. It's fucking incredible."

"Shona, I think you're delirious."

"I wish I was. I can't take much more of this. We've got to get out of here!"

"We've got to figure out what's going on."

She lowered her voice to a whisper. "Your new friend isn't figuring anything out. He's just repeating a lot of alien conspiracy crap he's heard on YouTube. He should be wearing a tin-foil hat!"

"I don't know. It makes more sense than anything anyone else has suggested."

"Santa Claus space ants?"

He shrugged. "After everything else we've seen today, why not?"

"Curtis, listen to me. Forget about aliens. You saw what those kids did to Beatrice."

He winced at the memory. "Yeah."

"They get in here, what are you going to do?"

"They're not getting in here."

"But if they do?"

"I . . . I'll . . . "

"You're going to shoot them? Kill them?"

"I'll do what I need to do. To protect us." It was a bullshit answer and he knew it.

"Maybe. Maybe you will." She nodded in Hank's direction. "Maybe he will. But maybe you won't. I know I can't. I can't do it." Tears gathered at the corners of her eyes. "They're only kids. They're *my* kids. I can't . . . I can't go through that."

"Yeah. Yeah, okay."

"They know we're in here. They will find a way in sooner or later. We need to get away before that happens."

He thought it over. "I don't know. Rear exit's sealed up pretty tight. Maybe we could get out through the roof, try to get into one of the other buildings. Can you walk?"

"I have to."

He nodded and turned his eyes on Dan, who sat at his desk,

humming to himself, lost in a world of his own. "Hey Dan! Can you take a look and see how many of those kids are out front now?"

Dan stared back at him for a moment, his gaze unfocused, like he hadn't registered the question. Then he flinched, blinked and said. "Sure, sure." He stood, strolled over to the window and peered across at the square. "Looks like ten!"

"That's more than half my class," Shona whispered. "All watching the front. We could slip away."

"What are they doing?" Curtis called.

"Not a lot," Dan answered. "Just singing."

"Singing?"

"Well, yeah. Who did you think that was?"

"I don't hear any singing."

Lonnie Price, who had been keeping himself entertained cutting snowflake decorations from paper, laughed. "Take the stuffing out of your ears, son. How do you not hear that?"

"I don't hear anything either," said Ling, the discussion having captured her attention. "What is it?"

"Christmas carols," said Lonnie.

"Sound just like angels," said Dan.

A quick census was taken, revealing Dan, Lonnie, and Terry—all born and raised in St. Nicholas—could hear the children singing in harmony. Of the rest—the outsiders—none did.

"But you can," said Will, directing the comment at Ling. "You can if you really want to."

"What do you mean?"

He pressed himself up against the bars of his cell, sliding his arms through and holding his hands out toward her. "You can see what they see and hear what they hear. Easy as breathing once you know the trick."

She crossed her arms. "And what trick would that be?"

"It's simple." His fingers twitched, caressing the air. He looked like an imprisoned mesmerist, attempting to guide her mind with his movements. "All you need to do is forget you're afraid. Just for a moment. Forget about your fear."

She watched his hands. It was a comical display. An adolescent's clumsy attempt to play the mystic. But she let herself play along, closing her eyes and letting the tension go out of her muscles. She took a deep breath and sighed it out, imagining all her fear was leaving her body in one big cloud. She emptied herself of emotion, letting her mind go blank, relaxing into a state of calm she knew could never last longer than a few seconds. And then . . .

Do you hear what I hear, they sang. *Ringing through the sky, shepherd boy. Do you hear what I hear?*

She opened her eyes. "I hear it."

Will smiled and nodded. "Yeah, you do. Beautiful, isn't it?"

It was. Not only the song. Not only their voices, which rang clear as polished crystal. There was a warmth that draped itself around her, carried in on the melody, soaking into her skin. A sensation of wonderful comfort. It felt so very right, she knew it had to be wrong. And so her fear returned, creeping back up her spine, chasing the veil of contentment away with prickling goose-flesh. Yet the song endured. She shivered. "I can't stand it."

Will laughed. It sounded sad and cruel. "I know. Trust me, I know."

Curtis had seen enough. "Okay." He took Shona by the arm and helped her up, onto her feet. "Let's go."

"Where are you two going?" Hank called as they passed by the cells, heading for the stairwell.

"Bathroom," Shona replied, yelling the word through gritted teeth as she limped painfully forward, her arm linked with Curtis's.

Hank rose from his seat and came after them. "You know where you're going?"

"We can find it," Curtis said, waving at him to stay where he was.

He didn't follow, but kept watch on them as they reached the end of the corridor and turned left. "You know, we really ought to stick together."

"Don't sweat it, buddy," Will told him. "You've still got me. I mean . . . " He gestured to indicate the cage in which he'd been trapped. "I'm not going anywhere."

"Um . . . guys?" The voice—small, hoarse and loaded with concern—belonged to Kendra. Hank, Will, and Ling turned to her, then looked where she was pointing.

Dan was at the main doors, against which a small barricade of furniture and boxes had been piled up. While the others had been talking, he had quietly and carefully begun taking the barricade apart.

"Dan?" Hank called, striding toward him. "Dan, what are you . . . ?"

Lonnie stood and got in his way. The scissors he'd been using to cut snowflake patterns were still in his fist, suddenly looking a lot bigger and sharper and meaner than they had. "Just hold it there, Hank."

"What's going on?" asked Ling, pressing the fingers of one hand against her temple. Though her fear was back—and pronounced—it had not caused the children's singing to recede. They continued with a new song, louder than the last, drilling into her brain.

Come, they told me pa-rum pum pum pum. Our newborn King to see, pa-rum pum pum pum . . .

Hank held up his hands. "Lonnie, what are you doing?" Behind him, Kendra stood and went to Ling.

"We're going to let them in, Hank," said Lonnie. "That's all there is to it."

"All there is to it," Dan echoed, shoving the last bench out of the way. "They're only kids. Can't leave 'em out in the cold all night."

Our finest gifts we bring pa-rum pum pum pum . . .

"Hank, buddy?" said Will. "You're not going to want to let him open that door."

"Shut up." Hank looked over Lonnie's shoulder, to the desk on which he'd set his rifle down. He'd have to go through Lonnie to get to it. He could do it, too. But then Terry strolled over and picked it up.

"They're only kids," Terry told him, cradling the rifle in his arms, his face wearing the same bland smile as Lonnie. "And it's Christmas."

Will snapped his fingers in frustration. "Ah, shit. Sorry, Hank. I should have known this would happen."

To lay before the King pa-rum pum pum pum, rum pum pum pum, rum pum pum pum . . .

Dan had his keys in the lock. They could all hear the mechanism open with a heavy *thunk*. That only left the bolts at the top and bottom.

"Fellas, now, just think about what you're doing," Hank said. "Remember what we discussed. There's a very strong, very real possibility your minds are being manipulated by an insectoid alien entity with psychic powers."

"That's telling 'em, Hank," said Will.

So to honor Him, pa-rum pum pum pum . . .

Resolute, Dan slid back the top bolt. Clutching each other, Kendra and Ling began to inch back, into the corridor beyond Will's cell. Hank's gaze switched back and forth between the scissors in Lonnie's hand, the rifle in Terry's arms.

When we come . . .

"They're only kids," said Dan, sliding back the bottom bolt. "And it's Christmas." He pulled the door open. "What's the worst they could—"

A child came soaring out of the night, moving with the speed and power of a cannonball, and knocked him off his feet. Its legs wrapped around his neck and its hands, both clutching knives, hammered into his head. The blades pierced his cheeks, temples, and scalp, pounded in and out in furious staccato rhythm. By the time he hit the floor, his face was a mangled mess of spurting red meat.

There wasn't a soul in the room who missed it. Every pair of eyes was locked on what remained of Dan's head as it smacked against the tiles, splashing blood in every direction. Ling and Kendra screamed, the girl twisting away from Ling's arms and racing down the corridor. Will instinctively drew back from the bars of his cell. Hank didn't move. He kept on staring past Lonnie and Terry, watching the child—a blond-haired boy—as he kept on stabbing, swinging down with one arm then another, a mad grin stretched across his face. Dan was already dead, his legs jerking in postmortem spasm, but the kid was having too much fun to stop.

Lonnie and Terry were watching too, strange smiles on their faces, and Hank couldn't begin to imagine what kind of fanciful festive scene they thought they were watching. All that mattered, in the moment, was they were distracted. He seized his chance, rushing Lonnie, shoving him into the desk, grabbing the hand that held the scissors and twisting it. For all his bravado, the other man had been unprepared for a fight. He crumpled under the weight of Hank's attack, crying out as the desk's sharp corner bit into his back and folding to the floor, yielding the scissors. Hank brushed past him, reaching out his other hand to grab the barrel of Terry's rifle. Terry turned at the sound of Lonnie's yell and frowned at Hank, briefly confused about what was happening, his mind soft from thoughts of Santa Claus. But then his grip tightened on the rifle, pulling. "Hey," he said, the word sounding strangely high pitched, uttered like a toddler wrestling for a Christmas present.

Hank swung at him with the scissors, striking one of the blades against his hand, cutting a gash across his knuckles. And Terry relented, giving up the rifle and clutching his wounded hand to his chest, the expression on his face twisting in a confusion of infantile outrage and betrayal.

They *were* children, Hank thought, staggering back with the rifle, his attention shifting from Terry—his feelings hurt as bad as his hand—to Lonnie, twisting on the floor, hand at the small of his back where the desk had caught him and whining, "Ow, ow, ow, ow, ow, ow, ow, ow!"

The blond boy had finally ceased his attack on Dan and the desecration of his corpse. He sat on the dead man's chest, staring down into his ruined face and holding the knives out at his sides, letting the blood pour from their tips in a steady stream. Behind him, the night wind blew through the open doors, carrying with it the manic giggling of his brethren as they crept toward the entrance.

Hank raised the rifle, putting the stock against his shoulder and training the sights on the boy. At the same moment, the blond head tilted up, snow- and blood-soaked hair whipping out of his face to reveal a cherubic smile he knew. There was a split second of dissonance as he tried to place the image, then it came to him. The counter of the general store, sinking tiny teeth into an oatmeal cookie under the watchful eye of his grandfather, while his mother attended art classes in MacArthur Point. It was the same way every Saturday morning, every time Hank went in to buy more materials to fix up his lodge. The same kid. The same face. The same smile.

His finger tensed on the trigger. If he got anywhere close to him, he knew without doubt he'd end up the same way as Dan. No question. But he couldn't put a bullet through the head of the little boy from the hardware store. The boy whose mother and grandfather were likely at home right now, lost in some hazy celebration of Christmas Eve, relaxing in all the love and warmth of the season. He just couldn't do it. And he could tell, from the look in the kid's baby blue eyes, that he knew.

"Damn it." He lowered the rifle, turned, and ran.

"Hank?" Will watched him, a blur of color as he sprinted past his cell and down the corridor. "Hank? Hank! Hank!"

No reply. Not even a glance by way of apology.

Will felt the rumble of fear in his gut and turned back to face the entrance. Sensing the approach of the rest of Santa's servants, he backed up against the wall, but there was nowhere else to go and nothing to do but watch.

Their laughter preceded them, dancing a few paces ahead, followed by their grins. Gleaming white teeth shone in the darkness, appearing to hover in the air, before they stepped through the door, into the light, and their faces were revealed. They all still looked like children, for the most part. Their skin was pale and shiny. Their limbs were long and skinny. There was something crooked about the way they moved. But they were still recognizably kids.

All eyes were trained on Will as they filtered into the room. Even the ones who marched straight over to Terry and Lonnie. Even as they drew knives and slit their throats and stood beside them, calmly drenched in the spray of their blood. They kept their eyes on Will.

That job done, a couple broke away from the main group and took off in pursuit of Hank. Then, with the last of the town's security force curled up and gurgling in spreading pools of their own liquids, the remaining children gathered at the bars of Will's cell, stared in at him, smiled and wiggled their blood-smeared fingers in greeting.

Lacking anything better to say, all he said was, "Hi."

29.

Curtis and Shona were only halfway to the roof when the screams tore up through the stairwell.

"Ah hell," he groaned, then bent down and grabbed Shona around the hips and knees, taking her into his arms once again.

"Hey," she said. "I can walk!"

"Not fast enough." He ran, carrying her up the next two floors and the small flight of stairs to the access hatch. Shona grabbed the bar and gave it a shove. It relented with a grinding metallic howl, releasing a blast of icy air into their faces.

She stepped out and glanced around, but there was nothing to be seen beyond the black sky and vaguely rectangular shapes of buildings, half-hidden by snow. She looked back through the hatch as Curtis was about to close it. "The others might be coming up behind us."

"We can't wait around to find out. We don't have time."

"No, you don't." The voice wasn't human. It was a helium-powered parody. The kind of voice one might hear issuing from the animated lips of a video game goblin, mangled by a dozen different distortion filters. But it was coming from the mouth of a creature that had once been Devon McCulloch. His head looked like it was made of porcelain, polished and sharpened at the edges, like the tapering tips of his ears, nose and chin. It hung heavy on the end of a neck that had stretched and thinned, the nubs of his vertebrae visibly poking through the skin. His eyes had become solid slits of neon yellow and, when he turned them on Shona, he smiled. The needle teeth Curtis recalled had grown since he'd seen them that morning, getting so big they were beginning to crowd each other out, making an untidy protrusion from his gums. He ran his tongue along their crooked ridges before he spoke, carelessly drawing blood. It trickled down his chin in a thin yellow stream. Not that he seemed to mind. "Hello Miss Fleming."

If Shona had a response in her head, she didn't know what it could be. It never made its way to her lips.

Curtis stepped in front of her. "Stay back," he tried to warn Devon, but the way he said it sounded more like a question, shaky and uncertain. He swallowed and tried again, aiming for a lower pitch. "Stay back."

Devon ignored him, focusing all his attention on Shona. "I liked your class, you know. You made teaching fun. Not like Miss Gulliver." He made a sickened face. "Good riddance to her."

"Devon . . . " She spoke the name like she'd only just recognized him. "What happened to you?"

He grinned. "I'm becoming who I was always meant to be. You wouldn't understand because you're not from here."

"I'll go away again, if you'd like." She put a hand on Curtis's arm and squeezed. "We both will."

"Maybe you could," Devon said. "Maybe I'd let you. If you tell me where Kendra is."

"What do you want with her?"

Devon's grin widened and he chuckled, his hot breath making clouds in the air. "I want . . . " He hesitated, like it was the first time he'd considered the question. Then he found the answer. "I want her. She's all I want." He looked at the hatch. "She's inside, isn't she?"

"No," said Curtis. "We don't know where she is."

"Don't lie. I know you've seen her."

"We did, but she ran away. We don't know where to. But if she's what you want, you better go look somewhere else."

Devon's searing eyes narrowed and he turned them on Shona. "Is that true?"

She nodded.

Slowly, he raised his hand. "I wonder." It drifted into the light from the hatch and they saw it was transformed. The gnarled, thin fingers—long enough now to fully encircle either of their necks—stretched out toward Curtis. When they curled, gripping air, he felt their movement in his chest.

"Curtis?" Shona grabbed for him as he fell to his knees, clutching at the wounds the child had made that morning. Wounds that were now opening and deepening. Fresh blood soaked through his bandages and shirt.

Devon laughed. It sounded like the kind of noise that would issue from an old toy. A manufactured approximation of mirth.

"Look what I can do now!" His claw twisted in the air and Curtis's mutilated flesh twisted with it. "Look!"

"Stop it," Shona cried. She hated how powerless it sounded, but it was all she could do.

"I'm not even touching him," Devon said, relishing the power as Curtis sank further to the floor, face twisted in pain, feeling invisible probes as they dug their way through muscle and sinew, closing in on his heart. Devon managed to suppress a giggle as he flexed his fingers and prepared a new, more devastating attack. "Now watch this."

His wrist exploded in a plume of yellow gore that sent his hand spinning away from his arm and over the roof's edge. He screamed and made a grab for it with his other claw, nearly following it down as it tumbled into darkness.

Curtis didn't see it happen, but Shona did. She watched his narrow limb shatter, the skin, flesh and bone rupturing all at once and the hand go spinning off into the night. She saw it, but didn't understand why it had happened or why it had made the sound it did. Like a gun going off.

Then Hank sprang from the hatch, rifle in his hands. He grabbed it around the barrel, swinging it like a club, and charged Devon. The boy was crouched up against the low wall at the edge of the roof, bleeding arm still stretched out toward his lost hand, face painted yellow with hot neon tears. He turned to face Hank just as the man let loose a howling battle cry, then clocked him in the face. The force of the blow knocked a spray of yellow into the air and pitched the boy over the side of the roof. He plummeted to the street below in silence.

"Was that him?" Hank asked, racing back to the hatch and slamming it shut. "Was that Santa Claus? Wasn't quite what I was expecting."

"That was Devon McCulloch," Shona said, trying to help Curtis back to his feet.

Hank blinked. "It was?" He looked at the space where the boy had been standing a moment ago, before he'd shot his hand off and thrown him from the building. "Oh shit."

"Don't worry about it," Curtis said, the words laced with pain as he struggled to stand. "Trust me. You did us a favor."

"We've got to move, anyway." Hank aimed a thumb at the hatch. "More coming."

They moved quickly over to the roof of the adjoining building and found a way inside. The upper floors were undergoing renovations and the door to the stairwell was unlocked. They followed it down as far as they could, emerging into a storage area packed to the ceiling with shelves and boxes. They moved through it in darkness, Hank leading the way, Curtis and Shona holding each other up for support.

"What happened back there?" Shona asked.

"They got in," Hank answered. "Wasn't pretty. I had to leave the poor kid in the cell behind."

"And Kendra? Ling?"

He looked at her. "They didn't come up ahead of me?"

"No. We didn't see them."

"Then I don't know where they went. They must still be inside, somewhere. Which means . . . dead, probably."

"Oh God . . . " Shona groaned. "We just left them."

"Don't feel too bad," Hank told her. "Survivor's guilt is for survivors. And we're not out of the woods yet." He halted, looking back the way they'd come, halfway along an aisle of neatly stacked shelves, then ahead, squinting through the darkness. "You hear something?"

Shona didn't think she did. Curtis could only hear his own labored breathing. But they indulged him, doing their best to silence themselves and prick up their ears.

Jingle bells, jingle bells, jingle all the way.

The melody sounded small and hollow, filtered through tin and plastic. Only ten notes were played, then silence. Hank shuffled forward a few steps, before the melody resumed.

Oh what fun it is to ride on a one-horse open sleigh.

"Look." Shona patted him on the shoulder, pointing to one of the shelves up ahead, its metal edges flashing dimly with the reflections of dancing colors. They glowed only for the few seconds when the song was playing.

Hank motioned to them both to stay quiet and crept forward, slowly cocking his rifle. He kept low as he approached the spot where the colors had been seen, then jumped to his feet, rifle leveled, ready to open fire.

Jingle bells, jingle bells, jingle all the way. Oh what fun it is to ride in a one-horse open sleigh.

The expression on his face—illuminated now with the same

blinking reds, oranges, and greens—relaxed from tense concentration into a relieved smirk. He lowered his gun, reached over and plucked their mystery singer from its entrenched position behind a cardboard box. It was a ten-inch-tall dancing snowman, with a sack of multicolored gifts that lit up when he sang.

"Merry Christmas from Coldwell," Hank said, reading the message printed on the toy's base. "We're above the Christmas store."

Shona would have liked to share in his relief, but she was thinking about the toy—the kind of kitsch triviality that would not have looked remotely out of place among the decorations in her home. She'd seen many of its kind before, their singing and dancing activated by a motion sensor. But Hank had only been close enough to trigger it when he pounced with the rifle. Which meant, before that, something *else* had been moving.

She wasn't given time enough to warn him. A giant hand smashed through the boxes from the other side of the shelf and closed around his torso. Each of its pale fingers was as long and thick as one of his own arms. They ensnared him completely from his waist to his shoulders—and squeezed. He let loose a manic scream, dropping the rifle and toy as he was lifted off his feet. Then the hand closed into a fist around his body, crushing his chest. His scream was silenced by his own blood and organs, forced up his throat and exploding from his mouth in a frothing fountain of viscera. Much of the rest of him, turned to pulp by the sheer force of the pressure exerted by the hand, spurted out between its fingers, pattering on the floor in a thick sludge.

The sound of it echoed through the storage room. Curtis and Shona, both clinging tightly to one another, bore witness to Hank's instant pulverization without uttering a sound.

The silence which followed was finally broken by the thing on the other side of the shelves. It peered between the dented boxes of Christmas trinkets, regarding what remained of Hank with one round yellow eye, and spoke a single word. "Naughty."

30.

KENDRA HAD TURNED and run from the sight of Dan's face being pulverized by daggers. She slid from Ling's grasp, throwing herself past Will's cell and down the corridor. She had moved without thought of where she was going or what she might do when she got there. Her only aim was to get away from the blond-haired boy and whoever or whatever else might be following behind him.

"Kendra," Ling called, following after her, ignoring Will's pleas as he grasped for her between the bars, desperate not to be left behind.

Beyond the cells, the corridor split in two directions. Down the right was Owen's office and the break room. On the left was the door to the stairwell, leading to the roof.

Kendra went right.

"Wait," Ling yelled, but the girl didn't listen and didn't look back. Ling only glanced behind her briefly when somebody cried out and saw Terry and Hank wrestling over the rifle, Lonnie collapsing to the floor. That was all she caught sight of before taking a right turn, chasing Kendra into Owen's office. "Kendra!"

The girl stood in the middle of the room, her whole body tense, eyes frantically combing the walls for an escape route. There were no doors and the only window was barred. Aside from that was a desk, a few chairs, and some filing cabinets.

"There's no way out," she said.

"It's the other way!" Ling pointed behind her, through the open door. "Come on!"

"There's no time! We have to hide!" Adrenaline surging through her system, Kendra launched herself over the desk and dropped down to the floor.

"No," said Ling, hovering at the entrance. "No, no, no. Don't do this to . . . "

There was a clamor of noise from behind her and she turned to see Hank going around the corner and sprinting off down the hall, toward the stairs. In his wake came the sound of two pairs of small, booted feet, slapping their way down the corridor. There was no chance of getting past them. If she moved now, she'd run right into them and, a moment later, be on the floor with knives in her flesh. All she had time to do was close the door and turn out the light.

And that's what she did, immediately stepping back to hide herself from the mottled glass window in the door. On the other side, two waist-high shapes appeared, lingering only for a moment before shrinking away, the sound of their giggles and footfalls going with them, after Hank.

Ling tip-toed her way over to the desk, scanning the shadows for Kendra. "Do you have any idea what you just did?" Whispering was more noise than she wanted to make, but her anger was so immense she couldn't help herself.

"Go away," Kendra answered, from under the desk. "Get out."

"You've killed us. That's what you've done. You think they won't be able to find us in here? You trapped us, you stupid . . . " She bit her lip to keep herself from saying any more, squeezing her eyes shut and her hands into fists as she fought to get a grip on her fury. Attacking the girl wouldn't do any good.

"Nobody told you to follow me in here. And there's no space under here for you. So you should probably just fuck off."

Ling was briefly filled with the urge to drag the girl out from her hiding place and slap her. Instead, she started searching the desk, rooting through the drawers and struggling to identify the contents in the dark.

"What are you doing?" Kendra asked.

"Looking for weapons."

"Are you serious? That's not going to . . . "

"Shhhh!" Ling cut her off at the sound of voices from out in the corridor. She heard a child say, "Check the other rooms," and felt her stomach flip.

She backed away from the desk clutching the closest thing to a weapon she could find—a ballpoint pen—and slid in between two filing cabinets. It wasn't the greatest hiding spot, but if nobody turned on the light, there was a chance, nestled in the shadows, she would escape discovery.

Then the door opened, someone leaned in, and immediately hit the light switch.

Despair and embarrassment swamped Ling in equal measure as the room was illuminated, instantly revealing her, awkwardly sandwiched between the cabinets, clutching a pen like a flick-knife. Kendra was similarly exposed, her entire body visible where she crouched beneath the desk.

The girl in the doorway glanced briefly between them both, her expression blank, then put a finger to her lips, reached up with her other hand and turned out the light. Turning her head, she called over her shoulder, "This one's empty!" Then she backed out and closed the door.

For close to a minute, there was only silence. Then, out in the lobby, the sound of Christmas carols resumed.

Easing herself out from her disastrous hiding place, Ling dared to take a breath and whispered, "What just happened?"

"I think I peed myself." Kendra's reply was a muffled groan.

"I'm serious. Who was that girl? Do you know her?"

Slowly, awkwardly, Kendra emerged from beneath the desk. "I don't know her name. She was at the house." She thought for a moment. "Someone had to cut me loose from the couch, but I didn't see who. Maybe it was her?"

"But who is she?"

Kendra's shrug was barely perceptible in the gloom. "She's vegan."

The statement hung in the air for a long moment, before Ling said, "I'm not sure how that helps us."

"It's all I know."

Ling crept toward the door, listening keenly for anything that would help her assess the situation beyond, but all she could hear was singing.

On the second day of Christmas, my true love gave to me . . .

She turned back and went to join Kendra on the floor behind the desk. "For now, we stay here and we keep quiet. She . . . she'll come back." It was a pretty desperate position to be in, she thought to herself, when all your hopes of survival were pinned on the actions of a little girl whose name you didn't even know. But here they were. "It'll be okay. Try not to worry. She'll . . . "

Her words of hope were silenced by an ear-shredding roar that shook the floor on which they sat and sent framed pictures and certificates flying from the walls. Ling covered her ears, but it did little to block the sound, which vibrated up through her limbs, pulsing in her gut and rattling her clenched teeth. Nothing she'd heard in her life—not the sonic boom of a fighter jet, the explosion of a volcano or the sound of a rocket blasting off into space—could compare with the cacophonous din of whatever beast bellowed now.

As its sound died away and the vibrations in the walls and floor subsided, Ling was comforted—if only in a slight way—to realize it wasn't coming from within the security station, but from the building next door.

31.

THE HAND CLUTCHING Hank's corpse sprang open to reveal the compressed mess of bones, flesh and clothing—all now mashed into the same darkly-red pulp—that had once been his torso. Cradled briefly in its palm, his body resembled a tube of tomato paste, squeezed in the middle till it burst at both ends. Then the fingers unflexed and he fell, joining the rest of his mangled remains on the floor.

Shona side-stepped left, tugging on Curtis's sleeve, trying to pull him around to the far side of the puddle. She held her breath, hoping against any sense they wouldn't be spotted if they kept quiet. But Curtis stayed where he was, his sleeve slipping from between her fingers as the creature's yellow eye, peering out from between the shelves, found her.

Its bloody claw reared up before her, blocking her path. "Shona Fleming from Scotland." It spoke with a voice like bubbling syrup.

She froze, gasped. "Morgan?"

"No, not Morgan. Come closer, won't you?" When he opened his mouth to speak, she heard thick saliva spatter on the floor. His fingers curled toward her, ready to pin her in place if she tried to get away. "Sing for me. Sing for Santa."

"What?"

"Please. There's so much naughtiness in the world. It makes me sick. And the only thing that soothes me . . . is music. Won't you worship me?"

Curtis was only a couple of paces behind Shona, but out of Morgan's line of sight. He held himself still, making not a sound, wishing he could move.

Don't do this, he told himself. *God damn it, not again. Don't freeze up. Don't freeze up.*

His eyes were on Shona, hemmed in by Morgan's hand. He

wondered if he were quick enough whether he could pull her free of the monster's grasp. If he failed, she would be crushed just as surely as Hank had been. At the thought, he couldn't help glancing down at what remained of the survivalist's carcass. And there, nestled in the blood and viscera, lay the rifle.

"You sang for me once," said Morgan.

"I did?" Shona asked, baffled by the surreal exchange.

"You did. In my dreams . . . You sang me Christmas songs. Won't you do it again?"

Though she didn't dare look away from his bulging yellow eye, she was aware of Curtis in the darkness beside her, lowering himself ever so slowly to the floor. Whatever he was trying to do, it wouldn't work unless she held Morgan's attention. So she coughed, sucked her tongue, tried to get a little moisture in her mouth and croaked out, "Jingle bells, jingle bells . . . "

"No!" Morgan rapped his huge, swollen knuckles against the shelves at her back, sending violent vibrations through her body. "Not that one! We just *heard* that one! I'm not even *mentioned* in that one! Sing something else. Something special. Praise me. Praise Santa Claus."

His fingers inched toward her, carrying the stench of Hank's blood and internal organs. It was all she could think of. That and how she would certainly meet the same end if she didn't give Morgan what he wanted. And suddenly, plucked from the hidden recesses of her mind, a song presented itself. A song from her own childhood. One she hadn't heard in years.

She sucked in a breath, then, "When Santa got stuck up the chimney, he began to shout. 'You girls and boys won't get any toys if you don't let me out.'"

Morgan gave out a low, rasping grown. "Yes. Oh, yes . . . "

"'My beard is black, there's soot in my sack, my nose is tickling too . . . '"

"That's better." His eye winked shut in something close to ecstasy. "That's so much better . . . "

"When Santa got stuck up the chimney, a-choo, a-choo, a—"

"Go!" Curtis cried and squeezed the trigger.

There was a click. And that was all. Morgan's horrid eye rolled around to spy Curtis. He withdrew his hand to make a grab for him.

"Shit," Curtis yelled and launched himself forward, diving into the warm, putrid mess of Hank's remains and thrusting up with the rifle, stabbing out with it like there was a bayonet on the end, plunging it into Morgan's eye. It popped like a yellow blister. He tilted back, disgorging a fountain of fluorescent soup from the ruined socket, then made a blind grab for Shona. The tips of his fingers grazed her hip, but the shelves were in his way. They bucked and groaned as he shoved his weight against them. Curtis dropped the rifle, grabbed Shona and pulled her under the grasping claw and away, hurrying to the end of the aisle and a door to another set of stairs.

"What the fuck was that?" she said.

"I don't know."

"What happened with the rifle?"

"I don't know. Something . . . It wasn't loaded right."

"My luck I end up with the only American who doesn't know how to use a gun."

"Hey, I used it, okay? It worked, okay? We're alive, okay?"

"Okay, okay, okay."

The stairs led to the story below and they chased them down, emerging on the main floor of the Christmas store. Here, everything packed into the boxes upstairs had been put on display. Lights, wreaths and trees of every shape and color. Giant candy canes nestled between ceramic reindeer and inflatable polar bears. Christmas tree baubles the size of beach balls dangled from the ceiling, while a model railway snaked through candle displays and toy villages, its red and brass engine pulling wagons spilling over with glittering trinkets. In the very center of the room, behind a white picket fence, stood a faux log cabin. The sign above the door read 'Santa's Grotto'.

They moved toward it, instinctively following the trail of broken ornaments littering the carpet, to find a hole had been torn out of one wall, as though an animal, frustrated by its own girth, had attempted to smash its way inside. The same half-blind animal they could hear crashing through metal shelves upstairs, struggling to find his way toward them through the fog of his own pain and murderous rage and unleashing a howl of such magnitude it caused the very building around them to quake.

It was some moments before either of them could make themselves understood over the ringing in their ears. "Where now?" Shona asked, too scared to trust her own sense of direction.

Curtis looked around them, searching for a way out, but the

building's geography was obscured beneath a sparkling jungle of holiday paraphernalia. Though most of the store was in darkness, a few twinkling bulbs had been left on among the displays, offering a warming glow to passersby in the street and deepening the shadows by contrast.

Curtis looked again to the broken cabin. For some reason Morgan had come here, driven by motivations unknown, to swathe himself in the symbols of Santa Claus. He'd probably smashed his way into the store the same way he'd tried to smash his way into the grotto.

As soon as he thought of it, Curtis became aware of the draft blowing through the store. He could smell the night air filtering in from the other side of the shelves. He pointed down an aisle garlanded with a trellis of frosted, plastic mistletoe. "We have to go, this—" He was silenced by a golden bauble hurtling out of the shadows and smashing into the back of his skull. It surprised more than it hurt, but it was enough to nearly knock him off his feet.

"Curtis!" Shona wheeled around, hunting for a sign of whomever had thrown the bauble, but Curtis clutched her hand and pulled her along the aisle.

"This way," he urged, rubbing at the nape of his neck where a few golden shards had succeeded in piercing the skin. "We have to—" An ornament bounced off his shoulder—a porcelain Santa this time—and shattered on the floor.

Shona flinched as something hit her back. She turned and managed to dodge a snow globe as it sailed over her head. "What the fuck is this now?" She ducked, dodging further projectiles as they popped and burst around her. "Who's doing that?"

Curtis pulled her onward, throwing up a hand to cover his face as more trinkets fell, the volley becoming a bombardment. "I don't—" Snowmen tumbled from the shelves ahead of him and rolled underfoot. "It's not—" Silver stars and snowflakes hailed from the ceiling. "Hell! Aw, damn!" He finally understood what was happening as tinsel and tree lights slithered out from the bottom shelves and tried to lasso his ankles. No children hid in the shadows, hurling missiles. The store itself wanted them dead. "It's the Christmas shit!"

"What?" Shona could hardly hear him over the sound of exploding baubles.

"All this Christmas shit! It's trying to kill us!" He pulled her through the aisle and into the path of a battalion of knee-high clockwork Santas, marching toward them, hatred burning in their painted eyes. "Christmas shit!" Curtis grabbed at a bargain barrel loaded with teddy bears in Santa hats—too soft to do any damage to him—tipped it on its side, and kicked it into the army's path. It rolled through them, scattering Santas like bowling pins and clearing a route to the checkout desk.

Curtis and Shona raced past it, still cowering under a barrage of Christmas shit spiraling around them like debris caught in a tornado, and reached the exit. The doors were closed and locked, but Morgan had smashed his way in through the glass panels in the bottom. They ducked down and escaped through the hole he'd made, gasping in the night air like swimmers breaching the water's surface.

"Come on," Curtis urged, pulling Shona behind him, knowing they couldn't afford to pause to catch their breath. Morgan's howl of fury chased them into the street. He'd found his way back to the first floor now, smashing his way through the store in search of them.

They headed south, away from the Christmas store and security office, veering east when they reached the edge of the square. They crossed Sixth Avenue, then Seventh, and had nearly gone beyond Eighth, at the edge of town, when Shona forced him to stop. "Wait, wait, wait," she said, limping badly. "Where are we going?"

"I don't know," he admitted. All he could think to do was run. He pointed ahead of them, toward the edge of town and the road to MacArthur Point, buried beneath nearly five feet of snow. "Maybe we just keep going? Take our chances?"

Shona let out a laugh, which turned to fog on the air. "I can't," she said, indicating her leg.

"I'll carry you."

She studied him for a moment, the way he stood, hunched over from the pain in his chest, already shivering. "*You* can't."

He didn't argue, but it was painful to see the understanding of their plight register in his eyes and the hope go out of them. He shook his head. "I don't . . . I don't . . . "

"Shhhh . . . " She stepped forward and put her hands on his shoulders, comforting him the way she would a child. "It's okay. Let's just . . . take a moment to think things through." She looked back the way they'd come and ahead, up the street and down. Then she thought for a moment, nodded and said, "Okay. Okay, I think I've got an idea."

Walking to The Malamute didn't take nearly as long as climbing its rickety stairs. Every step and every inch of the rail was encased in ice, and neither Curtis or Shona was physically fit enough to fully support the other. They had to go carefully and very, very slowly.

The bar's facade showed no signs of life. The bulb over the door was out, and no light shone through the window. Even the Molsons sign had been switched off. They'd decided to risk the climb anyway, though it risked proving a fruitless endeavor. Their next, closest option for shelter—beyond knocking at random doors—was Curtis's place, which would mean walking to the top of Nugget Hill. In their current conditions, that seemed an even more daunting prospect than the Malamute's staircase.

On reaching the top, they tried the door and found it locked tight. "Hello," Curtis yelled, pounding his fist against the wood. "If there's anyone in there, please open up!"

"Please open up," Shona echoed.

"Let us in!"

"Please!"

And a voice called from within, "All right, already! Shut the hell up!" There was a sound of furniture being moved, then locks being turned and bolts slid back. Then the door creaked open to reveal Einar, bloodied and bruised, shotgun clutched in his hand. His hair hung in greasy strands over his bearded face, a haggard shadow of the one that had greeted them the previous evening. His eyes moved between them, assessing. When he saw they'd been beaten as badly as him—if not worse—he nodded over his shoulder. "Come on in."

He wasn't alone. Curtis and Shona rushed inside, grateful to be enveloped in the saloon's warmth, and found Sergio and Richie sitting at a booth. Both men were nursing cuts and bruises and were surrounded by evidence of a furious battle, the shattered remains of stools, tables, glasses and broken bottles scattered throughout the room.

"Hiya." Shona's voice trembled when she spoke, a surge of emotion catching her by surprise at the sight of their relatively friendly faces.

"Welcome back to party central," Sergio said, his own voice monotone. His bandaged hand gripped an open bottle of mescal from which he'd clearly taken more than a few slugs. "Grab a seat if you can find one."

Einar slammed and locked the door, then shoved some broken tables up against it. "Don't tell me," he said, peering out the window to ensure no-one had followed them. "You want the first-aid kit."

"If there's anything left in it," Shona said. The adrenaline of their flight from the Christmas store and desperate trek across town had dissipated, returning the feeling to her frozen limbs—along with the pain.

"I'll take a look." Einar sounded less than hopeful, moving toward the kitchen.

Shona followed for a few paces, but stopped when she caught sight of what sat behind the bar, strapped into a chair. "Oh my God!"

Realizing what her exclamation was about, Sergio chuckled. It was a depressed, exhausted noise. "Oh yeah, *that*." He lifted the mescal bottle to his lips. "I'll tell you . . . it's been one hell of a long night."

32.

IN HIS WHOLE LIFE—even the part of it predating his antipathy toward Christmas music—Will didn't think he'd heard the song 'The 12 Days of Christmas' sung in its entirety. But he endured it now, from the lone partridge in the pear tree, all the way up to the twelve drummers drumming and back down again, sweetly serenaded by the children gathered around his cell. They gripped the bars in their chubby fists, stared in at him and sang their little hearts out, while he watched the progress of Terry Cabot's blood oozing its way toward him across the floor. It slowed and finally stopped in the same moment the song ended.

Will looked then at the girl opposite him, the one who had wielded the knife that opened Terry's throat. "Why did you do that?" He asked her.

She couldn't have been more than six years old. He'd seen her around—the same way he'd seen all of St. Nicholas's schoolchildren around. She had ginger pigtails, eyes as big as a cartoon's and big, buck teeth with a gap in the center, giving her a lovable, goofy grin. It was the same grin she was showing him now, though her teeth suddenly looked too sharp to be considered goofy. "Don't know," she said, answering his question in an elated whisper that told him, beyond not knowing why she'd murdered Terry, she didn't particularly care.

Until now, Will had been standing on his bunk, back against the wall, but he lowered himself down and took a tentative step forward, careful not to get within arm's reach. "You know . . . he used to eat children. Just children. You've heard the stories, right?" He looked around at all the faces watching him between the bars. All wore the same eager grins, staring at Will with unblinking yellowish eyes. "At some point I guess he realized children were more useful to him alive. He could command them easier. Take advantage of the fact they could move around without drawing attention or suspicion. It's useful to have an army at your disposal, ready to do your bidding without question. So he started feeding on grown-ups instead. And I guess, for now, that's what he's sticking to. But what do you think will happen to you when all the grown-ups are gone and he's still hungry?"

A sound escaped the buck-toothed girl's throat, the tiniest hiss of a mocking laugh and she whispered, "Don't know."

Don't know, don't care.

The faces of the others were just as indifferent. Will sensed this was a losing pitch, but he had to keep trying. "You can stop this," he told them. "You're the only ones who might stand a chance. The only ones he might let get close enough. He'd never suspect you because he thinks you're weak and stupid. But I know you're not stupid." Will looked to each of the children crowded around his cell, beseeching them to act, to turn the tables on Santa Claus. They watched in silence, their attentions seemingly held fast. Yet when he focused on any one child for longer than a second, he saw their smiles were cold and their eyes empty. Finally he looked past them, across the room to a young girl. She had curly brown hair and a glittering purple coat and stood with her back to the wall. She stared silently like the rest, yet something in her face—in her eyes—appeared different. Was there still something behind her vacant expression that could be reasoned with? "You have the power to stop this," he said, now directing his words entirely to her. "You can save your parents. Your friends and family. You can save yourself."

The girl watched him, her eyes drilling into his, and he could see—though she tried to hide it—there was something there. She wasn't like the rest. There was a chance here. For a brief moment, he felt something approaching hope.

Then a voice snuffed it out. "Naughty."

The children all drew breath at once, their pointed teeth chattering in excitement.

"He's here." The buck-toothed girl peeled herself from the bars so Will could see behind her, across the room, past the desks and dead bodies, to the open doorway. A shape lingered just beyond, a great shadow framed in the frosted blue glow of the streetlights.

Will's mouth suddenly felt very dry. He swallowed and straightened up, trying not to show any signs of fear as the children stepped away from his cell, like a pack of wolves making way for their leader.

The figure swept in through the door, stepping over Dan's mangled body and advancing to the center of the room. It wore a cloak of crimson velvet with white trim, draped over its entire body, dark and wet in patches where snow had melted into the fabric. Dozens of silver and gold baubles dangled from the cloth, rattling against one another as the thing lumbered forward. Lengths of glittering tinsel trailed behind it like so many fabulous dead snakes. Its composition was a challenge to make sense of. Only when it was a few paces away did Will realize it was hunched over, its head bowing toward the floor, bent spine grazing against the ceiling. If it raised itself to its full height, it might be close to three stories tall.

Instinctively, Will shrank back against the wall, eyes scanning his cell the way a rodent might, desperately hunting for some means of escape, though he knew there was none. "I'm not afraid of you," he said, sounding terrified.

The cloaked figure let out a low growl and lifted its head. All that was visible beneath the shroud was a beard of silver curls—the nylon hairs stained with blood—and, leering out from darkness as black as the bottom of a well, a single yellow eye. "Will Douglas."

He knew the voice. It was distorted, like the speaker had two sets of vocal chords layered one atop the other, too many tongues twisting against its over-sized teeth. Yet at its core were tone and speech patterns he'd been hearing all his life. Though how they could be emanating from this monstrosity was beyond him. "Morgan?"

The creature's shoulders shook—bells and baubles jangling down its back—and a tortured wheeze erupted from its throat, disassembling into laughter. "Morgan? You must have me confused, sir . . . "

Its hot breath wafted across the room and into Will's cell, smelling of nutmeg, cinnamon, hospital disinfectant, and stale blood. "Shit, Morgan, I . . . You've got to know I'm sorry for what I did. Truly, I . . . I thought you were Santa Claus."

At mention of the name, Morgan laughed and so did the children. "I *am* Santa Claus!" A hand emerged from beneath the folds of the cloak and reached for the cell, its thick, pale fingers closing around one of the bars. "Will Douglas. The problem child."

Will studied the hand, huge and ape-like, brown blood crusted in the wrinkles of its knuckles. "Fuck man, what happened? What did he do to you?"

"Will . . . " Morgan sighed, his voice more recognizably his own. "What is it you want for Christmas, Will?"

It was hard not to laugh. Will glanced around, inviting all present to bear witness to his bemusement. "You want to give me a present?"

"I'm Santa Claus. I want to give you exactly what you deserve."

That wasn't quite so funny. Will licked his lips and tried not to stammer when he spoke. "I . . . I don't . . . It's cool, man. I don't want anything."

Morgan sucked in a deep breath, his fingers tightening on the bar. "But you do. And I think I know what it is."

"You do?"

Morgan nodded, slowly. "You want out of this cell." He jerked his arm back and the bar buckled.

The children laughed.

Will screamed as the hand slid through the gap it made and closed around his head. He slapped Morgan's rubbery arm and struggled to pull himself away, but there was nowhere to run. The fingers dug in, seizing his skull with intense pressure and dragging him across the floor, up to the bars. The gap was wide enough that his head slid through easily, but then his shoulders crunched against metal. With a groan of irritation, Morgan shoved him back through, then tensed his arm to try again. Will tried to call out, to beg him to stop, to wait, but all his attempts were muffled by the wall of clammy, sour-smelling flesh pressed across his face. His legs kicked and hands clawed blindly at the air, hunting for something that would save him, but none of it was any use.

With inhuman strength, Morgan heaved him forward again. This time, when his shoulders struck the bars, muscles tore and bones snapped. A wave of scorching pain erupted through Will's body in the same moment all feeling went out of his limbs. It was a horrifying, contradictory sensation he was given no time to process. The sharpened tips of Morgan's talons pierced his neck, slicing through his throat and windpipe, digging through the flesh under his jaw and finally anchoring themselves in bone. Then, scored to the sounds of children cheering, gurgling and gushing blood, he gave one last tug and wrenched Will's head from his neck.

The children applauded, caught in the arterial spray as Will's decapitated body stumbled back from the bars and slumped to the floor. Above the collar of his T-shirt was only a ragged red wound, a small section of his snapped vertebrae gleaming through the mess of mangled flesh.

Morgan lifted Will's head up to his own, inspecting his ruined, slack-jawed face and eyes gaping from their sockets, frozen in his final moment of terror. He clucked his tongue before letting the useless ball of meat and bone drop to the floor, and sighed. "Free at last."

Behind him, having watched every moment of the gruesome spectacle as any good little servant of Saint Nicholas would, Cindee Joyce finally permitted herself a moment's respite and turned her face to the wall.

33.

"OKAY." After doing her best to patch Curtis up—for what felt like more than only the second time—Shona eased herself onto The Malamute's last standing bar stool and looked to Richie and Sergio. "Explain yourselves."

The contractors exchanged tired looks, each one gesturing for the other to take up the responsibility of telling their story, before Richie finally sighed and capitulated. "Let's see now . . . It was still early when all you folks left. Einar closed the bar, but he let me and Sergio stay and keep drinking a few more hours. Guess he wasn't in any hurry to be left here on his own. Then we walked back to the hotel around four, and . . . uh . . . " He trailed off, struggling to articulate what it was they'd witnessed.

"A bloodbath," said Sergio, finding the words his friend couldn't. "A fucking massacre. Children turned to devils and . . . Killing everyone. I never sobered up so fast in my life."

"What did you do?" Shona asked.

"We ran," said Sergio. "We tried to find help, but all we found were more of those . . . things."

"They were all over town," said Richie. "Going in and out of people's homes. Killing and laughing and . . . "

"We had to keep hidden," said Sergio. "Crouching low, sticking close to the shadows. When we found a storage shed with an unlocked door we hid inside and stayed there. Didn't dare move till daylight. When we came back here, we found the door busted open and Einar with . . . that." He aimed a finger at the other side of the bar and the bloodied child who sat there, strapped to a chair.

"He paid me a visit a little while before they did," said Einar, picking up the story. "Damn near killed me." He tugged at the rag wrapped about his neck, revealing the knife wound—deep enough to leave a nasty scar, but no deeper. "It was a strange thing. He passed out right in the middle of slitting my throat. Was out cold for over an hour. I tied him up, but as soon as he woke, he got loose, tried for me again. I was lucky these two showed up when they did."

"Took all three of us to bring the little shit down." said Sergio. "He's strong. Vicious."

Shona nodded. "We've seen what they're capable of. But what have you been doing since?"

"Waiting for help to arrive." Sergio poured himself a fresh measure of mescal. "And a little drinking. To help steady the nerves."

"Kid smashed up my radio," said Einar. "We couldn't call out."

"And we weren't going to go back out there," said Richie. "Not after seeing what they did. It'd be suicide."

Shona looked between the two contractors, then at Einar. "Well if that's the best plan you've got, you're going to be waiting here a very long time."

"Fuckin' A." Sergio raised his glass. "Let's get comfortable."

She turned to Curtis, who lay sprawled in the same booth at which they'd shared drinks the previous evening, trying not to breath too heavily in case it caused the wounds in his chest to tear back open. "I don't suppose you've had any further thoughts on courses of action?"

He gave out a groan, like the very idea of being asked to turn his mind to something caused him pain. "Sitting tight sounds pretty good to me."

"Fair enough." She could see he needed rest. "I guess we're all tired and sore and fresh out of ideas." She spun around on her stool to face Einar. "You wouldn't have anything to eat, would you? Bar snacks? Chips? Peanuts? Pork rinds? Anything at all?"

The barman shrugged. "I might be able to throw together a few more sandwiches."

She reached out and grasped his hand, squeezing it tight. "Einar, make me a sandwich and I'll marry you. No joke."

He blushed. "It's really no problem." Extricating himself from her iron grip, he shuffled into the back, to the galley kitchen, leaving her with the hostage.

The boy had been tied to the chair with what looked like maybe twenty feet of nylon rope, wrapped around and around and around his limbs and torso, and tightly knotted. His hands, untethered, had clawed frantically at the armrests, tearing out thick splinters of wood with fingernails turned to claws. His head had puffed up, turning almost as smooth and colorless as Devon McCulloch's. His narrow eyes, regarding her with undisguised contempt, held the same unearthly glow as Devon's and the dried blood around his nose and mouth—evidence of his prolonged battle with Einar and the rest—was yellow. No-one had bothered to put a gag in his mouth and she could see why. Teeth like broken porcelain shards protruded from his split lips, sure to slice through any cloth put near them—and any fingers that got too close in the process. In spite of his mutation, which was severe—worse than she'd seen on any child except Devon—she recognized him as ten-year-old Lucas Grenier.

"How's it going, Lucas?"

The boy only hissed in reply, black tongue wriggling behind his teeth.

"Guess he's not in the mood for conversation," said Sergio. "You should have been here a few hours ago. We couldn't shut him up. Droning on and on about how we're all going to die. How the town has to be saved from us outsiders. How Santa Claus himself has come to the rescue."

"Saint Nicholas," Lucas barked, foamy spittle flying from his lips. "His name is Saint Nicholas!"

"Aye," said Shona. "We've heard all about that." She turned to Sergio. "I don't suppose he told you what their plan is?"

It was Lucas who answered. "Death! You'll die for coming here! For trying to destroy our home!" His voice was an octave or more higher than it should have been, making him sound like a cartoon chipmunk. Shona couldn't decide if it made him sound terrifying, ridiculous, or both.

"That's a bit steep isn't it?" She asked him. "I came here with the best of intentions. All of us did. Isn't slaughtering us a bit of an overreaction? And not—it has to be said—terribly Christmassy. Wouldn't letting us leave if we want be more in the spirit of the season? What do you think Santa would say to that?"

"His name is Saint Nicholas!" Lucas screeched like a tantruming toddler, high and loud enough to shatter the mirror behind the bar—if it hadn't already been shattered.

"Fine, fine, Saint Nicholas. And what a saint he is. Have you seen what he's done to you?" She dropped down from her stool and limped around the bar to pick up the biggest mirror shard she could find, thrusting it into his face. "Take a look! You happy with this? Whatever that stuff is he fed you, it's destroying you!"

The boy studied his own reflection for only a moment, then looked away. "It's making me better. And it's not finished yet. You'll see."

Shona let the mirror shard drop.

"Lucas . . . You were such a sweet wee boy. Why would you want to be a part of this? Why would you let him do this to you? What's it all for?"

Lucas fixed her in a penetrating gaze and, for the briefest moment, she saw within his eyes all the innocence and vulnerability she thought had been extinguished. "For Christmas. Christmas every day. No sadness, no fighting. Only fun, forever. Only . . . happiness." Then the light went from his eyes and his face contorted into a demonic scowl of murderous intent. "Everything you were going to take away from us! Everything you would have destroyed!"

It was a monstrous image, but it didn't frighten Shona to see it. All she felt was sad. "Oh Lucas. You're so lost, aren't you?"

"There's no point trying to reason with him," said Sergio. "He's not going to get you out of this hell."

"Neither is sitting here, drinking, waiting for his friends to come find us." She reached into her pocket and produced the Christmas card she'd been carrying around with her. The one the children had presented on her arrival at the school. "Now look at this," she said, holding it out to Lucas. "You remember it, don't you?" She pointed to the image he'd drawn of himself in colored pencil. A brown-haired boy with rosy cheeks, waving in welcome. "You remember doing this for me?"

For a few seconds he resisted, but then his eyes rolled around to the card, focusing on the image. Again, she saw them soften, a hint of the boy he'd been leaking through the yellow. "I remember." His voice, still comically altered, sounded more like his own, its monstrous edges tempered by sadness.

"I don't believe the boy who drew this, who was so sweet to me, who made me feel so welcome, would ever want to do anything to hurt me. Not him. Not the real Lucas."

He stared a long moment at the card, then lifted his gaze to meet hers. "But I will." There was no menace to the way he said it.

No anger. But there was certainty. "I'll be free soon and the second I am, I'll kill you." There was an undercurrent of helplessness to what he said, speaking like an addict lost to his addiction, resigned to commit actions that were beyond his control. "It doesn't matter if I want to. I'll kill you and it'll feel good."

She felt the compulsion to shiver but tried to hide it. "You're not a murderer, Lucas. Not really."

The boy snorted an agonized laugh. "Tell that to the priest."

Shona drew back. His words were like a bucket of acid poured over her certainties, melting them all away. "You killed Father McHattie?"

Lucas nodded, giggling madly as tears rolled down his grinning cheeks. "He fought. He begged. He prayed. And then he died!"

"Why did you do it?"

"Devon said we had to."

"Why?"

He gave her a look like she was stupid. How could she not know? How could anyone not know? "Because of the story."

She wanted to ask what story he was talking about, but suddenly his face went slack, all features slumping into passivity and eyelids dropping shut. His head drooped forward and body went limp.

"Lucas?" She reached out to him, letting the card fall.

"Hey," Sergio called. "I wouldn't do that!"

"I know you wouldn't." She placed her hands on the boy's shoulders and shook him. "Lucas?" She patted his cold, damp face, but there was no response. "He's unconscious."

"A small mercy," said Einar, returning from the kitchen with a plate of sandwiches. He set it down on the bar. "You should eat, if you don't want to end up the same way."

She nodded, stepped away from the boy and hobbled around to the other side of the bar. "It doesn't make sense."

"Can say that again." Richie poured himself another slug.

Shona picked up a sandwich and took a bite, pondering as she chewed. "This Saint Nicholas character arrived some time yesterday evening. He fed them whatever it is that turns them into monsters and then, while most of the town was asleep, they went to work. They destroyed radios, sabotaged vehicles . . . and they murdered people. But why, hours before any of that, in my classroom, in broad daylight, would they kill Father McHattie?"

"Because of the story," said Sergio. "That's what the kid said."

"But what story?"

"You weren't there?" asked Richie.

She shook her head. "I stepped out. I never heard it. But there must have been something in it. Some secret worth protecting. They must have heard it and decided they had to kill him there and then to keep him from sharing it with anyone else."

"A pity," Sergio sighed. "That could have helped us, maybe."

"Yeah." Shona sank onto the bar stool, dejected. "Maybe."

And Einar said, "Probably the one about how St. Nicholas got its name."

Shona turned to face him. "You know it?"

The barman nodded. "McHattie was a drunk. He hid bottles of whiskey all over the church so he never had to be more than five feet away from a drink. And he was in here at least three nights a week. Came late to try and avoid his parishioners and stayed till closing. Some nights, when the bar was empty except for the two of us and he'd drunk so much he could barely move, he'd start telling me that story. Always seemed like he thought he was telling me for the first time."

Her sandwich finished, Shona reached over and grabbed two more—one for each hand. "How did it go?"

Einar ran a hand over his bearded face and thought a moment. "Let's see now . . . The way I remember it, he always started by talking about Boyd McCulloch, a homesteader, lay preacher and prospector who, more than a hundred years ago, bought a parcel of land stretching from the foothills of Mount Coldwell all the way down to Carrick River, hoping it might yield a fortune of a kind he couldn't guess. In the meantime, he settled here with his wife and six children and raised hogs and planted an orchard. And he called the land Applecross . . . "

34.

THE DOOR CLICKED open and Cindee Joyce said, "You can come out now."

Ling tentatively raised her head above the desk under which she'd been cowering. "What does that mean?"

The girl paused before answering, struggling to think of another way to say it. "You can come out."

"Are they gone?"

"It's safe." Cindee's silhouette shrank back from the doorway, beckoning them to follow.

Ling grabbed Kendra by the arm and hauled her up. "Come on."

"Seriously?" The teen groaned as her stiffened limbs were put to work.

"We're not staying here."

They couldn't have been hiding in Owen's office for more than an hour, but it felt like days. They had huddled together in the dark, terrified, trying not to move or make a sound and doing their best to ignore the apocalyptic sounds raging through the walls. Now they emerged, blinking under the hallway's fluorescent lights and following the child as she led them into the lobby.

The floor was littered with bodies. Ling recognized a few of them. There was Dan, of course, still lying where she'd seen him fall, his face looking like a pulverized wreck of chewed-up gristle. There was Lonnie and Terry too, sprawled in pools of their own blood. And in his cell lay what remained of Will. Ling only caught a glimpse of his ravaged corpse before turning away. She and Kendra had been able to hear his awful final moments from their hiding place—Morgan's arrival, their conversation, the boy's screams, the pounding of flesh against the bars, the breaking of bones and tearing of muscle, the splash of his blood as it doused the tiles. At the memory of it, Ling felt the bile rising in her throat. She put a hand to her mouth, squeezed her eyes shut and swallowed, trying to maintain her composure.

Cindee, watching her reaction, said, "At least you didn't have to see it."

"Jesus," Kendra muttered, her tone equal measures sadness and awe.

Ling sucked a deep breath in through her mouth—the thick stench in the room, if she'd allowed it into her nostrils, would surely have sent her gag reflex over the edge—and told the girl, "You're a tough one, aren't you."

Cindee only stared back, her expression betraying no emotion whatsoever.

With her gut under control—for the moment, at least—Ling surveyed the rest of the room and the other bodies slumped in corners, on benches and on top of desks. There were as many as ten of them—she wasn't about to count them—and all children. The same ones that had stormed the entrance, slaughtered the security staff and taunted Will with Christmas songs. "What happened to them?"

"They're sleeping."

"Sleeping?" Ling immediately lowered her voice to a whisper, terrified she might wake one of them up.

"It's okay," said Cindee. "They sleep when Saint Nicholas does. After he's eaten all he can eat, he has to rest. And that's when . . . That's when they change. While they're asleep. They won't wake up until he does."

Trying to understand what she'd said, Ling turned to the child nearest her—a boy in a bright blue snowsuit—and watched him, noticing now the way the fabric of his clothing moved, slowly swelling not with breaths, but as the flesh and bone beneath stretched and shifted. A process of fermentation was at play beneath his skin, transforming him at a cellular level. Ling thought of Morgan's mutation into the monster that had chased her from the clinic and wondered if this boy's metamorphosis, when it was complete, would be as bad—or worse. She didn't look at his face, deciding she'd seen enough horror for one lifetime.

To Cindee, she asked, "Why isn't this happening to you?"

The answer was delivered in a monotone. "They drank the eggnog. I didn't."

"Why not?"

The girl shrugged. "I'm vegan."

"Yeah, me too," said Kendra. "Starting right fucking now."

Ling wheeled around, scanning the room for a third time. "Where's Morgan?"

"Gone," said Cindee. "He wasn't here long."

"That's what we need to do," said Kendra, her eyes fixed on the desk that had once been Lonnie's. She approached it and reached out to touch the pistol that sat there, neatly presented alongside a scattered handful of fat, brass cartridges—relics from the point earlier in the night when the men had been counting their guns and ammunition, for all the good it did them. The handgun was a chunky, silver revolver, the kind some of the town's hunting enthusiasts favored as a last-resort self-defense weapon against bears. She picked it up and imagined pressing its cold weight against the brow of the creature she'd seen hollow out Bailey's corpse. "We should go back to my place."

Ling stared at her in disbelief. "What are you thinking of?"

"I had the chance once," Kendra said. "I should have taken it then. I could hear him . . . *it* . . . snoring from my bedroom. I had the chance. But I didn't have a gun."

"You think a gun's going to . . . ?"

"A bullet in the brain kills most things." Kendra opened the cylinder and snatched up some cartridges. "And these look pretty big."

"You want to go on a suicide mission, you're on your own." Ling turned to Cindee for backup. "Tell her."

The girl looked suddenly nervous. "I don't know where he is now. Saint Nicholas, I mean."

"He'll be back at my place," said Kendra, loading one cartridge after another after another. "In my bed. He slept there once and found it very comfortable. Why wouldn't he go back?"

"We don't have time," said Ling.

"We have time." Kendra spoke with icy certainty.

"We don't!" Again, Ling looked to the girl for support. "We don't have time, do we?"

Cindee shrugged. "I don't know. An hour? Maybe less."

"That's plenty," said Kendra, and snapped the cylinder shut.

"No." Ling strode over to her, put one hand on the gun and another on her shoulder. "No, no, no. This isn't it. This isn't the way we're going to do things."

"Suddenly you have a better idea?"

Gently, Ling slid the gun from Kendra's hands into her own. "We're going to get help. We're going to get out." She turned to Cindee. "My satellite phone. You know where it is?"

The girl furrowed her brow. "What's that?"

"It's a special phone we can use to call for help. It was in my desk in the town hall. But somebody stole it."

Cindee thought a moment. "We have choir rehearsals in the town hall. There's a space under the stage we used to hid e things. If one of them took it, it'll be there."

"Then let's go."

They dashed from the building and across the square, through freshly falling veils of snow, to reach the town hall. Cindee led them to the stage where, the previous afternoon, having murdered Father McHattie, the children had practiced their Christmas repertoire. A wooden panel slid out to provide access to the area underneath, where old props and equipment were stored, relics of past productions and celebrations.

Ling still clutched the gun. She placed it on the floor of the stage, shrugged off her coat and ducked into the crawlspace, shoving her way through dusty boxes of old tools and forgotten decorations, to reach the stockpile at the back. Here were most of the items the children of St. Nicholas had seen fit to steal from their families and neighbors. There were knives and flashlights, spark plugs and car batteries, cellphone chargers and radio parts—anything that might aid their attacks or assist others' escape attempts. But there were also dolls and teddy bears, beloved books and family photos—treasured trinkets from their lives in St. Nicholas. Things they didn't want to leave behind when they journeyed with Santa Claus to whatever North Pole paradise he had promised them. She had to wonder what kind of blissful Eden he could have described that would have made murder seem a price worth paying. Or did he never offer anything so specific? Was it enough that he was the one they'd worshiped all their young lives, the one they were preconditioned to please? A man who'd never let them down all the ways their parents and teachers had. Someone whose very existence proved magic was real and all the dreams they'd ever wished for—no matter how absurd—lay just beyond their fingertips.

Such idle musings melted away as her eye fell upon the red case containing the satellite phone. “Yes, yes, yes!” She grabbed for it, dragged it over through the piled souvenirs of the children’s war-like campaign, popped the locks and opened it up. “No, no, no!” Nestled in the foam padding was what remained of the phone. Shards. Metal and plastic pieces broken utterly beyond repair. Dejected, she tossed the case away, into the shadows, then turned and crawled in the opposite direction, into the light.

Cindee was crouched at the exit. “Did you find it?”

“Broken.” Ling clambered out from under the stage, wiping at the dirt and cobwebs on her clothes. “They smashed it to bits.”

“I’m sorry.”

Despite the maelstrom of thoughts and emotions careening in her head, Ling felt an acute twinge when the girl said that. She stared into her delicate, innocent face and wanted to tell her she had no reason to apologize, but suddenly saw they were alone in the hall. “Where’s Kendra?”

Cindee looked behind her, at the spot where the older girl had been standing only moments before. “I . . . I don’t . . . ”

Ling’s eyes went to where she’d placed the gun and saw it too had vanished. “Oh no,” she groaned, understanding immediately where Kendra had gone and what she intended to do. “Oh God damn it!”

She grabbed her coat and ran for the doors, Cindee trailing behind. Halfway across the hall she realized she had no idea where Kendra lived. If she hoped to stop her, she had to pray she hadn’t gone further than a few feet from the town hall. Crossing the lobby, a part of her wondered if she should even try to intervene. Perhaps the girl’s crazy, suicidal gambit was the best chance any of them had of getting out of this with their lives. But no, she told herself. She couldn’t let her do it. She had to make her turn back.

Then Ling threw open the main doors, saw who was in the square . . . and froze.

35.

EINAR TOLD THE story twice. Both times, the others kept their mouths shut, listening intently. The first time he got through it, Sergio sighed and said, “I don’t see how that helps us.” After the second time, during which they listened even more intently, he said: “I still don’t see how that helps us.”

“We can figure it out,” said Shona, speaking around a mouthful of sandwich—her fourth. “Saint Nicholas told McCulloch to name the town after him.”

“But he isn’t the real Saint Nicholas,” said Sergio. “He’s . . . what . . . the Devil?”

“Devil’s too big. Sounds more like some Native Indian tree spirit,” said Richie, then added, as if by way of qualification, “I’m one sixteenth Cree myself.”

“The theory the others were working on was insectoid alien,” said Shona.

Sergio scoffed. “Sounds like a lot of horseshit. Why not a space vampire? Or a were-elf? Or a pookah?”

Richie snapped his fingers. “Like Harvey!”

“Or a god,” said Einar.

Sergio gave the Icelander a withering look. “It’s not God. And if it is, count me out. That’s a fight you ain’t gonna win.”

“Not *your* god,” said Einar. “*A* god. There have been lots of mythical beings people worshiped as gods over the centuries. Maybe some of them were real. Maybe one of them had to go into hiding when its followers turned against it or were wiped out by Christian crusaders. It could have stayed hidden in these mountains for hundreds of years. No-one would have known.”

“Imaginative,” said Richie. “You ever share that theory with Father McHattie?”

Einar winced at the thought. “He didn’t like to talk theology.”

Shona, who had been chewing through the last of her sandwich while the rest had been talking, now aimed a finger in Einar's direction and swallowed. "There's something in that."

"The god theory?" Sergio sounded skeptical.

"Saint Nicholas. He wants to be worshiped. Whatever he is, he operates on a different level from us. Different levels. We're talking about someone or something that can communicate with people in their dreams, that can manipulate the minds of an entire town. Turn inanimate objects to his will, control the weather, transform people into monsters. He's not bound by the same laws of the physical world that limit our abilities and perceptions. He can go beyond all that."

"Esoteric cosmology," said Einar, extending the sandwich plate to Shona, its stack now reduced by more than half. "McHattie didn't like to talk about that either."

"Exactly," said Shona, picking up another neatly sliced triangle. "That's it exactly. His big advantage is he's operating in two realms at the same time—the physical realm and . . . the *other* realm. And if we can't get to him on the physical, we need to try the other."

"Jesus fucking Christ," Sergio exclaimed. "Lady, what the fuck are you even talking about?"

"No, no, no, no, no." Shona jumped off her stool, eyes wild with excitement at where her line of reasoning was taking her. "Hear me out. This makes sense . . . sort of. Just . . . just imagine for a second that thoughts and prayers actually mattered. Like every thought you put out into the world had an intrinsic psychic worth that could be measured in units of energy. And every thought someone had about you existed somewhere on another plane of reality. And if you could somehow reach those thoughts and prayers and claim them, they could fuel your influence over the physical world. To ordinary people your abilities would seem like magic and you would be considered . . . a god."

Reaching to tip the dregs of the mescal bottle into his glass, Sergio shook his head at Richie and muttered, "Can you believe this is what they're teaching in schools these days? First he's an alien, then a god, now a magician." He pointed at Lucas. "That look like magic to you?"

Shona was unfazed. "What is magic, Sergio? Just a trick that hasn't been figured out yet. Any sufficiently advanced technology is indistinguishable from magic. Arthur C. Clarke said that."

He groaned. "And we're back to aliens."

Shona continued. "The point is if you had that power, that ability, then there would be quantifiable value in being worshiped. It would be like . . . " She looked at the sandwich in her hand. "Like food."

Sergio stifled a laugh at that, but none of the men made any direct comments.

She went on. "Morgan went to the Christmas store because all that stuff . . . it nourishes him. He wanted me to sing to him, to praise him, because it made him stronger. Whatever Saint Nicholas is, nobody worshiped it or was even thinking of it before McCulloch came along. Whatever name it might once have had was forgotten, meaningless, leaving it starved of energy. Until he mistook it for Saint Nicholas. Gifted it a new name. And all the spoils that go with it."

"So any time some kid in this town thinks of Santa Claus, writes him a letter or sings a song about him, that's power he can use?" asked Richie.

Shona nodded. "And the greater the myth of Santa Claus gets, the more powerful he becomes."

Richie clucked his tongue, thoughtfully. "Maybe we shouldn't be talking about him."

"But we can," said Shona. "Because we're not a part of it. We're not locked into his psychic network the way the people who come from this town are. Our minds aren't clouded the way theirs are. We don't see the things they do. We can't be manipulated like they can. That's why we're dangerous. That's why he wants us dead."

"I don't feel dangerous." Sergio swirled the liquid in the bottom of his glass. "I feel . . . too fucking sober." He poured the shot down his throat, then tossed the empty glass over his shoulder. It smashed against the wall.

"Thanks," said Einar.

Sergio lifted the empty bottle. "Got any more?"

The barman waved a hand at the shelves of spirits lined up beneath the broken mirror. "Help yourself."

While the contractor rose drunkenly to his feet and made his way to the bar, Richie said to Shona, "If we're dangerous, that means there's got to be something we can do, right? What can we do?"

She considered the question, then turned to Einar. "The town belongs to him, because he put his name on it. Isn't that what you said?"

The barman cleared his throat and again quoted the line from McHattie's sermon. "Rename your land in my honor so that when I am weak and starving I may claim whatever grows upon it as my own, share in your bounty, and be fortified."

"The name is the key," said Shona. "He took the name for himself and with the name he claimed the town."

"So now he's Rumpel-fucking-stiltskin," Sergio muttered as he rooted through bottles, knocking a couple onto the floor.

"Hey, there could be something in that, Sergio," said Richie, getting on board with Shona's theorizing. "Names are important where demons are concerned. They say you can control a demon by knowing its true name."

"And now it's demons." Sergio turned to face Lucas, still behind the bar, still tied to the chair and still unconscious, drool pouring from his misshapen mouth in a thick, quivering stream. He nudged the kid with his foot and got no response. "Sure looks like a demon. I'll give you that much."

"It's the same with the occult," said Shona. "Black magic, chaos, Satanism, they're all based around symbols. Different words and emblems contain power that can be utilized for protection or destruction. When you think about it, that marries up pretty close with what we know about Saint Nicholas. He wears the personification of Christmas like battle armor. Wields its tropes and images like weapons. So does Morgan, now."

"So he's a Satanist?" said Einar.

Sergio snorted a laugh as he uncorked a bottle of white rum, his hunt for more mescal abandoned. "Satanist, demon, god, alien . . . why not all of the above?"

Shona ignored him. "But nothing wields more power than the name. It's the greatest symbol of all. He controls everything the name touches, which . . . in *this* town . . . is everything."

"That's right." Einar nodded. "Entitled to share in the land's bounty for as long as it bears his name. That was the deal."

"Yeah, it's a great fucking theory," said Sergio, rum dribbling down his chin. Turning his bloodshot eyes on Shona, he said, "You got some imagination to come up with all that. All credit to you. I almost want to believe it myself. But you're forgetting one thing."

Shona could smell his overproof breath from the other side of the bar. She watched him a moment, the way his head bobbed and body swayed from side to side. There was a good chance he'd pass out drunk before managing to articulate what he wanted to tell her, but she indulged him anyway. "What's that?"

He leaned across the bar toward her, lowering his voice to a conspiratorial whisper. "This town's name is *not* St. Nicholas."

"What do you mean?"

"Exactly what I said. As of December first, this place officially became Coldwell Slopes. Signed, sealed, notarized. So if this wannabe Santa Claus fuck came here to raid the pantry before the locks got changed, he's about twenty-five days too late. St. Nicholas the town don't exist any more."

There was silence for a long moment, before Shona said, "I didn't know that."

"No." Sergio took another swig. "The truth is, it don't matter what this place is called. And we're never going to know where the son of a bitch came from, what he is or what he wants. And we're sure as shit never going to be able to Sherlock Holmes a way to stop him that doesn't involve a stack of dynamite and, more than likely, taking an ax to a bunch of fucked-up mutant schoolkids. But me?" He belched, shaking his head. "I don't want any part of that. No thank you." He tapped a finger against the bottle. "I'm all right where I am."

Shona didn't have any response to that. She felt like she'd been holding a balloon that Sergio had just stuck a pin in. Perhaps it was true she'd let herself get carried away, but for a while she'd thought she was onto something—at least in the right ballpark. She turned to Curtis and asked him, "What do you think? Curtis?" He reclined in the booth, eyes closed, jaw slack, his body perfectly still. It occurred to her then he hadn't spoken a word since Einar started telling the story. *He's sleeping*, she told herself, moving closer. *Almost certainly definitely sleeping*. She slid in beside him at the booth, her mind throwing up images of the damage Devon had done trying to tear his heart from his chest. *Not dead, not dead, not dead, not dead.* Biting her lip, she placed her fingers against his neck, checking for a pulse, then let out a sigh of relief. "Thank fuck for that."

He stirred, eyes fluttering open. "Hmmm?"

"It's okay." She patted him gently on the arm. "Just making sure you were still alive. You can rest."

He looked like he was drifting off again, when Richie slammed his fist down on the table. "It's the signs!"

Curtis's eyes sprang open. "The what now?" he moaned, speaking for the room.

"The signs," Richie repeated. He went into the pocket of his coat, produced a folded wad of work documents in a plastic bag and began waving it like a winning lottery ticket. "My team was tasked with changing all the town signs, swapping out ones that said 'St. Nicholas' for ones that said 'Coldwell Slopes'. We did a whole bunch on the roads and some of the buildings on the outskirts. We changed the signs on the town hall after Miss Wong moved in and at the police station. But there were some—historic, treasured—Morgan asked us not to change until after Christmas, so as not to upset anyone. Said St. Nicholas deserved to have one last Christmas Day before the beginning of a new era."

Sounds like Morgan, Shona thought.

Richie stabbed a finger at his stack of papers. "We were supposed to take them all down first thing on the twenty-sixth. I've got the list right here!"

There was a moment of silence as everyone considered what he'd just told them, wondering if it could be right. Then all the men looked to Shona, wanting to hear her verdict before offering any comment of their own. "It's . . . possible," she said. "Tenuous, but . . . maybe? It could be."

"It's got to be," said Richie, rising from his seat, more animated now than any of them had ever seen. "The signs are the symbols that mark his territory. While they're still around, the town still bears his name! That's why they killed the priest! In case someone heard his story and figured that out!"

Einar, at the far end of the bar, on the other side of Lucas, leaned over to catch Shona's eye. "You think he's right?"

"Maybe." She shrugged and turned to Curtis. "What do you think?"

He shifted uncomfortably, trying to push himself up into a sitting position. "I, uh . . . I think I might have dozed off for most of what y'all were talking about, but uh . . . If that's what you think . . . I'll try anything."

And Sergio scoffed.

"Oh for fuck sake, man!" Shona rolled her eyes, losing patience with the contractor's dismissive attitude. "We know you think it's all bullshit! We know! But what else do you expect us to . . . ." The sentence died on her lips as she turned to face him.

He snorted. And blood sprayed from his lips and nostrils.

"Sergio?" Richie's voice was suddenly so timid it could barely be heard over the sound of rattling from behind the bar.

Sergio's whole body was shaking, convulsing against the countertop, sending vibrations through the bottles, glasses and assorted detritus littering its surface. His face was a sweating, bleeding knot of pain, eyes bulging from their sockets, pleading for help. Einar, standing on the other side of Lucas, was closest. He rushed to assist, then halted, cursing in Icelandic as he saw what was happening.

The boy was awake. And in contrast to when Lucas had passed out, there was hardly anything about him that still resembled a boy. His arms had grown spines like shark teeth, slicing through the ropes binding him to the chair. He'd struck out with the gnarled, leathery claw that had once been his right hand, sinking its hooks into Sergio's back, between the shoulder blades, punching holes in his lungs, blood fizzing out through the wounds. The fingers curled in his flesh, closing into a fist around his spine. Sergio tried to scream, but could only hiss blood through gritted teeth, his whole body shaking uncontrollably. Then Lucas lashed out with his other arm, his pinched hand crunching into the back of Sergio's skull.

From where they sat, Curtis and Shona had an unobstructed view as Sergio's eyeballs popped from his head, forced out by the jutting prongs of Lucas's talons and twin jets of pulverized brain matter. The ejected orbs were still in mid-air as Lucas drove the contractor's head into the bar, digging his nails into its surface. With his claw anchored in the wood—and what remained of Sergio's head—Lucas jolted upright, his chair smashing against Einar, knocking him to the floor, and, like an Olympic gymnast, he swung himself up and over to land prone atop the bar.

Shona saw what had become of the boy's head—a gray ball of snapping jaws and teeth—and all lingering hope for him extinguished. While he'd slept, his skeletal structure had reformed and pale skin tightened across his bones, flattening his features till no trace of them remained on his face. No trace of humanity in his eyes, set hard and yellow, deep within the recesses of gaping sockets. As they met hers, she heard again the promise he'd made to her, echoing within her skull.

I'll kill you . . . and it'll feel good.

Then he pounced.

36.

THE PREVIOUS EVENING, as St. Nicholas's Wintertainment celebration had gotten underway, Kendra had met up with her friends to eat, drink, quietly mock the crowds and make tentative plans for how to spend the rest of their night. They had lingered past the closing of the show, watching as all the stall holders packed up their wares and drifted home. They remained the last stragglers in the square, huddled around a burning fire pit, till Dan finally came and extinguished it. Kendra had left then with Bailey, noting as they crossed the square all the evidence of celebration abandoned in the snow, like wreckage left on the battlefield. Tray tables and folding chairs were stacked next to collapsed fairground games and dismantled rigging, half-hidden by tarp. Wintertainment banners, adorned with Coldwell the Singing Snowman's welcoming face, still fluttered from the lampposts. She knew the members of the town's festival committee—her father among them—had agreed to do a proper job of packing everything away a few days later, once they'd all sobered up. For the moment, all the apparatus of merrymaking would sit out in the square, meaning that if the townsfolk so desired, the celebration could, at the drop of a hat, begin again.

Now, as Kendra burst through the doors of the town hall, she saw it already had.

In the few minutes she'd wasted inside, humoring Ling as the woman fruitlessly combed through the children's stash of broken trinkets, before she'd finally come to her senses, grabbed the gun, and fled, the square had filled with people.

Apparently en masse, the townsfolk had poured from their homes and into the street, conglomerating at the bandstand. Some carried trays of food or pots of coffee, even bottles of wine and liquor. They sang and laughed and began pulling tables and chairs from the snow. They plugged the lights back in, re-lit the fires and got the audio system working.

Kendra, racing down the steps and across the street, was met with a human wall of conviviality. It swallowed her up. She staggered through the mob, disoriented by its heat, the cloying warmth of joy and laughter pressing in at her shoulders. The crowd felt bigger than it had the night before. It seemed every single man and woman in town had decided to make the pilgrimage. Everyone who was still alive.

Caught up in the mania of the moment, Kendra's mind struggled to make sense of what was happening. Overwhelmed by *deja vu*, she felt as though she'd been transported back to the previous night, all the horrors she'd endured undone. She spent a few moments searching for her father's cider stall before snapping out of the fantasy and remembering he was dead. They'd all be dead soon.

"Kendra!" She spun about at the sound of a voice she knew. Noah Fessenden and Marshall Boyd loped toward her through the crowd. Her friends. Her *only* friends, now Bailey was dead. She'd last seen them on this very spot when she'd assured them she'd be back in twenty minutes with booze. Noah's long face wore a sardonically outraged sneer. "Fuck have you been? We were supposed to be getting fucked up."

"Yeah," said Marshall, matching the grouchy tone. "We waited for like . . . an hour."

"It wasn't an hour," said Noah. "But still, it's like . . . the fuck? Y'know?"

"Yeah," said Kendra, still too confused by all that was happening around them to articulate a coherent explanation of all she'd suffered in the past twenty-four hours. "I'm sorry, guys."

"It's cool." Marshall shrugged, the slight already forgotten. "Just don't bail tonight. We've got the sweetest pad picked out."

"Yeah, guess fucking where!" Noah grinned.

"I . . . " She wanted to speak to them. Wanted to find the words that would allow her to communicate something worth saying, but it was beyond her. In their eyes she saw the same looks Dan, Terry, and Lonnie had shown her a few hours earlier, utterly oblivious to what was happening around them. She knew her face was bruised and swollen. There was blood in her hair. Blood on her scratched and torn snowsuit. And in her right hand she clutched a gun. She knew Noah and Marshall were both idiots. It was one of the things she really liked about them. But as dumb as they were, they weren't *that* dumb. They genuinely couldn't see the state she was in. To them, the veil covered their eyes and everything was sugar cookies and candy canes.

When she didn't answer them, Marshall blurted out, "The church!"

"The church?" she echoed, not entirely sure what they were talking about.

"The doors are unlocked," said Noah. "Nobody's there now McHattie's dead. And the basement's heated all night."

"Right." Kendra nodded, finally understanding. "You want to party."

"I mean . . . after this," said Marshall, gesturing to the crowd around them.

"What is this?" Kendra asked.

The boys stared at her a moment, both squinting as they valiantly tried to think through their brain fog to recall why they'd come to the square. "Something's happening," said Noah. "Some kind of show, I guess. That's what I heard, anyway."

"Who told you that?"

His squint intensified and he laughed. "I don't know, man. It was like . . . Somebody said it, y'know? Otherwise . . . why would anyone even be here?"

That was a good question, she thought. And worried she knew the answer. "Okay. Take care of yourselves." She pushed past them, determined to reach the edge of the square, hurry back home and kill Saint Nicholas before it was too late.

"If you're going to get booze, remember to bring it back this time," Marshall called after her.

"Yeah," Noah added. "Don't make us do Christmas Day sober!"

Ling never found Kendra in the crowd. She hunted for her, calling her name, but there were too many people dancing around her, too many grinning faces shoved into hers, too many attempts to shake her hand or fill it with a drink, too many over-familiar greetings.

"Great to see you, Miss Wong!"

"Merry Christmas to you, Miss Wong!"

"Are you having fun?"

"How will you be celebrating?"

"You must come to ours, Miss Wong! You must!"

She tried to tell them they were all in danger. Told them the security office and Samuel Street Hotel were littered with bodies. Tried to explain an evil entity had taken control of their children and had been methodically murdering members of their community. Gertrude dead. Owen dead. Morgan transformed into some kind of hell-beast. But none of the snatches of sentences she managed to utter without interruption made any sense. And nobody cared to listen. They were all having too great a time. In the midst of a town-wide massacre, they were throwing a party.

"Oh, isn't this wonderful," the half-deaf choir teacher, Ms. Beaverbrook, gushed. "To think I was just sitting at home, all alone, no TV, no radio, watching the clock countdown to midnight. And suddenly I got it in my head to take a stroll into town and found . . . this! Oh, you do deserve the credit, Miss Wong. Do you know what you've done? You've made this place feel like a true community again!"

"Ms. Beaverbrook." Ling gripped her by the shoulders, over-enunciating so she could read her lips. "The children are monsters!"

The old woman laughed. "Yes, they certainly can be a handful. But I must say their singing has come on leaps and bounds in the last few weeks."

"Don't you understand," Ling yelled. "If you stay here, you are all going to die!"

Beaverbrook tilted her head forward, straining to hear over the noise of the crowd. "To what, sorry?"

"To die!"

"Today? Why, today's Christmas day, of course! Or very nearly!" She tapped her wristwatch. "Would you excuse me? I must get a drink to toast the bells!"

Ling staggered away from the conversation dejected, bereft of ideas. She found Cindee sitting on the steps of the bandstand, looking just as lost. "I don't know what to do," she told her. "I'm sorry. I . . . I don't."

The girl stared back at her with an expression that said nothing at all. Then somebody yelled, "Cindee!"

Ling spun around to see a woman fighting her way through the crowd. She had curly brown hair like Cindee and was dragging a man behind her in a hand-knitted scarf and ratty red duffle coat. Both were skinny and pale to the point of appearing sickly. *Look like vegans*, Ling thought.

"Mom?" Cindee said. "Dad?"

"My God, I thought you were in bed," the woman replied, without anger. "How long have you been here, all alone?"

"I've been keeping an eye on her," said Ling. "There's no cause for concern." There was, of course, plenty of cause for concern. But she knew she wouldn't be able to convince Cindee's parents of that. Their eyes were as clouded as the rest.

"Oh, Miss Wong," the woman exclaimed. "Thank you so much. That's too kind of—"

"What are you doing here?" Ling asked her.

The couple exchanged nervous glances. "We . . . heard about the party. Thought it sounded like fun."

"Who told you?"

The glances grew more confused. "I think it was . . . You know . . . I'm not sure I can . . . "

"I don't remember who said it," said Cindee's father. "But I do remember thinking it sounded like fun."

He finished his sentence in the same moment the sound system erupted into life, filling the air with the opening bars of the Jackson 5's 'Santa Claus is Comin' to Town'. The noise shocked Cindee onto her feet and sent her running to her mother, throwing her arms around her waist, burying her face in the folds of her overcoat.

Mr.s Joyce laughed. "Oh dear. Honey, it's all right." She patted the girl's head and smiled at Ling. "Poor Cindee's always had a bit of a phobia where Santa Claus is concerned."

"Santa Claus-trophobia, we call it," said Mr. Joyce.

"No explanation for it. Just . . . frightens her, for some reason."

"Imagine," Ling said, then grabbed each of the couple by the arm, pulling them in close. "What if I were to ask you both to leave right now? Go straight home and take Cindee with you? In fact, how about if I came with you?"

They kept smiling, though their eyes showed only bafflement. "Why would we do that?" Mr. Joyce asked.

"Indulge me. I promise to make it worth your while."

Still looking perplexed, they agreed and left the bandstand, heading out of the square. But as they reached the perimeter of the crowd, Ling brought them to a halt.

"Didn't you say you wanted to leave?" Cindee's mother asked.

"No," said Ling, her eyes on the child standing out in the street, his body a twisted horror in the glare of the lamps, his yellow eyes studying the crowd. "We're staying right here."

Kendra had only made it as far as Third Avenue—two streets over from the square—when loud music started, making her flinch. *Saaaanta Claus is comin' to town! Saaaanta Claus is comin' to town!* She was glad to be walking away from it, the lyrics growing more indecipherable the further she went. But then she stepped into the alleyway connecting Third and Second—and heard something so much worse. "Keeeeendra . . . "

She froze, watching his shadow as it took form ahead of her, a crooked corpse rising from the snow, an oily demon bubbling up from the earth, his voice now so warped it no longer sounded his own. Yet she recognized it. "Devon?"

37.

IN THE MOMENT before he leapt, while his claw was still embedded in what remained of Sergio's skull and the others looked on in stunned silence, Lucas opened his mouth and roared. His jaws no longer operated like a human's but like a snake's, stretching wide enough to swallow a bowling ball, exposing twin rows of gleaming, crooked teeth and a tongue studded with razor-sharp spines like the ones along his arms.

It wasn't a great distance from the bar to the booth in which Shona and Curtis cowered. It took less than a second for Lucas to go from one to the other, crossing the gap in a single bound. That didn't leave enough time for Shona to grab a weapon or get out of the way. Yet she had time to imagine how it would feel when that mouth closed over her face, teeth chewing through her neck and serrated tongue winding around her head, its barbs lacerating her skin, stripping the tender flesh from her cheeks.

He landed with one foot on the table in front of her, one on the seat behind, the pointed hooks of his toes piercing the upholstery. He swiped at her, spraying Sergio's blood and brain matter into her face but failing to connect as Curtis pulled her back and into his arms. Even in the midst of the chaos, she registered his embrace, recalling how it felt when his hands had squeezed her that morning, a long, long time ago. She'd enjoyed how it felt—his strength, his heat, his tenderness—and had been in no doubt she wanted more. Dying in his arms, however, had not been in her plans. Nevertheless, she appreciated his efforts to protect her, futile as they were. Lucas pivoted back with his other claw, and this time there was nowhere for her to retreat and nothing she could do but close her eyes.

There was a sound she mistook for the apocalypse. The end of her world. The noise of her soul being ripped from existence. But there was no pain. If Lucas touched her, she didn't even feel it. She heard an explosion. A mighty clap of thunder that sent waves of chaos rippling through reality, tearing open the universe and scattering its stars like so many fragments of broken crystal.

Then silence. And winter flooded the room.

She opened her eyes, breathing in the frozen air, to find she was still in the booth, Curtis still holding on tight, both of them covered in broken glass and Lucas . . . gone. Slowly, she raised herself up, glass shards spilling from her clothing. She looked over to the bar and saw Einar with the shotgun raised to his shoulder, smoke hissing from the barrel. As the ringing in her ears faded to a low buzz, she realized what had just happened. He'd blasted the kid out the window.

"Sergio?" Richie spoke from his table on the other side of the room. He'd stood up from his chair but hadn't taken a step away from it.

"He's dead," said Einar, giving the contractor's mashed head a cursory glance as he stepped around the bar. He racked the shotgun as he approached the window, reloading with a shell taken from the pocket of his sweater. "You okay?" The question was directed at Shona.

"I think so." She extricated herself from Curtis's grip, then turned to face him. "You okay?"

He nodded stiffly, his eyes wide, as if frozen in panic. "Sure. Let's . . . let's go with that."

The Malamute's window was gone, along with most of the neon Molson's sign. Einar pushed aside what remained to lean out, then sighed. "Shit."

Shona joined him at the window and peered down, expecting to see Lucas's broken, buckshot-riddled body. But the boy—the creature—was gone. Fresh footprints trailed through the snow, leading toward the center of town. "Shit," she echoed.

"Y'all hear music?" Curtis asked, poking a finger in his ear. "Tell me that ain't just me."

Shona's own hearing was still recovering from the shotgun's boom, but she listened and, after a moment, was able to detect the words carried on the wind. *You better watch out. You better not cry. Better not pout. I'm telling you why . . .*

"I think we're running out of time." She turned away from the window and limped over to Richie. "You feeling pretty confident about the signs idea? Think it'll work?"

"Huh?" He stared at her dumbly for a moment, like he'd forgotten who she was, before returning his gaze to Sergio's mangled corpse.

"Richie!" Shona slapped him, hoping it would snap him out of his stupor. "If we want to take the signs down, we'd better go now. Do you agree?"

"Yeah." He nodded, his breath shallow, trying to maintain his composure. His hands fumbled as he went through his documents to find the map. "There . . . there are six." He unfolded the page and pointed out the markings with a shaking finger. "One on the road into town, one at the park, the school, the post office, old fire station and the mining museum."

"Three on the north side of town, three on the south," said Shona, studying the plan. "Simple enough. So we split up."

"What?" The booth rattled, scattering glass shards as Curtis clambered awkwardly out of it. "We're not going to split up."

"We are. And we don't really have time to talk about it. Look here." Shona showed him the map. "The road, the park, the school. It might take you twenty minutes, but it'll take me over an hour."

"You don't—"

"My leg is *fucked*, Curtis. I'll slow you down too much. But this . . . " Her finger traced a line from the post office to the fire station to the museum. "It's a few hundred yards in what's basically a straight line. I think I could manage it."

"If your leg's really that bad, you shouldn't go anywhere. You should stay right here!"

"And wait for Lucas to come back? Or one of his wee friends? No. We need to put a stop to this—if it's even possible—and we need to do it now."

"I'll go with her." Einar emptied a box of shotgun shells onto the bar and began stuffing them in his pockets. "Watch her back."

"Thanks," Shona said, then turned to Richie. "What do we need?"

He shrugged. "Some are just wood, some metal, at least one brass and brick. I can't remember which are which. Saws, hammers, and axes will do for most. A chisel, if we can find one, or a crowbar. A blowtorch would be good."

"There's a workshed downstairs, around back." Einar tugged on his cap. "Let's go."

He and Richie spent the next few minutes gathering together

what tools they could find, while Shona made her way slowly back down the staircase, Curtis at her side to keep her from falling.

"I really . . . I'm not sure we should be doing this," he said.

"I'm not sure about anything. But it's worth a shot."

"We'd be safer sticking together."

"Not necessarily."

"If this is because . . . " He trailed off, sighed, frustrated with trying to explain himself. "I know I haven't done the best job of protecting you."

She paused before taking another step. "What?"

"In the truck, at your place. On the roof with Devon. Back there . . . with Lucas. I know I could have done better. Acted faster . . . It's like a bad habit I can't break. When shit goes down, more often than not . . . I freeze."

"Curtis, just . . . shut up." She gave him a sympathetic pat on the arm. "It's sweet, honestly, that you would worry. But the truth is I haven't had the time or energy to take a mental note of everything you've done today—or haven't done—and judge you on it. I'm not giving you marks out of ten. I just want to survive. I want us all to survive."

"I just . . . wouldn't want to let you down."

She sighed, not unkindly. "I'll tell you what your problem is, Curtis. You think too much."

His eyes widened in surprise. "I've never been accused of that."

"You haven't let me down. And you don't need to worry. You and me? Whatever we've got here? I'm committed. For at least the next couple of weeks. Okay?"

He smiled at that. "Okay."

"Only . . . do me a favor?" She moved her hand from his arm to his cheek. "Don't die. That would really spoil the holidays."

He nodded, leaned in and kissed her.

"Hey, look at this!" Einar returned, interrupting the moment. In one hand he clutched a canvas bag full of tools, his shotgun sitting on top. His other hand held a rope dragging an old, wooden sled. "Forgot I had it." He nodded to Shona. "Jump on!"

She limped over, with Curtis's help, and took a seat. "Comfy."

Einar set the bag down beside her. "I'll pull the sleigh. You keep watch for . . . children."

Richie came crunching through the snow with a toolbox and

hammer. He looked ashen-faced, haunted, like he was barely holding it together.

"You ready?" Curtis asked.

"Ready as I'll ever—" He flinched, ducking down as a firework tore through the night sky and exploded in a burst of green and red light. Others followed in its wake, screaming in ascent and roaring like cannons, painting the town below in nauseating festive colors. It was clear they were coming from the town square, where a celebration was in full swing.

Shona checked her watch. "Midnight. Merry Christmas, everyone."

38.

KENDRA PEERED THROUGH the darkness, studying the way Devon's body moved, swaying like it was underwater, his silhouette undulating like liquid. "What . . . what happened to you?"

He laughed and his teeth shone through the shadows, white as scorched magnesium. "I fell. But then I got better. So much better. Come closer and I'll show you."

She took a step back. "Stay away from me."

The smile dimmed, like a flame going out. "You don't have to be afraid, Kendra."

"I'm not." Her fingers closed around the grip of the gun, hidden in her snowsuit pocket. "I'm warning you to stay away."

He sucked in a long, deep breath and exhaled it in a billowing mustard cloud. "I'm not going to hurt you. I never wanted to hurt you."

"Your little friends are killing everyone."

"I don't care about them."

"You brought that fucking *thing* into our house! You caused all this!"

"And it's all been worth it. You'll see. Soon you'll understand." He took a step toward her.

"Stay back."

He sucked at his glimmering teeth, making his disdain for her attitude apparent. "You hated this town, Kendra. You were never happy here. Never wanted to be here. You hated your life. So why cry over it, when we're about to get something so much better? We can be happy in the new world he's building for us. We can be together. Learn to love one another."

Despite her mounting terror, Kendra couldn't suppress a laugh. "Love? That's the sickest thing you've said yet. I don't love you, Devon. I don't even *like* you."

"I know." He took another step. "But you will. When I show you what I've learned. What I've become." His next step brought him out of the shadows, into the light.

Kendra felt her stomach lurch. "What . . . the fuck."

She was staring at a living cartoon. A Christmas elf that had clawed its way out of a Merrie Melodies short, its long limbs twisting like nervous snakes, skin pulsing like Technicolor film stock and eyes a pair of swollen lemon light-bulbs. He stretched a hand toward her, its four fingers splayed beneath a soft, white glove. "I lost this hand." He uttered the words with a kind of dazed reverence. "And I fell a long way down. I broke. But I went to sleep and when I woke up, I was all better. Better than better. Thanks to him. This is his power. He makes magic real."

It sounded like the start of a song. Kendra took another step back, afraid he might begin dancing toward her on his bowed legs, accompanied by an off-key chorus of clockwork toys. "This isn't magic."

"Oh, but it *is* . . . " The painted-on colors of his costume—green tunic with candy-cane striped stockings, a pointed cap and boots with curved toes—glowed like electric lanterns when he spoke. "It's the oldest magic the world has ever known. He's teaching me how to use it. I can teach you."

"Not interested."

"It's wonderful. It's so, so wonderful."

"Devon." Her voice cracked as, for the first time, she realized how truly lost he was, and sadness overwhelmed her. "There's no coming back from this."

He giggled. "But I don't want to go back. What I want . . . is you." Again, he stretched his hand toward her.

She wasn't sure if he expected her to take it. "That's a sick joke."

"I'm not joking. All I want for Christmas . . . is *you*." His gloved hand closed into a fist and he pulled his arm back.

Kendra felt her body pulled with it, like he'd thrown an invisible leash around her torso. She screamed, couldn't help it, tried to take out the gun, but then he did it again. He squeezed his fist and her arms snapped to her side, her body clutched in his projected grip. He tugged and she lurched forward, the toes of her boots dragging through the snow.

"Now . . . " His breath steamed toward her as she drew close enough to touch and he opened his hand, reaching out to caress her face. The instant his fingers spread apart, the force binding her body melted away. She dropped, but didn't fall, coughed, drew the gun and fired.

It was like shooting a television set. The bark and flash of the gun was answered by an eruption of white light and a sound like shattering glass. Devon crumpled, falling back into the shadows. Kendra, swaying unsteadily on her feet, squinted through a mist of curling gun smoke, its tendrils twisting between the clouds of her panicked breaths.

"Devon?" Her voice quivered as much as the hand holding the pistol. She didn't want him to answer. She wanted him to be lying dead in the darkness. But she had to make sure. She edged forward, prodding the shadows with the gun's barrel. "Devon?"

His hand struck out from the darkness. No longer plush, plump and white-gloved, it had transformed into a bony black claw, the scraggy fingers tipped by spears of yellow bone. They struck Kendra's arm, slicing into her wrist and sending the gun spinning away. Yelling, she dove after it, snatching it up from snow dappled red in the geyser of her blood. She turned back to see Devon stepping out of the alley, his deformed and distended body flickering and hissing like static.

She knelt in a slush of blood and snow, trying to apply pressure to her gushing wrist with one hand while gripping the gun with the other. There was no feeling in her fingers, no sense of control, but she managed to line up a shot and fired. The bullet went wide of the mark and the gun, again, slid from her grasp. This time she didn't see where it went.

"Must we keep doing this?" Devon pressed a hand to his own wound, a hole in his stuttering abdomen leaking yellow. His face crawled and disassembled around his eyes and teeth, like his flesh had been traded for a disorganized swarm of roiling maggots. "You hurt me, then I hurt you . . . It can't go on."

Kendra scrambled in the snow, searching for the gun, struggling to see beneath flashes of red, pink, and green—the first of the fireworks bursting overhead. It couldn't have fallen far, but she went back and forth, fearing every swipe at the snow only buried it deeper. She couldn't find it. She heard herself whimper before Devon spoke again.

"We're family." He inched closer. "We shouldn't be fighting." She was nearly in his arms now. "Not on Christmas Day."

She turned, bolted up onto her feet, and ran.

39.

It's the mooost wonderful tiiiiime of the year . . .
Have a holly jolly Christmas, it's the best time of the year . . .
Everybody's waiting for the man with the bag . . .

ONE HOLIDAY CLASSIC after another after another blared over the sound system while fireworks lit up the sky. Ling was surrounded by smiling faces, the crush of the crowd and the strength of their spirit creating a warm, cozy atmosphere—hot enough to make her sweat, even in the sub-zero depths of Canadian winter. She pushed her way through them, ignoring invitations to chat and rejecting offers of freshly grilled hamburgers, toasted marshmallows and chilled champagne. The people of St. Nicholas were celebrating like it was their last night on Earth, unaware it almost certainly was. She navigated her way to one corner of the square, then another and another, hunting for a way out. Each time she reached the edge of the crowd, she met another child, patiently standing guard, ready to catch anyone who tried to escape.

Ling wished she had a weapon. The pistol would certainly have been useful to have right now. She thought back to the hunting knife she'd found in the clinic and how tightly she'd held onto it. Now she couldn't recall what had become of it. She supposed there might be something in the square she could turn to her defense—perhaps a marshmallow skewer or a broken beer bottle—but everything she set her eyes on looked ineffectual against the whetted teeth and claws of the schoolchildren.

There was still a chance, she knew, that Kendra would succeed. She'd searched, but hadn't been able to find the girl anywhere in the crowd. That meant there was a chance she'd escaped the square before the children had woken up. And there was a chance she might be able to intercept Santa Claus, either at her home or in the street. And a chance she might get the drop on him, blow his head off and save the day. A chance, a chance, a chance.

Don't panic, she told herself. *Don't freak out. Don't be afraid, don't be afraid, don't be afraid.* She repeated it over and over in her head, part of an effort to slow her racing heart. What she wanted was to clear the terror from her mind so she had room to think, to devise a way out. But the more she repeated the mantra, the more she began to believe it. Maybe, after all, it was true. Maybe things weren't as bad as she'd first thought. Maybe there was no reason to be afraid. Not anymore.

"Miss Wong." She felt a hand on her arm and turned to greet the grinning, grizzled face of Jake Hodgkiss. He stood alongside his wife Hilary, her face entirely hidden beneath a hood, scarf and goggles. "I know I've said it before, but I'm going to say it again. Merry Christmas!"

She stared at him, briefly lost in the study of his wrinkled, weather-beaten skin, the wisps of white hair sprouting from his scalp. He was tall but frail, spine bent so his rheumy eyes were level with hers. Hilary was short and stout, with one arm permanently locked around his, acting as ballast to keep him from toppling one way or the other. Both so, so old.

"Mr. Hodgkiss." She reached out to him. "You shouldn't be here."

"Ah, bull-pucky!" He brushed off her concern. "Where else would we be?"

"At home, in bed. It's so late . . . and so cold."

He grinned. "I'm used to the cold, Miss Wong. Spend enough time in this part of the world and it'll chill the blood to the point you don't even notice it. Might take a man a while, but ninety-odd years will do it."

She shook her head, suddenly so sad for reasons she couldn't articulate, even to herself. "You'll die out here."

His smile didn't falter. It was like he'd heard the same line a million times before. "If we thought like that, we'd never leave the damn house! Now here!" He thrust a cup into her hand. "This'll warm you up!"

She lifted it to her lips, sniffed, and took a sip. Mulled wine. As warming as he claimed. "Thank you."

"Added a shot of amaretto for extra heat," he said. "Wanted to congratulate you."

"Whatever for?" She didn't deserve congratulations. It was her fault they were all trapped here, penned in like cattle ready for the slaughter. "I haven't done you any good."

"Why certainly you have. Be in no doubt about that. Miss Wong, I . . . I owe you an apology. The things I said to you yesterday, why I couldn't have been more wrong. I see that now. Hilly and me, we've lived in St. Nicholas all our lives. That's the best part of two centuries between us. We've known plenty of good times and plenty of bad. The best were always at Christmas. But in all that time we've never known a Christmas like this one. It's . . . it's magical, is what it is. You can feel it, can't you?"

She could. A warmth beyond the sweetly spiced alcohol. Thick in the air, dampening the brain and clouding the vision, smoothing the edges, making everything soft.

"I can feel it," she said.

He raised a cup of his own. "And wouldn't you agree it's wonderful?"

It was. She had to concede it most certainly was.

The fireworks ceased in the same moment the music stopped and Hodgkiss lifted his cup high over his head and cried, "A cheer for Ling Wong! The savior of St. Nicholas!"

And all around, the people cheered. Ling felt a wave of adoration wash over her. Into her. Through her. A torrent of emotion audible, physical and ethereal that wrapped around her like a scarlet ribbon and squeezed, squeezed, squeezed until it had wrung all the fear and anxiety and terrible, distressing thoughts right out of her. Until nothing remained but love, wonder and joy.

She was laughing. She was crying. She was alive.

Everything would be all right. She understood now. At last. All the horrors of the last day and night were cleansed from her mind in an instant, smashed to pieces under the weight of this community's love, their fragments dissipating into the ether. It was like waking from the most awful nightmare to discover it had all been a dream—and suddenly it was impossible to recall what she had been so worried about.

Sleigh bells. She could hear sleigh bells, their rhythmic jingling bouncing through the square. Vaguely, she wondered which song was playing now. So many of the old hits began the same way. But the jingling continued. No drums kicked in. No guitars, no brass, no vocals. After a moment, she realized the sound wasn't being played through the speakers.

It was coming from the sky.

"Ho, ho, ho!" His voice boomed as loud as any firework, echoing through the clouds. "Ho, ho, hooooo!"

The crowd moved as one, tilting their heads back, smiles and eyes wide, to bear witness to his arrival. Disbelieving, Ling looked with them. *Surely not*, she told herself. *It can't be.*

But it was.

40.

CURTIS WAS GLAD of the music and the fireworks and the pervasive roar of the crowd as he and Richie raced down Eighth Avenue, scurrying rat-like through the shadows as they made their way to the road out of town. The noise was a reassuring signal that all the townsfolk and, presumably, all the children were still gathered in the square, their attentions focused on celebration. Hopefully it meant Morgan and whatever had been passing itself off as Santa Claus were there too, though that didn't stop him glancing nervously over his shoulder every two seconds.

They followed the road a quarter mile out, to the sign which stood at the very periphery of the town's light. Beyond, all was darkness.

The sign was simply built from galvanized aluminum, designed to withstand the elements. The town's name was spelled out in a quaint, old-fashioned font, written in reflective paint above a slogan Curtis had never heard before. It read: 'Welcome to St. Nicholas! Santa's home from home.'

It was six feet wide and ten feet high, which meant Richie had to climb up on Curtis's back to reach the bolts securing the sign to the posts. Working them lose required a wrench and a hammer and a hell of a lot of panting, cursing and pounding on metal with hands numb from the cold. By the time they got it down, both men were sweating, sore and exhausted. Then, with it lying on the ground, they used whatever sharp-edged tools they had to scratch and score the name till it was unreadable. It took more time and a lot more energy than Curtis would have liked.

"One down," Richie said, dragging himself onto his feet.

Curtis didn't answer. His ears were full of the sound of his strained breaths and his jack-hammering heartbeat. As it eased, silence descended and he noticed the music and fireworks had stopped. He looked back along the road into town and saw there was still a glow in the sky over the square. But all sounds of merriment had ceased.

"Guess the party's over," Richie said, then shrugged. "Or just getting started."

Curtis turned and looked the other way, along the snow-blanketed trail that led to the world beyond St. Nicholas. Hidden more than four feet down was the black tarmac that could take him away from here, back to the life he'd left behind. Four thousand miles back home to Mobile. Three-and-a-half thousand miles to his children in Toronto. It was all still there. All he had to do was go to it. He squinted into the gloom, willing a pair of headlights to appear. Rescuers coming to get them. If they appeared now, would he go?

Most men never get the chance to prove themselves, to sacrifice themselves, to show how just and honorable they are in the face of danger. Most men only get to wonder how they would behave. And here he was, even now, still wondering.

Not Shona, though. Given the chance to save herself—and only herself—he knew exactly what she would do.

In any case, all he could make out on the darkened road were the spiraling patterns of the eternal blizzard raging just beyond the town's borders.

"It's about a hundred miles to any kind of help," said Richie. "In case you were thinking of walking."

Curtis smirked and rubbed a hand across his chin "Shit, is that all? That don't sound so far." Then he snatched up his satchel of tools and started back to town. "Come on. Two more to go."

For Shona and Einar, the job was easier, but took longer. The signs outside the post office, the old fire station and the mining museum were all made of wood, with the town's name painted in delicate lettering that had been lovingly restored every year or two, whenever the mayor's office could find funds within the budget. Destroying them with a saw and hatchet was relatively simple, but the route from one to the next was all uphill.

Einar wheezed as they made their ascent, dragging Shona

behind on the sled. She felt a little bad about it, but there wasn't much she could do in return except keep watch for signs of Lucas or other children. So she sat, shivering and watching and listening to the sounds of Einar as he struggled more, gasping and coughing, the incline growing steeper the closer they got to the mining museum. It was situated in an elegant building that, in the town's early days, had been the local theater. Its historic significance made it an ideal place in which to display the records and remnants of St. Nicholas's gold-mining past, but its location, nearly at the very top of Nugget Hill, made it a challenge to get to, especially in deep snow.

As if to emphasize the point, when they were only fifty yards from the museum, Einar stumbled and fell, plunging face-first into the snow, the reins to the sled slipping from his grasp. Shona barely had time to register what had happened before she was sliding back downhill, the sled quickly picking up speed. Panicking, she threw out an arm and managed to grab onto a hitching post—another historical artifact from the town's frontier past—and hugged it tight, struggling to keep the sled under her legs, while Einar dragged himself back to his feet and shuffled over to her.

"Sorry for that," he said, speaking between heavy breaths, his face a deep, dark shade of red.

"It's okay," she said, still straining to keep the sled from sliding out from under her. "I can probably walk the last wee bit anyway. If you help me up."

He slung the sled's reins over the hitching post and helped her clamber her way over to the boardwalk. From there she was able to half limp and half crawl the rest of the way to the museum. She slumped back against its locked door to catch her breath, staring into the unpainted side of the sign. Beyond it, another fifty yards or so up the hill, was the barbershop on the corner of Eighth Avenue, and above it Curtis's apartment. Seeing it made her a little sad and wistful for the time they'd spent there the previous morning, before all the pain, bloodshed and horror. Before everything she thought she knew about the way the world worked was turned on its head.

"You hear that?" Now that he wasn't dragging the sled any more, Einar's panting eased long enough for him to hear the world around him. "It's quiet."

"Yeah." She nodded, then, because she couldn't help herself, added, "Too quiet."

He frowned, tilting his head as if to train his ears on the dead silence all around them. “You’re right. It’s too damn quiet. What does that mean? Could something have changed? You think Curtis and Richie . . . Could they have done it?”

“I doubt it.” She took the map from her pocket, unfolded it, held it out to him. “It’s a lot of ground to cover. At best, they might just be reaching the school.”

He took the map, studied it for a moment, then slipped it inside his jacket. “Okay. Then we might as well make some noise.” He threw his satchel down on the boardwalk and took out a saw and heavy mallet. While he began sawing through the narrow wooden struts holding the sign aloft, Shona kept watch.

In the time since the final firework had burst, it felt like the night had grown darker. She couldn’t tell if the inky black cloak over their heads was sky or clouds. It was colder now, too. Colder than she’d ever known. But that was good, in a way. The numbness in her extremities covered up the pain. Again, she cast an eye toward the window of Curtis’s apartment. They’d said they’d meet there when it was all done, when they were through with the signs, whether the plan worked or not, to figure out their next move. He’d put his door key in her hand and told her, the first chance she got, to get inside, get warm and wait for him. He’d said it with the air of a man who didn’t think it likely he’d be coming back. Imagining letting herself in now, perhaps crawling into his bed, she couldn’t help picturing him the way she’d seen him the previous morning, asleep, face-down in his long-johns, a photograph of his children nearby.

“Shit.” She still hadn’t asked their names.

Einar halted in his work. “What is it?”

“Nothing.” She spoke through chattering teeth. “Keep going.”

He’d already cut through one of the struts. Wagering that might be all it took to bring the sign down—with a little brute strength—he grabbed one edge and began yanking at it. It budged but didn’t quite break. He stepped around the side and tried a few blows with the mallet. This time something snapped and the sign tilted forward, but still didn’t fall.

“Damn it.” He dropped the mallet, returned the saw to his right hand and crouched down by the second strut. “Almost there.”

Click-click-click-click-click-click-click-click.

It was impossible to tell, at first, where the sound was coming from. Shona, sitting on the opposite side of the sign from Einar, couldn't see his face, but she could see his hands, one gripping the strut, the other holding the blade of the saw against one corner, both froze the instant he'd heard the clicks. She looked on as his hand slowly lowered, placed down the saw and reached for the shotgun.

"Einar," she whispered.

"Shut up." His voice was calm, serious and softer than hers. "Stay hidden."

Click-click-click-click-click-click-click-click.

The same sound, but slower now. Metallic. Familiar yet alien, devoid of context.

Shona shuffled forward and peered out from behind the sign to see Einar on his feet, his back to her, walking away. He held the shotgun in front of him, aiming into the alley across the street. A narrow wall of shadow. She could see nothing moving within.

Click. Click. Click.

Einar halted when he was a few paces from the alley. Whatever the cause of the sound, he knew it was directly ahead of him. He held the gun level, waiting, watching and listening with the patience of a hunter. Shona clamped a hand over her mouth to muffle the sound of her chattering teeth. Then, for an agonizing few seconds, there was only silence.

It was broken by a shrill, robotic grinding, emanating from within the darkness of the alley. It started loud and got louder until the source came marching out of the shadows.

A twelve-inch-high clockwork Santa Claus. Shona remembered seeing a dozen just like it in the Christmas store. It strode proudly out to meet Einar, shortening the distance between them to only a yard or two before a mound in the snow caused it to tilt and topple over. It lay on the ground, legs still chugging uselessly in rhythm with the key slowly turning in its back.

"Show yourself, demon!" Einar yelled into the alley. "Stop being a coward! Face me like a man!"

The response came not from in front of him, but from behind. To Shona, cowering on the other side of the half-broken sign, it appeared like the collapsing of a great, black curtain upon a stage. A monstrous shadow dropped into the street, swooping down from the museum's roof to land softly upon the snow, its billowing robes unfurling behind, their dark, damp folds glittering with innumerable adornments like a rippling galaxy of stars. Its sound was like a velvet pillowcase full of wind chimes.

Einar didn't hesitate. He spun around to face the beast and fired. Racked the shotgun and fired again. And again. The barrel might as well have been spitting cotton candy for all the difference it made. Morgan gave no sign that so much of a sliver of lead had touched him. He moved into the weapon's roaring spray and swung his great claw.

The gun ripped from Einar's grip as his jacket, shirt, and chest were torn open. He fell back screaming, a confetti of blood, torn fabric and scraps of flesh spraying into the air where he'd stood.

Shona, desperate to go to his aid, reached a shivering hand into the toolbox, clenching it around the handle of a crowbar. But it was a futile gesture. There was nothing she could do.

Morgan had grown even larger since their encounter in the Christmas store, increasing in height and nearly doubling in weight. The shroud he'd fashioned for himself could barely contain his girth and in places where his spines and rough edges had split the fabric, portions of his flesh could be seen—black and hard, dappled and wet, like the skin of a lizard gone to rot.

He stepped over to Einar, broad feet sinking deep into the snow, and leaned in, close enough that his drool splashed on the barman's ruined chest. "Einar Steffanson from Selfoss." It wasn't Morgan's voice anymore. Not a trace remained. It sounded too deep to be human. He reached out a hand, running the whetted tip of his finger along the slash he'd left in the man's torso. "Tell me . . . what is it you want for Christmas?"

Einar groaned out a curse in Icelandic. It sounded defiant, unafraid.

"I know," Morgan said. "I remember. You'd like to get out of town for a while. I can grant that."

His claw closed around Einar's leg, gripping it so tightly Shona could hear the bone crunch. Einar cried out in pain and then, appearing to exert no effort whatever, Morgan threw up his arm. Einar was dragged up with it and lifted into the air. Then, at the apex of his reach, Morgan let go, sending Einar cartwheeling through the sky. It was like tossing a ragdoll. A man of the barman's size and weight could not be expected to be thrown far—even by the most monstrous giant, gifted with supernatural strength. But Einar tumbled up and up and up, rising with such speed it seemed possible he might reach the moon. Shona watched his ascent, saw him disappear into the darkness, his screams fading on the chill night air. Then he was gone.

"Enjoy your trip," Morgan called after him. Then, exerting much more effort than had been required to pitch the man into space, he hauled himself around, both of his scorching yellow eyes scanning the boardwalk. "Now . . . Where are your friends?"

Shona huddled behind the sign, trying to make herself as compact as possible, trying not to breath, not to shake, watching through the gap between the struts as Morgan approached.

"I know you have friends," he said. "I know they're still here somewhere. I know they've been . . . " He paused when his foot crunched against a piece of paper.

Stepping back, he looked down and saw the map. It lay on the snow where it had fallen when Morgan's attack had released it from Einar's jacket, stained at the corners with the barman's blood. Morgan leaned in to study it, only curious at first, then wryly amused as he noted each of the circled locations and began to decipher what he was looking at. Then, when he finally understood, he stiffened, his breath caught and glowing eyes grew wide.

"Naughty," he whispered, his voice equal parts incensed and awed. "Naughty, naughty, naughty."

He turned and ran, dashing across the street, leaping up onto the roof of the opposite building and away, out of sight. Shona knew he'd be going to check on the other signs, to make sure they were all intact. That meant Richie's theory about their power was probably correct. It also meant there was an equally strong possibility both he and Curtis would very soon be dead.

She couldn't let that happen. She grabbed the sign and used it to drag herself up onto her feet, then stepped off the boardwalk, onto the snow.

She fell back again when Einar landed right in front of her. He plummeted back to earth at twice the speed at which he had been propelled into the sky, his body smashing upon the ground, exploding with the force of impact. The collision made an instant soup of blood, bones, organs and effluent, spraying out across the street like the pulp from a rotten pumpkin. Shona was slapped down by a wave of blood and gristle. It coated her clothes and face and got in her mouth—a hot, coppery stew. She spat chunks onto the boardwalk as she scrambled back onto her knees, wiping thick sludge from her eyes to see where he'd fallen.

He'd made a crater in the snow. At its center, what remained recognizably human—a pair of boots on broken legs, poking out from a mound of red mush—steamed like freshly laid dog shit.

Shona wanted to scream. A howl of rage and sadness more than fear. She choked it back and picked up the crowbar, smashing it against the back of the museum's sign. She hammered at it again and again, gouging out the wood with the bar's metal prongs. In a few seconds of furious activity, she'd torn a hole in the center and made splinters of the name 'St. Nicholas'. And maybe that was enough, but odds were it wouldn't do Curtis any good. Not if Morgan got to him before his own work was done. But what could she do? What could she do?

In a fit of impotent fury, she dropped the crowbar and threw herself at the sign. The second strut snapped and it fell forward, taking her with it. They both hit the snow and began sliding downhill, her riding it almost like a sled, until they arrived at the one Einar had transported her on from the bar.

She stared at it for a moment, then looked at the map, still lying where Morgan had left it. Beyond that was Curtis's apartment on the corner of Eighth Avenue, right at the top of Nugget Hill.

The thought hit her like a bolt of lightning. Fully formed, flawless, undeniable.

She could save him.

Ordering herself to stay calm, she slid off the sign, grabbed the sled's reins from the hitching post and slowly, steadily, began crawling her way back uphill, pulling the sled behind her. It was slow going, much too slow, but she had to be careful. Couldn't afford to slip and begin drifting back down the slope. She paused near Einar's body—or what was left of it—to collect his shotgun, the crowbar and the map. She checked it over, confirming what she already knew.

From the top of Nugget Hill was a simple route to the school. Only a couple of turns. All of it downhill. Going by sled, she could get from one end of town to the other in only a couple of minutes. If she kept her nerve. If she didn't crash. If she was very lucky, she might get to Curtis and Richie before Morgan did. There was a chance.

"Come on, for fuck sake," she told herself. "You can do this. Come the fuck on."

The incline steepened as she ascended. She clawed her way up through the snow, straining for purchase. She couldn't feel anything now. No pain, not even the cold. Only a burning sense of determination.

The road leveled out at the summit. She rounded the corner onto Eighth Avenue and saw the road stretching out beneath her, the steepest hill in town, the fresh snow untouched. The perfect piste.

She was no master of the sled. It was something she'd tried maybe only half a dozen times in her childhood. Never anything like this. She pushed Einar's rickety wood and rusted iron toboggan up to the edge of the slope and climbed on. When she was settled in a seated position, reins in her lap, as secure as she could be on what was, in essence, a few wooden boards nailed together over a pair of runners, she twisted around to collect the shotgun from the snow.

And then she saw him.

Lucas stood only a few yards away, in the middle of the street. He was hunched, frozen in mid-creep, like a child playing 'What's the Time, Mr. Wolf?'. His bulging head pulsed rhythmically with his shallow, excited breaths. His long, razor-tipped fingers twitched, readying for attack.

Shona snatched up the shotgun, swung it toward him and pulled the trigger.

What damage the blast did him she never saw. But its kick jolted her back, causing the gun to slip from her hands and tipping the sled over the rim of the hill, into the drop. She felt her stomach lurch, forcing a small, frightened yelp from her mouth.

And then she was flying. Like the first, sudden plunge on a roller-coaster. Plummeting down the slope. Fast. Unstoppable.

Completely out of control.

41.

LING COULDN'T BELIEVE what she was seeing.

He came roaring in on a blaze of silver, his gilded sleigh carving its way through the clouds, a dozen deer pulling majestically at the reins. They traced a circle through the sky above the square, sweeping the perimeter the way a bird of prey might, before taking a hard turn and plunging down, fearlessly, to land.

The crowd opened a path for them and they galloped gracefully down to meet it. They were magnificent beasts, with sparkling dark hides and huge, varnished antlers, mightier than any reindeer ever seen in captivity or the wild. Their hooves made a thunderous sound as they struck the snow, the sleigh following shortly behind, its garland of silver bells jingling all the way.

"Ho! Ho! Hoooooooooooo!"

And there he was.

Santa Claus tugged on the reins and brought the deer and his sleigh to an abrupt halt alongside the bandstand. Then he stood, held out his arms, and turned to address the crowd.

"Merry Christmas!"

They all cheered. Ling cheered. She'd never believed in Santa Claus. At least, that's what she had always told herself. After more than fifty years of not believing she was being confronted with undeniable proof that she had been woefully, terribly wrong—and she couldn't be more delighted. There were tears on her face. Tears in her eyes. She blinked them away to get a better look at the man who now stepped down from the sleigh and marched up onto the bandstand.

"People of St. Nicholas!" He addressed them without a microphone, his booming voice doing a better job of projecting itself than any modern-day sound system could ever hope to achieve. "Thank you for welcoming me to your wonderful town. I am flattered that you would throw a feast in my honor!"

The townsfolk cheered once again. Briefly, a few of them displayed expressions of confusion, like they hadn't any idea this was a feast being thrown in honor of Santa Claus. But only briefly.

"I suppose many of you are surprised to see me here, knowing it is, after all, my busiest night of the year." He paused for laughter and duly received it. "Some of you might be surprised to see me at all, having heard an enduring and perplexing rumor that I don't exist!" He was answered by cries of consternation and theatrical outrage. Almost ape-like, he beat his fists against his velvet-padded chest, then threw out his arms, imploring. "Well? What do you have to say to that? Do I exist?"

This time the response was rapturous. An overwhelming, incomprehensible volley of cries that somehow came together into a clear, emphatic chant. "Santa! Santa! Santa! Santa!"

The man up on the stage breathed in the adoration, chest swelling, shoulders rising, smile spreading beneath his downy-soft beard. Then, with a relaxed ease, he waved for the chanting to cease and was obliged. "I have come here in response to a letter, answering the request of a young lad by the name of Devon McCulloch. Is he here?"

Heads turned this way and that, the townsfolk searching among themselves for young Devon, his mother Erin, perhaps his stepfather or sister. But none could be found. Even the children, at the periphery of the crowd, took a quick look around.

The kind, twinkling eyes of Saint Nicholas narrowed ever so slightly. "No matter. I'm sure he'll be along. In his letter, he told me this town treasured Christmas like no other. He said the spirit of the season was celebrated here perhaps more fervently than anywhere else on God's earth. He worried that with the changing of the town's name, with its transformation into something new, this would all come to an end."

Ling felt eyes on her and a stab of guilt in her gut.

"But I can see now such fears were unfounded," Saint Nicholas said. "A town is so much more than its name. And I know this town, this community, this family of special souls, will embody the truest spirit of Christmas forever more—whatever its name!"

Again, the people cheered. And Ling cheered with them, jumping up and down, weeping from a mix of joy and relief. It would all be okay. Everything was going to be okay. All her fears and anxieties dwindled away to nothing now she finally understood. Santa Claus was real.

"I feel truly blessed to come here and be received with such warmth and hospitality. And I wish, so much, that I could stay a little while longer. However, I am expected back home for another party. And believe me, at the North Pole, Christmas Day is celebrated with a feast so extravagant it rivals even this. It simply wouldn't do to be late!"

Disappointment washed through the crowd like a sickness. Ling's own joy disintegrated, all happiness and sense of rightness with the world turned to ash at the thought of his leaving. It was too cruel an idea to comprehend. She found herself mute, unable to communicate her devastation, though the moans and boos from around her did an effective job.

Saint Nicholas chuckled at the sudden change in the atmosphere, the people vocally turning against him. Then his mustache twitched with a mischievous thought. "Well . . . would anyone like to come with me?"

The question stopped the groaning dead. The silence which followed was long and awkward, each man and woman pondering what he meant, whether he was proposing what they imagined, though it could not possibly be that.

"I'm serious," he told them. "Hospitality such as this deserves to be reciprocated. Who here can say they've never dreamed of visiting the North Pole? This is your chance! Step forward if you're so inclined!"

Dozens moved, requiring no further invitation. Working her way through the crowd to get to them, Ling was astonished and impressed to find the people of St. Nicholas forming an orderly queue at Santa's feet. She immediately got in line.

"Well look at that!" Saint Nicholas grinned, watching the queue take shape. "I don't know if there's space for everyone in my sleigh. But let's find out!"

42.

KENDRA DIDN'T KNOW where she was running to until she saw the church. In trying to evade Devon, she made a mad dash through different streets, darting down alleys like a scared cat, racing around the sides of buildings and doubling back on herself, hoping she could lose him by forcing him through a confused maze of her own invention. But he kept up the pace, hot on her tracks, his injury causing no impediment to his progress.

"Kendra!" His call echoed through the night, a strained rasp both childish and demonic. "Kendra, wait up!"

Then she was back in the middle of the street, panting, quivering, unsure of where she was and trying to think where to go next. That was when she saw the flowers and cards for Father McHattie, all the tributes tied to the railings of St. Nicholas Church. At the sight of them, she remembered what Noah and Marshall had told her. Now McHattie was dead, the place was empty. The door was unlocked.

Kendra loped toward the main entrance on legs that burned from all they'd been through. She hurled herself up the steps and into the heavy wooden doors, with their traditional wrought-iron handles. She heaved one open and slipped inside, slamming it shut behind her.

The darkened silence of the vestibule felt like sanctuary. She sank down onto the cold stone floor and rested her forehead against its smooth surface. Her whole body felt like it had been lit on fire. Beyond the sound of her ragged breaths and hammering heart, she could hear her own blood pattering on the floor. She was afraid to look at her wrist.

Devon had destroyed her in more ways than physical. Stripped her of all she had, leaving behind a ruin of the person she'd once been. And he hadn't even been trying.

Tears fell, mingling with the blood. She wanted this nightmare over. More than anything else, she wanted him dead.

"Kendra . . . " His mocking voice was at the door, fingers drumming on the wood. "I know you're in there!"

Her body moved ahead of her frantic mind. Muscles charged with adrenaline, she was on her feet, into the nave and halfway down the aisle before her brain knew what was happening.

Behind her, Devon's drumming turned to hammer blows, his fists smashing the door to pieces. "Stop running away from me!"

She kept moving, not thinking about where she was going, only knowing she had to get away. She ducked around the altar and through a narrow doorway to reach a spiral stairway going up. She was halfway to the top before she realized she was climbing the shaft of the bell tower.

"Why do you keep running?" Devon's voice reverberated up the stairwell. "You've got to know you can't get away." He'd followed her into the tower. She couldn't go back down. "You make it so easy. Footprints in the snow. Blood trails on the floor. It's like you want me to find you."

The wound on her arm blared pain when he spoke. She clutched it to her chest, cursing herself for her stupidity, for exhausting herself by running in madcap circles without giving any thought to all the ways he could track her. And now she was trapped. Nowhere to go but up.

"You can admit it," he said, voice growing louder as he approached. "Admit you want me. We can take it from there. Start all over again."

She pressed on, up, through the shadows, forced on to whatever awaited at the top.

"Or I can make you want me. That's the painful way. You won't like it much. But I will."

The stairs ended in the belfry. No trapdoor. Nothing to block the way behind her. Starlight poured in between the broken wooden slats in the windows, inelegantly mended with chicken wire, illuminating the bare outlines of her surroundings. She stood halfway out of the stairwell's mouth, scanning the small room for something she could use.

Like most of the town's oldest buildings and monuments, the belfry was littered with the detritus of halfhearted attempts at preservation and restoration. In this case, the attempts had been made by Father McHattie himself, during infrequent bouts of sobriety when he'd dreamed himself capable. He had wrapped the bells up in plastic, nailed up planks to reinforce the timber beams and stuffed the cracks in the masonry with paste and old newspapers. In one corner was a bucket and a stack of cardboard boxes. Kendra ran to them and rifled one-handed through the contents, finding bags of powder, brushes and duct tape—but no tools. He'd had the sense to take his hammers, saws and anything useful back down below, out of the elements. Finding nothing she could make into a weapon, her fear and rage matched in their ferocity, she threw the boxes aside. And then her eye caught the gleam of something metal hidden behind them, nestled against the wall. She reached for it, unable to discern what it was until it was in her fist.

The cross from the church steeple. Cast from copper and plated with gold, it had for the best part of a century pierced the sky, a shining beacon to God's love. Until McHattie, like a crazed, drunken steeplejack, had climbed up and retrieved it, determined to keep it safe from potential looters.

The cross was heavy, four feet long, tapering to a fine point at the base. When held from the top, as Kendra held it now, it looked like a sword.

"I've been wondering something." Devon stood behind her.

After shaking the building's foundations with his cacophony for so much of the chase, he'd ascended the last few steps and closed the distance between them in silence. And she was crouched in his spreading shadow. Cornered.

With a defiant scream she spun toward him and thrust out with the cross, aiming at the center of his chest. Devon caught its tarnished tip an inch from piercing his ribs. He held it there, squeezing the cold metal in his fist, refusing to yield to Kendra however much she pulled or pushed.

His electric smile lit up the darkness between them. "I said . . . I've been wondering something."

Kendra pulled frantically at the cross, which felt like it was embedded in stone. Her whole body twisted as she tried to wrestle it free, feet digging against the floor.

Devon leaned into her and she stumbled back, falling into the cardboard boxes, scattering their contents. Something rolled out from under them and touched her foot. Something that clinked.

With her free hand she reached for it, blood-slick fingers fumbling in the dark.

"I've been wondering . . . " Devon's mouth changed as he spoke, teeth stretching, multiplying, sharpening and brightening as his tongue slithered out across them to whip at Kendra's face. "What you *taste* like."

Her fingers closed around the neck of the whiskey bottle and she swung it into his chin. The blow snapped his jaws shut, teeth slicing through his twisting tongue and spraying her face with yellow blood. He gave a muffled howl of pain and reared up, grip loosening on the cross long enough for her to shove it into his abdomen. The point pierced his scrawny torso, driving him back, across the floor.

He staggered away from Kendra, blind with the pain, arms flailing. She rose, one hand still on the cross, the other gripping the bottle. She chased after him and swung the bottle again, this time smashing it against the side of his mad, bubbling head.

The light within him flickered and for a moment Devon's face was lost behind a rain of booze, blood, and glittering glass shards. He fell back against the wall of the belfry, its loose stones immediately collapsing under his weight, scattering into the street below through a cloud of plaster dust and old newspaper. The slats in the window tumbled along with the stones, opening up one side of the tower to the air.

Sprawled over the disintegrating masonry, he cried out, mangling her name with his mutilated tongue. He made one last grab for Kendra, but she thrust again with the cross, pressing its metal deeper into his poisoned flesh.

He fell into the night.

It didn't take long to travel the hundred feet or so to the street. Yet he found time to think on the journey. He thought how funny it was that the same things kept happening. Twice that night he had fallen from the top of a building. Twice his sister had attacked him with a bottle of alcohol. He had recovered the previous times and would again. Far from weakening him, those experiences had left him stronger. Such was the transformative power of Saint Nicholas.

This time, when he recovered, he would have so much more strength than before. So much more vigor. He would be monstrous and unforgiving. He would find Kendra again—as he always did.

And this time, he would leave no room for negotiation, for flight or defense. She would be consumed in every way conceivable.

Santa would save him. Santa would transform him. Santa—

The thought was extinguished the instant a metal spike pierced the back of his skull and exploded from his eye socket.

43.

FOR THE FIRST few seconds, crashing had felt like an inevitability. Shona lay face down on the sled, hands gripping its edges, her whole body shaking from the vibrations of the wood and metal beneath her. She couldn't see where she was headed but felt sure it was probably into a wall or a lamppost. At this speed, she'd break bones. Her best hope of avoiding serious injury was to throw herself off the back and take her chances in the snow. It might hurt, tumbling her way down the rest of the slope, but at least she'd survive. But then what about Curtis?

She had to try to regain control of the sled. It bounced over a bump in the road, launching her body into the air, and for a terrible moment she thought she would be thrown clear, but then she dropped back down onto the rickety slats, seizing the momentum to roll herself onto her back.

She saw the sky. The blanket of clouds had peeled back to show her a sea of dancing stars, their dazzling beauty bright enough to light her way. In the same moment, the sled bounced once more, its nose tilting up, taking her into the air.

The vibrations ceased. The rattling and creaking cut out. For a second there was only the whoosh of air rushing past her ears and a sensation of weightlessness, like the sled and her body both had thrown off the shackles of gravity and taken flight, aiming for the stratosphere. A strange sliver of serenity amid the madness.

She tore her eyes from the heavens to see the ground racing violently up to meet her. She hunched forward and grabbed the front rails, holding on tight as the sled crashed back down to the snow, fishtailing frantically, almost like it was trying to throw her off. It tilted up on one runner for a perilous moment, threatening to tip over, but then righted itself, gaining speed all the time.

She had to get it under control. The wind whipped frost into her eyes, but squinting through her icy tears she could make out the corner of Copper Street approaching fast on the right. That was where she needed to go, but the sled was on a collision course with a concrete salt bin. In her mind she could already hear the crunch her body would make slamming into its side.

She pulled tight on the reins and leaned back, trying to use the full weight of her body to make the damn thing brake. The nose lifted a little and it slowed—slightly, but not much. The bin kept on coming toward her, impact only seconds away.

Come on you silly cow, she told herself. *Kids know how to do this shit. It's easy!*

She leaned right, trying to get the sled to lean with her, but it hardly budged. Panic mounting, concrete wall looming like a piston-powered tombstone, she swung her right foot out over the side, digging her heel into the snow.

It was an act of desperation, but it worked. The sled pivoted away from the bin, lining up with the center of the street. She dug her heel in again and it swung further, taking the corner of Copper Street in a smooth, graceful arc.

"Yes," she cried, catching a mouthful of slush and not caring. "Yes! Yes! Fucking yes!"

She was off Nugget Hill now, still heading down but at a much gentler incline. The sled was slowing. As soon as she realized, she threw her whole body forward, using her weight to boost her speed.

I'm getting the hang of this, she thought as she accelerated past the next two blocks and around the corner of Copper and Third. *I am. I can go faster.*

Racing down Third, she straddled the sled like the figurehead at the prow of a ship, her face aimed stubbornly into the wind, eyes fixed on the way ahead, uncaring of the icy wind that slashed her cheeks and stung her gritted teeth, wanting only to go faster, momentum building like a rocket.

She might have been doing no more than twenty miles an hour, but from where she sat it felt like sixty. Seventy. Eighty. For a moment she heard cheering, like crowds at the Winter Olympics urging her on and couldn't tell if it was real or in her head. She supposed it could have been real. It wasn't far to the square and whatever crazed celebration was happening there.

Not far to the school either. And downhill all the way.

After dealing with the sign at the edge of town, Curtis and Richie moved on to the park. A walled garden between the road and river, it boasted a series of walks through deciduous trees, quaint flowerbeds and play areas for children and really came alive in the summer. This time of year it was a desolate scene of bare branches and ice-encrusted swings. At the entrance, bolted together from old railway sleepers, stood a sign that simply read, 'Welcome to St. Nicholas'. The bright blue letters were painted galvanized steel and had been screwed into place. Removing them was easier than bringing down the first sign—especially given this one only came up to chest height—but was still a painstaking process.

When all the letters had been taken off and cast over the wall, into the park, they headed north to Service Street and the school. This was the sign Richie had been worried about. Over fifteen feet high, fashioned from solid brick and brass. The name was, at least, a single plate—not a bunch of individual letters. But it was secured to a metal bracket with heavy rivets, frozen tight by the cold.

"We'll need a ladder and a blowtorch," Richie said.

"Wait here," Curtis told him, then went through the school gates and around the side of the building, letting himself in through the staff entrance. He returned with a telescopic ladder on his shoulder, carrying a welding torch and gas canister. "Got a light?"

Richie threw him a Zippo. "Guess I forgot who you were. What else are you hiding back there?"

Curtis passed him the ladder without answering his question, deciding this wasn't the time to regale him with tales of the previous custodian Mr. Elliott and his pack-rat habits that had turned the school basement into a fuel dump.

They took it in turns, one holding the ladder steady while the other climbed to the top with the welding torch. A minute or so under a blue flame was enough to melt the thick layer of ice capping each of the rivets and soften them up a little. Patient yet firm application of a hammer and chisel shaved off the heads. Each one removed brought them closer to being able to force a crowbar between the bracket and the nameplate and pop it loose. While they worked, the sounds of the cheering crowd in the square, just a few streets over, grew in volume and intensity.

"What do you think is happening over there?" Richie choked the question out through gasps as he sweated and strained to chisel the second-last rivet head away.

"I don't want to know. Try and ignore it."

"Sounds almost like they're celebrating. Sounds like . . . sounds like they're happy." He lowered the chisel. "Could we be wrong about this?"

"What are you talking about?"

"Just what I said. What . . . What if we've got it all wrong?"

Curtis stared up at him, trying to make sense of the expression on his face, the strange look in his eye. A look he'd seen before. "I don't think this is the time to be—"

"Listen to them."

"Richie . . . "

"Listen to them!"

Curtis wasn't entirely sure what was happening. He considered grabbing the other man by the ankle and dragging him down from the ladder, into the snow. He could wrestle the chisel and hammer from his grasp, climb back up and finish the damn job himself. Or he could listen.

In truth, he couldn't help but listen, the crowd so loud now, the jubilance of their raised voices soaking the atmosphere like a warm mist. There was something so calming about the sound. So enticing. When he deigned to pay attention to it for a moment, he began to understand what Richie meant. He wanted to be there. Part of the crowd. Wrapped up in all their excitement. Their joy. Their embrace of the present, untroubled by whatever the future might hold. It sounded good. It sounded like somewhere he ought to be.

It wasn't far, of course. Once they were finished with the sign, they could walk straight round and be there in only a few minutes. They'd be there a lot sooner, though, if they forgot all about the sign and left right now. He was on the cusp of suggesting the same to Richie when he heard something else.

"Tiiiiiiiiiiiiiiiiiiis!" A small, shrill sound coming from far away, just loud enough to cut through the joyous drone from the town square. "Cuuuuuuuuur-Tiiiiiiiiiiiiiiis!"

Curtis stared at the row of buildings across the street, trying to discern where the cry was coming from.

"Cuuuuuuuuur-Tiiiiiiiiiiiiiiis! Morgan is coooomiiiiing!"

He stepped out, into the road, moving toward the intersection with Third. "You hear that?"

"I hear it," Richie answered, meaning the crowd, climbing down the ladder. "I hear it."

"No, no, no. That." Curtis pointed a finger up Third Avenue, at the small, distant shape rapidly making its way down the hill toward them. "Is that . . . ?" He squinted. "Is that Shona?"

"Look out," she cried, speeding down the ice like a missile. "Look out! Morgan is coming to k—" The warning was cut short as she plowed into a snowdrift concealing a fire hydrant and twin parking bollards. There was a crunch and clang of wood and metal as the sled shattered and she was catapulted from it and into the road.

"Shona!" Curtis was about to run to her but saw Richie had descended the ladder, leaving the sign intact, and was now walking in the direction of the square. "Hey! Hey, Richie! What are you doing?"

The contractor shook his head but didn't turn around. "I'm just going to check it out." He looked in a trance, a hungry dog following the scent of roasted meat.

"Richie!"

"I'm just going to check it out," he repeated, jogging now. "I'll be back." He crossed the road, approaching the corner of Service and Fourth.

Morgan stepped out to meet him.

The man had become a huge, hulking darkness. A swollen black mass. An unnatural thing, moving with the speed and power of a bear, jangling like an avalanche of sleigh bells. Whatever hallucinatory madness had a hold on Richie's brain, it dissipated the moment Morgan's shadow fell across him. He turned immediately around and tried to run, but a claw swept his legs out from under him. He fell into the street, planting his face in the snow. His limbs scrambled frantically, as though he thought he might crawl his way to freedom, but Morgan stepped forward, placing one huge foot on his back, pinning him in place.

"Richard Quigley from Winnipeg." Morgan's eyes glowed bright as headlamps, their golden beams trained on their unfortunate target. "Don't tell me what you want. I think I remember."

Richie made a muffled protest, his hands clawing weakly at the snow, mouth full of ice, the pressure on his back compressing his lungs.

Curtis's own breath was trapped in his chest. He wanted to intervene, to race to Richie's rescue, but all he did was lean forward a little. Some instinct for self-preservation kept his feet rooted to the ground, prevented any cries from escaping his lips. Preservation or panic. He didn't know which. He glanced at Shona and saw her try to lift her head.

You're doing it again, he said to himself. *You're freezing up.*

Then Richie screamed.

"I *do* remember," Morgan growled through a grin. "You wanted a back massage."

He drove his foot down, grinding it like a piston into Richie's spine, squashing the man like a bug under his full weight and strength. The contractor's ribs and vertebrae popped noisily under the pressure, his organs crushed, blood spurting up through splitting flesh and between Morgan's toes. The scream was short and singular. He hadn't the breath for more.

Still frozen in place, Curtis watched as much as he could stand, then looked back to Shona.

She managed to drag her bloodied face out of the snow, lifting herself up on quivering arms. Her eyes peered out between strands of damp, tangled hair to find his and she breathed a single word. "Run."

He couldn't hear it from where he stood. Could only see the shape of it on her lips. But it was like a starting pistol going off in his head. He spun around and threw himself into a sprint, leaping up on the sidewalk and through the school gates, lifting his legs high as he dashed through the snow.

The halogen searchlights of Morgan's eyes found him as he was bounding across the schoolyard. "Curtis Tate." He spat the name like a curse, while giving his foot a final sadistic twist through the macerated pulp of Richie's torso. "From Alabama."

Curtis knew he would follow. He kept running and didn't look back till he reached the staff entrance. Even then, the brief glance he stole was nearly too much.

With monstrous speed, Morgan came. His arms held out and fingers splayed, eyes ablaze with demonic light. Strides so long he appeared to be gliding. Silent but for the tinkling of chimes. Robes billowing out behind him. An enraged, advancing, poisonous storm cloud.

It was almost enough to send Curtis's mind fleeing for cover and his muscles into shock, but he held on. He kept moving, into the building and down the darkened corridors, ice water on his boots making him slip and stumble but not going down, throwing himself through one set of double doors after another.

Morgan followed at speed. He smashed through the entrance and gushed into the building like an upturned barrel of black water, sloshing across the floor and up the walls. His head, bobbing on the end of his elastic neck, thudded against the ceiling and he let out an involuntary cry, liquid limbs battling the environment to slow his momentum.

He relaxed, crouching down, reshaping his over-augmented frame to fit the narrow corridor. His undulating movements became more feline, imitating the sinister prowl of a jaguar. There was no need to rush. He knew the school better than Curtis did. Knew where he was going and what he would find when he got there. His prey had nowhere to run.

"Curtis the custodian." He drummed ossified fingers against the wall, announcing his approach. "What is it you want for Christmas, Curtis? Tell me and I can get it for you. Tell Santa Claus . . . " The dancing fires in his eyes lit up the corridors ahead, throwing sharpened streaks of yellow and long, deep shadows across Curtis's path. "I bet I know what you want."

Curtis didn't see the plastic floor sign forbidding students and staff from entering the gym till he was tripping over it. He flailed, just managing to stay on his feet, then kicked it away, down the hall. He crashed through the doors to the gym, tearing away reflective safety tape like cobwebs. Starlight shone through the high windows along the opposite wall, painting silver squares on the warped wooden floor. He sprinted across the boards, only vaguely registering the way they bent and groaned, to reach the fire exit. He grabbed for the push bar.

It snapped off in his hands, fixtures clattering to his feet in a shower of rust particles. Morgan's eyes lit them up, revealing their sparkling, bloody color, as he entered the hall.

"That door is on your list of repairs, custodian." Laughter surged from his chest as he spoke, as if escaping from gills. "Perhaps you never read down that far. It is, I suppose, a long list."

Curtis couldn't bear to turn around. His trembling hands still clutched a piece of the push bar. He wondered briefly if its corroded steel could be made into a weapon. A spear, maybe. But it felt light. Warped by age and water. Like everything else in the gym.

Morgan took a step forward and the board beneath him creaked. "Now tell me what you want." Twin circles of yellow light stained the wall, Curtis's shadow shivering between. They expanded as Morgan drew closer, illuminating the wall bars stretching from the floor up to the windows. The kind little kids climb in gym class. Curtis hadn't even known they were there.

"Shall I guess?" Morgan's voice was deep enough to send vibrations rippling through the moisture-laden air. "You want that pretty little schoolteacher. And I can give her to you. Yes, I can. I'll give her to you."

Curtis spun and hurled the spear. Morgan's eyes followed its path as it spun across the room, missing him by yards. It clattered to the floor and lay in the corner, its potential spent.

"Hmmmm." Morgan stared at it, perplexed by the pointless display, then returned his gaze to Curtis, only to find he was halfway up the wall, climbing toward the window. He laughed again. "Where are you going, you naughty child?"

Curtis ignored him, clambering on to reach the window, grabbing the handle and shoving it open, letting in the night air.

"Such ingratitude," Morgan sneered, marching across the floor. "Santa wants to do you a favor. I said I'd give her to you. And I will! Piece by bloody, rotten, ragged piece!" Each word punctuated with another stomp of his foot. And on the last, the brittle boards beneath him snapped.

The weakened wood disintegrated under his weight, shattering in an eruption of splinters and sawdust. He tumbled through a crumbling rain of shredded oakwood, down through a whirling cloud of debris, into the cavern below. His body smashed gracelessly into the stores of machine parts and power tools, generator spares and engine fuel, kerosene drums and gas cans. All the treasures Mr. Elliott had left behind with no concept of how they might be put to use. The impact tossed them high into the air and brought them crashing back down through a churning cloud of dust, dirt, and woodchips, covering Morgan like a blanket of dead leaves. Rusted containers split and bottles broke, spurting jets of oil and gas.

The flashlight beams of the monster's eyes winked and blinked through the maelstrom and, for just a moment, Curtis caught sight of Saint Nicholas's servant sprawled out in the demolished stockpile, his gangling limbs twitching in confusion, the hood of his robe thrown back to reveal his face. His head was little more than a skull now, encrusted with a thin layer of hard, black skin that looked as if it had already rotted and decayed. Curtis hoped it would still burn.

He climbed up into the open window and straddled it, halfway outside. He took Richie's lighter from his pocket and the soccer scarf from about his neck.

"You asked what I want for Christmas," he called down to Morgan, touching the flame to the fabric. "I want some heat."

He tossed the burning scarf into the crater below, lingering in the window long enough to watch it land in a pool of oil, flickering fingers of blue and yellow flame quickly spreading to encircle the dazed and squirming would-be Santa Claus, catching his robes alight.

Then Curtis turned to face the night and jumped.

"Come on!"

Shona hammered her open palm against the crowbar, attempting to pry the sign from its fixings. Drained, panting, broken and bloody, she had crawled her way from one side of the street to the other. She had lifted the crowbar in her numb and shaking hand and dragged her shattered body to the top of the ladder. She found the corner edge at which Richie had managed to make a dent with his chisel and, with what brute strength she could muster, had forced the crowbar's claw into the gap, working it till it was embedded firmly behind the panel, the bar prone before her. She threw up her fist and brought it down hard on the shaft.

It didn't move.

She tried again.

"Come on!"

Again.

"Come on to fuck!"

Again, again, again.

"Come on to fuck you fucking c—!"

On the final syllable, the plate popped free. In the same moment, the school's basement exploded in a plume of flame that tore through the gymnasium, rupturing its walls and roof, shaking the ground and lighting up the night.

Shona toppled from the ladder, grabbed the sign, and all came tumbling down.

44.

THEY EACH WAITED their turn, like good little helpers. Ling no doubt ranked among the most excited. Of all the ambitions she'd dreamed of realizing, all the things she wished to experience, and goals she hoped to achieve—and there had been a great many—she couldn't recall a ride on Santa's sleigh ever being one. Yet at this moment, there was nothing she could imagine wanting more.

At the apprehension of such an adventure, she felt her eagerness might explode out of her, sending her rocketing into the air. It might send her fists flying, all of their own accord, pummeling the people before her, knocking them out of her way and clearing a path to Saint Nicholas, such was her boundless, extraordinary elation at the thought of putting her hand in his and being led wherever he might take her.

Yet, calling upon reserves of patience she could never have imagined she possessed, she held her emotions in check and, like all the rest, stood composed and serene, quietly awaiting her turn. This she managed somehow, in spite of herself, even as she watched the sleigh begin to fill with passengers.

It was not a vehicle with unlimited capacity. It was big, yes. Certainly, it was big. But as more and more of the townsfolk were guided into it and directed to take a seat on one of the polished wooden benches, she saw there could not possibly be enough room for everyone.

Ling began counting the people ahead of her, struggling to remain calm against a growing suspicion she would be left behind. Forgotten. No, she couldn't bear that.

She kept a closer eye on the men and women taking their turns to climb the steps, one at a time, ascending into Saint Nicholas's rarefied orbit. He embraced every man, pulling them into his powerful arms for a vigorous, reassuring hug. The women he kissed. The merest, most gentle peck on the cheek. The lightest touch of his lips, the tickle of his beard. Yet it seemed to Ling the kisses lasted some time longer than mere pecks should. But of course they did. This was only Santa being Santa. Time played merry games in his presence. And when he'd finished with his greetings, he personally guided each of his new passengers into the sleigh, directing them to their seat.

Ling watched them, jealously studying the passively pleasant faces of the townsfolk seated side by side, waiting for lift-off. She counted them, attempting to gauge how many spaces were left, then counted the heads of the people in front of her. And breathed a huge sigh of relief. There was room. There was still room. For her and just a few more. She would get to see the North Pole yet.

She felt a tug on her sleeve and looked down to see Cindee. The girl's pink fingers clung fiercely to her coat.

"Don't." She wept, her voice small and desperate. "Don't do it. Please, don't. Please. Please!"

"Cindee?"

"Oh don't worry," her mother said, making a gentle effort to pull the girl away. "She's okay, she's fine."

Ling suddenly realized Cindee's parents had been in line behind her all this time. That meant they'd be coming with her in Santa's sleigh. Cindee too, she supposed. If the girl could be mollified. "Are you sure?"

"She's fine," her mother said, stretched smile fixed tight on her face. "Honestly."

"Look at it," Cindee sobbed, fingers digging through the fabric of Ling's sleeve, into her flesh. "Look what it's doing to them! See it! Why won't you see it!"

Ling wished she understood, but had no idea what the girl was talking about. She looked at the line ahead, dwindling now, only a few folk left between her and the stage. They remained, for the most part, fully engaged in the moment, lost in the joy and wonder of Christmas. But Cindee's piercing voice, rising in volume, managed to catch the attention of one or two. They turned curious heads their way.

"Come on now, honey," her mother cooed, sweet as syrup. "Don't make a fuss."

Cindee shot her a look of righteous fury, then screamed.

It was a horrid sound. The kind of petulant shriek Ling only ever heard while passing playgrounds, in supermarkets, at weddings, or other social functions where tantruming toddlers could not be avoided. The kind of awful noise that made her grateful she'd never had children of her own. Terrible enough to sour even the magical atmosphere within the square.

Others cringed among the crowd, unable to hide their discomfort, while Cindee's tear-streaked face got redder and angrier, the hellish screech defying nature's laws to become louder still. Even the other children, patiently standing guard for so long around the perimeter, found it too much to bear. They moved in, weaving their way through the crowd. Ling caught glimpses of their heads bobbing between the shoulders of others, looking much more like children now than they had earlier. When was that? And what had they looked like?

It was all so difficult to recall now. The revelation of Santa's existence and the invitation to go with him had overwhelmed everything else. Ling felt a stabbing pain at her temples, a headache brought on by more than Cindee's wailing. She looked to Saint Nicholas, seeking some reassurance, but he seemed not to have noticed the girl's cries. He was entirely preoccupied with greeting his new passengers, making a quick thing of it, racing through the cuddles and kisses, increasing his fervor to compensate for their brevity.

There was only one person ahead of Ling in the queue now. Ms. Beaverbrook of all people, the children's choir teacher. She went giddily up the steps, into the arms of Saint Nick. At the same time, Ling tried to catch his eye, but lost it. It was a strange thing, the way his image shivered and melted ever so briefly in her vision, coinciding with another scream from Cindee. His face blurred out, becoming a hazy smear, like a stain on her cornea. Something moved behind it, a shadowy form rising to the surface . . . But then she blinked and his jolly red face was just as it should be, his lips puckering up to give the choir teacher a kiss.

Cindee's cries were silenced, and Ling felt her hands pulled away from her sleeve. She turned to see two of the other children carrying the girl away, their hands clamped over her mouth, and was relieved. They'd know how to calm her down.

"Miss Wong."

Ling shivered, hearing her name spoken in his rich baritone.

Turning to face him, she saw his arm was still around Ms. Beaverbrook, the woman practically wilting with joy in his presence, but his twinkling eyes were fixed on her. "Yes?"

"I've heard so much about you." He held out his hand. "Will you be joining us?"

She swallowed, feeling very suddenly like a timid high-school girl being asked to the dance. "If you'll have me."

He grinned. "Oh yes. I'll have you all."

Heart pounding, she reached out to take his hand in hers. And felt the earth move.

The explosion was louder than Cindee's screams and the rumble beneath their feet jostled the crowd. Stalls rattled and the fairy lights flickered and died. People searched the skyline for the source of the roar now echoing across the square and, looking south, saw a great ball of flame rising up over the buildings. It burst like a great orange bubble, sending a streak of fire and smoke up across the night and coaxing cries of shock from the crowd.

Ling watched it with the rest, wondering what could have caused it, where it was happening.

"It's the school," someone said, panic rising. "It's got to be the school."

A chill went through Ling's body—instant and shocking, like she'd been doused in ice water. From the gasps of others, she was sure they all felt it, as though the warmth of the celebration had been swiftly sucked down into the earth, taking their shared merriment with it. She blinked against the darkening light, trying to understand why the strung bulbs suddenly lost their glow, the shadows deepening, the sharp edges returning. It felt very much like being shaken out of a lovely dream to be confronted by the harsh, ugly truth of reality.

Dizzy, queasy, unsure of herself and her surroundings, she looked away from the tower of flame, turning to face Santa Claus, certain if anyone could provide comfort in such a distressing moment, it would be him. She reached for his hand . . . but it wasn't there.

The appendage ready to clasp hers was no hand at all. It looked more like the pincer of a crab, with twin prongs black and glistening. The same spiked, hardened shell coated its narrow, brittle wrist, halfway wrapped in rancid red rags. Ling's eyes traveled up the bony arm and across a chest that heaved and swelled with the pulsations of innumerable gelatinous yellow sacks, poking out through the holes in its tattered tunic and between battered copper bells like bilious neon tumors. The head that sat atop its shoulders was an incomprehensible configuration of dark, red, alien eyes and twitching mandibles capped with a moth-eaten red-and-white hat. Its mouth was red and wet and dripping, strings of moist meat hanging from its chin.

Ms. Beaverbrook, who only seconds earlier had been luxuriating in the embrace of the great Saint Nicholas himself, saw the same thing Ling did. The woman tried to twist free of the creature's grasp, eyes stretching wide and opening her mouth to shriek—but all that escaped her lips was blood.

Ling looked down and saw the woman had been sliced open from her waist to her collarbone, the gash leaking fluids in a heavy stream, pattering on the floor of the bandstand, its boards painted red with the blood of all who had gone before her.

Santa's passengers, the ones sitting in his sleigh so patiently, who Ling had eyed so enviously, were all dead. He'd chewed the throats from some and gouged death wounds in the chests of others. Their mangled corpses were piled up in a rusted flatbed trailer hooked to an ATV. Not a sleigh or reindeer in sight.

Somebody screamed.

Ling was fairly certain it wasn't her. Fairly certain she hadn't inhaled or exhaled since laying eyes on the thing that had called itself Saint Nicholas. Revealed to her now as he truly was. She couldn't be sure her heart had continued to beat since its dozen glowing insectile eyes found her own.

Others, wrenched back into reality from a dream longer and deeper than her own, looked now and saw the beast, the woman spurting blood in his grip. They screamed too. The children screamed, waking from their own delusions to find their bodies poisoned and deformed, falling into fits at the feet of parents too afraid to touch them. It took only moments for the entire gathering, faces lit by the flickering flames stretching up across the sky, to descend into outright hysteria.

From what Ling could see, no-one was consumed by panic more quickly or completely than Saint Nicholas himself. At the sight of him, most fled, but a few brave souls charged the stage, hoping to rescue Beaverbrook or the friends and loved ones who had already passed through his hands—not realizing they were dead. The beast quivered like an enraged hornet, his multitude of limbs rattling defensively. He snatched back the claw offered to Ling and drove it up into the choir teacher's parted flesh, grasping a handful of intestines and wrenching them out of her, arming himself with a whip of glistening viscera. He used it to lash the people advancing on the bandstand, slapping them down. Ling herself was struck in the face and thrown onto her ass, the length of red tissue making a sound like taut leather against her cheek.

For a moment she was blind, her senses overwhelmed by pain and confusion. She recovered in time to see a man make a grab for Saint Nicholas as the monstrosity attempted to leave the stage. He was rewarded with a claw to his face, the pincers punching through his skull and unleashing a vibrant volley of gore.

No one else tried to get in his way after that. Few even watched him as he clambered awkwardly down from the bandstand and slunk away, behind the trailer. They were too preoccupied with the children, their own rising mania or attempts at escape to pay any attention to where Saint Nicholas was going.

Little Cindee Joyce stood somewhere in the carnage, yelling through her tears. "You see? You see it now? You see!"

Ling's ears filled with howls of terror and despair from all around her. It was the sound of Hell itself, willing her own mind to break and plunge her into a state of lunatic paralysis from which she might never recover.

But she knew where she was. Unlike the rest, she understood what was happening. And her eyes stayed locked on Saint Nicholas.

Ling climbed to her feet and followed him to the other side of the corpse-laden trailer, to the edge of the square and across the street. He crawled along the ground like a crocodile, his scraggy legs splayed and belly dragging through the snow. His movements were jerky, frantic, but his progress was slow, making it easy for her to keep up. He wheezed, coughed and spat between muttered expletives, struggling with the toll the exertion took on his wasted limbs. Ling imagined he'd probably been faster back before he'd eaten, before his stomach had swollen with the organ meat of dozens of victims and his bulging golden glands had filled with the yellow venom that turned children into demons. Once he might have been able to dance lithely through the shadows, but now, lit up in all the blazing colors of the school inferno, his grotesque, bloated body was easy to track.

Maintaining a safe distance, Ling followed him down Fifth Avenue and through an alley to Fourth. She might have followed him further still, had her attention not been drawn to the girl slumped against the wall of the building across the street, her snowsuit spattered with blood, trying and failing to stand up on legs too weak to function.

"Kendra?"

45.

CONFUSION REIGNED FOR a long time after the explosion. In the absence of Saint Nicholas's comforting influence, the community was destroyed, horrified, and dismayed, unable to comprehend reality or the terrible violation it had endured. Thoughts were chaotic, behavior strange, dialogue insensible.

For Shona the problem was compounded by a blow on the head suffered in her fall from the ladder—one more injury to add to an exhaustively long list. When Curtis found her she was conscious, but babbling incoherently, uncertain of where she was or what had happened to her. The brain fog didn't begin to clear till they were nearly at the square. He carried her all the way there in his arms.

The scene they found was a grim one. The wreckage of the impromptu Christmas feast remained, the tables of food and drink toppled, smashed, and trampled in the fleeing stampede. The bandstand wore a scarlet sheen—a layer of frozen blood. There were bodies too, some sprawled on the ground, others piled in the trailer, partly covered by a piece of tarp too small for the job. In the midst of it all, a handful of broken survivors—kneeling, wailing women and silent, ashen-faced men—lamented the loss of friends and family members, the absolute destruction of their lives.

Inside the town hall, the situation was only slightly better. Long designated the community's disaster relief center, it had ample stores of bunks, blankets, general medicines, and first-aid supplies—much of it now being put to use. Most of the children slept, worn out from shock or the trauma their young bodies had undergone. A few were still awake, crying for their parents through misshapen mouths. Some of their mothers and fathers sat with them, offering what comfort they could. Others kept their distance, too appalled by their hideous transformations to get close. Some were dead.

Many people were dead, they learned. Perhaps as many as forty of the town's citizens, plus all the contractors. Among them was almost everyone with any knowledge of how to repair telecommunications or sabotaged engines. Many survivors fled to their homes and barricaded the doors. They included the parents of Cindee Jacobs, who hid their daughter in the basement, baffled as to why their child should be the only one in town to be spared hideous mutation, but grateful. Anyone left who still had their wits about them had been tasked either with tending to the injured and grief-stricken or searching the north side of town for other survivors and working vehicles. All this was relayed to Curtis and Shona by Ling, standing behind a folding table on which a map of the town and lists of supplies had been laid out, delivered in succinct chunks when she wasn't barking orders.

As they lacked the resources to put it out, the decision had been taken, she said, to let the fire at the school keep burning. "You don't think it'll spread, do you?" she asked Curtis.

He shrugged. "I hope not."

"Me too."

A bunk was found for Shona beside Kendra, swaddled in bandages and blankets and still awake, her dark-rimmed eyes staring off into nothingness. Jake and Hilary Hodgkiss huddled together on the next bunk over.

"Hasn't spoken a word since I found her," Ling said of the girl. "I suppose she's in shock. It's a wonder more of us aren't."

"What about You Know Who?" Shona asked, her voice trembling like the rest of her, weak from pain and exhaustion but clinging on for a resolution.

"Gone."

"You're sure?"

"I'm sure." Ling spoke with inarguable authority, sounding unreasonably calm. "Don't worry about him. He's gone and you're safe."

Shona nodded to the other side of the room, to the children lined up along the wall in their varying states of monstrosity. "What about them?"

Ling hesitated, unsure how to answer. "They're . . . alive. Excuse me." She turned to deal with the problems of another group, providing them curt answers and clear directions. They listened attentively, following her instructions the way soldiers would a commanding officer. No-one had any doubt who was in charge. When she strode away, Curtis followed her.

"Hey, we need real help here," he said, casting an eye back at Shona and Kendra, both looking frail and pale as ghosts. It was a miracle either was still alive. "We need real doctors. And soon. If we don't—"

"Radio and phones are still out," Ling said. "That hasn't changed. So far, the only vehicle we can find capable of going beyond the town limits is sitting outside." She directed him to the ATV by the bandstand. "I guess he needed it to transport the bodies back to his . . . lair. If they didn't lose their way in the snow, a person could use it to reach the highway maintenance camp at Carrick Crossing in about four hours. So I'm told."

"Let me go," Curtis said, not a trace of hesitation in his voice. "I want to go."

He was persuaded to wait until dawn, when the light would lower the risk of him hitting a rock on the trail and dying alone on the ice. As Ling put it, a "heroic but dumb" way to die. In the meantime, they had the chance to trade stories about the things they had witnessed, the actions they had taken and why they'd taken them, the people they'd seen die and who had killed them. By sunrise, Ling had a more or less complete picture of all that had transpired.

An hour after Curtis set off, she left the controlled madness of the town hall and returned home to grab a quick shower, something to eat and a change of clothes.

The streets looked so much worse in daylight. Evidence of atrocity was everywhere. Broken windows, blood stains in the snow, scattered clothing and weapons torn from the children's victims as they attempted to flee. The servants of Saint Nicholas had worked diligently to ensure anyone he could not control was removed from his path. The ones who survived the slaughter could be counted on the fingers of one hand.

Men could be heard yelling a few streets over, continuing their random, inexpert sweeps of various buildings in search of the villainous demon who'd ruined their town and condemned their children to a nightmarish existence. Every man was armed and every now and then an impotent gunshot sounded. Ling thought it would be a miracle if none of them killed themselves before the day was through.

She had told the others she would be back within the hour, but after visiting her home she did not immediately return to the town hall. She turned south, heading into the shadow of the tower of black smoke still staining the sky over the school.

She walked to the church, where the body of Devon McCulloch hung from the spiked iron railings. Six of them had skewered his head, neck, and back, making wounds from which blood had dripped down and stained the tributes to the town priest a sickly shade of yellow. His frost-bitten form had not reverted to that of a child in death. As with the others, all the heinous ways his flesh had been warped remained in evidence.

She went in the unlocked door and found her way down to the heated basement. It stank of something thicker than damp. An aged, bitter rot that soaked the air.

“Hello?” She spoke to the shadows. “I know you’re there. You don’t have to hide.” She waited, listening for his answer, watching to see if he appeared from among the stacked plastic chairs and boxes of hymn books. “I thought this is where you would come. Warm, quiet, empty. A good place to hide. And it’s the only place in town that still has your name on the door . . . for all the good it does. Does it do you any good? Can you still exert any influence down here?” She paused again, eyes scanning the gloom. “Guess not. You might as well talk to me. You wouldn’t be risking anything. I’m not going to run and tell them you’re here. I don’t have any weapons. And I’m alone.”

There was silence. Then the shadows gave a sadistic sigh. “How foolish.”

A shiver of fear and excitement traveled up Ling’s spine. She took a breath and told herself to resist the urge to run. “You know who I am. And I think we’re overdue a talk.”

There was a sound she couldn’t quite comprehend. A dark rattling that echoed in spiraling circles around the room. He was chuckling. “Do you? Do you, indeed?”

“You know there are men out there now, armed, searching the town for you? Sooner or later, one of them will realize what I did and come here, find you and kill you. Maybe you’re hoping you can hide out till sundown, then make your escape, back to whatever barren wasteland you call home? If you're lucky maybe you can remain there, undiscovered, as you slowly starve to death. But odds are, you'll never get away."

His mandibles clicked irritably. "You sound very certain."

"I don't doubt you can handle yourself in a fair fight. But I've seen you. You're fat, slow and outnumbered. Up against a handful of men with rifles, it'll be a sad, bloody end. At least it'll be over quickly."

"You came here to gloat?"

"I came here to say that you have bargaining power. There is scope for . . . negotiation."

A bitter laugh. "Power? What power is that?"

"The children. The ones you . . . fed. What will become of them?"

The creature, still unseen, drew in a deep breath. Ling felt the walls around her close in ever so slightly, as if caught in the vacuum. "Pain upon pain upon pain. Agony upon agony. And finally, eventually, when they can take no more . . . death."

"Could you prevent that?"

"Oh yes. I could cure them of affliction. Remake them just how their doting parents remember them. It would be easy to do. And I'm the only one who can."

"Will you? If I can guarantee your life, will you save them?"

Another deep breath. Another long sigh. Relishing the moment. "No."

"Why not?"

"You said it yourself. If I leave this place I will die. Slow, excruciating starvation. I will perish cold and miserable and hungry, and it will take a long, long time. Better to be butchered by a pack of vigilantes, perhaps even take a few of them with me. And let the brutalities endured by their children in their sickened, dying days be my legacy. I would prefer to die with the comforting certainty of their continued suffering on my mind. This would please me." In a corner, hidden by stacked crates and shadow, his dark chuckle rattled again. "As would your blood."

Ling still couldn't see him, but she stood her ground. "Perhaps I could sweeten the deal."

"Your flesh would be sweet."

She started talking faster, worried her time was running short.

"You made a deal once with the man who owned this land. That's true, isn't it? Well for all intents and purposes, I am its owner now. I am in a position to negotiate a new arrangement. One that could benefit us both."

Though she couldn't see him, it felt like he was all around, like a snake winding his way around her in ever-decreasing circles. But then he stopped. "Explain."

She swallowed.

"I don't know what you are. I don't need to know. I have seen what you can do. I have felt the power of it. And I believe I have a general understanding of what I would have to provide in return." She reached into the inside pocket of her overcoat and produced a folded sheet of paper. With a hand she couldn't keep from shaking, she held it up. "I've taken the liberty of preparing a provisional contract. Take a look if you'd like."

There followed yet another unbearably long silence which she endured, fighting back her own fear, watching, waiting for him to make his move. Finally, he poured in from the darkness and reared up in front of her, revealing himself in all his towering, putrid glory. "Show me."

She looked down, so as not to be driven into a trance by the sickening machinations of his face, unfolded the paper with trembling fingers and held it out. "I left the space for your name blank. Obviously, Saint Nicholas is worthless now, but then . . . it was never your true name, was it?"

His myriad eyes studied the typed words for a time, then flicked up to focus on hers. "You had another in mind?"

46.

Three Years Later

WHENEVER SHE WALKED past the former site of St. Nicholas Elementary—which was most days—Shona couldn't help picturing herself lying beneath the sign in a bloody, battered mess, the way Curtis had found her. She was concussed and mostly incomprehensible and still remembered very little of what happened then or in the hours following. But Curtis told her what she had said to him when, staggering away from the burning building, he had knelt down in the snow and taken her into his arms.

"What are your kids' names?"

In the moment, it had been the very last thing he expected her to ask, but she repeated the question, insisting he tell her, until finally he relented.

"Good," she'd said. "That would have annoyed me."

She had immediately forgotten his answer, of course, along with any memory of the exchange. Later, in a MacArthur Point hospital bed, when he'd prompted her on the subject, she had to admit she still didn't know their names.

There were other holes in her memory—some significant, some less so. She had no recollection whatsoever of being airlifted out of town or the periods leading up to and between her various surgeries. Entire days had passed her by without her brain retaining a moment when she woke to find her parents at her bedside.

They informed her of the story the rest of the world had already heard. Of the freak gas explosion that ripped through the St. Nicholas school building while it had been playing host to a Christmas celebration. More than sixty people had been killed outright, including entire families and almost all of the out-of-town workers. In a contrite statement to the international press, the Bingzhen Group promised a full investigation and compensation for victims' loved ones. However, all indications from the authorities were that no-one was to blame. It was a tragedy that nobody could have foreseen and no-one could have prevented.

Time and again, while she was recovering in hospital, and later, as they marked New Year in a modest way at a local hotel, her parents told her how lucky she was to have survived. She didn't disagree and didn't dispute the 'official' story about what had happened, but in her own head she knew better.

Curtis paid her a few visits while she was still in hospital. He told her of the tale Ling had concocted to explain away the death and destruction. It was a fiction the rest of the townsfolk quickly agreed to propagate. They seemed to prefer it to the truth, which for many had been too difficult to accept. Their violation at the hands of Saint Nicholas had been long and deeply traumatic. They preferred to lie, grieve, and move on with their lives rather than confront it. This was made easier by one small miracle. Shortly before Curtis arrived at the highway maintenance camp and made the call that would send the rescue teams into action, the children of St. Nicholas were cured. It happened in an instant. Some seizures, a little light vomiting, and every one of the afflicted youngsters was relieved of their physical malformations. Their transformations were so quick and pain-free, they appeared effortless, like casting off cheap Halloween costumes. Better still, not one claimed to have any memory of the atrocities they had committed or why.

But Shona remembered. Curtis remembered. They sat together in her hospital room, waiting for the police or someone to come ask them for their version of events. They wondered if they would be able to stick to Ling's story. The truth, she'd insisted, would be too outlandish for the outside world to comprehend. Tell it and they would be hounded the rest of their lives by investigators, journalists, lunatics, and conspiracy nuts. They would lose any chance of living normal, decent lives. It was a solid, practical argument—tough to argue with. Even so, Shona wondered if she wouldn't end up blurting the truth out anyway—because the truth was what it was and it had to come out.

She needn't have been concerned. In the end, nobody came to

interview either of them. No statements were sought or taken. The official story became exactly that. Curtis went to Toronto to be with his family. Shona stayed in MacArthur Point with hers.

It was some weeks before she made the journey back to Coldwell Slopes—as it was now called. She flirted with the idea of returning to Scotland, as her parents begged her to. But the plan for the resort was pressing ahead, the Bingzhen Group was paying her medical bills and Ling assured her she still had a job. Soon there would be a new school and the children needed a teacher.

Beyond all that, she had questions. The cover-up did not sit well with her. Most troubling was how easily the story had been accepted. She struggled to imagine what kind of investigator would arrive on the scene, see all those mutilated bodies, and accept they had all died in the same way. Unless Ling had burned them. And scorched any other evidence. And bribed any and all officials to ensure the truth never came to light. The thought of such a grand conspiracy being thrown together at short notice and succeeding . . . it simply wasn't tenable. The idea of it made her queasy.

So she returned, seeking answers, determined to dig and keep digging until she got to the truth. Right up until the moment she passed the billboard which read, 'Welcome to Coldwell Slopes. The town that Christmas calls home.'

It was not the same town she had left. In the weeks she had been away, Ling's company had been busy, drafting in an army of contractors to rip out and upgrade infrastructure, tear down buildings, throw up new ones and sculpt Mount Coldwell into the skier's wet dream that had so long been promised. Scars made by Saint Nicholas remained—in the form of broken buildings and fractured families—but they were fading fast. And the community was utterly transformed.

People she'd barely spoken to in December now welcomed her the way they would a beloved and long-lost family member. While they mourned those who had been lost, conversation was dominated by talk of the future, of all they hoped to achieve in this new era, for themselves and their children. Positivity was rife. Hope abounded. Discussion of the massacre felt perverse in such an auspicious atmosphere. Whenever Shona tried to bring up Saint Nicholas, Morgan, the deaths or the cover-up, all anyone wanted to do was move on. By the time she finally saw Ling, that was all she wanted herself.

And move on they did. After three years, the only time she thought of Saint Nicholas and all the horrors he'd unleashed was when passing the old school sign. And even then, the thought was only a fleeting one. The sign itself had been repurposed as a memorial to those who had died in the gas explosion. As such, it was one of the only signs in town not to bear a depiction of the resort's mascot, Coldwell the Singing Snowman, as a mark of respect.

On the morning of the 23rd, three years to the day since the death of Father McHattie, she passed the sign on her way to the town square, to join the annual Coldwell Wintertainment Spectacular. Popular with residents and tourists alike, it was professionally catered, but the Coldwell Community Council—of which she was a prominent member—encouraged the preparation of homemade crafts and treats to lend the celebration a more congenial air. So she had worked through the night to produce three trays of vegan marshmallow snowman pops—the spitting image of Coldwell himself.

"Can I give you a hand?" A stranger asked as she marched down the street, the trays stacked in her arms.

"No thank you, I can manage."

"Do you need some help?" said another.

"No, no, I'm fine. Thanks."

"Help you out there?"

"I've got it," Curtis said, stepping out from the passing crowd to lift the trays from Shona's hands and put the minds of all the various good Samaritans at ease.

"I was carrying it fine," she grumbled. "It's only marshmallow."

"You know what folks round these parts are like." He grinned. "Can't stand to see a good-looking woman carry a damn thing. It's unchivalrous."

"Yeah, I know. It's a burden. Where's Shawn and Chrissy?" Curtis's kids had come to spend Christmas with their father—something they'd been demanding since their first visit to Coldwell Slopes when they had fallen in love with the place and the idea of celebrating the season here. Their mother had no option but to allow it. "I thought you were taking them up Dasher today."

"People are being told to stay off Dasher," he said, referring to one of the more advanced runs on the south face of the mountain, one of the few the kids hadn't been down yet. "I don't know why. Right now they're watching the ice-carving competition."

"Probably for the best." While Curtis had discovered an untapped passion for winter sports since the resort's opening, Shona's enduring memory of her experience on Nugget Hill was enough to put her off such activities.

They reached the square, today playing host to an ice rink, funfair and thriving Christmas market, weaving their way through the chatting, laughing crowd to reach the community council's cocoa and cake stall. Kendra stood behind it, waving them over. Up on the bandstand, someone hidden in a puffy Coldwell costume kept the youngest children entertained by dancing and pretending to be crooning the Christmas classics playing over the sound system.

"Who's in the suit?" Shona asked.

Kendra shrugged. "Noah or Marshall, I think. I'm just glad it's not me." She'd worn the suit herself during the first winter seasons. An easy way to make a little cash, if exhausting. These days, between her job at the Coldwell Kids' Club, studying for a teaching qualification and volunteering for the community council, she didn't have the time. "You guys hear about Dasher?"

She buttoned her lip when someone called her name. "Kendra!" Cindee popped out from the crowd, curly brown hair spilling out of her Coldwell the Singing Snowman bobble hat. Having undergone a growth spurt in the last year, she was now taller than Lucas Grenier, who trailed behind her. "Is the cocoa ready?"

"It is." Kendra tapped a finger against the urn in which she'd prepared a gallon of hot cocoa with coconut milk. Since lodging with Cindee and the rest of the Jacobs family, she'd quickly adapted to the vegan lifestyle. "Want a cup?"

The girl nodded. "Two please."

"How are you, Lucas?" Shona asked.

"Fine thank you, Miss Fleming."

The boy still had scars on his face from where buckshot had ripped into the skin, but they were barely visible now. Like the rest of the children—Cindee, as ever, the exception—he claimed to have no recollection of the days around that Christmas when he had become a crazed killer in the service of Saint Nicholas, but Shona wasn't sure. He never seemed able to hold her gaze longer than a second without looking away, a trace of guilt forever in his eye.

She offered them both a marshmallow pop. Then they went on

their way, eager to join the rest of their friends at the funfair for a spin on Coldwell's Carousel, racing each other in Coldwell's Carnival Cars or trying their hand at one of the games to win either a stuffed or animatronic singing Coldwell.

The town was awash with children now, at all times of the year. The number enrolled at the elementary school had increased tenfold and Shona's own class now numbered thirty. Come December, the population felt close to evenly split between adults and kids. Coldwell Slopes lived up to its slogan, generously amplified by the countless travel agents, journalists, bloggers and influencers who all rated it as the number-one holiday destination for those who loved yuletide. Beyond the expertly crafted ski runs or the peerless powder—the condition and consistency of snowfall had been second to none, since opening—it was the atmosphere in its quaint, historic streets that was most highly prized. It was truly remarkable how many families had come this year without any intention of hitting the slopes at all. They were here simply to immerse themselves in the magical feeling of a small-town Christmas—better than any Hallmark movie.

Shona could understand it. Her own love of the season had not been spoiled by Saint Nicholas. Slightly tarnished, perhaps, but as soon as she set foot back in town and breathed in the chill, revitalizing air, it had bloomed once again, stronger than ever. And so it continued.

"What about Dasher?" Curtis asked.

Kendra leaned across the table, lowering her voice so none of the grinning, rosy-cheeked tourists would overhear. "Apparently some couple from South Africa decided to go night skiing and never came back down. They think there might have been an avalanche or something."

"That's terrible," said Shona.

"Rescue squad's up there now, but . . . " Kendra gave a shrug that finished her sentence for her.

Shona understood what it meant. It was a big mountain. It didn't matter how many safety precautions were put in place. Ultimately, those who journeyed up its slopes were dicing with the dangers of a harsh and unforgiving wilderness. It was surprising—and fortunate—that there had been so very few such incidents since the resort had opened. Shona could think of only one, the previous Christmas. Another tourist who lost his way on the slopes, his body yet to be recovered. She viewed such tragedies as a reminder to count her blessings and be thankful for all the treasures in her life, all the things that made her happy to get out of bed each morning. That thought in mind, she linked her arm through Curtis's, put her gloved hand in his and squeezed.

He squeezed back, then nodded over her shoulder. "Better look professional. It's the boss."

"I heard that," said Ling, wagging her finger. "You know I don't like it."

"I know you *say* you don't."

"Ling!" Shona broke away from Curtis to embrace her friend. "How are you? I haven't seen you in ages!"

Ling laughed, awkwardly returning the hug. "I'm fine. Busy, busy, busy. Conferences, board meetings, interviews. It never stops."

"What about New York? I heard they want you back."

"Oh, you heard about that?" Ling cast an eye toward Curtis and Kendra, wondering whom from within her small circle of confidence had been gossiping and concluded probably everyone. "They want to look at franchise options. I guess it was inevitable, after the year we've had, the kind of numbers we've sent. They see our success and want to replicate it in other territories. Naturally, they want me to return to head office to lead on strategy."

Shona's face fell. "But you . . . "

Ling held up a hand to silence her. "I told them I'm happy to help however I can, with guidance, proposals, investors, whatever . . . But I do it remotely. I'm not going back. I told them . . . I'd miss my family too much."

"Oh!" Shona's voice cracked. She could feel herself tearing up. "Oh, Ling . . . "

"Oh Jesus," Kendra groaned, rolling her eyes.

"Good for you," said Curtis. "Place just wouldn't feel like home without Mama Bear around."

"I think I prefer 'boss' to 'Mama Bear'." Ling flashed a mischievous smile, then glancing over at the bandstand. Jake and Hilary Hodgkiss were on stage, waving her over. "I'd better go. They want me to make a speech." She began to move off, then turned back. "Dinner at my place tonight?" She pointed at Curtis. "Bring the kids." Then at Shona. "And your appetite."

"We'll be there," Shona said, fighting back a grateful sob.

Curtis put his arm around her, whispering, “And here I thought you never cry.”

“I don’t.” She sniffed, wiping away a tear. “You know that.”

“For a second there, you really thought she was going to leave, didn’t you?”

“Absolutely no more than a second,” she said, nestling against his chest. “She’s too smart for that. She knows Coldwell Slopes would never work anywhere else. They don’t have what we have.”

She watched Ling stride away, into the crowd, then looked out across the sea of faces. Some she knew, most she didn’t. But it was true, what Ling had said. It was a family. They all felt the same way. The same spirit of kinship. The same deep, rumbling undercurrent of brotherly love. Whether someone chose to visit for a week, a month or a year. Whether they chose to make a life here, the way she had, or only flew in for the holidays. For however long they were in Coldwell Slopes, they were a part of the community. From the ashes of St. Nicholas, she and Ling and Curtis and Kendra and all the rest had managed to build something truly spectacular. A place where everyone, whoever they were and from wherever they’d come, felt like they truly belonged. And if anyone were to ask her how they’d managed to do it, she would have to admit she truly didn’t know.

Lost in her thoughts, her gaze settled momentarily on a Coldwell snowman in the midst of the crowd, his foolish grinning face turned toward her, his painted-on eyes apparently trained on hers.

It was impossible to tell who was in the suit, but it had to be someone she knew. Acting on instinct, she gave him a little wave.

And he waved back.

About the Author

John McNee is the writer of numerous strange and disturbing horror stories (many collected in John McNee's *Doom Cabaret),* as well as the novel *Prince of Nightmares.*

He is also the creator of Grudgehaven and the author of *Grudge Punk*, a collection of short stories detailing the lives and deaths of its gruesome inhabitants, plus the sequel, *Petroleum Precinct.*

He lives in Glasgow, Scotland, where he is employed as a journalist, and can easily be sought out on social media and through his website, www.johnmcnee.com (sign up to the newsletter and get a free book).

And yes, he still believes in Santa Claus.

BBB

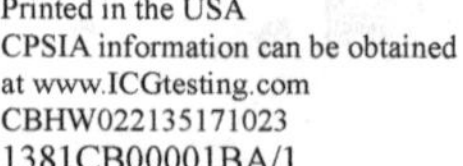

Printed in the USA
CPSIA information can be obtained
at www.ICGtesting.com
CBHW022135171023
1381CB00001BA/1

9 781940 250601